PASSIONATE ADVERSARIES

"O' all the greedy, thieving—"

"Listen to me!" Niall gave Anne a small shake. "I'll be chieftain soon. If we legalize our union at year's end, in a sense we will have joined our lands anyway. So you see, there's really no problem."

It took all of Anne's control not to slap what she saw as a smug look off Niall's face. "A year is too late! You legally own your lands as o' today. 'Tis no longer ours, don't you see? No wedding will change that!" She turned her back to him. "I beg leave to return to my people."

"Don't even think it!" Niall growled. "We are handfasted for a year. Willing or no, you'll stay here for that time and not a moment less."

He began to walk away from her when her tear-choked voice halted him. "I hate you, Niall Campbell. Mark well my words. If 'tis the last thing I do, I'll make you rue the day you brought me here."

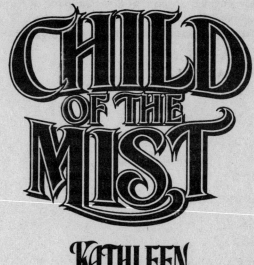

CHILD OF THE MIST

KATHLEEN MORGAN

LEISURE BOOKS NEW YORK CITY

Acknowledgment

Acknowledgment is made to *Complete Book of Witchcraft* by Raymond Buckland, Llewellyn Publications, St. Paul, Minnesota, for use of the handfasting ritual on pages 97-98.

A LEISURE BOOK®

January 1993

Published by

Dorchester Publishing Co., Inc.
276 Fifth Avenue
New York, NY 10001

Printed in the United States of America.

To Karen Johnson and Deborah Ulin. You sustained me during some pretty dark moments—for that I am deeply grateful. You were there to share the joy of my first book sale—a day I will cherish forever. And then, there were all those Saturday shopping sprees to the Chosun Gift Shop and Itaewon....

For the good times as well as bad, this book is dedicated to you.

Prologue

"N–Niall!"

The weak but insistent cry rose above the muffled sobbings, carrying desperately across the large, stone-walled bedchamber to the fireplace. A man, tall and powerful, jerked upright. With a resolute straightening of his shoulders, he released his white-knuckled grasp on the mantle and was at the bed in a few quick strides. Waving aside the midwife and maidservants, he lowered himself onto the soft down comforter. Gently, he grasped his wife's hand.

"Aye, lassie?" Try as he might, he could not hide the catch in the dark register of his voice.

Her slender fingers squeezed his. "Och, my brave, sweet Campbell." She smiled wearily up at him. " 'Tis sad I am . . . to leave you. I would never willingly cause you such pain . . . not in a hundred . . . thousand years."

7

He gathered her to him. "Hush, lassie. Don't worry about me. Save your strength for what matters. You . . . Your healing."

"N–nay," she quavered. " 'Tisn't a time . . . for false hopes. I pray only that our babe lives—" A sharp hiss of pain escaped as yet another contraction shuddered through her.

Niall swallowed hard against his angry, helpless anguish. Dear God, why must she suffer so? His grasp on her tightened, and he willed all the strength of his heart, his body, into hers.

The babe be damned. All he wanted was his sweet, bonny wife. How would he go on without her? She *must* live. She must. . . .

"*You* m–must go on. Take another wife." Her eyes, bright with understanding, stared up at him from a waxen yet still hauntingly lovely countenance. "A wife . . . who'll give you . . . a son. A wife . . . to love . . . as you have loved me."

"Love again?" Niall's bitter laugh pierced the air. "And how can that be, when you're the only one for me? Nay." He vehemently shook his head. "There'll be no other—now or ever!"

"P–promise me! *Promise*—" Her words were lost in a strangled scream. Her eyes widened in sudden comprehension. "The babe. Och, sweet husband. At last . . . our babe comes!"

For one final, exquisitely tender instant they clung to each other. Love, deep and bittersweet in this moment of truth, arced between them. Then there were hands, pushing them apart, drawing Niall away.

"Your pardon, m'lord," came the anxious voices. " 'Tis time. 'Tis women's work now. Step aside."

The tortured sounds followed Niall as he stumbled back to the hearth. Muted cries, choking sobs, mingled with the snapping, crackling clamor of the hungry fire. Time passed with lumbering slowness as Niall stared into the agitated flames, hearing it all from some place far away even as the night's horror charred its memory into his soul. Lord, never had he hurt so, not from any wound in battle, not from. . . .

He paused in his tormented thoughts. The sounds had ceased. His ears strained for some word, a babe's first cry—anything. There was none.

An awful fear flared. Niall turned.

His anguished gaze sought the form in the bed. She was still now, her beloved features relaxed, peaceful. A tight, smothering sensation constricted his chest. Niall wrenched his attention to the women surrounding her.

All but one averted their eyes. Niall's glance riveted on her. His features twisted in pain even as he sought to harden his heart against the imminent truth.

Old Agnes, his wife's loyal maidservant, returned his gaze, the answer to his question flickering despondently in her eyes. A shudder wracked Niall's big, hard-muscled frame. He shook his head, his black mane of hair grazing his broad shoulders in a movement of anguished disbelief.

The agony burgeoned, growing to explosive force even as he fought the inevitable acceptance. A cry rose in his throat, tearing past the strict control, the years of well-schooled discipline. His glance moved back to the frail, lifeless form in the bed, oblivious to the small bundle of white lying in her arms.

"Nay!"

The shout echoed across the room, reverberating off the walls to carry far beyond the chamber's thick wooden door. With staggering, stumbling strides, Niall returned to the bed, throwing himself down to gather his wife into his arms. Soundless spasms shook his body as he rocked the limp form to and fro, endlessly murmuring her name.

Quietly, the servants drew back to afford the grieving husband a semblance of privacy. They stood there, huddled in the shadows, uncertain what to do. All, that is, but one.

A dark-haired maid slipped out of the room. As she closed the chamber door, her glance swept the dim, torchlit corridor. A beckoning movement from a dark corner caught her eye. With a knowing smile, she scurried over.

"She is dead then?" a deep voice demanded.

The girl nodded.

"And the bairn?"

"Stillborn, m'lord."

A mirthless sound rose from the shadows. "Good. Very good. Then there's still time for the misfortunes of *my* family to be righted. Still time for the clan chieftainship to pass from Niall Campbell to me.

"Aye." He chuckled, an icy rim of triumph sharpening his voice. "Time enough indeed. . . ."

Chapter One

April, 1564
Castle Gregor, Western Perthshire, Scotland

Anne MacGregor paused on the castle parapet walk, gathering her long woman's plaid about her. Swirling vapors blanketed the winter-browned land, filling the low hollows and rills, curling restlessly about the trees, to spread ever onward in an eerie sea of fog. She smiled and turned to the man beside her.

" 'Tis fortunate the mists are heavy this day. 'Twill cover our going and, hopefully, my return as well."

Anne motioned toward the stout rope that dangled over the side. "Come, Donald. Lead on."

Wordlessly, the young, shabbily clad Scotsman scrambled over and down the wall, then held the rope taut as Anne nimbly followed. Without a backward glance, they hurried into the enshrouding whiteness. Until well out of earshot of the clansmen walking guard on the fortress battlements, their journey was swift and silent.

Grasping his long, gnarled walking stick, Donald plowed through the dense mists as if he saw through them, his steps sure and bold from years of traversing the beloved terrain. Anne, not quite so certain, kept close company, her large leather bag of herb powders, potions, and salves clutched tightly at her side.

Her thoughts raced ahead, planning the childbirth preparations. It was Fiona's first and Donald's young wife was frightened half to death. Only the promise that Anne would attend her had calmed the girl's fears.

Though barely eighteen, Anne MacGregor was already renowned for her skills in the healing arts. Both noble and poor alike called for her in their hour of need, and, unstintingly, she gave to one and all. *Aye, one and all*, Anne mused with a fleeting twinge of pain, and still the cruel tales about her persisted.

"I am grateful, ma'am," Donald said, slowing his steps to hers. "I know yer father forbade ye to leave the castle. If 'twasn't my Fiona's time, I'd have never asked . . ."

A pang of guilt at so willfully disobeying her father shot through Anne. Alastair MacGregor, clan chieftain and doting sire, had always given her free rein. Though she well understood his motives for now forbidding her to leave the castle, it couldn't be helped. At least not this time.

She'd made a vow to Fiona, long before the cattle raids had started up again, and was honor bound to keep it. The word of a MacGregor was sacred. Marauding Campbell reivers or no, she would see it through. Her father would understand, if there were ever a need to tell him.

Anne smiled at her companion, her silver eyes warm and reassuring. "Don't worry, my friend. 'Tisn't your fault the savage Campbells roam our lands. Life must go on in spite o' them, though I fear they'll never let up until they've stolen every bit o' MacGregor holdings—the thieving, heartless knaves!"

Donald's lips twitched at the mildness of Anne's censure. " 'Knaves'? Och, that's too kind a word for the likes o' them. And most especially for that young Campbell heir."

He shot her a worried glance. "I only wish ye'd worn yer short-sword. A bodice knife is nigh useless against an armed warrior. And they dinna call him the Wolf o' Cruachan without reason. Why, he's the most bloodthirsty, murderous—"

"Don't speak o' him!"

A sudden chill coursed through Anne. Instinctively, she touched the small, sheathed dagger nestled between her breasts. Holy Mary, it was enough to be out, virtually defenseless in such dangerous times, and then to have Donald dwell on the most feared Campbell of all!

Her pace quickened. "Time is short and Fiona needs us. We've more important things to concern us than some churlish Campbells. Besides, they haven't raided MacGregor lands in over a fortnight. Surely we've naught to fear on such an early morn."

"Aye, ma'am," her sturdy companion agreed, uneasily glancing about him. "As ye say. There's naught to fear. Naught at all."

"That's it. That's my girl," Anne encouraged, gripping Fiona's hand in hers. "You're a brave, brave lassie and will soon have your sweet babe. Are the pains still strong? Then take a breath and push again."

Fiona glanced up, a weak, trusting smile lighting her face. "A–aye. A sweet babe," she whispered, then tensing, bore down with all her might. The pains soon passed and she fell back, exhausted.

Anne lifted a cup to the girl's lips. "Drink a bit more, lassie. 'Tis the raspberry leaf tea. 'Twill hasten your birthing."

The brew was obediently sipped before Fiona fell into a deep slumber. It wouldn't be long before the next pains came, that Anne knew, but until then rest was the best thing for a laboring mother. She looked about her. It was long past darkness, the day having come and gone.

Anne hunched her shoulders in an effort to ease the ache of the hours spent crouched beside Fiona, then tucked an errant strand of russet-colored hair behind her ear. Glancing down at the young peasant woman, she sighed. Dear, frightened, trusting Fiona.

Her gaze wearily scanned the shabby little croft house. Despite Fiona's untiring efforts, the thatch-and-clay dwelling was little more than a hovel. *What a life to bring a wee babe into*, Anne mused. The only bed was a mound of peat covered with a coarse blanket, and the air was so smoke-filled one could hardly draw a breath without choking.

If only there were more we could do for our people. The thought stirred anew the old, angry frustration. Her father tried, but the years of endless feuding had worn him down. They were no match for the cursed Campbells—never had been—and still their enemies persisted.

Her hands balled into tight little fists. How she hated them! Would they never cease until they'd stolen all her clan possessed? If there were but a way to stop them. . . .

Fiona stirred in Anne's arms, a sleepy grimace twisting her face. *The pains*, Anne thought. *They come again.*

A damp blast of air swirled through the tiny cottage. She glanced up. Donald walked in, his arms laden with squares of dried peat to stoke the small hearth fire. At that instant Fiona moaned, her eyes snapping open in sudden anguish.

"Blessed Mother!" she gasped. "I . . . I . . . The babe!"

Anne scooted down to check her, then looked up at Donald. " 'Tis time. Come. Help me."

She motioned toward Fiona's head. "Hold her, talk to her while I—"

A scream of terror, followed quickly by others, pierced the night air. Rough, angry voices mingled with frantic cries and the staccato rhythm of hoofbeats pounding through the village. A hoarse shout of "Cruachan!" rose from the tumult of noise, slicing through the thin walls to the three people within.

At the dreaded war cry, Anne and Donald's eyes met in sickening realization. The Campbells. They were back and raiding the village.

Donald rose. "I must go help defend our people."

"And what good would it do?" Anne bluntly demanded. "If they mean to murder us, we've no chance. Mayhap they'll be satisfied with the animals as with most times. Stay, Donald. You're more use here than outside, no matter what happens."

Indecision flickered in the young peasant's eyes, then he sighed his acquiescence. "Ye're right. If I'm to die, I want to see my wee one first."

The minutes passed as they worked, Donald encouraging his wife while Anne struggled with the slowly emerging infant. Her heart leaped to her throat when the head appeared with the cord tight about the neck. It couldn't be loosened and it was vital the babe be free of the choking noose as quickly as possible. But nothing Anne did hastened the emergence of the shoulders, which suddenly seemed too large for easy passage.

The sweat beaded her brow as she struggled with the difficult birth, praying to God to help her as she encouraged the straining mother. At last the shoulders slipped free. The babe was born.

The tiny girl child lay there, unmoving, her body blue and lifeless. Frantically, Anne worked to tie and cut the cord, then gently rubbed the infant dry. The babe remained silent.

Anne's gaze lifted to the two anxious parents. "I . . . I can't . . ." She stopped, mesmerized by their pleading expression. She was all they had.

In an instant slowed in time Anne harked back to the day Fiona had first revealed her pregnancy, of the look of utter joy and anticipation on her face, of the eager plans. They had so little, Fiona and Donald, but they were rich in love and giving. Of that, they had an abundance. So very, very much for each other . . . and for their babe.

She *had* to do something.

Anne turned back to the limp little form. Her gaze scanned the tiny, perfectly shaped girl. What could she do?

Breathe, she silently implored. *I beg you. Breathe.*

Her lips moved. Anne's head slowly descended, her own breath wafting over the babe. Dared she share the life-sustaining air from her own body? Dare she even try? Yet, dare she not?

Gently, she lifted the little girl, and, before she realized it, Anne's mouth settled over hers. Tentatively at first, then more forcefully when she saw the tiny chest rise with each breath, Anne blew small puffs into the infant. At first nothing happened, the only sound her own panting breaths mingling with the ragged rasps of the two parents. Then, after what seemed an eternity, the babe gasped, then choked, finally uttering a strangled cry.

The cry, weak at first, grew in strength and intensity until it filled the small croft house. And, with each shuddering, indignant little breath, the joy, the immense satisfaction, grew within Anne. She raised her eyes to Fiona and Donald, eager to share their happiness. But their gazes, suddenly bright with terror, were no longer directed at her.

Anne whirled, steeling herself for the sight she knew must lie behind her. She could never prepare herself, however, for the look of unmitigated revulsion on the face of the tartan-clad man standing in the doorway. Gleaming with a half-mad light, the full force of his stare was riveted upon her.

"Witch! Vile, devil-whoring witch!"

Once more the man with the crazed eyes shoved Anne forward, sending her sprawling in the dirt outside the croft house. She tried climbing to her feet but, with her hands bound behind her and the hindrance of her long skirt, she tripped and fell again. Her thick hair tumbled loose, falling about her face and into her eyes.

Anne fought to catch her breath, striving to calm her pounding heart. The nightmare that dogged all her waking moments had finally come to pass. The vicious rumors, the unkind tales about her healing skills, had caught up with her at last.

She was to die—condemned as a witch.

Anne flung back her hair and stared up into a dozen hostile, torchlit faces. She scanned their plaids. Campbell men. Anne's breath caught in her throat. In their eyes gleamed superstitious fear—and an absolute certainty of death.

The injustice of it all welled in her, mingling with her fierce MacGregor pride. From somewhere, from some place buried deep within, a blazing anger burst forth.

Anne's eyes flashed silver fire and, for an instant, she thought she saw the raiders quail. Good. If they feared her for the powers they imagined she possessed, so be it. She had nothing to lose.

"Be gone you cowardly, thieving knaves!"

She climbed to her feet, noting, out of the corner of her eye, a large form—another Campbell?—edge into her line of vision. It was of little concern, one man more or less. She turned the full force of her gaze on the clansmen already facing her.

Anne threw back her shoulders and stood there, defiantly proud. "You trespass at your risk, for this village is mine. Do you think binding my hands will stay my powers or save you from damnation? Think again, Campbells, fools and cowards that you are!"

A low, angry growl rumbled through the men. Anne knew she'd stung their fierce Highland pride by questioning their courage. It was a dangerous game, for their affronted dignity might yet override their witch fears, inciting them to attack her in a mindless rage. But to cower before them now was even more foolhardy.

"Come forward, any who dare face me," she challenged. "I grow impatient with your girlish fears."

Slowly, she surveyed each man. "Och now, my wee laddies, won't one o' you come forward?"

The Campbell with the strange look in his eyes took a hesitant step toward her. He withdrew his sword from its scabbard. All eyes, including Anne's, turned to him.

"Aye?" Anne's hands clenched until her nails scored her palms, but she managed to maintain her air of feigned indifference. "And what does this wee bairn think he can do against me?" She laughed. "Is he the best o' you then?"

"Aye, the best and your death giver, whoring witch!"

The man leaped forward, his eyes blazing in an insane rage. Before Anne could dodge him, he was upon her, roughly grabbing her by the hair to force her to her knees, his sword hand arcing high above his head.

Blessed Mother. I'm going to die! The thought flashed through Anne's mind. A sharp, anguished pain twisted within her. Nevermore to see the beloved heath bloom on the hillsides. Nevermore to gaze upon the snow-capped peaks of MacGregor land. Nevermore to feel the warmth of her father's arms. . . .

"Enough, Hugh!" a deep-timbred voice cut through the air.

The man hesitated, his hand twisting painfully in Anne's hair. For an instant, she thought he'd strike her anyway. Then slowly, blessedly, his grip loosened. With one last, vicious kick that sent her sprawling into the dirt, he stepped away. She heard the rasp of metal as he resheathed his sword, then the tread of footsteps moving toward her.

Anne struggled to rise, but the sharp pain in her side kept her gasping on her knees. Tossing the hair out of her eyes, she satisfied herself with gazing up at the two men now standing before her.

His hand still gripping his sword hilt, Hugh glared at another tall Campbell, also wrapped in a belted plaid. The bulk of the fabric, forming both kilt and mantle, only added to the other man's imposing size and aura of power. As Anne's glance scathingly raked him, a realization flashed through her. He was the raiding party's leader.

He looked to be in his early thirties, with thick, gleaming black hair that just grazed his shoulders. His nose was straight, his jaw square and stubborn, and his full, firm lips had a cynical twist as he quietly listened to his compatriot's rantings. His eyes, when his glance briefly followed Hugh's gesture in her direction, flashed tawny-brown, intense, and coldly assessing.

Once more, anger flared in Anne. The villain, the rogue! How dare he look at her like she was some piece of vermin, because he was Campbell and she

MacGregor! She opened her mouth to berate him, then thought better of it.

"My orders haven't changed," he was calmly saying. "No MacGregor will suffer unless they raise a hand against us. We came for their livestock—and nothing more."

"And you're a fool if you let this witch live!" Hugh spat, drawing near so none but the three of them could hear. "You know the law demands her death. Will you go against it?"

"Hold your tongue, man!" His leader's voice slashed through the air. "You cut close in calling me a fool. Cousin or no, if you utter one word more . . ."

At the ominous tone, the color drained from Hugh's face. "I—I meant no offense." He began to back away. "Do what you want with the witch. 'Tis on your soul, not mine."

The dark-haired leader watched him go, then turned to where Anne was still kneeling on the ground. He pulled her to her feet.

For a long moment they faced each other. His cool gaze missed nothing, from her tousled hair and defiant silver eyes, to the torn and dirty dress. A strange, indefinable light momentarily flickered in the brown depths of his eyes, then died.

His hand moved to her breasts. For the space of a sharply inhaled breath, Anne thought he meant to ravish her—right there before his men. Then he withdrew her bodice knife.

"Turn. Give me your hands."

The order was brusque, emotionless. Anne obeyed. It wasn't the time to argue or curse him for being a Campbell. She'd barely escaped death and the look in his eyes warned that his patience had worn thin. Cold metal touched her as he cut through her bonds. Then she was free.

Anne glanced down to rub her hands. "I'll not be thanking the likes o' you, for 'twill never make up for what you've done here." Her eyes rose to meet his. "Nonetheless, I owe you a debt."

His mouth quirked. "A debt? Between Campbell and MacGregor? I think not, lassie. There can never be anything between us but the deepest enmity."

He flipped the knife in his hand and offered it back to her, handle first. Wordlessly, she accepted it, then watched him turn and walk away. His long, muscular legs, bare beneath his kilt, swiftly carried him to the black stallion waiting nearby. In one agile leap he mounted, then reined his horse about to look at her.

"You're an impertinent, foolish wench to taunt my men. Though I admire your spirit, mark me well. I didn't spare you because I feared you, for I don't believe in witches. But if our paths ever cross again, think twice before opening your mouth. We Campbells don't take kindly to disrespect—especially from MacGregors."

With a wave of his hand, he signaled his men forward. Out of the village they rode, driving the stolen MacGregor stock before them.

Anne watched them go, filled with a helpless, roiling rage. *Curse you foul Campbells! Curse your thieving, heartless ways!* she silently screamed after their retreating backs, her knife still clasped in her hand. *And, most of all, curse the dark, arrogant man who leads you!*

Alastair MacGregor reread the missive one last time, then crushed it in his large fist and threw it onto the fire. Recalling the scribbled words, a fierce emotion flared in his breast. Was it possible? Dare he hope for a way to end the feud before MacGregor pride was irretrievably broken, ground into dust beneath the Campbell heel?

And yet as dearly yearned for as peace was, dared he believe, dared he trust the man whom he awaited even now—a hated Campbell, assured, just this once, safe passage through Castle Gregor? How could anyone trust a clan that so blithely instigated a vicious feud during the happy occasion of a marriage feast, refusing to see any side but their own?

Alastair shook his head despairingly. Nay, it wasn't likely any good would come of this night's meeting, yet what else. . . .

A fist rapped at the door. Alastair wheeled about, paused to stare at the portal then, squaring his shoulders, strode resolutely toward it. A man, shrouded in a rain-soaked MacGregor tartan, was shown in.

Alastair shut the door and bolted it behind him. He walked to a small table that held a whiskey decanter and several cups. The MacGregor glanced over his shoulder. "Do you fancy a dram o' the potents to chase the chill from your bones?"

"Aye, that I do."

Alastair poured a liberal dose into two cups, then, as an afterthought, sweetened his with a splash more. Tonight of all nights, he'd need every bit of courage he could muster.

The two men sipped their drinks silently, allowing Alastair a moment more to assess his visitor. The MacGregor tartan had been his idea, for he wanted none to suspect what was afoot. The Campbell guest's face was difficult to make out. Despite the fire's warmth, he seemed reluctant to remove the plaid from his head and shoulders.

He doesn't want his identity known, Alastair thought. The realization sent an inexplicable chill down his spine. He was a cool one, and no mistake, whatever he was up to, the man didn't care to be implicated. Suddenly, the MacGregor wanted this night's meeting done with as quickly as possible.

Alastair cleared his throat. "Er, your letter spoke o' an offer. About a plan to end the feuding. What exactly might that be?"

"The Campbell is ailing and won't last the summer. With a new chief comes new policies—and an end to the feud."

"And I'm not fool enough to think Niall Campbell will end a feud his father began. If you've come to offer me hope the Wolf will go against his sire, you can leave the way you came, and be making it quick!"

"And who was saying Niall Campbell will be the next chief?"

Alastair's brow wrinkled. He tilted his head to study the man before him speculatively. "He's clan tanist, the Campbell's chosen successor. Short o' an untimely death . . ."

White teeth gleamed in the mantle's shadow. "Aye, an untimely death. Niall leads many raids on your lands. If you were to know in advance when and where he'd strike, you could set your own men there. Niall's band is always small for he claims his success lies in swift, unexpected attacks. Outnumber them and you could kill them all—Niall included. Then the Campbell would be forced to chose a new chief."

"And who might that be?"

"Someone sure to see my way o' things."

There was a finality in the man's voice that brooked no further discussion. Alastair decided not to pursue it. It didn't matter anyway. Any choice but the Wolf of Cruachan was bound to be an improvement. But what if the offer led MacGregors into a trap?

"And why should I trust you?" The MacGregor strode back to the whiskey table and poured them both another dram. "What assurance do I have you'll not betray me and mine in the end?"

He returned and handed the visitor his cup.

The man shrugged. "My word. The word o' a Campbell, to be sure, but then, what is there to lose? If I fail you, are you any worse than you were before? 'Tis a gamble, but are not the stakes well worth it? Take it or leave it."

Alastair emptied his cup. The fiery liquid seared a hot trail down his throat, spreading rippling fingers of warmth throughout his chest. It calmed him a bit, allowing him the opportunity to sort through his jumbled thoughts.

Take it or leave it. Had it come to this then, when a MacGregor was forced to accept whatever leavings a Campbell threw his way? Lord, what a bitter draught to swallow! Yet swallow it he must if his clan were to survive. One thing for certain, Alastair vowed with a fierce determination, Niall Campbell would rue his birthing day before he was done with him.

"Tell me when the Wolf plans his next raid." The MacGregor sighed. " 'Tis as you said. Any chief would be better than he. Help me capture him and your troubles will be over."

"I want him dead, MacGregor."

Alastair's bitter laugh cut through the air. "Och, he'll die, and no mistake. Just how and when I leave to my own pleasure."

Aye, the man across from MacGregor thought as he once more drained his cup. *And your pleasure will be short indeed. I'll make certain my clan learns of the Wolf's death. Before he's cold in his grave we'll be back in full force, to exact a savage revenge. Then I'll finally have it all—the Campbell chieftainship and control of all MacGregor lands. . . .*

Chapter Two

Through a red haze of pain, Niall Campbell gazed out upon the castle's outer bailey. The early-morning sun stained the sky with lavender. Save for the MacGregor sentries guarding the parapets, no one was about. He clenched and unclenched his fingers to ease the numbness in his hands, the only movement allowed by the tight ropes binding his limbs in a spread-eagled position to the wooden cross posts.

Had it been but two days now since his capture? It seemed an eternity. He licked his dry, cracked lips, the thirst raging through him like wildfire. His battle wounds ached fiercely, but none were severe enough to kill him before the lack of water did. But then, wasn't that the MacGregor's plan—a slow, agonizing death?

With a weary sigh, Niall leaned his head against the stone wall supporting the cross posts. If only he'd fallen with his men, brave lads one and all. But that fate had never been meant for him.

It had been a trap from the start; that was more than evident. He and his small band had no sooner ridden into the narrow draw leading to one of the MacGregor villages then the attack began. Surrounded on all sides, the MacGregor crossbows quickly thinned the Campbell ranks. Then the hand-to-hand combat began.

Though they'd fought with all the courage and ferocity of Highlanders, one by one his men fell. Eventually, the MacGregors managed to separate him from his remaining warriors and a heavy net dropped on him from the cliff above. Pinned to the ground, his sword useless in the stout rope snare, he'd turned to his dirk with desperate effect.

At the memory, a grim smile touched Niall's lips. Before they'd finally beaten him senseless, he'd hamstrung more than a few MacGregors.

Yet, in the end, it had all been for naught. To a man, his lads were dead and he was now a MacGregor prisoner. Not for long, though. Niall didn't delude himself as to his eventual fate. After all these years, the animosity between the clans ran deep and bitter. And he of all Campbells, clan tanist and leader of the debilitating raids in recent months, was hated most of all.

Nay, his death was a foregone conclusion. Niall could accept that with a certain equanimity. What he couldn't accept was the galling realization he'd been betrayed—and by one of his own.

A foul, black-hearted traitor in their midst! But who and why? The question had tormented him all the long hours of his capture, nibbling away at his strength as inexorably as had the lack of sleep and water. A traitor, and naught he could do, neither discover who he was nor warn his clan. Naught left to do but die, with the terrible knowledge unspoken, unshared.

Once again a frustrated rage grew within him.

Damn the man to hell, whoever he was! Niall twisted futilely in his bonds, accomplishing little more than abrading the bloody sores of his wrists and ankles further. The pain only fueled his anger and he fought the harder. Finally, his rapidly draining strength exhausted, Niall Campbell fell back, his wounds and tormenting thirst beckoning him toward a blessed oblivion.

Anne hurried across the outer bailey toward the keep. The thought of her own bed, covered with its plump down comforter, had never seemed so attractive. But then, never had she felt so exhausted!

It was early morn and she'd been up all night nursing a feverish servant, not to mention all the clansmen who still needed tending after the skirmish with the Campbells two days past. Though the victory had ultimately been MacGregors', the outnumbered raiders had sold their lives dearly.

Aye, the victory had been dearly won, but perhaps it would bring an end to the raids. After all, didn't they now hold prisoner the Wolf of Cruachan himself? His death, her father had assured her, would make the Campbells think twice about venturing onto MacGregor lands.

Though it was a cruel necessity to tie the man in the castle's outer courtyard, and doom him to a slow, thirst-maddened death, it still did not sit well with Anne. Enemy though he was, even the thought of watching him succumb, inch by agonizing inch, made her stomach churn.

Her steps quickened in her eagerness to cross the courtyard's broad expanse as swiftly as possible. Perhaps all the years of trying to save life made it so hard to bear to look at him, but in the two days since he'd been tied in the bailey, she'd not once glanced in the prisoner's direction, nor ventured past him unless absolutely necessary. In some way, not seeing him seemed to spare her the harsh reminder of his presence.

A low groan floated across the bailey. In spite of herself, Anne's eyes lifted toward the prisoner. His head was down, his full weight hanging from his hands as if he were unconscious. Mayhap the sound was her imagination, she thought, but, as she turned away, he moved. Anne halted, then took a hesitant step toward him. There was something familiar. . . .

He stirred again, attempting to lift his head, but couldn't seem to muster the strength. The slight movement, however, sent a premonitory shiver through her. She had seen him before, but where?

She inched her way over. As Anne studied the bent head, dread insinuated its oppressive tendrils about her heart. His form was powerful, awesome in size and inherent strength, even half-dead and trussed like some criminal awaiting execution. The mane of unruly black hair hid his features, and the Campbell plaid and torn, bloodied shirt gave no hint as to why she should recognize him. Yet, for some inexplicable reason, she felt compelled to know more.

Laying aside her leather herb bag, Anne raised trembling hands to cup his face. It would take but an instant, she assured herself, and he'd never know. Slowly, ever so carefully, she lifted his head and brushed aside the dark hair.

At the sight of the finely hewn features, Anne gasped. Her fingers tightened into his flesh. His eyes flickered open, tawny-brown and pain-glazed, then slid shut.

Bruised and bloodied though his face was, his cheeks darkly shaded by a heavy growth of beard, Anne could no longer deny recognition. It was the Campbell leader who'd rescued her from his crazed cousin! The Campbell leader . . . Niall Campbell . . . the Wolf of Cruachan!

With a shudder, Anne released his head and stumbled backward. Gathering up her bag, she hurried away. Holy Mary! Not him, *anyone* but him!

Anne scrambled up the steps of the keep and into its dark, stone coolness. Up the winding staircase she went, never pausing until she was safely in her own little room, the door bolted behind her. Flinging herself onto the bed, Anne buried her face in her hands.

Long minutes passed as she struggled to still her pounding heart. It was he, the hated, the greatly feared and despised Wolf of Cruachan—the MacGregors' fiercest enemy—and the man who'd saved her life. Never had she dreamt the day would arrive when he'd be in need, and it would be in her power to save him. Yet, in but a few weeks' time, the day had indeed come.

Now, the debt was hers to repay. But at what cost? To spare his life now, to set him free, would most certainly lead to dire retribution.

Yet, Anne reluctantly admitted, she owed him a debt, a life for a life. To turn from him now would be a dishonorable act. But if she didn't, she might well jeopardize her people's welfare.

Och, what to do, what to do? she inwardly cried. Still, as the hours passed in agonizing indecision, the choice was always the same. At long last, when day had faded to early eve, Anne rose from her bed and went to seek her father.

"You did what? You owe him what?"

Anne cringed at the explosive force of her father's rage. Never, in all her years, had he so much as raised his voice to her. Now to see the pain, the anger on his face, and know she was the cause . . . She stifled the uncharacteristic urge to flee and faced the man standing across the room.

" 'Tis as I said." She swallowed hard, then continued, "The Wolf spared my life. Now, I owe him a debt of honor. You can't kill him, Father."

"Can't? Can't kill him, you say?"

Alastair MacGregor covered the distance between him and his eldest daughter in a few quick strides. Grasping her by the arms, he jerked her to him. "Do you know what you're saying, lass? If I let the Wolf go, do you think he'll not try to avenge his men? Until now his raids have lost us our cattle, a few horses from time to time, but no lives. But now—now Campbell blood has been shed. Do you think he'll stop until MacGregor blood flows as freely? Most likely even more freely," he muttered, "knowing that black-hearted fiend."

Anne hung her head. "I—I'm sorry, Father. I didn't want to go against your orders, but I'd promised—"

"Promised? Promised?" The MacGregor's face turned a mottled red. "I ordered you to stay within the castle for your own safety and still you wouldn't listen! And now you've done it, for well you know your honor is MacGregor honor. To deny a debt such as this shames not only you, but the entire clan. Och, lass. You've gone and muddled things now!"

He began to drag her toward the door. Anne dug in her heels. "Where are you taking me?"

"To the Wolf," her father growled. "I'll hear the truth from his own lips."

Through the keep he led her, and Anne died a little death at each pair of questioning eyes and raised brows encountered along the way. Out into the early-evening sunshine they went, toward the lone, shadowed form tied in the outer bailey.

He must have heard them, for he lifted his head at their approach. "Time for another . . . gloating visit, is it?" Niall croaked, his voice raw and rasping. "Sorry to disappoint you . . . MacGregor. I'm still . . . very much . . . alive."

Alastair shoved Anne in front of him, pushing her almost into Niall's face. "Do you know her, Campbell? Tell me true!"

Reddened eyes, one purpled and nearly swollen shut, quietly studied her. Anne saw the recognition flare, then purposely flicker out. For an instant, she thought he might deny he knew her. But why? Did he think her in danger if he spoke true? Did he hope to protect her by lying? Fleetingly, she almost wished he'd mistake the situation, even if it meant his death. It would solve everything.

"The truth," she forced herself to whisper. " 'Tis your life that hangs in the balance. Tell him the truth. No harm will come to me."

His suffering eyes knifed into hers, probing deeply until Anne felt an unwilling compassion flow through her. Then his dense black lashes lowered. He sighed, the sound one of utter weariness.

"Aye, I know the lass. What's it to you, MacGregor?"

"What's it to me?" Alastair nearly choked in frustrated rage. "Rather, ask what's it to you? She's my daughter, man! You saved her life. Her debt to you is *my* debt. I cannot kill you now, as much as I yearn for it, no matter what happens. MacGregors have little else left, thanks to you and yours, but we still have our honor. *That* will never die, until you wipe the last o' us from the Highlands."

"Then . . . you'll let me go?"

The MacGregor shook his head. "I haven't decided. Content yourself with the fact you'll live. Debt or not, you're no guest here. You're merely trading the cross posts for the dungeon."

He turned to Anne. "And you, lass. I haven't decided what to do with you yet, either. In the meantime, I task you with tending our prisoner. Your need to nurse every beggar who crosses your path led to this. See how you enjoy nursing him!"

Her father shot Niall one final, contemptuous look, then stalked off, shouting orders at two guards to take the Campbell prisoner to the dungeon and clasp him in chains. Tears stung Anne's eyes as she watched him stomp away. She'd heard the pain, the deep concern in his voice beneath his anger as he'd spoken to Niall Campbell. She'd backed him into a corner in revealing her debt, that she well knew. And, indeed, what choices *were* left? He seemed damned if he freed the Wolf, and just as damned if he didn't.

"I wouldn't cause you trouble, lassie."

At the sound of the deep voice Anne turned to him. "And why should one MacGregor more or less matter to the likes o' you? Don't waste your pity on me, Campbell! My debt is paid. 'Tis my only comfort, and little will it be in the coming days o' caring for you!"

Anne strode away. Soon Niall Campbell would take his rest in the damp, fetid depths of MacGregor dungeons. He'd need food, water, and his wounds tended, and he was now her responsibility.

Even the thought of touching him sickened her, vile, vicious beast that he was. But touch him she would, nurse him in the best way she knew how. Until her father decided the proper course of action, Niall Campbell's welfare was now of utmost concern. For her people's sake, Anne would care for the devil himself.

"More," Niall gasped, thinking he'd never get enough to slake his thirst. "Give me more."

Anne pulled back with the cup and water pitcher before he could reach it with his chained hands. She firmly shook her head. "Nay, 'tis enough for now. You'll only make yourself sick if you drink too much so soon. Give your belly time."

Niall wiped his mouth with the back of a grimy hand. "Och, and aren't you the heartless wench? Is this but another MacGregor torture? Tormenting me with a sip or two, not enough to slake my thirst but only tease it?"

"Call it what you will." Anne set the pitcher and cup aside and took up her herb bag and a box filled with bandages and bowls. "One way or another, you'll get no more to drink until I deem fit."

She paused to eye him closely, her glance moving down his body with a coolly detached air. "Your leg looks the worst. I'll tend it first. Raise your kilt."

Dark eyebrows arched in weary amusement, for Niall's thigh wound was long, extending nearly to his groin. "Are you certain you want me exposing myself? You're a maid, aren't you?"

She expelled an exasperated breath. "And sure, don't you suppose I've seen a man's body or two in my years o' healing? 'Tisn't your privates I'm wanting to tend, only your leg. Do you want your wounds seen to or not?"

Niall shrugged and lifted his kilt to expose the full length of his leg. "I only thought to spare your sensibilities." He gestured toward the jagged cut. "Have at it, lass."

Silence hung heavily over the dank chamber as Anne worked in the flickering torchlight. She could feel his eyes upon her, sense them slide over her body as she carefully labored on his leg. It angered her, though she knew it for the normal masculine act it was. That realization disturbed her most of all.

Gritting her teeth, she forced her attention back to the task at hand. The wound was shallow. Apart from some redness at the edges, it appeared it would heal well enough.

Her gaze moved outward from the cut, noting the powerful, iron-thewed thigh. He was in superb physical condition, the muscles and sinews bulging under tautly stretched, hair-roughened skin. *A terri-*

ble, lethal enemy in battle, Anne mused, *the murderer of many a fine MacGregor lad*. The thought once more stirred her anger. Her touch, as she applied her herbal healing salve, was brisk.

"Why are you so angry at me, lass?"

The unexpected query startled Anne. Her head jerked up. Her eyes careened into his. Calm brown eyes, flecked surprisingly with gold, stared back at her. For a moment, no words would come.

"A–angry?" she repeated in disbelief. Was he daft? What did he expect, Campbell that he was? Anne shook her head, perversely refusing to give him the satisfaction of admitting he was right.

The faintest glimmer of a smile touched his lips. "You nearly bit my head off earlier when I told you I was sorry to cause trouble between you and your father. And now you're tending me with less than a gentle hand. I haven't said a word since you began, so how have I suddenly angered you?"

Anne opened her mouth to reply, then clamped it shut. She didn't owe him an explanation and he'd not get one. Inhaling a calming breath, she turned back to the bandaging of his leg.

"I'm not here to be your companion, only to see to your wounds and nourishment. 'Tisn't necessary to make nice talk with me."

"Mayhap not," he agreed quietly, "but I'd like to nonetheless."

The chains that bound him to the wall clanked as his hand moved to raise her chin gently. Silver eyes flashed at him, but Niall persisted. " 'Tisn't your fault, lass, no matter what your father's told you. My death would've set far worse on MacGregors than my living ever will. Your father will see that, once his anger cools."

"Och, will he now?" She wrenched her chin from his grasp. "And will your living end the feuding? Tell me that, Niall Campbell!"

Aye, he thought, *if I can discover who the traitor is, if your father willingly reveals his name.*

A sudden, horrible thought assailed him. The traitor. How long had he been behind this? Since the very start of the feud? It was too terrible even to think such a thing, for the feud between Campbell and MacGregor had burned hot and bloody for over eight years.

Niall shrugged. " 'Tis possible, lass. It depends on your father."

"Hah! Lay it all on my father's back, will you? 'Tis so like a Campbell to stoke the pot, then claim he was nowhere about when it boils over!"

Anne stepped back, her hands settling on her hips. "And why should you even want the feuding to end? The sanctity o' a wedding wasn't enough to keep you from starting the feud. And 'tis well known how you like the raiding, the bloodshed. You're slowly wearing us down with your greater numbers. Why should you want to stop until you've stolen all we possess—including the land itself?"

His mouth tightened. A hard look glittered in his eyes, but Niall managed to control his temper. It wasn't her fault she'd been led astray as to the true cause of the feud. "We don't want your land, lass." He sighed wearily. " 'Tis a matter o' clan honor. If the MacGregors would stop, then so would we. And I think you've been misled as to who truly caused the feud."

Anne arched a skeptical brow. "Really now? And how would you know?"

"I was there. 'Twas my wedding day. While all were feasting after the ceremony—MacGregor as well as several other neighboring clans—one o' our villages was raided, the people murdered to a man, woman, and child, and the livestock stolen."

"Aye, I know the tale," Anne finished impatiently. "And the only clue to the raiders' identities was a scrap o' MacGregor plaid. More than sufficient evidence that we'd been the reivers, despite my father's protests to the contrary. Thank the Holy Saints my people were safely back on MacGregor lands before you discovered the village. No doubt you would have murdered them all, right there at your wedding feast."

"What would you have done, if the crime had been against your clan?" Niall asked softly. "Wagged your finger and asked them not to do it again?"

"I'd have waited a bit, investigated more thoroughly, before beginning a blood feud! Such a crime as raiding can easily be laid at some innocent clan's feet, if the reasons are right. A scrap o' plaid is hardly a fair piece o' evidence!"

"And how thoroughly did the MacGregors investigate their own?" Niall countered. "Have you no renegades who might have done such a thing? But, nay, we never heard o' any MacGregors brought to trial, nor ever received one word o' apology."

"Apology for what? For a crime we didn't commit? Highland honor wouldn't permit such a thing!"

Niall shrugged. "Aye, 'tis true enough. But, one way or another, the feud is set and there seems little either o' us can do about it. For my part, I had yet to be named clan tanist and wasn't privy to the rest o' the evidence, or part o' the final decision. I accepted the council's decision, though, as any good Highlander would.

"As far as your other accusation that I like raiding and the shedding o' blood, well, I do admit to enjoying the thrill o' occasionally lifting a few cattle—what Highlander doesn't?—but I don't like bloodshed. Feud or no, neither I nor my men have killed any o' yours save in retribution for the death of one o' ours, or in justifiable self-defense."

"And I say you lie!"

The words slipped out before Anne could stop

them. Niall struggled to his feet, then sank back to the stone bench, his face pale with the sudden exertion.

"Don't say that!" he growled, his sweat-damp features tight with anger. "Don't ever, *ever* call me a liar! I've never lied and I'll certainly not begin now just to please you. Think o' me what you will, but don't justify your clan's shortcomings with false accusations!"

Eyes wide, she stared down at the man before her. She'd been a fool to taunt him. Grudgingly, Anne had to admit Niall Campbell seemed to place great store on his word. His reaction had been too immediate, too violent, not to have sprung from the heart. And if he hadn't been privy to the decisions surrounding the beginning of the feud, he might truly feel justified in accepting the Campbell view of things. Yet how could she believe him, for to do so could perhaps place blame, at least some of it, upon her own people?

Confused emotions whirled in her head. Blessed Mother, what was she about, that a hated enemy could stand here and make her doubt her own kind? He was clever, that was all.

Tread lightly with him, Annie, she told herself. *'Tisn't important what he says. Humor him and then be gone.*

"I—I beg pardon," she forced herself to say. "My tongue is too sharp at times and forges ahead o' my good sense. My purpose here isn't to upset you, or to relive the feud, but to see to your needs."

She motioned toward his battered face. "Let me finish tending your wounds. You must be sore weary. I'll bring you some food before you take your rest."

The anger left Niall with a rush. In its place flowed heavy exhaustion. He leaned back against the stone wall with a deep sigh. "Aye, that I am, lass." He grinned up at her. " 'Tis mayhap why my anger boils so close to the surface."

Anne picked up a clean cloth and wet it in a bowl of water. She studied him for a moment, then began to wash the gash over his left eyebrow.

"This cut is deep and won't cease its oozing. I'll apply witch hazel to stop the bleeding, then some o' my marigold ointment. 'Tis excellent in the healing of wounds."

Niall grunted his assent, well aware she didn't wish to discuss the subject of their families further. Instead, he occupied himself in watching her. For the first time, he took his leisure in closely studying the woman before him.

Her hair, now pulled into a long, thick braid down her back, was a rich, glowing color. Its dark red hue set off the ivory radiance of her flawless skin to perfection. Her nose was straight, short and charming, her lips full and delightfully pink as she bit into them in her intense concentration.

His glance slid from her arresting face, moving down her small, slender body. The plain woolen dress wasn't meant to entice, but its simplicity flattered her curving figure better than the stiff, exaggerated outlines of courtly gowns ever could. Her breasts were small but most pleasingly rounded, her waist narrow, her hips provocatively full.

She was a beautiful woman. When engaged in something she loved, as Niall sensed she loved her healing, she radiated a serenity and strength that made her seem almost ethereal. The lass was different, and no mistake. In his younger days, before he'd wed, Niall knew he'd have found her attractive. Aye, most attractive, but not now, and perhaps never. . . .

He quickly shook aside that painful memory. There was nothing wrong with him. Perhaps all he needed was a lovely witch's potion.

She'd certainly been bewitching that eve of the raid. Standing there before his men, her hair wild and tousled, defiantly taunting them, Niall couldn't help but admire her spirit and courage. He'd guessed her ruse, her intention of using the prevailing witch panic to turn them away and protect the village. And it would've worked on a sane man. But Hugh wasn't quite sane, not all the time. She'd nearly lost her life because of it.

"That night we raided the village." He took her hand to stop her ministrations. "Why did my cousin think you a witch?"

Surprise flickered in her silver eyes. *Why would he ask such a question, or even care for that matter?*

"He thought I'd used witchcraft to bring a wee babe back to life."

"And why would he have thought that?"

Anne hesitated. *If I tell him, he may think the same o' me.*

For some inexplicable reason, she didn't want him to, though she knew his opinion of her shouldn't matter. In the past she'd never let the whisperings, the clacking tongues, give her pause. Yet gazing down at him, into the measureless depths of his rich brown eyes, she felt herself falter.

"A misunderstanding, as are most claims o' witchcraft," Anne finally replied with a small shrug of her shoulders, averting her eyes to dig into her bag for her ointment.

"Aye." Niall chuckled. "Misunderstandings, rumors. I can well understand how they grow until the tales faint resemble the person."

A sudden realization assailed him. "I know you now. You're the one they call the Witch o' Glenstrae."

Anne nodded, intent on applying the healing salve to his brow. "I've been called that. Does it disturb you?"

"Nay. I told you before. I don't believe in witch-craft. Besides, I've been called a wolf, yet I feel no more one than I imagine you feel a witch."

In spite of herself, a smile sprang to Anne's lips. She put aside her ointment and looked at him. "Rumors, I fear, move faster, last longer, than truth ever can. And with far more damage."

"Yet you persist in your healings, knowing full well the danger o' the tales spread about you."

"And would you have me stop my work? Cower in a dark corner because o' idle gossip and the mouth-ings o' ignorant minds?" Anne vehemently shook her head. "Nay, I've a life to lead. I'll not hang back in fear because my talents lie in other paths than most women."

Laughter rumbled deep in his chest.

"And what's so amusing?" Anne demanded.

"Och, 'tis naught, lass." Niall grinned. "I was but wondering how your future husband will look upon all this."

She tossed her head. " 'Tis o' no import. I'll never wed, for I'll not be constrained by the rules o' some blustering, narrow-minded fool. And besides, I've no worry. None will have me because o' my reputation. My poor father, though he hated to shame me in such a manner, was finally forced to marry off my two younger sisters before me."

Anne laughed. "But I didn't care. What was one more broken custom among so many I'd already tossed by the way?"

Admiration mingled with bemusement in Niall's eyes. "Och, you'll run a man a good race before he's tamed you, and no mistake. Never fear, though, lassie. There are men aplenty who'll not turn from the task. A spirited filly, if gentled well, is o' greater value than a plodding nag."

"So, now I'm compared to a horse! Your opinion o' women is sorry indeed, Niall Campbell!"

He threw back his head and shouted with laughter, then stopped, clutching his side. A grimace of pain twisted his handsome features. "Och, I forgot my bruises. Have a heart, lass, and don't make me laugh again." He cocked his head. "Tell me your name. We've never been properly introduced, you know."

An unaccustomed warmth surged through Anne, followed quickly by a flash of irritation. She shouldn't feel so ... so friendly, so flattered by his interest. He was still her enemy, no matter how pleasant he could be. Her lips tightened and she forced down her natural affability.

"I can't fathom the import, your knowing my name. It changes naught. All that matters is you are Campbell and I, MacGregor. But since you asked, I am called Anne."

The color drained from Niall's face. His expression hardened. Anne thought she saw a flash of pain in his eyes, but it passed so swiftly she could have been mistaken. There was no mistaking, however, the physical distance he meant to put between them as he leaned away.

"You're right, o' course," he growled. "I was wrong to ask. It changes naught. Naught at all."

Chapter Three

Anne hurried up the dungeon steps, thankful her task of caring for Niall Campbell was over. His wounds had been tended, a light meal served, and he was now resting, a thick fur provided him against the room's chill. Later, after he'd had time to sleep, she'd return with some wash water and a fresh shirt to replace his dirty, tattered one.

But later was hours away, from the haggard look of exhaustion on his face. For the time being, she was free of him, free of the disconcerting emotions he so easily stirred. And she meant to spend it outside, breathing the fresh Highland air.

The day was nearly spent. Savory smells of roasting meats and yeasty breads filled the air. Anne sighed contentedly. How she loved this time of day, when the dying sun cast its mellow glow upon the land, when the day's struggle and strife were over, and the only labor left was the satisfying contemplation of one's accomplishments. It was so peaceful, so. . . .

A loud commotion reached Anne as she strode into the main hall and toward the huge, open doorway. From the outer bailey came the sound of men's shouts, the clang of weapons, and the stamping and snorting of nervous horses. She stepped out into the keep's inner courtyard. No one was about. Anne's pace quickened.

She was out the gate and halfway across the outer bailey before a servant scurried by, a harried look on her face. Anne grabbed her by the arm.

"What's amiss? Why is everyone rushing about?"

"R–rushing about?" the little maidservant panted. "Dinna ye know, ma'am? 'Tis the Campbells! They're at our gates, a whole army o' them! Och, 'twill go bad for us now, very bad!"

Her silver eyes turned to the parapets where, even now, MacGregor clansmen were massing, the stiff wind flapping their red tartans about their legs like crimson flames. The stout form of her father paced the walkway. She headed toward him.

He was staring out over the hills, his features grim. Anne followed his glance and gasped. There, in what seemed an endless mass of tartan hues, was a huge army. Though Campbells were most prevalent, Anne could also make out the colors of several other clans. Campbell allies, one and all, she thought bitterly, and armed to the teeth for war.

"Give him to us, MacGregor!"

Three Campbell men rode forward. From her vantage point, Anne recognized one of them as Niall's mad cousin, Hugh.

"Give us our tanist or you'll rue the day you so foully took him!" the oldest of the trio, a tall, bearded blond man, shouted.

"And who are you to threaten me, Campbell?" Alastair MacGregor boomed back at him. "I'll keep your man as long as I please, and no amount o' threats will make me give him up before I'm ready.

You'll not menace me from my own castle!"

"Och, and will we not?" The sandy-haired Campbell gestured about him. "Think long and hard, man. Tomorrow, at dawn's first light, we'll ask you again."

Before her father could reply, the leaders turned their horses and galloped away, their army following swiftly behind. On a distant hillock they halted. As Anne and her father watched, the warriors began to set up camp.

"What will you do, Father?"

"And what do you suppose?" he snapped, his eyes burning with an admixture of rage and frustration. "They'll lay siege if we don't give him up, and how long could we last?"

Alastair gripped the stone wall, his shoulders hunched in despair. "Och, curse the day I ever laid eyes on that man," he muttered, half to himself. "Curse the day I ever entrapped Niall Campbell! I should've known a traitor helps neither side."

"What are you saying? How did you entrap Niall Campbell?" Anne's nails sank deep into the flesh of his arm. "And what do you mean, 'a traitor'?"

He shook her hand away with an exasperated gesture. "Leave me be, lass! I've got to think! Got to find a way out o' this that'll save both our hides *and* our honor."

Her father stalked off, his head bent in deep concentration. Anne turned back to the scene outside the castle walls. Lovingly, her gaze swept the wooded glens, the bracken-strewn hills and meadows, the rocky crags. MacGregor land.

For eight years now they'd borne the periodic raids, the dreaded attack of intruders. But today was the culmination of their deepest fears, for the nightmare had at last become reality in an army that stood ready to destroy them. And there was naught—naught at all—they could do about it.

*   *   *

"What do you want with me?"

Niall stood before Alastair MacGregor, groggy from being dragged from a heavy slumber, his hands and feet in shackles. His glance strayed to the deep, stone-cut window across the chief's room. It was pitch black outside. What time was it? Midnight or past?

Alastair watched the guards shut the door behind them before answering. "We have a problem."

Niall's attention riveted on the older man. "*We* do? And what might that be?"

Damn him, the MacGregor cursed silently. Even in chains the arrogant young whelp refused to make it easy. Something inside Alastair hardened. *Well, he'll not best me in this, for I've naught left to lose. . . .*

"Your clan lies outside the castle," Alastair said. "They demand your return."

Niall shrugged. "Then 'tis simple. Give me to them."

"Nay, 'tisn't simple at all. MacGregor honor couldn't bear such disgrace."

Tawny-brown eyes studied him. Alastair saw the understanding flare in their depths.

" 'Tis as you say," Niall admitted at last. " 'Tis never a simple matter where Highland honor's concerned. What do you want o' me?"

The MacGregor's hands clenched. His heart quickened in excitement. "An end to the feud."

"And how do you propose we do that?"

Alastair walked to the whiskey decanter and leisurely filled two cups with the potent brew. Prolonging the effect of his reply, he handed one of the cups to Niall before answering.

"How else, but in the age-old custom o' joining the clans? You'll take my Annie as wife."

Niall stared at him for a long moment, then

downed the contents of his cup in one gulp. He handed it back to Alastair.

"Nay, it can't be. I am honored by your offer, but I cannot wed your daughter."

"And why not?" Alastair calmly inquired. To find offense at the refusal would only weaken his plan. " 'Tis a marriage made in heaven. My Annie's a beautiful, kind-hearted lass, a wee bit headstrong but from what I've seen and heard o' you, you're just the man to tame her. She's well built, healthy, and will bear you fine sons. What more can a man ask? 'Twill join our two clans *and* put an end to the feud."

"Indeed, she seems everything you've said and more." Niall ran a hand raggedly through his hair. "The problem lies not with her, but with me. I still mourn my wife."

Alastair nodded sympathetically. "I can well understand your hesitation. I, too, lost a beloved wife. But it has been a year, a fair time for a mourning. You're the chief's son and clan tanist. You, o' all men, recognize that the peoples' welfare comes before your own desires, however justifiable they may be. None will condemn you for ending your mourning, not when 'twill bring an end to the feuding."

"And I don't care what anyone thinks, one way or another!" Niall rasped, his tall frame tensing in anger. "Who is to say a year is long enough? I'll not shame the memory o' my wife for anyone! Do you hear me, MacGregor? *Anyone!*"

Alastair's jaw clenched. This was proving more difficult than he'd anticipated. He hadn't counted on the man's deep emotions for his wife clouding his judgement.

"And I say, think again. You're hardly in a position to refuse. Though you managed to escape death once, I've naught to lose now—and you've everything."

Niall laughed. "And do you think I believe you'd

dare kill me with a Campbell army outside your gates? Your castle would be overrun and every man, woman, and child put to the sword. 'Tis the Highland code."

"Who said I'd kill you?" Alastair shook his head, a grim, deadly smile twisting his mouth. "I'm not fool enough to make a martyr o' you, to return you to them clothed in the glory o' death. Nay, I thought rather to send you back a little less a man than when you came." His bushy gray brows arched. "If you get my meaning?"

Niall stiffened. The man must be addled even to suggest such a thing! He shuddered at the thought then, regaining his composure, looked deep into the MacGregor's eyes.

His enemy's gaze was as firm as his own. *He's backed to the wall*, Niall realized. *All that's left is his honor*. And that, Niall well knew, was a life-or-death matter.

But where was the honor in shaming his beloved's memory? Though he was far from wanting another wife, the MacGregor lass was comely and many marriages had been made for less than romantic reasons. He never hoped to have again what he'd once had anyway. That kind of love came only once in a lifetime. But to wed before he'd mourned as he saw fit. . . .

"And if you did such a thing, what good would I be to your daughter then, man?" Niall inquired coolly, determined not to give the MacGregor an inch in this battle of wills.

The look of surprise on the man's face salved some of Niall's wounded pride. He made his decision. All issues of love and honor aside, he knew he had to survive if for no other reason than to discover the traitor.

"You're a hard one, MacGregor." He sighed. "I'll give you what you want, but you must meet me halfway. After all, I've my pride to consider, too."

Alastair smiled, sensing the victory within his grasp. He'd won, so why not be generous?

"Ask, and if 'tis within reason, 'tis yours."

"I'll need another year before my mourning's done. I'll handfast with your daughter for that time, then wed her. 'Tis the best I can do."

Handfast, the MacGregor thought. Lord, Annie would balk at that unwed state worse than at marrying a Campbell. To live together as man and wife without a church-sanctioned ceremony might be acceptable to many, a "trial marriage," so to speak, where both could go their way if things didn't work out, but he knew his daughter. For all her flaunting of a woman's customary strictures, she'd never go against the proper religious morals her mother had instilled in her. Yet, noting the determined set to his prisoner's jaw, he also knew Niall Campbell wouldn't budge from his offer. Annie would just have to understand.

Alastair extended his hand, a huge grin on his face. "We've a bargain. My Annie's yours." His expression turned serious as Niall clasped his hand. "I'd be obliged if you treated her kindly. 'Tisn't her fault, whatever bitterness you may feel toward me because o' this. Don't take it out on her."

"Don't concern yourself, man. I'll not harm her."

Niall then remembered the Reformed preacher who'd just a year ago returned from Edinburgh to take up residence once more on Campbell lands. His father's bastard brother, Malcolm Campbell, was a narrow-minded witch fanatic who'd already managed to stir the clan to the edge of panic. Niall wondered what the man's reaction would be to Anne.

He turned to Alastair. " 'Twill go hard for her, nonetheless. Her witch's reputation has spread far and wide."

A wild fear sprung to the MacGregor's eyes. "You'll

protect her, won't you? She's not a witch. 'Tis her great skills with healing and those strange gray eyes o' hers that give some folk pause. But she's not a witch."

"I know that, man. I'll do what I can." Niall gestured toward the whiskey decanter. "I'd like a wee more o' the potents, to seal the bargain as it were."

"Och." Alastair chuckled. "A man after my own heart."

He hurried over and refilled both cups. When Niall's was once more in his hand, the MacGregor raised his in a toast. "To an end to the feud once and for all, and to your—"

"One thing more." Niall halted him. "As we're soon to be family, I can expect your full measure o' loyalty, can I not?"

The older man's gaze narrowed. "You already know the answer to that. What is it you want?"

"My capture. 'Twas too easy, you knowing when and where we were to attack. Who told you, MacGregor?"

"I—I don't know what you—"

"No games, man! Don't protect a Campbell from one o' his own. Besides, who knows? He may have been the one responsible for the feud. Stranger things have happened. Tell me his name. You owe loyalty to me now, not him."

Alastair shook his head. "I can't tell you that, for I don't know the man. He came to me alone and kept his face covered. He was a crafty one and full o' hatred for you, but why, I don't know. He was careful to say little. I fear I can't help you."

"Damn!"

Frustration swelled in Niall until it nearly choked him. Save for having his suspicions confirmed, he was no closer to discovering the traitor than before. His only advantage lay in the fact the man didn't know that Niall yet suspected. It was small indeed, but all he had. But not for long. He'd see to that.

"No one must know, MacGregor. You must reveal the fact that you told me this to no one. Do you understand?"

"Aye. You have my word on it."

"Good." Niall raised his cup. "Then to the union o' our families. May it forever bring an end to the feuding."

Alastair once more lifted his cup. "To our families. May the Children o' the Mist once more live in peace with Clan Campbell."

The two men downed their drinks.

"How soon can the handfasting be done?" Niall asked. "I've a need to return home as quickly as possible."

Alastair's brow knit in thought. "I must tell Annie, give her time to accept it. And her possessions need packing. Do you desire an elaborate ceremony?"

"Nay. We'll save that for the wedding."

"Then why not have it at midday? 'Twill give you time to rest and me time to break it to my daughter."

"As you wish, but we must depart immediately thereafter. Also, I'll need one o' my own as witness."

"Your clan will return at dawn's first light. You can come with me to the walls and call one inside. But no tricks. I'll not have you shame my daughter by telling her I forced her on you. Your word on it, Campbell."

Och, man, Niall thought. *Suddenly you're caring for your daughter's feelings, after all but trading her off like some prize cow?* He controlled the sneer that threatened the corner of his mouth.

"You have my word on it, not that 'twill matter. Your daughter is too smart not to guess the truth." Niall laughed. "I don't envy you the task o' convincing her. I may as yet get out o' this. Then what will you do?"

The MacGregor's face reddened. "My Annie's an obedient daughter, for all her spunk. She'll obey her father, and no mistake."

Niall's dark brows arched challengingly. "Then call her, man. Now. Let's get this settled once and for all."

Anne awoke to her serving maid shaking her. "Ma'am? Please, ma'am, yer father's calling for ye."

"Wh–what?" Anne sat up, brushing the hair from her eyes. "Father? Did he say what he wanted?"

The little maid shook her head. "Nay. I was only told to dress ye, fix yer hair, and send ye on yer way as quickly as possible."

"Then let's get on with it." Anne sprang out of bed. "At this hour, I fear it must be important."

It had to have something to do with the Campbells, perhaps even Niall Campbell himself, Anne mused as she hurried down the chill stone corridor toward her father's chambers. But what would her father need her for? How could she be of any help? Well, no matter, she firmly told herself as she paused to smooth her dress and hastily braided hair before knocking on the door. One way or another, she'd discover the answer soon enough.

"Come in, lass," her father's voice beckoned at her first knock.

Hesitantly, Anne pushed open the door. Her father and Niall Campbell stood together, warming themselves at the hearth. She walked in.

"Close the door and come here, lass."

Anne quickly did as she was told. "Aye, Father?" she murmured an instant later, her eyes searching his face in concern. "You called me. What troubles you?"

Alastair gestured toward Niall. "We've come to an agreement that'll end the feuding."

Her eyes swung to meet those of Niall Campbell. "Is it true? You've agreed to end the feud?"

Niall nodded.

"But how?" she eagerly persisted. "What common ground could you two possibly find? What honorable recourse to ease the wounded pride o' both sides?"

A strange light flared in Niall's eyes. "I've no talent for smooth words to ease your pain, and I won't lie. Ask your father. 'Twill come better from him."

He looked at Alastair. "I'll wait at the window. 'Twill give you a few moments alone together."

Alastair nodded. Both he and Anne watched as Niall walked and took his seat across the room. Then Anne turned to her father.

"What did he mean? Why should an end to the feud cause me pain?"

"Och, lass." He sighed. "Now hear me out before you fly into a rage. 'Twas the best, the only thing, I could do." He took her by the arms. "I've given you to him."

Shock warred with anger until Anne's arresting eyes darkened to stormy gray. "Wh—what? You did what?"

"You heard me, lass. I gave you to Niall Campbell."

"You *gave* me to . . . to *him*?" Anne's voice rose on a thread of hysteria. "But why? He doesn't want me!"

Niall winced at the naked anguish in her words, knowing full well their truth. Pity slashed through him. Though it was evident she was just as adamantly against their union as he, Anne would suffer far greater consequences. She'd be the one to leave her home and adjust her life to his. She'd be the one to lose the freedom she so dearly cherished, not to mention the opportunity to heal, for it would be far too dangerous for her to roam about ministering to his more superstitious clan.

Perhaps she didn't realize that yet. Niall prayed

so, for the knowledge might be more than she could bear. Better to break it to her later, after she'd had time. . . .

"Nay!"

The cry wrenched free of the muffled speech coming from across the room. Niall's head jerked around. At that moment Anne turned to him. Their eyes met, regretful brown ones locking with tear-bright silver.

"N–nay," she whispered, the entreaty so direct and personal it sliced to the depths of his heart.

He fought the impulse to go to her, gather her into his arms and comfort her. Instead, he forced his glance back out the window. It would do no good, Niall told himself.

What could he promise her anyway? He didn't know if his people would ever accept her or if she'd find happiness at Kilchurn. And he had no hope of love to offer. Better she seek what comfort she could from her father.

"How can you do this?" Anne demanded of Alastair, the tears now coursing, unchecked, down her cheeks. "How can you give me to a man such as you know Niall Campbell to be? He's ruthless, cruel, and will probably ill treat me solely out o' hatred for MacGregors. You forced him into this. I know you did!"

Alastair gently wiped her tears away. " 'Tis for the good o' both our peoples, lass. He saw the wisdom, as you must. Don't fear him. He's an honorable man. I know that now. He'll not mistreat you."

"B–but I don't want a husband!" she wailed. "I don't want to wed!"

"Er, 'tisn't a marriage," her father mumbled, coloring fiercely. "Or at least not for a time. You're to be handfasted to him for a year and a day, until his mourning for his wife is over."

Anne jerked away, her tears staunched in her

scorching anger and disbelief. "*Handfasted*? You're *handfasting* me? I don't believe it! Why not just give me to him as his whore? 'Tis one and the same as far as I'm concerned!"

"Now, lass." Alastair moved toward her, his voice low with warning. "Calm yourself. 'Tisn't the same at all. Handfasting is an ancient, honored custom. There's no shame in it. Besides, he's agreed to wed you when the year is up. You can't blame him for wanting to mourn his wife, can you?"

"Let him mourn the rest o' his life for all I care!" Anne hotly replied. "It doesn't matter to me! 'Tis my right as a Scotswoman to refuse this. I *will not* handfast or anything else with him!"

"And I say you will!" her father roared, losing his patience at last. "You're still my child, my firstborn and heir. The welfare o' our clan, nay, its very survival, is now in your hands. You know where your duty lies."

He pointed toward the door. "Now go, and not another word from you. The ceremony will commence at midday. The Wolf wishes to depart immediately thereafter, so see to your preparations. I don't wish to discuss this further!"

Anne opened her mouth to protest then, seeing the tense, rigid expression on her father's face, thought better of it. It was no use, she realized. It would all be the same in the end. She couldn't refuse her father in a matter such as this.

He was right. She did know her duty. She was MacGregor and the plight of an entire clan mattered more than her own wishes. But to handfast with a man such as Niall Campbell!

With a choking sob, Anne ran from the room.

The ensuing hours until midday flew by in a flurry of activity. From a place far removed, Anne watched the preparations for her departure. Her gowns were carefully folded, her slippers and small collection of jewelry wrapped in soft cloths, her beloved clarsach safely tucked among them all.

A heavy pain settled around her heart. Would there ever be reason to strum the curved wooden harp in Kilchurn Castle?

Soon, nothing remained save the traveling gown of deep emerald velvet and a heavy woolen cape to ward against the blustering spring winds. Her entire life, Anne mused sadly, had quickly condensed into a few bulky parcels.

One last time, she walked out into the keep's private garden. The sturdier plants that had over-wintered were beginning to sprout fresh shoots of green. Her beloved herbs. Life-giving, heart-and-body soothing. Would there be a place for them in her new life?

A sob rose in Anne's throat. In but the span of a few hours her life had completely changed. Now, she was a helpless pawn to be manipulated at the whim of others. The freedom, the control she'd once had, were now lovely illusions.

Aye, illusions indeed, Anne thought, *for they were never more than that in anyone's mind but my own. I've never had any power over my life save what was permitted me.*

She knelt to brush a bit of dirt gently from a chamomile plant. *Soon their delicate, daisy-like flowers will bloom,* Anne mused wistfully, *and I'll not be here to see them.*

The realization stirred something, firing her resolve, feeding her wounded spirit. She rose to her feet, her hands clenched at her sides. Let them all be damned! Though the circumstances of her life may have changed, why should she relinquish her life's work? The censure of others had never stopped her before. Why should it do so now?

She'd risked death for a long while now. Even in

Campbell lands, there was nothing more they could threaten her with than that.

Anne hurried away, soon returning with a trowel and an empty wooden box. A grim smile on her lips, she carefully dug up a sampling of every herb in her garden and placed it in the container. Somehow, someway, she'd find a spot to transplant and grow her precious friends at Kilchurn Castle. She had to. In some symbolic manner, their rebirth would also assure hers.

An hour later Anne stood in her father's chamber, dressed in the green gown with fitted bodice and tight sleeves with their trailing edges, her hair gathered in a pearl-studded snood and topped with a small green velvet cap. Her only jewelry, in deference to the journey ahead, was a long pearl necklace, knotted just below the high-collared neckline. Nervously, her glance scanned the empty room as she waited for her father, who had gone with Niall Campbell to fetch one of his men as witness to the impending ceremony.

She jumped at the heavy tread of footsteps in the hallway. Before Anne had a chance to compose herself, the door swung open. In walked her father, followed closely by Niall Campbell and another man. Anne swallowed hard and forced her gaze to meet that of the tall, dark-haired warrior, who strode over to stand before her.

"Lass," Niall's deep voice rumbled, "allow me to introduce another o' my cousins, Iain Campbell. Iain, this is Anne MacGregor."

At the mention of her name, the equally tall, darkly golden-haired man jerked his admiring gaze from her to Niall. "Anne?"

"Aye," he replied tersely. "Pay your respects."

Iain, who looked to be several years younger than Niall, looked back at Anne. He accepted her proffered hand. A pair of intensely blue eyes studied her for a moment, then his head bowed to kiss her hand.

" 'Tis my greatest pleasure to make your acquaintance, ma'am. You are truly one o' the most lovely women I've ever laid eyes upon."

"And you are as gallant as any court gentleman to say so," Anne murmured stiffly. "I hope we can be friends."

A reckless grin split Iain's handsome face. "I'd have liked to be more than friends, if Niall hadn't claimed you first. But fate being what 'tis, I suppose I'll be pleased to settle for a friendship."

At his blunt, forthright manner, Anne couldn't help but smile. Here was one Campbell, at least, who seemed willing to accept her. Perhaps there was hope.

Niall cleared his throat. "Now that my cousin is finished charming this gathering, let us get on with the handfasting. We've several hours' journey ahead and I wish to be home before dark."

Iain merely quirked an amused eyebrow, but Anne, irritated by his rudeness, shot him an icy glance. "Aye, by all means. I've no wish to deter you from more important matters."

He opened his mouth to snap something back at her, then thought better of it. *It isn't her fault,* he reminded himself for the tenth time. *Be gentle. It's even worse for her than for you.*

Niall addressed the MacGregor. "The ceremony, if you please."

Alastair's gaze skittered anxiously from his daughter to Niall. *Let this go smoothly,* he prayed, *or all will be lost.* He opened the small book he held and, after a prolonged bout of throat clearing, began to read.

"There are those in our midst who seek the bond o' handfasting. Let them be named and brought before us." He raised his eyes to Anne and Niall. "Take each other's hand and step forward."

A large, heavily calloused palm extended toward Anne. After a moment's hesitation, she placed her trembling hand in Niall's. There was a momentary squeeze, as if he were trying to reassure her. Then, as one, they moved to stand before the MacGregor. Out of the corner of her eye, Anne saw Iain take his place beside his cousin.

Alastair directed his gaze to Niall. "Repeat after me. I, Niall Campbell, do come here o' my own free will, to seek the partnership o' Anne MacGregor. I come with all love, honor—"

"I'm not a hypocrite, MacGregor!" Niall interrupted him harshly. "Leave love out o' this or I'll not make the vows."

"A—as you wish," the older man stammered, unnerved by the vehemence in Niall's voice. "I meant no offense. 'Tis the customary rite."

"And I don't give a damn what the custom is!" Niall hissed through clenched teeth. "Now, get on with it!"

"I—I come with all . . . honor and sincerity, wishing only to become one with her whom I lov—honor."

He paused as Niall repeated the words. "Always," Alastair then continued, "will I strive for Anne's happiness and welfare. Her life will I defend before my own. All this I swear. May I find the strength to keep my vows."

Niall spoke the words after him. Then Alastair turned to Anne, guiding her in her pledge. Once she'd finished, he withdrew two rings from his pocket. Of plain gold workings, the pair gleamed with the patina of age and loving use.

"These were your mother's and mine." His eyes misted with memories as he smiled down at his daughter. "There wasn't time to fashion new ones for the ceremony. I'd be pleased if you'd wear your mother's."

"Aye, Father," Anne whispered, tears of bittersweet joy welling in her eyes. " 'Twould please me, too."

He handed the ring to Niall. "Place it upon her finger."

Niall slid the golden circlet onto the third finger of Anne's left hand. Then his gaze returned to Alastair's.

"W–would you consider wearing my ring?" the older man asked. " 'Twas part o' a long and happy union once before. Mayhap 'twill bring the same fortune again."

Niall gritted his teeth, a muscle twitching furiously in his jaw. *'Tis a farce, all o' this,* he inwardly raged, *yet the old man persists in trying to force some romantic symbolism into it. Well, this goes too far! I won't compromise my honor.*

A gentle squeeze of his hand halted him. Turning, Niall found himself captured by a mesmerizing pair of silver eyes. Warm with silent entreaty, they pulled at him. He knew, for Anne's sake at least, he couldn't refuse.

"I—I'd be honored, MacGregor," Niall mumbled, still ensnared by the strange feelings roiling within him. Benumbed, he watched as the man presented his daughter with the ring and she placed it on his finger.

"As the grass o' the fields and the trees o' the woods bend together under the pressures o' the storm," Alastair once more intoned, "so too must you both bend when the wind blows strong. But know as quickly as the storm comes, so equally quickly it may leave. Yet, will you both stand, strong in each other's strength. As you give lov—honor, so will you receive strength. Together you are one; apart you are nothing."

He raised his eyes to gaze at them. "Ever honor, help, and respect each other—and know that now you are truly one."

A broad smile lit his face. " 'Tis over, the hand-fasting. You may kiss her."

Kiss her, Niall thought. Ah, well, she was his now and if it would but put an end to this odious ceremony. . . .

He pulled her to him. His powerful arms encircled her.

In rising horror, Anne watched the approach of Niall Campbell's ruggedly hewn face. *Holy Mother, 'tis too much after such a day!* she protested silently. *I can't bear it! If he kisses me, I'll surely swoon!*

She shook her head wildly in an attempt to evade the hard, inexorably descending mouth, struggling in his arms. A hand seized her head in an iron clasp. In helpless fascination, Anne stared up at him, a cry clawing its way to her throat. Before it could break free, his mouth captured hers.

Chapter Four

Strong, hard lips slanted over hers, forcing Anne back against the unyielding grip of Niall's hand. For a moment slowed in time, she fought him, her fingers digging into his broad, linen-covered chest, before finally surrendering to his overwhelming power— and the cruel reality of her fate.

She was a fool to fight him; Niall Campbell owned her now in body and life. To resist would only shame her before the clan. There was nothing left but acceptance, but that acceptance would be as cold and unyielding as she could make it.

Anne relaxed in his arms, neither pulling away nor returning his kiss. The change in her response startled Niall. He drew back to scan her face. Silver eyes, devoid of expression, stared up at him.

So, this is how it's to be, he mused wryly. *A frigid bedmate.*

Disappointment shot through him, then Niall reminded himself of the true purpose of the handfasting. She was comely enough, but he'd neither the time nor inclination to woo a wench, willing or not. Issues of far greater import demanded his attention. Like the identity of a certain traitor.

The realization, hovering at the edge of his consciousness, rushed back with disconcerting force. With a low, angry curse, Niall released Anne.

His frowning glance found the MacGregor. " 'Tis done then, the vows said and sealed."

He nodded to his cousin. "Let us be gone."

Iain grinned. "Not so fast, cousin. Custom, not you, dictates the pace. As clan witness to this handfasting, I'm required to give your lady a kiss. Would you have her feeling unwelcome to the family?"

Niall's gaze narrowed. He gestured toward Anne with an impatient sweep of his hand. "Make it quick, then."

As she stood there in stunned surprise, Iain took her into his arms. His intense blue eyes, deep and fathomless as the waters of mighty Loch Awe, smilingly swept over her. Then his lips touched hers, gently covering her mouth.

It was too much. First the cold ownership of Niall's kiss, and now Iain's expert assault. She'd never kissed a grown man, aside from her father's affectionate caresses, and now to have two in one day! Anne groaned in dismay, moving to push Iain away.

"Enough, cousin." Stirred by the unexpected surge of possessiveness Anne's small sound evoked in him, Niall stepped forward to grasp his cousin's arm.

The flare of irritation—or was it jealousy?—burning in Niall's eyes was not lost on Iain. With a reluctant grin, he released Anne.

"Welcome, lass. You'll make a fine Campbell, and no mistake."

Anne shook her head. "N–nay. 'Twill never be. Though I journey far from home and hearth, I'll always be a MacGregor."

"And journey you shall," Niall's steel-timbred voice intruded. "Your belongings are packed; the horses await. Let us be gone."

Anne glanced toward her father, unable to hide a look of silent supplication. He paled. Remorse surged through her at the expression of pain and regret that crossed his face.

With a determined thrust of her shoulders, she faced Niall. *'Twill do no good to bemoan your fate, Annie girl,* she told herself firmly. *You're handfasted now, and that's that.*

"Aye," she murmured, returning Niall Campbell's glittering stare with a resolute one of her own. "Let us be gone. 'Twill do no good to linger over things that cannot be changed."

She extended her hand to him. "Better to face bravely what life brings, to forget the past and forge on—for the good o' all, MacGregor and Campbell alike."

The lowering sky, heavy with dark, moisture-laden clouds, precluded overlong farewells. For that, at least, Anne was thankful. If she'd lingered a moment longer, she'd have surely burst into tears in front of them all, mortifying both herself and her father, and no doubt adding to Niall Campbell's rising exasperation. But the thought of several hours' ride, in what rapidly threatened to turn into a typical Highland downpour, was enough to put a damper on leave-takings between travelers and well-wishers alike.

They mounted quickly. The huge castle doors swung open. For a moment, Anne stared out upon an assemblage of tartan-clad warriors. Then Niall urged his mount forward. As he cleared the fortress' portals, a cheer rose from the army outside the gate.

"The Wolf! The Wolf o' Cruachan lives!"

At the outcry Niall rose in his saddle, his right

arm lifting in a close-fisted salute. "Cruachan!" he shouted, the harsh Campbell battle cry echoing across the hills.

Urging his horse onward and followed closely by Anne and Iain, Niall rode to the head of his forces. With a motion of his hand, he signaled the journey to begin.

Anne never looked back. She didn't dare or the tears would have surely flowed. Riveting her gaze on Niall's broad back, riding ahead with his cousin, Hugh, and the older man who'd been the spokesman for his return, she steeled herself to the sight of the beloved land she was leaving behind.

The road turned south along the River Strae, its current turbulent with melted winter snow. A fine mist rose from the water-battered stones. Anne inhaled deeply of the scent of rich, damp earth.

The meadows were alive with springtide flowers, gallant little daffodils, delicate snowdrops, and yellow primroses. The milk-white petals of the delicate Star of Bethlehem gleamed among the rank growth of ivy and fern in the nearby woods. Everywhere she looked she saw the heartbreaking beauty of her land. A lump rose in Anne's throat.

"Don't fret so, lassie," Iain Campbell gently intruded as he rode up alongside her. " 'Tisn't as if you'll never see your home again. In time, when the feuding cools, I'm sure you can talk Niall into bringing you back for a visit. We're nearly neighbors, after all."

She gave him a misty-eyed smile. "My thanks for your kindness. I don't think your tanist will have much time for humoring the likes o' me, though."

Her gaze turned to rest again on Niall, riding ahead, deeply immersed in conversation with Hugh and the sandy-haired man. "He seems to find Campbell concerns o' far greater import. I wonder what clan he's planning to raid now that MacGregors can no longer be his enemies?"

Iain's mouth quirked at the bitterness in Anne's voice. "Och, lassie, don't be so hard on him. With his father ailing, Niall's had a heavy burden o' responsibility laid on him these past few years. Give him a chance. He's not a cruel man, just a wee bit harder since his wife's death."

"Aye," she muttered, "I know how deeply he mourns his wife. Too bad he didn't mourn her enough to prevent our handfasting."

"Well, I'll not speak about something I know little about." He turned toward her. "Would you like to learn a bit about our clan, before we reach Kilchurn Castle? Mayhap 'twould ease your way."

Anne nodded. It was hard to stay glum with a man as handsome and charming as Iain Campbell at her side. "Aye, that would be nice."

She pointed to the older man riding on Niall's right. "And who might he be? Surely someone o' power, for he spoke for your clan in demanding Sir Niall's return."

A bitter smile touched Iain's lips. "Och, a man o' power, and no mistake. He's Duncan, laird o' Balloch Castle on Loch Tay and the Campbell's younger brother. He's also my father."

She shot him a sideways glance. *He doesn't get on with his father*, Anne thought, noting the tight expression on Iain's face. She quickly stifled the impulse to ask him more. It wasn't her concern. She had problems enough without seeking more.

"And Hugh, the witch-hater." Anne gestured to the brown-haired man riding on Niall's other side. "Where exactly does he hang on the Campbell family tree?"

"Mad cousin Hugh? His mother is Lydia Campbell, sister to the Campbell and my father."

"Is he really mad?" Anne asked, recalling the crazed look in Hugh's eyes the day of the raid.

"In some ways, aye. And yet, there are times when

I wonder if there's not a method to his madness . . ."
Iain paused. "At any rate, when he commits himself
to a cause, he can be quite fanatical, going on for
hours, even days, on the same subject. He bears a
heavy grudge that his mother was born female, for
it puts him fourth, after Niall, my father, and myself,
in line for the chieftainship. As you can imagine, 'tis
one o' his favorite topics. We tend to ignore him
when he starts up about it."

"Poor man," Anne murmured pityingly.

"Niall told me Hugh tried to kill you." Iain shook
his head in wonder. "Yet you can still say that, after
what he almost did to you? Och, you're a rare one."

She glanced at him. "I'm a healer, Iain. My heart
goes out to those in distress, whether o' the body or
mind."

"Well, don't concern yourself with Hugh. He'd not
appreciate your efforts. On the contrary, 'twould be
very dangerous for you. He hates witches above
all else."

"And why is that?"

Iain shook his head. "I don't know, lass. It makes
about as much sense as most things Hugh takes a
disliking to. But for your own sake, stay clear o'
him."

"Aye," Anne muttered uneasily.

Movement up ahead distracted them into silence.
They watched as Niall, with a wave of his hand, sent
a rider galloping off down the road. Stretching tall
in his stirrups, Niall stared after the man until he
disappeared from view. Then, with a dark frown, he
settled back onto his horse.

A plan. He must have a plan for discovering the
traitor. Niall glanced behind at the ruddy, good-
hearted faces of his warriors. To question the motives
of even one of them sickened him. But he must, for
more was at stake than his personal safety.

His clan was also in grave danger. If the traitor

had truly stirred the feud all these years, ambition was evidently a higher priority than Campbell welfare. And he as tanist seemed to be all that stood in the way of that ambition.

But who would want him dead? There were several lairds to consider, ones he'd had as tanist to deal with severely in the past. And he didn't dare discount someone who might hold a secret grudge, one he'd no way of knowing about. Yet, as thoroughly as he tried to sift through every possible motive, the spectre of the chieftainship rose above them all.

His own family. Could one of them possibly covet it enough to eliminate him as rightful heir, to become a traitor? There were several males in direct line for the eagle feathers of clan chief—his uncle and two cousins closest of all. To add their names to the list, much less actually consider them, twisted like a dagger in Niall's gut. But consider them he did and, gradually, one name rose above the rest.

Iain. Who else would have better cause than Iain to see him dead? When his father had first turned ill, Niall, thanks to a faction highly in favor of Iain, had not automatically been chosen tanist. In the end the position had finally fallen to him. He'd thought Iain had accepted it but now he wondered. Perhaps, even after all these years, Iain was biding his time.

But his boyhood friend, gallant, courageous Iain? Niall flung aside the gnawing suspicions with a violent shake of his head.

Proof. He had no proof and there were others. He mustn't forget the others, like Hugh and Uncle Duncan.

But cousin Hugh, though well known to covet the chieftainship, was far too unstable to be accepted by the clan. And Duncan, though his father's brother and a strong advisor, might be considered too old to bring much long-term stability. But Iain . . . Iain was young, strong, and very capable.

Suddenly, proof or not, Niall couldn't stand the thought of Iain near anything that was his, and that included Anne. He growled a brief word of explanation to Duncan, then wheeled his mount around and rode back to join the pair.

He pulled up alongside Anne. Niall's keen glance scanned both of them before finally settling on his cousin. "Your father wishes to speak with you. Ride ahead."

Iain laughed. "Have a need to be with your lady, have you? Och, cousin, why not just come out and say it? You've never couched words so gently before."

"Ride ahead and no more o' it!"

"M'lady." Iain nodded to Anne, then urged his mount forward.

She waited until her blond companion was out of earshot, then turned to Niall. "Was it necessary to be so rude? He only tried to keep me company, to distract me from my sorrow."

Niall snorted disdainfully. "And did he now? I think he sniffs a little too closely at what's not his."

Indignation surged through Anne. "Why, you crude, churlish knave! We may be handfasted, but I'm not some piece o' chattel you must protect from your lust-crazed warriors. And I won't abide you telling me who I may and may not take as friend. There'll be few o' those at Kilchurn as 'tis."

"Fear not, sweet lass." Niall chuckled grimly, refusing to allow her to anger him. "I've already taken steps to remedy that wee shortcoming. The rider I sent ahead will notify the castle o' our arrival. And I've ordered a feast this eve to welcome you to the clan. So you see, you'll soon have more friends than you'll know what to do with."

"A—a feast?"

Anne swallowed hard. *He thinks to unsettle me,* she thought and shook her head firmly. "Pray, don't go to such trouble for my sake. There's no need to make pretenses you do not feel. 'Twill fool no one, at any rate."

Niall clamped down hard on an angry retort. "And I say you mistake yourself, madam. All pretense aside, the only way you'll ever gain acceptance is if I accept you. The feast is but my way o' showing that. So don't turn up that haughty little nose o' yours. 'Twillna endear you at Kilchurn."

"I don't care—".

"And I say, don't let fly what you can't call back. For better or worse, Kilchurn is your home, the Campbells your people, for the next year at least. Besides," Niall continued in a gentler tone, "I don't wish you ill. You saved my life, after all, and at great expense to yourself."

"And I don't need your pity," she snapped back at him. " 'Twas a point o' honor that saved your life and naught else."

"Then attend the feast as a point o' honor, for to hide in your room would only confirm what my clan already thinks o' MacGregors."

Anne's hands tightened about her horse's reins. "And what might that be?"

Niall's glance moved casually to scan the countryside. "Och, naught really. Just that MacGregors are all cowards."

"Why, you big, arrogant—"

"Now calm yourself, lassie." Her dark companion laughed. "Those weren't my thoughts. *I* certainly have never doubted your courage. I was thinking o' what others might say, if you failed to show your face this eve."

"I'll be there," Anne muttered, "and no mistake. Are there any other surprises you've planned tonight? If so, tell me now."

He coolly assessed her, his eyes moving over her face and body until Anne's cheeks flushed with exasperating warmth. Realization of his interpretation of her words flashed through her mind. Disgusting, ruttish stag!

Niall returned her anger-bright glare. "Nay, no others. I'd imagine you've already envisioned far worse than I could ever surprise you with. Now, if you'll permit me, I'll remove what must surely be my unpleasant presence. Will you mind riding alone, or shall I send back one o' my men?"

Anne shot Niall a contemptuous look. "Don't concern yourself about me. Considering the choice o' company, riding alone is far more to my liking."

He grinned, then signaled his mount forward. Anne watched him ride away, relief flooding her at being free of Niall Campbell's loathsome presence. Her gaze sought the form of his golden-haired cousin riding up ahead.

Och, she silently mourned, if only Iain had been her father's choice. He, she could have come to care for. And his bedding of her, if not pleasant, would have at least not been the terrifying, degrading experience she feared awaited her at the hands of the legendary Wolf of Cruachan.

She'd seen it all, guessed her fate, in that last look he'd sent her. Her fate—and horrible it was.

The rain that had held off all day began to fall. Anne pulled her cloak tightly around her to ward off the encroaching dampness, shivering even as she did. Up ahead, through the mist that rose from the land, she could make out the white-capped, twin peaks of Ben Cruachan. Soon, they'd clear the last of the hills. Soon, the deep waters of Loch Awe would come into view.

Loch Awe and Castle Kilchurn, that great stone fortress of Clan Campbell. Soon it would imprison her as mercilessly as it held others out. And soon, all too soon, she must face Niall Campbell alone there—across the unlikely battlefield of a bed.

* * *

"Here, lassie," Old Agnes murmured soothingly as she stepped away from the tub of steaming water and bustled over to Anne, "let's get those wet clothes off and ye into this nice warm bath. 'Twill take the chill from yer bones. Ye dinna want to catch the ague, do ye?"

The ague, Anne thought humorlessly. Folk sometimes died if its fever and lung sickness couldn't be controlled. It would be the answer to all her problems. She'd escape this unfriendly place, not be forced to face Niall Campbell and his unwelcome advances. Aye, the ague for once seemed a most welcome fate.

Numbly, Anne felt hands touch her as the old maidservant worked free the fastenings of her gown. The air of the bedchamber, though warm from a roaring hearth fire, still made her tremble when the sodden clothes finally fell away.

Agnes wrapped an arm around Anne's shoulders, firmly guiding her to the large wooden tub. "That's my lass," she crooned. "Just step into this nice warm water and ye'll soon feel better. We've enough time before the feast even to soap yer hair, then dry it before the fire. Ye'll look glorious when I'm through with ye, and no mistake."

Anne obediently climbed in and sank beneath the water. As the heat gradually replaced the shuddering spasms, her eyes closed and she sighed.

A gnarled hand stroked her head. "See, lassie? Didna I tell ye? 'Twill be all right soon enough. Now, let me wash yer hair with some o' this fine soap. Doesna it smell heavenly?"

Anne inhaled deeply of the sweet lavender scent. The gentle, kneading motion of the maid's fingers lulled her into a deeper and deeper state of relaxation. She sank lower into the water. It was so blissful, so comforting, Anne thought dreamily, after the tense, uncomfortable journey and arrival at Kilchurn.

The rain had continued for hours and their party had arrived miserably soaked to the skin. Though Niall immediately hustled her upstairs to her room, insisting she get out of her clothes before she took a chill, Anne couldn't help but notice the sullen stares and raised brows that followed them through the keep. *News travels fast*, she'd thought grimly, *and bad news fastest of all*.

Hostility pervaded the Great Hall as they'd walked across it, hounding her down the cool stone corridors, tailing her to the very door of her chamber. Only now, safely inside, the cold finally seeping from her in the gently lapping water, did Anne at last allow herself to relax. If only she didn't have to ever leave this room. . . .

All too soon, it seemed, Agnes was urging Anne from the rapidly cooling water. "Come along, lassie." The old woman wrapped a bath sheet about Anne's water-slick body. "Come, sit before the fire and I'll comb out yer hair. 'Twill be so lovely when it's dried, as thick and wavy as 'tis. How would ye like me to dress it for the feasting?"

Anne lowered herself to the cushioned stool before the fire. She shrugged. " 'Tis o' no import. Do with it what you will."

Agnes frowned. "Now, lassie, dinna talk like that. O' course it matters. Ye want to be looking as pretty as ye can for the young lord, dinna ye? 'Tis past time he find happiness again, and no—"

A cool gust of air halted the maidservant's good-hearted ramblings. Both turned to the door, now standing ajar. In its opening stood the tall, slim figure of a girl of about the age of fourteen, her long, black hair wafting gently about her shoulders in the back draft of the hallway. Even from across the room, Anne could see the flashing brilliance of her turquoise eyes, flashing angrily—at her.

"L–Lady Caitlin," Old Agnes gasped in surprise. "What brings ye here so near the feasting? Why havena ye dressed—"

The old servant's words died as Caitlin strode across the room. She eyed Anne, then sniffed disdainfully. "So, this is the wench Niall brought back from MacGregor lands. You're comely enough, I'll warrant, at least for warming my brother's bed, but I can't understand why he'd willingly bind himself to a MacGregor slut."

Anne went rigid, barely hearing Agnes's horrified cry. Clasping the sheet to her, she rose and moved the few feet to stand before Caitlin. Though the girl was taller by half a head, Anne stared steadfastly up at her, returning the hostile glare with a calm one of her own.

So it begins, she thought. *And I must be the one to swallow my pride, to offer my hand in peace, if I'm to survive this year. Well, she's little more than a child after all.*

"Aye," Anne admitted quietly, "I'm MacGregor, and no mistake. But I'm not a slut and I'll thank you to remember that. Otherwise, we can never be friends."

Caitlin's lips curled contemptuously. "Friends? Hah!"

Water-damp hair brushed Anne's shoulders with her nod. "Aye, friends. 'Tis past time for the feuding to end. Can it not begin with us? 'Twould set an example for all to heed."

Surprise widened the girl's striking blue-green eyes. For a moment, Anne thought she saw hesitation flicker there. Then something passed across them, a memory perhaps. Caitlin's lips tightened with renewed resolve.

"Nay, it can never be. Though you saved my brother's life, too much has been ruined by this handfasting." The ebony-haired girl vehemently shook her head. "Nay, I cannot be your friend. 'Tis impossible!"

In a flurry of skirts and whirling tresses, Caitlin hurried from the chamber. Silence hung heavy in the room for a time, until a fire-eaten log fell to the hearth in a loud explosion of wood and glowing sparks. With a deep sigh, Agnes went to shut the door, then moved to the curtained bed. She returned with a blue velvet dressing gown.

"Here, lassie," she said as she held it open for Anne to put on, "cover yerself before ye take a chill. 'Tis cold enough in this castle without ye enduring the stone damp on top o' it all."

Aye, Anne mused, wrapping the dressing gown about her, *the castle's dwellers are a chill lot indeed. And each, for his own reasons, resents my presence here.* Expelling a deep breath, Anne turned back to the fire's warmth, fearing it was the last comfort she'd find in the night ahead.

A firm knock at the door interrupted Agnes. Quickly brushing the long mass of dark red curls to cascade down her mistress's back, the old servant finished fastening the clasp of the heavy pendant necklace around Anne's neck. Then she hurried to the door.

Anne continued to stare into the hand mirror, her pensive gaze riveted upon the twinkling blue stone surrounded by its ornate silver setting. It had once been her mother's, but that gentle lady was now dead over five years. Anne cherished the necklace with all her heart.

She sighed. *'Twill give me the strength to see this night through*, she thought, *and all the days thereafter, if only I keep it close. 'Twill sustain my courage so I don't bring dishonor upon my clan.*

The creak of iron hinges intruded on her poignant musings, and Anne laid down the mirror.

"M'lord. Your lady's ready just this moment."

Anne's gaze jerked around. Tall and broad-shouldered, Niall Campbell's powerful form filled the doorway. He now wore doublet, skintight trews that molded to his hard-muscled legs, and plaid draped across his body and over his left shoulder. A high-collared white shirt peeked from beneath the close-fitting, long-sleeved jacket. Stockings and soft, heelless brogs covered his feet.

Niall moved toward her, his leg wound barely seeming to hamper him, his stride one of a lithe, confident Highland warrior. Anne swallowed hard, a strange, languid warmth flowing through her.

His eyes, though still bruised and swollen from his beating at MacGregor hands, glittered in the firelight as he stared down at her. A curious half-smile lifted the corners of his mouth. At his bold perusal, heat flushed Anne's cheeks. It angered her, this continued, uncharacteristic response to him.

"Are you quite done staring at me, m'lord? If I haven't dressed to your satisfaction, there's yet time to change."

A chuckle rumbled deep within Niall's chest. "For such a wee wisp o' a lass, you're certainly always looking for a fight. But you won't get one from me."

He glanced admiringly down the length of her body. "That particular shade o' pale blue does special things to your eyes. You've dressed to my satisfaction and more."

Warily, Anne eyed his proffered arm. "What are you about? 'Tisn't time for the meal."

"My father wishes to meet you. He's confined to his bed and won't join us for the feast. We'll visit him in his chambers."

Anne's heart gave a small flutter of trepidation. The Campbell. She was going to see the Campbell—the man, in the end, responsible for the long, bitter feud. The man who'd cold-bloodedly sent his son out to wreak terror and havoc upon MacGregor lands.

With a rush of renewed anger, Anne realized she despised the Campbell chief even more than she did his son. It was at his command that the feud had been allowed to continue. Niall Campbell, as ruthlessly competent as he was, was only obeying orders.

Her father's words came back to her. " . . . the welfare o' our clan . . . its very survival . . . now in your hands."

No matter her true feelings for the despicable Campbell leader, Anne knew she must mask them with courtesy and good will. She accepted Niall's arm. What did one more compromise in a day beset with them matter?

"As you wish, m'lord." Anne sighed, her glance resigned but resolute.

The journey down the long stone corridors, their dank walls decorated with tapestries and weaponry, passed all too quickly for Anne's tastes. Before she had a chance to compose herself, Niall pushed open the door of a brightly lit room. The chamber was graced with a large hearth, filled with briskly burning logs, and a red brocade-curtained bed piled high with fluffy pillows and a comforter. The frail form of a man seemed lost among the bedclothes.

He waved them over. "Niall? Is that you, laddie? Come closer and bring the lass with you."

Bright blue-green eyes peered up at her as Anne neared the bed. Blond hair, heavily streaked with gray, graced a weather-beaten, deeply furrowed face. Yet though the hair coloring and eyes were different, the features older, Anne noted the strong resemblance between father and son. She managed a tentative smile.

"Come closer, lassie," the Campbell urged kindly. He glanced at his son. "Niall, don't stand there. Pull up a chair for your lady."

Once Anne was settled, the older man leaned over to take her hand. "My son told me how you saved his life, lassie. I'm forever in your debt."

" 'Twas nothing," Anne began stiffly before a sound from Niall stopped her.

She glanced back at him. He was standing behind her chair, a warning light gleaming in his eyes. Anne knew he half expected her to brush aside his father's gratitude as "a point o' honor."

With a small smile, she turned to the Campbell. " 'Tis kind o' you to say that, but 'twas the least I could do. After all, your son first saved my life."

The Campbell lay back on his pillows, a wry grimace on his lips. "Aye, Niall told me how Hugh thought you a witch. He's a troubled man, my nephew. I hope you can find it in your heart to forgive and forget."

"I'll do my best, m'lord."

He cocked his head at her. "And aren't you the sweet one? My son did well in handfasting you. Beauty and goodness, all rolled into one delicate bundle. But then, he always was lucky with the lassies. Weren't you, laddie?"

"Aye, Father," was Niall's dispassionate reply.

The Campbell's gaze returned to Anne. "I'm glad the feud has ended with your joining. It went on far too long, no matter who was first to blame. 'Twas a wise idea, your father's. I only wish I'd thought o' it." He paused, a troubled look darkening his features. " 'Twill solve a lot o' things."

For a long moment the Campbell was silent, then he grinned, as if a sudden thought had assailed him. He looked up at his son. " 'Twill solve your problems, too, laddie. 'Tis past time you put off your mourning and gave me a grandson. Aye, a wee bairn. 'Tis just what this castle—" A hard, wracking cough cut short his words. He gestured to a nearby table. "W–water!"

Before Niall could react, Anne was at the table
pouring out a cup. Her emotions churned. How
could a man so bent on another clan's destruction
be so kind and warm? He hardly seemed the sort.

Her hand clenched the cup of water. The Campbell,
it was rumored, had been ill for several years now.
He'd been forced to delegate more and more responsibility to his son, finally naming him tanist just a
year ago. Had Niall Campbell taken it upon himself
to step up the raids, in the hope of finally ending
the feud?

Anger filled Anne. The bloody knave! Of course,
that would explain everything. And the Campbell
probably didn't even know . . . poor, old man.

She returned to the bed and gently lifted his head.
"Drink, but slowly, in small sips," she instructed,
struggling to contain the rage that shook her voice.
" 'Tis the best way to soothe the catarrh."

He swallowed half the cup's contents before falling wearily back onto the bed. "Th–thank you, lassie."

Anne plumped the pillows behind his head and
pulled up the comforter. "I've done naught. Tomorrow, if you'll allow me, I'll brew you a tea o' lavender
flowers. 'Tis wonderful for the catarrh."

"Och" he weakly smiled up at her—"and won't
that be a pleasant change from my physician? He
gives me no relief with his endless purgatives . . .
and bloodletting. I get so very . . . very . . . tired . . ."

The Campbell's eyes slid shut. Soon the deep, even
breathing of slumber filled the room.

Niall's hand settled on Anne's shoulder. "Come,
lass. 'Tis time we were leaving."

Gently, so as not to disturb him, Anne disengaged
her fingers from the old man's clasp. They left the
room. Before she could turn to walk down the hallway, Niall gripped her arm.

Anne halted. "Aye?"

" 'Twas kind o' you to treat my father so gently. I know you must hate him as much as you hate me."

Anne stared up at him, aware he'd yet to make his point.

"My father's dying."

The brutal truth of his words startled her. "Aye, 'tis evident."

"He spits up blood most times now. There's naught you can do."

"I can ease his sufferings, make his last days less painful."

Niall inhaled a shuddering breath. How could he make her see the danger of using her healing skills in Kilchurn? His father would die no matter what she did, but none would remember that. In the end, all that would be recalled is he died of her ministrations.

He shook his head. "Nay, you can't, lass. I want you to stay away from my father with your potions." His grip tightened painfully on her arm. "Do you hear me? Do you understand?"

Anne wrenched free, both hurt and angered by his words. Did he think she'd harm his father? That because of the years of bitter feuding she'd stoop to using her skills for revenge? Her fists clenched into tight little fists. Well, what did she expect?

She glared up at Niall with burning, reproachful eyes. "Have it your way, *m'lord*. Your unfair suspicions will only make your father suffer and hasten his death, but then, mayhap you cannot wait to claim your chieftainship. And what should it matter to me? One Campbell is as bad as another!"

With a mutinous flounce of her hair, Anne turned to go. Before she'd taken her first step, his ice-rimmed voice halted her in her tracks. "Madam, don't walk away from me," Niall growled. "I haven't finished with you yet."

Chapter Five

Anne turned, every muscle tensed for battle. Her silver eyes flashed, her cheeks flushed with fury.

"*Not finished with me?*" she slowly ground out the words. "Surely you jest, m'lord. You've all but named me a despicable murderer, completely unworthy o' your trust. What more is there to say?"

Niall's own anger rose to meet Anne's. His dark eyes slammed into hers. Damn, he'd neither the time nor patience for this! He'd more pressing problems. Why couldn't she see beyond. . . .

He paused. There, flickering behind the thin veneer of rage, Niall found her pain. *Unfeeling bastard!* he mentally cursed himself. Once again he'd hurt her, viciously clawing away the few consolations she had left like some Highland wildcat, without warning, without mercy. All his good intentions to the contrary, he seemed to wound her at every turn.

Niall ran a hand through his thick, black hair, the gesture ragged, exasperated. "I don't despise you, lass, nor think you a murderer. But as far as trust goes, I don't give that easily to any man, friend or foe."

His reply nonplussed Anne. What was she to do with his abrupt changes in mood? One moment he was the cruel, ruthless enemy she expected him to be and the next. . . .

Anne's face clouded in confusion. "Then why did you forbid me to help your father? I have a calling to heal. 'Tis sacred to me. I'd never turn from anyone in need, nor cause harm, no matter—"

"Och, so there you are, nephew."

Duncan Campbell's voice intruded from the shadowed hallway. He strode into view and halted before them. "The folk are gathered, the tables laden with food and drink. We await only you and your lady for the feast to begin."

"Aye." A small frown darkened Niall's brow. "We were just now on our way."

Frustration and relief warred within him. He hadn't expected the matter of forbidding Anne's healing in Kilchurn to come up quite so soon. He'd hoped for time to ease her into life here, then break the news. If it hadn't been for his uncle's timely intrusion. . . .

Niall cast aside his confusing clash of emotions. The confrontation wasn't over, just delayed. He offered Anne his arm. After a moment's hesitation, she accepted it.

Duncan eyed them. "Er, I've never had the pleasure o' an introduction . . ."

The tension of the past few moments drained from Niall. He chuckled. "Lass, this is my uncle, Duncan Campbell." He nodded toward the older man. "Duncan, Lady Anne MacGregor."

Duncan bowed. "Welcome, lady. You are long overdue in my nephew's life. 'Tis my pleasure at last to make your acquaintance."

As she extended her hand to him, Anne studied Niall's uncle covertly. He was tall, as were all the Campbell nobility and, though not as powerfully built as his nephew, an imposing, substantial man nonetheless. His sandy-colored hair was pale with a generous scattering of gray. His full beard was even paler, nearly white-gold. He possessed the same strong, ruggedly handsome features as his son, Iain. If not for his eyes, Anne would have found Duncan Campbell a most attractive man.

But dark as the depths of an angry, storm-tossed loch, they were cold, their expression flat and unreadable. And the smile that touched his lips as he bent to kiss her hand, though correct in every way, never passed his mouth.

A small tremor coursed through Anne. *So, yet another Campbell unhappy with my presence. Is there no end to the enemies I'll discover in Kilchurn?*

Niall noted the shiver and mistook it for the chill of the corridor. "Come, lass. 'Tis warmer in the Great Hall. Time enough to talk further once we are there."

This time Anne was in a more receptive frame of mind to examine the Great Hall. It was a large, impressive room, in size as well as luxury. The walls were wainscot-paneled of carved fir, the upper portion of bare stone lavishly hung with intricately woven tapestries to brighten the room and absorb its chill.

Rushes covered the floor. The fragrant scent of the sweet woodruff scattered among them mingled with the tangy wood smoke wafting from the great hearth on the far wall. In front of the blazing fire were gathered several men and women, some standing, others seated on padded benches, laughing and talking in happy animation.

Anne found Iain there. Like a beacon in the night he drew her, the only person in the crowded room whom she knew to be friend.

At that moment, Iain looked up. He smiled and strode over to her.

Niall's grip on Anne's arm tightened when he noted the direction his cousin's path was taking. He forced his muscles to unclench, his breathing to even.

Iain. Can it really be Iain? he asked himself for the hundredth time. *I can't believe it. I won't believe it, not yet, not without proof. And it isn't the time to reveal your suspicions to Iain or any man. Play the fool awhile longer. Lure the traitor into the trap. The victory, when it comes, will be all the sweeter for the waiting.*

Despite the calming words of reason, a cold anger stirred in Niall at Anne's welcoming smile for the blond man. All his iron control couldn't mask the muscle that twitched in his jaw as a sudden thought assailed him. Could his cousin's flirtatious attentions toward Anne have a more sinister purpose than the light-hearted teasing it appeared? Could Iain somehow plan to use her against him? It would be the way of a traitor.

But it was too soon to place all his suspicions on Iain, Niall reminded himself. There were others just as suspect. He must remember that. He *must* remain in control and clearheaded. It was the only way to ferret out the traitor.

Niall inhaled a rasping breath. Damn, but the doubts, the constant questions, were eating him alive!

"Lady," Iain's deep voice intruded on Niall's tormented thoughts. His cousin rendered Anne a customary nod. "I'm pleased to see you're no worse for the journey's wear." His eyes gleamed in open admiration. "The blue o' that dress becomes you greatly."

Anne flushed. Grimly, Niall recalled she'd not reacted half so strongly when he'd complimented her earlier. He glared at the younger man. Iain seemed not to notice.

" 'Tis time to be seated," Niall growled, his decision made.

Until he could ascertain Iain's true intentions, every effort must be made to keep Anne from his cousin. It was the safest course of action. Niall turned to her, eliminating Iain from the conversation.

Anne pulled her gaze from Iain's smiling countenance. "Aye. As you wish, m'lord."

The hard glitter in Niall's eyes startled her. Whatever was the matter now?

She glanced at Iain. " 'Twould please me greatly if you'd sit by me at table. A familiar face, among so many strangers—"

"Iain will sit elsewhere."

Puzzlement darkened her eyes. " 'Tis a simple matter to move one person. Please, m'lord—"

"My mind is made. Now, no more o' it." Niall led Anne toward the table.

She considered protesting his highhanded manner but a glance at Iain quashed that idea. His deep blue eyes had narrowed to slits. Were they always so at odds with each other? Anne wondered.

The main table was raised above the others on a dais, situated perpendicularly to two other long tables. Though the lower tables were comfortably provided with padded benches, the chief's had English chairs covered in bright green damask. As Niall held out a chair for Anne, Iain took his place down at the far end of the main table.

It seemed too great an insult to one of the Campbell's immediate family when she knew Iain's rightful place was at center table. Her heart went out to the young man.

"How can you be so cruel to your cousin?" she demanded softly when Niall was seated beside her.

"He means you no discourtesy in his kindness to me."

"I've my reasons," he muttered. "Now, no more o' it!"

Anne's lips tightened but she withheld comment. Rebellious, uncomplimentary imprecations, nonetheless, roiled in her head. *If I were you, you pigheaded dolt*, she raged at Niall silently, *I'd withhold my good will from the father, not the son. He's the one to beware, with those dead eyes of his.*

Out of the corner of her eye, Anne noted Duncan Campbell seating himself on Niall's other side. At the memory of the older man's inscrutable expression, a premonitory chill prickled down her spine. Mad cousin Hugh, cold-eyed Uncle Duncan. The disparity between the Campbell's personality and his reputed conduct toward her clan. The strange circumstances surrounding the Wolf's capture. What had her father said that day of the Campbell army's arrival? Something about entrapping Niall . . . and a traitor?

Aye, there was indeed something dangerously amiss in the castle, but what, she had yet to fathom. And now, vowed to the Campbell tanist as she was, Anne sensed she risked full involvement—even to the endangerment of her life.

Niall signaled for the feast to begin. Anne found little interest in the sumptuous fare, though, at any other time, the fresh, fried Loch Awe trout, succulent slices of cured mutton, and stoved chicken surrounded by onions, potatoes, and carrots would easily have tempted her appetite. There was scant energy left for eating at any rate. All her efforts were needed in maintaining a calm, proud front for the curious, hostile-eyed Campbells.

Her lack of interest in the fare wasn't lost on Niall. He noted how she moved the food around on her plate to feign eating it, her refusal of the dessert of sugar rolls and honey cakes sprinkled with ground almonds, the pale, taut look on her face. The coolly restrained reception of his people didn't help he knew, nor did Caitlin's glaring animosity on Anne's other side.

Curse it all, Niall thought in exasperation. Though he knew a MacGregor wouldn't be readily accepted after years of bitter feuding, he'd hoped for a more pleasant evening. A sense of the long, difficult road ahead for Anne filled him. He made a silent vow to aid her as best he could.

Guilt at the memory of the look on her face earlier plucked at him. Perhaps he'd been too harsh with her. He knew she'd been upset over his refusal to allow Iain to sit with them.

Niall sighed. If only he dared trust her with his cousin. But he didn't dare trust anyone right now, not even his own family. Damn that traitor to hell!

The meal ended, and the minstrels with pipes and harps arrived to entertain the gathering. Niall sat through the singing, becoming more tense by the moment. Finally, when the fiddlers entered to take their seats and the rushes were moved aside for the dancing, he could bear it no longer.

His wounded leg be damned! Perhaps a turn at a reel would ease the unpleasant churning in his gut.

He offered Anne his hand. " 'Tis time for the dancing to begin."

She stared down at his large, calloused palm, well aware tradition dictated the lord and his lady lead the first dance. But to go down to the dance floor, to stand there and subject herself to the full examination of all. . . .

Anne rose in a rustle of skirt and petticoats, her expression inscrutable save for the resolute silver fire in her eyes. "As you wish, m'lord."

She allowed him to escort her onto the dance floor. Together with Iain, Duncan, Hugh, Niall's sister, Caitlin and two other women of the clan nobility, they formed lines, the men opposite the women, for the reel. As the music began, Anne turned to face Niall. Standing in place, they executed the intricate *pas de basque* steps recently popularized by Queen Mary's court. Then, moving in unison, the two of them crossed behind Iain and his partner to meet in the center with the third couple in line, Duncan and the dark-haired Caitlin. Joining hands in the middle above their heads, they moved in a circle to the music.

As they danced, Caitlin's seething animosity, barely restrained during the meal, flared into overt hostility. It grew until Anne thought, at any moment, the girl would halt and, in the middle of all, attack her. Fortunately, the dance just then required partners to be exchanged. Niall whisked his glaring sister away.

"You must be patient with our little Caitlin," Duncan murmured as he moved with Anne down the center of the line behind his niece and nephew. "She doesn't take kindly to a MacGregor in our midst, and hasn't the maturity o' years to hide it."

Anne shot him an assessing glance. "Indeed. 'Tis a trait in short shrift this eve. But do not lay the blame too heavily on Caitlin's shoulders. She, at least, has the excuse o' youth."

Duncan's mouth tightened. "That may be, lady, but you'll not win our hearts with an arrogant air. If compromise is needed, mayhap it should come—"

Once more they met in the middle with Niall and Caitlin. For a brief moment Niall scrutinized Anne's face. With a frown, he noted the anger burning in her eyes. Had Duncan said something untoward?

Niall shot a glance at his uncle before the two couples separated once more to dance away. The older man's features were calm, a slight smile on his lips. Niall relaxed.

He turned back to his sister. It seemed there was no need to look further than her for the source of Anne's discomfiture.

"You've played the role o' hostess poorly this eve, lassie."

Turquoise eyes glared up at him. "Och, and how so?"

"You know the answer as well as I." Niall steadily returned her gaze. " 'Tisn't proper to treat the Lady Anne so inhospitably. I expect you to set the example. No good will come o' continuing the feud at her expense."

"You're the only Campbell here who stands to profit from her presence." Caitlin's rosy lips curved disdainfully. "Couldn't you have found a bedmate closer to home, brother dear?"

Niall's eyes narrowed but he withheld comment. He swung his sister about and headed up the outside of the line to rejoin Anne and Duncan.

"She saved my life!" he finally growled. "I'd have thought that alone would've endeared her to you. But no matter. You've only to obey me in this. Do you understand?"

"Och, and all too clearly." Caitlin's eyes filled with tears. "I'll obey you but, though I love you with all my heart, I can never be *her* friend. Her presence here has ruined my life!"

She danced off to rejoin Duncan, effectively ending the conversation.

Caitlin's parting words echoed in Niall's head. More unsettled than before, he rejoined Anne to begin the same dance routine with the next couple, Hugh and his partner.

That set, though no words were exchanged, was equally disconcerting. Hugh never ceased his furious glaring at Anne. Only Niall's quelling presence, hovering nearby, prevented outright rudeness on his cousin's part.

To Anne, the dance seemed to drag on inter-
minably. One by one, she was forced to meet and deal
with a gamut of hostile gazes from the other dancers.
And what did you expect, she asked herself wryly time
and again, *open arms and Highland jigs?*

The music finally faded, signaling the end to the
dance. Niall glanced down at Anne, suddenly weary
of the evening's festivities. Her face looked pale and
strained.

"You're tired, lass," he murmured softly, leaning
close as he spoke. " 'Tis been a hard day. 'Tis past
time you were abed."

Silver eyes met his. "Aye," she whispered.
" 'Twould seem so."

They left the hall, the lilting tunes and happy
laughter following them like so many mocking spec-
tres. Yet as eager as she'd been to leave the prying,
unfriendly eyes in the Great Hall, the nearer they
drew to the bedchambers, the heavier Anne's heart
began to pound within her breast.

How would she ever bear what lay ahead? If only
she weren't so tired, so emotionally drained from
the events of the worst, the most confusing, day
of her life! She wanted so to endure with dignity.
If only he'd be gentle with her. . . .

Niall opened the door to Anne's bedchamber. Once
inside, he turned to her, searching for words to
express his regret at the night's unpleasantness. In
spite of himself, all he could think of was how lovely
the interplay of shadow and light was upon Anne's
face. Lord, had he ever truly realized how beautiful
she was?

Her hair fell like curling silk about her shoulders
before cascading down her back. The sight of it
filled Niall with a sudden yearning to touch it. Her
soft, moist lips were slightly parted. His heart quickened as his gaze momentarily narrowed to the lush
ripeness of her mouth. Yet it was the sweep of her

long, sooty lashes, lowering to rest gently against the curve of her high cheekbones, that was his true undoing.

Anne's delicate flowerlike scent wafted up to him. Niall inhaled deeply. Desire, unwanted, unexpected, swept through him, igniting a roaring conflagration in his loins like flame through dry tinder. His breath caught in his throat. His hand brushed her cheek.

She tensed, and the effort to restrain herself from stepping away was evident. It shattered the mesmerizing fascination that held Niall entranced.

Damn it to hell! This is madness, he raged at himself. *I want naught from her, and most certainly not her body. Nay, it* can't *be her body. I haven't desired a woman since. . . .*

The admission was painful, yet at the same time, oddly exciting. And it would explain the strange yearning, the heavy fullness that had settled in his groin at the sight of Anne just now. Aye, it would explain, but never justify it.

His hand cupped her chin. Apprehension flared in Anne's luminous eyes.

Niall shook his head, his voice ragged. "You've naught to fear from me, lass. Truly, I mean no harm."

"I—I don't fear you."

Niall's mouth quirked. "Och, and don't you now?"

She didn't answer.

"Well, no matter." His hand fell from her face. "If 'tis bedding with me that worries you, you've naught to fear. I won't force myself on you. 'Tisn't my way."

His eyes lowered. "I'm not ready to commit to a woman, to sire another bairn, no matter how dearly my father desires it. I spoke true in my reasons for our handfasting. The loss o' my wife . . . and wee son . . . pains me still."

With an effort, Niall lifted his gaze to hers. "I

don't know what you thought or expected, but 'tis too soon."

Anne stared up at him, deeply stirred by the undercurrent of intense sorrow, by his plea for understanding. How quickly he could change from an arrogant, self-possessed warrior to a vulnerable, tormented man! Och, it was too much to fathom, especially tonight of all nights.

She managed a small, tentative smile. "Don't concern yourself, m'lord. I am grateful you'll go slowly with me. 'Tis more than I ever dared hope."

Anne paused to scan his face thoughtfully. He, too, looked weary. The past days had been just as hard for him, with his capture and wounding. She suddenly remembered she hadn't tended to his wounds since yesterday.

"Your leg, m'lord," Anne began hesitantly. "How does its healing go? I should cleanse it and apply more o' my marigold ointment."

Niall stiffened. Though, in truth, he preferred her skills to the castle physician's, he knew he couldn't allow her to care for him, then forbid her doing so with everyone else.

He shook his head. "My leg fares well, lass. Our physician saw to it when I bathed. You needn't concern yourself."

There was a momentary prick of hurt, then Anne quashed it. Niall Campbell had no reason to trust her abilities to that of some physician, even if most were little more than purveyors of purgatives and bloodletting as treatment for every illness. It would take time to win his confidence, that was all.

Anne smiled, a soft, sweet movement of her lips. "Then 'tis good night, m'lord."

"Aye. Good night, lass."

For an instant longer Niall stared down at her, the firelight sending glinting shards of gold to dance in his eyes. Then, turning on his heel, he crossed the bedchamber and entered his own room through the connecting door.

Late the next morning as they were unpacking the rest of Anne's possessions, the maidservant discovered the box of herb plants.

"What would ye have me do with these, lassie?" Agnes held up the container.

Anne turned from the lace-trimmed nightgown she was folding to glance at the old woman. Her face brightened when she recognized the box. Her herbs! How could she have forgotten them?

She lay aside the nightgown and hurried to Agnes. Tenderly, her fingers caressed the delicate leaves, examining one, then the other. They all looked well, if a bit wilted, but needed replanting soon.

Taking possession of the box, Anne carried it to the sunlit window. She watered the herbs carefully. Only when her ministrations were complete did Anne turn back to the servant.

"Is there some patch in the castle garden where I might plant these?"

"Aye, lassie," the older woman replied, a distinctly uncomfortable look spreading across her face. "But 'tisn't my place to grant ye leave. Sir Niall instructed me to send ye to him with any requests."

So, Anne thought in exasperation, *and must I also ask him permission to breathe?* She smoothed the wrinkles from her skirt and tucked an errant strand of hair in place.

"Then so be it. Where might I find him?"

"Mayhap in the inner bailey, near the walled garden. He and his warriors always meet in swordplay at this time o' day. Shall I take ye there?"

Anne nodded. "Aye. 'Twill be awhile before I've fathomed the intricacies o' this castle."

As soon as they'd left the imposing bulk of the keep and stepped outside, the sound of clanging swords reached their ears. They passed quickly around the building's corner buttress to find eight men engaged in energetic sword practice. Anne easily singled out Niall's broad-shouldered form from the rest.

All were stripped to the waist, the excess of their belted plaids wrapped around and tucked into their belts. Their upper torsos and arms glistened with sweat. Anne swallowed hard and moved closer, Agnes following.

Niall's hands gripped the wooden handle of a claymore, the giant sword as long as its owner was tall and a weapon only of the strongest men. His arms moved in large, seemingly effortless arcs as he deftly parried the blows of his companions. A grim smile touched his lips and a fierce light gleamed in his eyes, the love of battle settling about him in some fearful, heated aura.

Only when his men began to falter, then cease their swordplay, did Niall at last pause to look about him. His searching glance found Anne's. A wrinkle of puzzlement formed between his brows.

Laying aside his claymore, Niall strode to a nearby water trough. After immersing his head, he straightened, the fluid sluicing down his chest and shoulders. He flung back his sodden mane of hair, scattering water everywhere, then, with a wry grin, approached her.

Sunlight glinted in the droplets that clung to him, reflecting across the water-slick planes of his muscled upper body. For an instant, Anne could only stare at the dark, wet hair that swirled across his chest and abdomen.

"I—I wish a word with you, m'lord," she murmured finally, forcing the words past the strange, hot ache in her throat. Distractedly, she motioned to the walled garden. "Away from the others, if you please."

Niall shrugged. "As you wish."

They walked in silence until the garden's wooden gate was shut behind them. Then Anne turned, gathering all the tact she possessed. " 'Tis a fine garden," she began, gesturing about her. "The soil rich, the sun shining full upon it for most o' the day. By your leave, I would plant my herbs here."

"And what purpose would that serve?"

Anne glanced up in surprise. At the set look to Niall's face, a sense of unease stirred. "Why, to use for my healing potions, o' course. Did you think I'd refuse to help your people because they were Campbells? Didn't I make my position clear last eve?"

" 'Twas quite evident what your feelings were, lass. Nonetheless, it cannot be." He reluctantly shook his head. "You will not plant, nor harvest, nor treat anyone with your herbs at Kilchurn. Do you understand?"

"But why—" Her voice broke off as she struggled with the surging frustration that roiled within. Holy Mother, to ask him for anything and then have it refused! And this, her precious herbs, her beloved healing, above all else!

Anne stared up at him, confused. "Why? Why would you refuse me such a simple request?"

"I've no heart to refuse you anything, lass," Niall replied, his voice rough with regret. "But in this matter I can do no less. You're well aware how strong the witch panic burns since the law passed. Have your already forgotten your admission that even some o' your own clan think you a witch? What do you think *my* clan will think if you resume your healing?"

"I—I don't care! I am good at what I do. There's no taint of evil in it. In time they'll see that, accept me."

Niall hesitated. He wanted to grant her this one request but knew it was unwise. Since the law enacted just a year ago making witchcraft punishable by death, the Reformed Kirk had been zealous in their persecution. When a hapless person, and it was almost always a woman, was accused, she'd be deprived of rest, food and water, and finally tortured to extract a confession. And, though confession meant certain death by burning or drowning, most eventually confessed. The instruments of torture were that effective.

He shuddered, harking back to the one victim he'd seen burnt at the stake. It had been Dora, his cousin Hugh's one and only love. Malcolm Campbell was responsible for that, one of his first acts upon resuming control of the village kirk. Poor, unstable Hugh had been easily swayed to the preacher's side, especially after finding Dora in the arms of another man.

She was dead before Niall could reach her, though the flames had yet to consume her body. That day he'd made a vow never to allow another burning on Campbell lands. Up until now, he'd been successful in keeping that promise.

"Nay, lass." Niall sighed, steeling himself for the task at hand. "I fear that will never be. My people are too superstitious, too easily led when it comes to matters o' religion, for good or bad. A priest o' the Reformed Kirk, my father's bastard brother, lives among us. His hatred o' witches runs deep. As deep as Hugh's, I fear. He may well stir them against you."

"And what o' you?" Anne demanded, her voice taut with rising anger. "Are you not clan tanist, soon to be chief? Can't you control your own people? Why, oh why, do you persist in being so . . . so pigheaded?"

Niall struggled to keep the irritation out of his voice. "A wise chief knows when and where to interfere in the lives o' his clan. Matters o' religion are not one o' them. I won't allow witch burnings on Campbell lands, but that doesn't lessen the danger to you all the same."

Anne made a move to protest.

Niall held up a silencing hand. "I've enough problems to deal with at present. As hardhearted as it may seem, I don't need you adding to them."

Two spots of red flamed Anne's cheeks as she fought to contain herself, to find some small thread of hope to cling.to. As harsh as his refusal was, she also heard the sincere regret in his voice. And she knew he had many problems and responsibilities. But not to plant her herbs. . . .

Well, he could not worry about the existence of something he knew nothing about, Anne consoled herself. She exhaled an acquiescent breath. "I don't wish to become a hindrance or an embarrassment to you."

His stern, finely chiseled mouth relaxed a bit. "Then you'll obey me in this?"

"Aye, m'lord. I won't plant my herbs in Kilchurn." Anne tilted her head in feigned consideration, eager to change the subject before he prodded her further. "But if I cannot heal, what can I do? I have little talent at sewing or most o' the other womanly arts."

A relieved grin spread across Niall's face. He'd feared a much more emotional, more protracted battle over the issue of her healing. Not that she didn't bear watching, for a time longer at least.

"Why not go riding? You've free access to the stables and Kilchurn and its lands. I ask only if you ride from sight o' the castle you take one o' my men with you. As powerful as we are, the Campbells are as prime a target for reivers as any other clan. I wouldn't wish you to fall into unfriendly hands."

Aye, Anne thought, her rebellion growing anew as she left the garden and walked back to rejoin Agnes. *'Twould surely add to the difficulties if you were forced to ransom me. But then, why should I care—one way or another? I warned you before I'd not be constrained by the rules o' others. And that, my arrogant rogue, includes you, no matter how beset with difficulties, no matter how tormented you may be.*

At the memory of those moments with him in her room last night a small, regretful smile touched Anne's lips. *Though perhaps I should, I cannot wish you ill, Niall Campbell.* She inwardly sighed. *Truly I can't, for you've been more than gentle with me. But my life's work will not be denied, not for you or any man. It cannot be denied—even to the sacrifice o' my life. Perhaps someday you will see that—and understand.*

Anne found a sunny clearing in the midst of a forest of fir, oak, and alder that covered the hills a short walk from Kilchurn Castle. There she planted her herbs.

The man be damned! she silently cursed as a pang of guilt swept through her. *I do this for the good o' all and someday he'll see this, but, truly, how can one reason with such a pigheaded man? I must be daft to care what he thinks, or how he would feel if he knew, but I do.*

She paused in her thoughts to pound the earth around a fragile feverfew plant. *Well, I will not let it matter,* she began again defensively. *I warned him, that I did, that no one. . . .*

"Och, ye will surely kill those wee plants if ye force them into the ground so cruelly."

Eyes wide, Anne quickly looked over her shoulder and saw an old, shabbily dressed lady. On her arm the woman carried a large basket filled with plants. Wispy, snow-white hair peeked from under a red linen kerchief, and the small face was weathered and lined. The eyes that studied her, though, were bright and alive, belying the age that bowed the old woman's shoulders.

"I . . . I . . . Who are you?" Anne rose to her feet.

The old woman chuckled. "I'm known as Ena. I live in the village over the hill from Kilchurn. I've birthed the babes and tended the hurts and ills o' clan Campbell all my life."

Her gaze narrowed as she examined the neat rows of herbs Anne had already planted. "Do ye know the healing art, then?"

Joy flooded Anne. Here was a kindred spirit, someone to understand and be understood by.

"Aye." A happy smile lifted her mouth. "Before I left home, I was healer to Clan MacGregor."

"Och, so ye're the one our young lord took in handfasting." Ena moved closer. "And what are ye called, lassie?"

"Anne." She motioned toward her plantings. "Would you see what I have, tell me what else grows well here and where I might find it? I'd be grateful for anything you'd share with me."

Ena squatted to examine the plants. "Hmmm, I see ye've the St. John's Wort, agrimony, colt's foot, as well as the soothing chamomile, and yarrow, and meadowsweet. All fine herbs for healing."

She cocked her head. "Do you know o' the leaf o' the fairy fingers? 'Tis a powerful remedy for the dropsy, but must be used with caution or it can kill."

Anne shook her head. "I've heard o' it, but never grown the plant."

The old woman smiled. " 'Tis also called bloody fingers, or gloves, or foxglove, but I prefer its ancient name. Ye dry the leaves and grind them into a powder. 'Tis bitter and sickening to the taste, so 'tis best to cover it with a strong drink. Too much, even a single leaf chewed and swallowed, can cause seizing o' the limbs and the heart to stop. Yet for those curs-

ed with the swollen limbs o' the dropsy, 'tis truly a
wondrous plant. Come to my hut in the village and
visit me someday. I'll teach ye o' it and more."

"I'd like that very much." Anne helped Ena to her
feet. "How will I find you?"

" 'Twillna be hard, lassie. Folk for miles know
where Ena lives."

She began to walk away, then glanced over her
shoulder. "Ye're a bonnie lass, and no mistake. Dinna
be afraid o' the young lord. He's a brave and good
man."

With a wave, Ena disappeared into the forest.
Anne stared after her. A friend . . . another friend. It
seemed for every obstacle Niall Campbell put in her
way, someone came forward to lead her around it.

The realization heartened her as she bent to finish
the transplanting of her herbs. Gradually, a feeling
of coldness, of eerie presentiment, wafted over her.
Anne shrugged the unpleasant feeling aside. It was
nothing, she assured herself, but a chill wind blow-
ing through the trees.

Yet as she continued to work the emotion grew,
burgeoning into a full-fledged sensation of being
watched. Watched by someone, something, evil and
full of hatred. A hatred that encircled her, cloaking
her in a smothering cloud of malevolence.

Anne rose. *Surely 'tis my imagination,* she thought.
My mind is but overstimulated, strung too. . . .

She heard a rustling behind her and froze. Her
hand moved to the small dagger nestled at her bosom. Withdrawing it, she turned. There was nothing
but the windblown leaves of the large, ferny brack-
en. She moved closer, her knife clenched in her fist,
yet found nothing.

Anne sagged in relief. Just then, a flash of lighter
color among the forest-dark shrubbery caught her
eye. She inched closer.

The shades took form in the colors of a tartan. A

chill, black silence enveloped her. Within it reverberated the sudden pounding of Anne's heart.

There, floating on a gentle breeze, was a scrap of Campbell plaid.

Chapter Six

"M'lady?"

Anne jerked to a halt. Her hand, halfway to her bedchamber door, paused in mid-air. The familiar voice beckoned her from the morose thoughts that had dogged her since she'd found that piece of Campbell cloth. And, as cowardly as she felt in the act, Anne turned and flung herself into Iain's strong arms.

He gathered her to him, pulling her against the hard-muscled wall of his body. Tenderly, he stroked Anne's hair. "What is it, lass? What has frightened you so?"

She started to reply, to tell him of the forest's evil intruder, then hesitated. If he knew, he might want her to take him there. Then he'd see her garden. And she couldn't risk Niall finding out, at least not for a time.

"Och, 'tis naught." Anne met his gaze. "You startled me, that's all." She glanced down at the arms that held her. "Please let me go. I'm fine now."

His gaze met hers. A flush crept up Iain's neck and face. He released Anne and took a step backward.

"Aye, 'twould help, I'd wager."

Anne felt the warmth rise in her own cheeks. Holy Mary, what must Iain think?

"I—I am sorry for throwing myself at you."

The tension eased from Iain's face. He chuckled. "Aye, and I immediately flung you from me, didn't I? Nay, I fear the blame for our extended embrace must be shared."

"Then so be it. I don't wish . . ." Her voice faded at the tenderness of his gaze. Heavy silence settled between them. In the emptiness, Anne could hear the blood rushing through her body.

He cares for me! The realization filled her with panic. She could never be his and, because of that, didn't dare examine the depth of her feelings for him. Nay, for then she'd also be forced to face her true feelings for Niall Campbell. And *that* was the most frightening realization of all!

"I—I must go." Anne stepped back.

"Wait!" Iain grasped her arm. "I came to ask you if you'd like to ride with me, see the loch."

"A ride?" The tension of the past few moments drained from Anne in the happy anticipation of going riding. "Aye. I'd dearly love a ride. When can we leave?"

Iain grinned at her eagerness. "Just as soon as you're ready. Shall I meet you at the stables?"

"Aye." She glanced down at her soiled skirt. " 'Twill take me but a few minutes to prepare myself."

Anne whirled and hurried into her room.

Iain was so good, so kind, she thought as she quickly stripped down to her petticoats. At every turn he attempted to think of her happiness. And now, it seemed he saw her as more than just a friend.

The warm glow in his eyes a few moments ago confused Anne. How was it possible he cared for her after such a short time? Was he, mayhap, as lonely as she?

She sighed. She must tread carefully with his heart, if 'twas true. There could never be anything between them, for she was vowed to another, whether she wished it or not.

'Twill do no good to curse the fate that bound you to him *instead o' Iain,* Anne fiercely chided herself as she donned a simple, dark green woolen dress. Yet, even as the sense of futility filled her, Niall's darkly handsome face rose in her mind's eye. She remembered how the sorrow as he talked of his lost love had deepened his eyes to an intense shade of brown, turning his voice husky with barely repressed emotion.

In that moment he'd opened his heart to her, shared a deeply personal part she sensed he revealed to few others. And, in that moment, Anne had felt herself irresistibly drawn to him. Aye, she admitted, drawn to him as woman to man.

That realization, most of all, disturbed her. She didn't want to care for the enigmatic, ruthless man known as the Wolf of Cruachan. He stirred emotions in her better left unexamined, the kind that sent a woman's heart to pounding and turned her brain to mush. And no man was ever going to do that!

Anne moved to close the chest when her glance snagged on the MacGregor plaid neatly folded within. After an instant's hesitation, she pulled it out and draped it around her shoulders, fastening the cloth with a silver brooch adorned with the form of her clan's beloved Scots pine.

Though she knew it wasn't wise to wear her clan crest and colors in Kilchurn, Anne suddenly didn't care. She wasn't ashamed of her heritage. Let them all, Niall Campbell included, know they must accept her for herself, and part of that identity was MacGregor. Why must all the adjustment be hers? *Aye, why indeed*, Anne angrily asked herself as she finished dressing and left her room.

Iain awaited her at the stables, garbed in a loose, snow-white shirt, snug-fitting tartan trews, and a sturdier, ankle-high laced pair of cuarans. At his side hung the ever-present dirk, across his back, his claymore. His dark blue eyes skimmed Anne as she walked up, but he made no comment about the plaid slung about her shoulders. He helped her mount, and they were soon galloping out of the castle and along the shore of Loch Awe.

The day was cool, the sky a clear, delicately cloud-strewn blue. The loch's aquamarine waters were placid. Long-necked swans floated serenely upon its mirrored surface, passing near the imposing stone castle.

Kilchurn, Anne thought as they rode away. Guardian of Loch Awe, standing lonely sentinel on its narrow outcropping of land. Tales were that when first built it had stood apart on an island.

Looking at it now, she wondered if the fortress might not someday break free once again, to float like some massive warship down the length of darkling water. It was indeed a beautiful land, this seat of Campbell power, of mighty, snow-capped mountains, forested hills, and heather-clad meadows, reminding her so much of Glenstrae . . . and home.

Anne shook aside the painful memory. She turned her glance to the blond man riding beside her. "And where are you taking me, Sir Iain? Do you plan to abduct me and hold me for ransom?"

Iain shot her a rueful smile and shook his head. "If you were still a MacGregor lass, aye, the idea would be foremost in my mind. Not that I'd ever give you up for any amount o' money."

His smile broadened into a grin. " 'Twould be an easy thing to hide you in these mountains. When we were boys, Niall, Hugh, and I used to explore Ben Cruachan, spending the summer days roaming its rocky heights and the nights sleeping beneath the stars, wrapped only in our plaids.

"Once we came upon an ancient, deserted tower high in the mountains. Surprisingly, it was still quite sturdy. All it needed was new floors and doors to make it habitable. Each summer, for several years, we'd journey up to it, to work on its repairs."

"Did you ever finish it?"

Iain laughed. "Aye, as a matter o' fact. But that was over ten years ago. I haven't been there since."

"And is that where you plan to take me?" Anne asked, a twinkle in her eyes.

He reined in his horse. "Nay, not this time."

Iain gestured toward a small burn that emptied into the loch. Huge oaks, their gnarled arms outstretched across the coldly gleaming torrent of water, grew nearby. Below, the grass was starry with wild anemones in vivid purples, reds, lavenders, and whites.

Anne gasped in pleasure. " 'Tis heavenly!" A radiant smile touched her face. "Thank you for sharing this with me."

He dismounted, then moved to take her hand. "I'm pleased you like it. 'Tis little to leave you with, but I wanted you to have this special place to come to, to be your haven, when I'm gone."

A shade of puzzlement darkened her silver eyes. "Gone? Are you leaving, Iain?"

"Aye, lass. 'Tis time to return home, to Balloch Castle."

Anne's head lowered, her thick curls tumbling forward to hide her suddenly downcast face. Her only friend in Kilchurn besides Agnes and now he was to be taken from her.

"When?" she whispered.

"On the morrow."

Her hand covered his. "Och, nay, Iain. Must you leave so soon?"

He sighed. "Aye. I must go. My father will stay a time more, awaiting some response from the Crown he and the Campbell have been working on all these months. But there's too much to be done at Balloch now that summer draws nigh. One o' us, at least, must be there to oversee things."

"But I've only been here a day . . ." Anne shook her head. "Och, I am selfish to think only o' myself. I beg pardon."

At the note of pain barely contained by her self-reproach, Iain's heart went out to Anne. He pulled her gently down from her horse but didn't let her go. Instead, Iain gathered her to him, partly to offer comfort and partly for one last feel of her soft woman's body. She was Niall's, but at this sweet moment of parting he no longer cared.

"You can't keep your hands off what's mine, can you, cousin?" a steel-timbred voice intruded.

Iain paled. His arms fell away.

Awash in a sea of grim foreboding, Anne turned around. Niall's dark eyes were cold, glittering with suspicion. She took a hesitant step toward him. "M'lord—"

A movement of his hand silenced her, for his glance had returned to Iain. "Well, cousin? I await your reply."

The younger man glowered back, uncowed. "I care for her, if that's what you're getting at, but I'm not low enough to sneak behind your back and cuckold you. 'Twasn't what you thought, at any rate. Anne was but sad to hear o' my departure and I—"

"Were but comforting her?" Niall supplied dryly. "Then 'tis well you're leaving, for if you ever touch her again—"

Iain reached behind him and unsheathed his claymore. "And what will you do? Have me thrown in the dungeon or mayhap flogged? Or would you prefer to just finish me off in a fight to the death?"

He moved into a warrior's stance, both hands gripping his sword. "I tire o' your foul mood o' late. Why not put it to rest once and for all? I'm not afraid o' your reputation with the claymore. Answer me, Niall. Why not here and now?"

Anne turned to Niall. His hand had swung to his own weapon's hilt, and his face was rigid with glacial anger. They were about to do battle, and all because of a simple misunderstanding!

Instinctively, she ran to her blond companion, knowing she'd have a better chance of reasoning with him. "Iain, do not fight your cousin," she pleaded. "If there's any fault, 'tis mine. I foolishly keep running to your arms and I've no right. The sin is mine, not yours."

"A hug o' comfort is hardly a sin," Iain muttered. "I won't leave you here to suffer his wrath. I'm not afraid o' him."

"He won't harm me. You know that. 'Twill be all right." Her hand gripped his arm. "Please, Iain."

Iain hesitated, indecision wavering in his eyes, but at last he resheathed his sword. Taking her hand, he raised it to his lips. "Farewell, lass. If ever you need me . . ."

Anne smiled. "Aye, well I know. Fare you well, my friend."

He mounted and rode away. Anne faced Niall. He'd sheathed his sword, but the look in his eyes remained hard and unforgiving. Slowly, like a person going to his doom, Anne walked to stand before him.

Her small chin lifted a defiant notch. Perhaps she was partly in the wrong but she was past weary of his suspicions.

"Well, m'lord? So at last you've caught me in my 'unfaithfulness.' What is my fate? I but await your pleasure."

"Don't mock me!"

"Then what would you have me say? I doubt you'd believe me at any rate!" Anne threw up her hands in frustration. "Why do you treat us like this? I've done naught, and neither has Iain. Are you trying to destroy our friendship? Is that it? Do you hate me so much you wish me friendless?"

"I don't hate you!" Niall growled. "Don't put words into my mouth, nor lay deeds at my feet not o' my doing."

He ran a hand through his hair in exasperation. "Why is it that every time we're together we fight? 'Tisn't my intent. I swear it."

"Then why such anger toward Iain?"

"I'm not at liberty to say, save that Iain may not be all he seems." Niall lifted her chin. "I'm sorry if that's not enough, but 'tis all I can offer."

Anne wrenched away, incredulity darkening her eyes to stormy gray. "You insult me with your suspicions, all but do battle with Iain, and then offer that most inadequate o' explanations? Nay, it can *never* be enough! Despite what you may think, I'll not shirk my vows, no matter how odious they be. And don't worry about my fidelity to you, not with Iain or any other man. I can bear anything for a year—and that includes the likes o' you!"

He cocked an amused brow. "Och, and can you? And exactly what have I done that's so unforgiveable? Raped you, beat you, locked you in your room? I've the right do all that and more, yet all I've asked is that you stay away from Iain—"

"Is that the truth o' it, now? Your truth, mayhap, but not mine. I say you've tried to take away my only friend, not to mention refused me my greatest joy in life, my healing. Why, you've really done naught, m'lord, but attempt to destroy my freedom, my very identity!"

His eyes strayed to the plaid she wore. "Aye, your very identity. MacGregor identity," he rasped. "And the source o' all our problems."

His hands moved to the silver brooch upon her shoulder and began to unfasten it. "You talk about having no friends, then flaunt this plaid in everyone's face."

Anne's hands halted his. "What are you about?"

"Isn't that obvious? I don't want you wearing this in Kilchurn."

She stared at him for a moment, and read the hard resolve in his eyes. What was the use? And she *had* been a fool.

Her hands fell to her sides. "As you wish, m'lord."

The cold irony in her voice vibrated along Niall's tautly strung nerves. With a force that surprised even him, his fingers tightened in the plaid and he pulled her to him. "Curse you, woman! Why do you fight me every step o' the way? Why must all the effort be mine? You say you want friends, then don't wear this for a time. Appear to them not as a MacGregor, but as a woman—my woman. And as for Iain," he continued, anger beginning to thread his voice, "why do you constantly run to him and shut me out? You are vowed to me, yet have you ever made one gesture of friendship?"

Anne's anger evaporated, leaving only confusion. Friendship? Was it possible? Could he truly want her friendship? Her mind whirled back to the events of the past few days.

The memory of his anger and arrogance immediately flooded her but, when the roiling emotions settled, she admitted many were the times he'd also been gentle with her, apologized for his earlier harshness. And last eve, when he'd lowered his defenses to explain why he wouldn't bed her. . . .

"I—I don't know what to say," she murmured, "how to answer you."

Anne grasped his forearms. How warm he felt beneath his linen shirt. She ran her fingers along the corded length, marveling at the crisp texture of hair where the rolled up sleeves met bare skin. Awesome power lay coiled beneath the rippling surface, yet he had never so much as threatened her. True, he'd tried to control her—and that was harm enough—raised his voice a time or two, but he'd never, ever, lifted a hand to her.

Her eyelids, weighted with growing languor by the heady nearness of him, reluctantly lifted. Compelling, gold-flecked brown eyes stared down at her, kindling a deep, aching fire. Niall's lips were clenched, his jaw rigid, but his erratic breathing belied his outward semblance of control. Strong fingers dug into Anne's arms but the pain was fiercely sweet in the spiraling current of excitement that engulfed her.

"Say naught, lass." Niall's head lowered, his voice rough velvet. " 'Tis past time for talking. *Show* me what you feel."

His mouth descended, capturing hers in a hard, hungry kiss. For a moment Anne struggled, then yielded to him. Her arms entwined about his neck, her small body stretching to press against the full length of his.

At her eager response Niall shuddered, then crushed her to him. His tongue moved to trace the soft fullness of her lips then, tentatively, slipped past her parted teeth. He kissed her slowly, thoroughly, the long-repressed desire rising to surround him in a red-hot mist. His tongue plunged into her mouth in growing abandon, becoming wilder, thrusting. His hands roved over her back, then down to her small, rounded buttocks to press her more closely to his swollen manhood.

She trembled but didn't pull away, her own tongue shyly meeting his. A harsh spasm wracked Niall's body. He groaned.

If he took her now, out here beneath the trees, Niall sensed she'd not resist. And, suddenly, he wanted that, wanted it with a fierce, fiery need. For this moment in time, there was nothing but the passionate urgency of two young, ardent . . . Niall groaned and pushed Anne away, his chest heaving, his fists clenched at his sides. God, but it was still too soon, no matter how strong his reawakened needs! And he didn't know her, had yet to trust her fully. He willed his breathing to slow, his body to relax, avoiding Anne's glance until he could handle the excitement that stirred anew at the sight of her ripe, kiss-swollen mouth.

"I—I beg pardon," he finally muttered, his voice still husky with desire. " 'Tisn't right, what we almost did. I told you before, I—I'm not ready."

Anne stepped back, wrapping her plaid protectively about her. "Aye, you said that, though your body speaks differently. But fear not, m'lord. I'll respect your request. I will not force myself on you."

She wheeled about and strode toward the horses. *Curse him!* Anne thought through her rising sense of shame and frustration. *He takes me and when I respond, he acts as if I'd been far too eager to throw myself at him.*

She stopped short. Well, mayhap she had. He *was* her clan's hated enemy. Eight years of bitter feuding should not be forgotten in but two days of hand-fasting.

Tears, maddeningly unwelcome, filled Anne's eyes. *I hate him!* she raged. *He toys with my heart at every turn! Och, how I hate him!*

A hand gripped her shoulder and jerked her around. Brown eyes blazed down at her.

"I didn't mean 'twas your fault, lass," Niall rasped,

his expression one of bewildered remorse. "I—I'm not angry at you, but at myself. Aye, angry—and totally confused." A wry grin twisted his rugged face. "And, truly, can you blame me? One moment we're talking about friendship and the next . . . Well, we're all but mating on the ground."

Anne shook off his hand, her fists rising to a position of exasperation on her hips. Enough of this maddening man!

"And what o' it? 'Twas a mistake on both our parts. Enough said."

"Aye," Niall agreed.

A soft smile grazed his lips as he moved to help her onto her horse. "Mistake or not, enough said . . . until the need arises to speak o' it again."

The hissing and popping of pine sap splattering onto hungry flames drew Niall's attention from the letter. He glanced up from the massive oak desk that commanded an entire corner of the library, his eyes moving wearily toward the stone hearth on the opposite wall. Outside, a heavy, late-spring rain slanted past the window, pelting the castle with wind-driven sheets of water.

A fine day to be indoors attending to clan business, Niall thought. *Warm and dry, with a glass of fine claret to chase away the ever-present dampness.* Yet the feathery script on the parchment spread before him seemed as illegible as some foreign language. Too many impressions, too many memories, bombarded him until he found himself reading and rereading the page in an unseeing daze. Finally, after a futile hour of little progress, Niall put away the letter.

With a sigh, he leaned back in his chair and picked up his glass. He swirled the crimson liquid, watching the interplay of firelight and shadow on the backdrop of fine crystal. It sparkled and shimmered in the hearth's amber glow like tongues of flame. Like the auburn glints in Anne's hair. Like the inner fire that flared in her eyes when she was angry.

Anne. When had he begun to think of her as Anne? A small, wondering frown puckered Niall's brow. The mention of her name—his beloved wife's name—no longer chafed the raw, festering wound of his loss. Yet when had that happened? He'd met her barely three weeks ago when she'd stood before all his men, a glorious, defiant beauty. Since then he'd spent but a few days with her, and most of those filled with constant conflict.

Already he looked at her in a different light. She stirred him like no other since the death of his first Anne. Stirred him deeply, yet what did he really know of her?

She'd been his enemy until a few days ago. In her heart, she might be his enemy still. What did he really know of her true feelings? What if, somehow, she was involved with the traitor?

Lord, what if *Anne* was conspiring with Iain to bring about his downfall? Had yesterday at the loch been the opportunity they'd been waiting for? Had their embrace been arranged to goad him into a fight?

The thought of Iain willingly raising his sword to fight sickened him. True, they'd sparred many times as boys and young men, but always in fun, always solely to improve their swordsmanship.

But not yesterday. Yesterday the blood lust flared brightly in Iain's eyes, so brightly Niall wondered if any quarter would have been given if he'd fallen victim to the younger man. Nay, as much as he hated to admit it, it appeared Iain had greatly desired his death.

It would also explain the seeming devotion that had so quickly grown between Anne and his cousin. Mayhap there was more there than affection, how-

ever platonic Anne claimed it to be. For that matter,
his and Anne's handfasting could also have been
part of a greater plan. After all, he'd only Alastair
MacGregor's word on the true circumstances of
his betrayal. What if they'd all been lies, twisted
to manipulate him to the ultimate MacGregor
revenge?

Niall's head lowered to rest in his hands. Lord,
how he wished he'd someone to talk all this over
with, to help him sift through the questions until
he found the answers! His father would listen and
understand, but he dared not burden him with this.
Robert Campbell already clung to life by the most
tenuous of threads. And, though he respected his
uncle Duncan's wisdom, for some reason—call it
instinct—Niall knew he dared trust no one with any
possible claim to the chieftainship.

It was past time to put a plan into effect. On
the morrow, he would summon several of his most
trusted warriors to a secret mission. He would send
them out across Campbell lands to visit secretly
all the higher lairds, instructing them to keep their
eyes and ears open for any sign of suspicious activity. He'd ask for the first report in a month's time.
Time enough for his men to uncover any plots outside Kilchurn, if that indeed was where the treachery lay.

In the meanwhile, Niall would continue to center
his efforts on his immediate family. Besides Iain, that
had to include Hugh, Duncan, and even Malcolm.
Preacher though he was, he, too, was a possible
traitor. Niall dared leave no stone unturned, no person unexamined. Now, *all* were suspect, including a
certain lovely, silver-eyed woman.

Of its own accord Anne's pale, delicate face insinuated itself into Niall's mind. A fierce anger swelled
at the thought of her possible deception, an anger
that, upon closer examination, more accurately

resembled pain. How could he misjudge her, for she seemed so brave and kind and good?

Mayhap his mourning heart had betrayed him. Mayhap he was so needful and she had happened along at the right moment. And mayhap, just mayhap, she saw him for the fool he was.

His head bent under the weight of such a horrible possibility. His fist unconsciously clenched until the curved bowl of his glass shattered in his hand. The claret ran between his fingers to mingle with his blood, but Niall was oblivious. With an angry motion, he swept the crystal shards from the desk.

Damn it to hell, he was no one's fool! Not his ambitious cousins', or any of his relatives' or lairds', and certainly no woman's! There wasn't time to cloud his mind with a beguiling lass, no matter how well-rounded and tempting. His clan needed him; his father depended on him.

He must harden himself to her, no matter how difficult, how cruel he might seem. Though Anne MacGregor might not be a traitor, he couldn't allow himself to forget the danger she presented from a less obvious side—his hungry, wounded, needing heart.

Anne barely saw Niall for the next two weeks, save at the supper meal. Even then he seemed reserved, remotely polite as he inquired after her activities, offered her an additional portion or tempting dessert. After that tumultuous day at the loch, she didn't know whether to be relieved or concerned over his behavior. Finally, she let the matter cease to bother her. There were more pleasant, less disturbing, matters at hand, even in Iain's absence. Like learning more of the healing art from Ena.

Brushing back a stray tendril of hair that had escaped the snug braid hanging down her back, Anne returned her attention to the little hut and the concoction of comfrey tea Ena was carefully pouring into a small earthenware cup. Her gaze followed the gnarled hands as the old women offered the brew to the young child held in her mother's arms. The little girl had fallen from a tree several hours ago, breaking her right wrist. She now looked at the liquid offered her with youthful suspicion.

"Drink it, lassie," Ena urged. " 'Tis the knitbone tea. 'Twill hasten yer healing." Her eyes twinkled with warmth and humor. "Ye wouldna want all yer friends to call ye a wee bairn, would ye?"

The girl grimaced, then hastily swallowed the concoction. Ena gave the mother a few more instructions. Both she and Anne assisted the pair out to the ox cart where the father waited.

After seeing them off, Ena turned to Anne. "Will ye share a spot o' tea before ye leave for the castle?"

Anne smiled. "Aye, but I can't tarry long. 'Twill soon be sunset and I must return to Kilchurn."

"Ye dinna wish to miss the evening's meal with yer lord, do ye, lassie?"

A teasing light gleamed in the old woman's eyes. Anne started to deny it, then thought better of it. It was true enough at any rate. The more she was with Niall Campbell, the more she enjoyed him.

She gave a rueful nod. "Aye, he's certainly not the evil man the tales would have him be."

They halted at the hut and Anne allowed Ena to enter first.

"The tales o' the evil, murdering Wolf o' Cruachan?" Ena sat and began filling two cups with rose hips. "Och, lassie, 'tis all one warrior's silly boasting to another, until the man scarce resembles the legend. Not that Niall Campbell isna a brave man."

She paused to pour a pot of simmering water over the rose hips. "He's just not a self-serving whiner, like some o' the Campbells these days."

Anne's brow puckered. Perhaps she could learn a bit about Niall's problems from Ena.

"There's trouble in Castle Kilchurn then?"

"Something's afoot," Ena mumbled, pausing to allow the tea to steep before handing her a cupful. "I am not certain exactly what, but I dinna like the feel o' things these days. The portents dinna bode well—"

"Are you a witch then," Anne interrupted eagerly, "to speak so o' portents?"

"Nay." Ena shook her head. "I'm no witch, just a watchful old woman with a bit o' wisdom after all these years." She shrugged. "Mayhap 'tis something in the air. I dinna know. What I do know, for I can feel it in every bone o' my body, is that the young lord is in great danger. Ye must help him."

Anne stared at her. "In danger? But how and from whom? And how can I possibly help him?"

Ena sipped her tea. "I dinna know, lassie. 'Tisn't something o' the head, but o' the heart. I feel it, that is all. And as far as helping him, why, keep yer eyes and ears open, give him all yer loyalty and devotion. Ye never know when ye might see or hear something, have some bit o' information cross yer path that could be o' use."

"He won't trust me or what I say over his kin." Anne sighed. "I mean naught to him. He doesn't want or need my help."

"Doesna he?" Ena's brows lifted. "I wonder. Ye've already won over the heart o' the Campbell. I hear ye visit him every day. How far behind can his son's heart be?"

"The Campbell's a sick and lonely old man," Anne protested. "Few will stay near him long for fear o' catching the consumption. I but try and bring a little cheer to his days. Why, I don't think Sir Niall even knows I visit him. If he did, he'd most likely forbid it."

"Mayhap, and then mayhap not." Ena eyed her intently. "Does it bother ye then, the fact that Sir Niall might find ye appealing?"

At the sudden turn in the conversation, Anne felt the heat flare in her cheeks. "Nay, o' course not. I don't care what he thinks o' me. Our handfasting is but an act o' convenience—clan convenience. I fully plan to return home as soon as the year is over."

"Och, and that would be a sad day for Campbell and MacGregor alike! He *needs* ye, lassie. Canna ye see that yet?"

"Nay." Anne vehemently shook her head. " 'Tisn't true. He needs no one, and certainly not—"

A firm knock sounded at the door. Anne glanced at it, then back to Ena. The old woman climbed to her feet and hobbled over. At the sight of the person who stood there, she dipped in an awkward curtsy. "M'lord. I'm honored—"

"Is the Lady Anne here, Ena?"

At the sound of Niall's deep voice, Anne rose. Had she violated yet another of his strictures by coming to visit the old healer? She moved to stand behind Ena.

"I'm here, m'lord. What do you wish?"

Niall's dark eyes swept over her. "Come away, lass. I've a need to talk with you."

Anne smiled at Ena. "Thank you for the tea. I'll return soon."

They were hardly out the door when a strong hand gripped Anne's arm. She turned to Niall. "Aye, m'lord?"

He began to lead her away. "You're determined to thwart me every way you can, aren't you?"

"How, m'lord?" Anxiety rose at the grim tone to his voice. "What do you mean?"

Niall halted, pulling her around to face him. "I asked you not to do your healing among my people, explaining all the while my reasons for it, my concerns over your actions being misconstrued as witchcraft. And still you keep company with old Ena. Don't you know she's thought a witch? What do you think the village considers your visits here to be? What do you think they consider you? Damn it, lass. Are you bent on your own destruction?"

"She's not a witch!"

"It doesn't matter what you or I think." An undercurrent of exasperation threaded Niall's voice. "I've discussed this all with you before. Why won't you heed my words? I grow weary o' talking."

"I don't mean to disregard your request, truly, m'lord, but it seems we are fated to always be at odds." Anne tried to temper her reply with reason, knowing, in his own way, Niall meant well. "I think it better you not try to control my life. Let it take its natural course. 'Tis best for the both o' us."

"And is it now?" Niall tiredly shook his head. "Do you think I could stand by and watch you go to your destruction? You're my responsibility now. I promised your father—"

Anne wrenched her arm from his grip. "I am no one's responsibility but my own! When, oh when, will you see that? I never asked for, or desired, your protection." She inhaled a steadying breath, forcing her voice to soften. "When will you allow me my freedom, m'lord? I can't live without it."

His brown eyes darkened in pain. "I'll give you all the freedom within my power, lass, but I won't, I can't, allow you to endanger your life."

He paused, noting the crowd of interested bystanders beginning to gather. "Now, no more o' this. I'll not allow you to entertain the people at my expense, either. Will you come o' your own accord?"

She stared up at him for a long moment more, confused by the strange mixture of frustration and compassion whirling inside her. Frustration at having her life so strongly held in check. Compassion for him in his sincere belief he was right in doing so. Yet what else could she do but continue to fight him on this?

With a deep sigh, Anne turned from Niall. Her brisk strides carried her quickly across the village commons, the acute sense of being watched following her. The feeling grew until it became one of almost tangible discomfort. Full of malevolent intent, it hung heavy on the air, filling Anne with the memory of another unsettling day—of that day in the forest!

She whirled to confront the sender of such evil thoughts. Her glance careened into that of three men, glowering at her from beside the village well. There, dressed in bright plaids, were Duncan and Hugh Campbell. Beside them was yet another man, a fanatic hostility burning in his eyes. He was dressed in the robes of a Reformed preacher.

Chapter Seven

Soft, lilting notes rose from the clarsach as Anne's nimble fingers plucked its strings, but the resultant melody fell on unheeding ears. Her thoughts were far away, flitting over rain-drenched loch and mountains to a place called Glenstrae. She stared out at the leaden landscape, her somber gaze following the torrents of water relentlessly pelting the earth. Was it raining just as long and hard in MacGregor lands? Anne sighed and laid down her harp.

It had been well over a month now since she'd left her home. Relegated to a life among a hostile people, little had happened to change her initial expectations. True, she'd found friends, but Iain was gone and the Campbell was dying. And her relationship with Niall Campbell, what little there'd ever existed from their mutual debt of each other's lives, seemed to be deteriorating slowly.

They hardly saw each other of late. The Campbell tanist rarely found time even to make it to the evening meal and, for the past week, had been far from the castle itself. It had been from this very window that Anne had watched Niall and his warriors depart on that mist-shrouded morn, in deadly pursuit of a band of reivers who'd burned several Campbell crofts and murdered the inhabitants. Seven long, lonely days without even the consolation of knowing that somewhere on the castle grounds was a tall, dark, unsettling man.

A mocking grimace twisted Anne's lips. Blessed Mother, but the solitude was beginning to turn her into some love-besotted fool! True, Niall Campbell was brave, strong, and revered by his men, but those weren't reasons enough for the small, needing ache she felt whenever she thought of him. Why, they hardly knew each other!

Anne paused. Aye, she hardly knew him. Yet the brief glimpses of his deeper side, those times he'd revealed a bit of that raw wound of his wife's loss, filled her with an inexplicable yearning to know more about him. Niall Campbell was a man like any other, and yet he was like no man she'd ever met before.

With a snort of disgust, Anne rose from the window seat and grabbed up her heavy cloak. The weather be damned! It was boredom that was driving her to such romantically melancholy thoughts. There was much to the man she still didn't know. She must stop placing so much value on the little she did know of him. And she must never forget all the damage Niall Campbell had wreaked on the MacGregors in the fearsome guise of the Wolf of Cruachan.

What she needed was a change of scenery. Old Ena would be in her hut, huddled before her small hearth fire for comfort from the bone-chilling dampness. There was sure to be a welcome there.

A timid knock halted her. Anne's glance swung to her bedchamber's thick oaken door. Who could it be? If it was Agnes, the servant woman would not sway her from her determination to visit Ena. Squaring her slim shoulders, Anne headed toward the door.

Instead of her maidservant, a small lad stood in the doorway. It was Davie, one of the Campbell's personal servants.

"Aye, laddie." Anne smiled down at him. "What is it?"

He swallowed a nervous laugh. "Th–the Campbell, ma'am. He wishes yer presence."

Anne tossed her cloak onto a nearby bench. "Then lead on, Davie."

The boy hesitated, his eyes scanning the room. "Er, m'lord wishes ye to bring yer clarsach. He's a need for some music to lighten the day."

"Och, and does he now?"

A soft smile lit Anne's face as she walked back to the window for her harp. In spite of her intentions to the contrary, Robert Campbell and she had grown close of late. Her initial impression had indeed been accurate. Unlike his enigmatic son, the father was open, warm, and sincerely seemed to enjoy her company.

In the social isolation of the past month, Anne had been surprised to discover how deep ran her need to be of service, to interact with others. She was well aware of her calling to heal but the strength of the drive, the spiraling ache deep in her gut when she found her natural instincts to be with others so stymied by Niall Campbell's well-intentioned if misguided constraints, was disconcerting. There were times she feared she might go mad from the pain. A slow death, indeed, and far worse than any fate the Campbell tanist might ever imagine for her.

With a determined shake of her deep russet curls, Anne flung the disquieting thoughts aside. Her mind had been made a long while ago; it was only guilt at her deception that pulled her back, time and again, to the same pointless reflections. Pointless, as were her tumultuous feelings for Niall Campbell.

"Come, lad." Anne paused before little Davie. "Your master awaits."

The Campbell sat in a huge English chair, his feet propped on a stool, his arms comfortably padded with pillows. His pensive gaze was riveted out the window. At the sound of Anne's entry, he turned. A smile brightened his pale face.

He motioned to her. "Come, lass. An old man requires a bit o' cheer on such a gloomy day."

Anne smiled as she lowered herself into the chair Davie pulled over for her. "On such a day, what cheers you cheers me, m'lord." She positioned the clarsach on her lap. "And what ballad would you hear? Your favorite—the Douglas tragedy?"

"Aye, lassie, but wait a bit. I want to talk."

The Campbell's eyes strayed to where Davie sat on his stool by the door. "Fetch me a bowl o' Maudie's cock-a-leekie soup from the kitchen, laddie. And a goblet o' claret."

He glanced at Anne. "And you, lass? Have you eaten your midday meal?"

Anne shook her head. "Nay, m'lord, but I'll see to my hunger later. I much prefer visiting with you."

He grinned, then waved Davie out of the room. His smile faded. "The old woman . . . Ena's her name, is it not? Niall told me you visit her often."

Uneasiness rippled through Anne. "Aye, that I do, m'lord. She is harmless enough."

Robert frowned. "She is thought by some to be a witch. 'Tisn't wise to be seen associating with her, lassie."

Anne stared at him for a long moment. "I find no harm in Ena. She's a good, gentle woman. Are you ordering me to stay away?"

"Nay, lassie." He took her hand. "I've no wish

to deny you your friends." The Campbell eyed her closely. " 'Tisn't Niall's desire to make you unhappy, either. He has spoken to me about his decision to forbid your healing arts in Kilchurn. As hard as it may seem, his choice is wise. Mayhap someday, when things are more stable, but not now. My clan is superstitious, and the witch law . . ."

Anne laughed wryly. "Och, well I know about that. Your son constantly reminds me o' the witch panic. But I'm a healer. I have already learned much from Ena that can help all."

He raised a graying brow. "And have you, now? Is a cure for the consumption part o' that knowledge?"

"Nay, m'lord." She smiled sadly. "But if you ever have the dropsy . . ."

Robert chuckled. "Och, lassie, you brighten my lonely days. My children love me, but I see them so little o' late. With Niall forced to take over the chieftainship in all but name—as well he should—and my Caitlin spending most o' her time visiting the MacArthurs, and the rest o' it mooning over the MacArthur heir, well, it seems life itself is slowly taking them from me."

He paused to shift to a more comfortable position in his chair. "Aye, they're both good and faithful children but life must go on, and a sickroom's a gloomy place." Robert squeezed her hand. "But you, lass, you come here everyday and spend hours with me."

"I don't mind, m'lord. I value your friendship—"

"And you've found few friends in Kilchurn," he finished for her. Bright blue eyes studied her closely. "And what o' Niall? Have you two grown close? I'd hoped for a grandson before I died."

Anne flushed. "M'lord . . ."

"Och, lassie, I'm sorry." Robert engulfed her hand between two of his own. "Forgive an old man's meddling. 'Tis naught but an honest concern for your happiness—and that o' my son's."

"I doubt our handfasting brings your son much happiness, m'lord. It seems all we ever do is fight. And there are even times when I think he must despise me, for he never calls me by my given name." She shook her head, a small frown marring her brow. "Truly, I don't understand it."

" 'Tis a simple enough explanation, lassie." The Campbell released her hand to lean wearily back in his chair. "Niall's first wife was named Anne. Mayhap 'tis still too painful for him to speak her name."

"I didn't know, m'lord."

Anne straightened in her chair. At every turn, despite her determination to view Niall Campbell as a hard, heartless villain, he instead proved himself a man of deeply felt emotions.

In spite of her resolve to keep her perspective regarding Niall Campbell, Anne couldn't help wanting to hear more. "He told me little o' his wife. If I knew more o' her, mayhap 'twould ease my understanding."

A faraway light shone in the old man's eyes. "She was a Stewart lass. Niall loved her from the first time he set sight upon her. It was at a *ceilidhs* one winter's evening. The Stewart chief had come for a meeting and brought his family. To honor him, I'd ordered the traditional gathering o' singers and musicians. Och, what a fine evening 'twas, with the storytelling, rousing music and dancing!"

He glanced at Anne. "But I ramble in my tale. She was a bonnie lass, Annie Stewart was, her hair o' palest gold, her form as sweet and lush as a summer-ripened peach, her nature o' the gentlest kind. Niall was devoted to her, and she to him. Yet their love, it seemed, was not sufficient to overcome the cruel fate that dogged Annie's childbearing. In the eight years they were wed, she miscarried three bairns, finally dying in the bearing o' the fourth, a stillborn son. Her death almost destroyed Niall."

"And I, because my name is the same, constantly remind him o' his beloved wife."

An unexpectedly savage pain slashed through Anne. Niall's first wife was everything she wasn't— meek, gentle, delicately feminine—and Niall had loved her madly.

"I didn't tell this to discourage you, lassie."

The Campbell's deep voice intruded on Anne's pensive musings. Startled silver eyes turned back to him. "Wh–what did you say, m'lord?"

"You must have patience with him. Someday Niall will allow himself to love again, and that lass will be the most fortunate woman in the world. It could well be you, Annie."

"Nay, 'twill never be!" She shook her head vehemently. "We have naught in common save the battleground o' our opposite opinions. He never even wanted to handfast with me. He only tolerates my presence as a clan necessity."

"Nonetheless, there is something growing between you. Even I can see it."

Anne stared at him, even as she struggled to contain the sudden swirl of hope within her breast. "Nay, 'tisn't true. Your affection for me only clouds your perception o' the situation. You see what you want, not what is."

He wagged a silencing finger, an affectionate smile on his lips. "Hush, lassie. I know my son. And, one way or another, time will tell. I only hope to live long enough to see that happy day."

Robert leaned back in his chair. "Now, I've a need for a song. Play the one you spoke o'. Play for me, lass, and have patience."

For a long moment Anne fought the impulse to deny once more the content of Robert Campbell's words, as if in the doing she could bury the persistent hope the speaking had stirred. Her gaze turned toward the narrow slash of window across the room.

The rain had ceased sometime during their talk. A furtive ray of light from the setting sun had escaped the clouds to find entry through the window. Like some happy portent after the long days of gloom, it illuminated the chamber, bathing it in golden light. Like the promise of happiness at the end of a terrible sorrow, Anne thought in rising joy, if only one could first weather the storm. If only one had the patience, the love, to persevere. . . .

She picked up the clarsach and strummed the opening chords, a smile on her lips. "Patience you say, m'lord? That I have aplenty."

The Campbell sighed, a look of peace on his face, as Anne began to sing.

"Rise up, rise up, now, Lord Douglas, she says
And put on your armour so bright;
Let it never be said, that a daughter o' thine
Was married to a lord under night.
Rise up, rise up, my seven bold sons,
And put on your armour so bright,
And take better care o' your youngest sister,
For your eldest's awa the last night . . ."

Niall strode down the long corridor leading to his father's room. He'd only just now returned from a week's pursuit of the reivers and he was wet, cold, and hungry.

For a fleeting moment, Niall allowed himself the fantasy of sinking into a hot bath and cleansing the filth from his body, of imbibing a glass or two of a fine claret. He could almost taste the dry red wine, imagine how the liquid would course down his throat to spread its sweet, mellow warmth thoughout his body. Then he sighed. No matter how pressing his own needs, his first duty was to his father, who'd be awaiting a report of the expedition.

The reivers to a man had been caught and hanged, but the effort had cost him two good lads, not to mention a varied assortment of wounds on several others. His hand rose to the ragged slash that wound its way from his left temple to his jawline. The outlaw leader, a huge bear of a man, had left his mark just before Niall had run him through with his claymore.

At the memory, a grim smile twisted his lips. The slight movement tugged painfully at his wound. Niall ignored it. Another scar was small payment for the safety of the clan and far less than the life price he'd exacted from his opponent. He'd have to take care, though, or he'd soon be so marred of feature Anne wouldn't be able to stand the sight of him.

Anne. Unbidden, her silver eyes flashed through his mind, followed swiftly by the vision of her finely sculpted features and slimly rounded form. How many times in the past week had his thoughts turned to her? And how many times had he jerked himself from the recollection only to find his breathing labored, his loins heavy with desire?

The heaviness had been with him almost constantly in the past few days. Niall knew he'd have to find release soon, before it became a physical pain. Aye, it had finally come to this. With a force that amazed him still, his need for a woman had returned—and the woman he needed was Anne MacGregor.

A sweet voice, accompanied by a harp, floated down the hall. Niall halted. It was Anne, singing to his father.

The melody flowed over him like a soothing balm. Once again, Niall grew warm with desire. With a low oath, he shook the languid feeling from him. Lord, the woman could stir him with but the sound of her voice!

A lad rounded the corner. Niall halted, the shadowed hallway effectively hiding him from discovery. As he watched, Davie knocked on the door to Robert Campbell's room.

The singing ceased and a minute later the door swung open. Anne's flame-dark head peeked through. When she saw the boy, she smiled. "Aye, laddie? Do you wish to see your master?"

Davie shook his head and shyly held up his right hand. "Nay, m'lady. 'Tis my hand. I spilled hot soup on it. Cook said ye've knowledge o' healing and asked if ye'd tend it."

Anne stepped out into the hall and closed the door behind her. She took Davie's small hand in hers. The skin on the back was reddened and beginning to blister. A simple poultice of nettle tea would alleviate the pain of the burn, and then. . . .

She stopped. Niall had forbidden her to treat anyone in the castle. Up until this moment, she'd obeyed him in that at least. Of course, until Davie, no one had asked for her assistance. That didn't lessen her obligation, however, to obey in thought if not in deed. It was just so hard to turn from someone in need.

"Please, m'lady," Davie interrupted her thoughts, his voice taut with pain. "It hurts so. Isna there anything ye can do?"

Anne stared down at him, chewing her lower lip in indecision. Why was the act, long ago determined to be good and right, suddenly so hard to carry out? Because Niall Campbell had asked her not to? Because she didn't want to hurt him, nor cause him further trouble? Was that it? Well, it wasn't reason enough to ignore Davie's plight.

She released the boy's hand. "Come to my room in five minute's time. I'll see to your hand as soon as I take my leave o' your master. And, laddie"—Anne stayed Davie as he turned to go—"for your sake as well as mine, no one is ever to know. Do I have your word on it?"

"Aye, m'lady."

"Good." Anne stepped back into the room and closed the door.

Niall watched until the boy once more rounded the corner and disappeared from view. The long dreamt of sight of Anne, bent over Davie's small hand, her beautiful features glowing with kindness and concern, filled him with a possessive pride. He could almost imagine her in the same role, examining the hand of one of their own children.

He caught himself. It didn't matter what his dreams were for the future. Reality was too harsh, too potentially dangerous to ignore. Anne had lied when she'd said she'd not heal in Kilchurn.

A spiraling rage grew inside him. *Damn her!* Niall cursed at the closed door. Despite his requests to the contrary, she stubbornly refused to listen. He hadn't the heart to deny the wee lad his healing, no matter how long Anne had been disobeying him in this. But . . . but . . . *damn her*!

Niall ran a hand across his jaw, stirring anew the raw, burning pain of his wound—and the memory of his concern over how its appearance would affect Anne. *Fool!* he fiercely derided himself. *While you waste precious time mooning over her, she has been going about her business of scorning your requests and flaunting them in your face. Not only does the woman have no feelings for you but she actively seeks to undermine all you've tried to build toward peace between Campbell and MacGregor.*

As he stood there, impotently fuming, the door once more opened and Anne slipped through. Niall watched her walk away, well aware her destination was her own room, her purpose the healing of little Davie. With the greatest of efforts, he stifled the impulse to go after her. He couldn't risk his father hearing them. This issue was Anne's and his alone.

A sudden thought assailed him. Did the Campbell even know? Despite the discussion he'd had with his father, had Anne managed to extract permission all the same? The possibility angered Niall but, at the same time, it offered him hope she hadn't completely disregarded his requests, only chose to obey a higher authority.

But, no, it wasn't possible. Anne had been far too quick to step outside his father's chamber when Davie had shown her his hand, closing the door carefully behind her. Those were not the actions of a person with the Campbell's permission.

Anne had no one's leave, yet still she persisted in her stubborn convictions. Niall paused, his eyes narrowing in renewed suspicion. Were her actions the result of her headstrong beliefs or part of the plot to undermine and destroy him? The doubts grew, scoring Niall's heart. Indeed, did Anne's continued disobedience arise from a carefully constructed scheme she shared with the traitor?

With a low growl, Niall forced himself toward his father's chamber. It didn't matter what her motives were. Either way, they ran against his desires. Either way, she'd betrayed him.

All thoughts of a pleasant interlude with Anne after the meeting with his father fled. He was far too angry to face her. If he saw her now, if she even dared give him one of those defiant little smiles, Niall feared he might lose control. And, thanks to a beguiling MacGregor liar, self-control was about all he had left.

"A flagon! Bring me another flagon and be quick about it!" Niall shouted to the servant standing watch nearby.

The man scurried in the direction of the kitchen. Niall turned back to his glass. With an exaggerated flourish, he emptied the last dregs of claret into his goblet, then threw the empty metal flagon aside. He stared at the glass, swirling the ruby liquid so hard it sloshed over the sides to course down his hand.

Blood, Niall thought, his bleary gaze following the sticky rivulets until they mingled with the hairy expanse of his arm. It might as well be his own blood he was spilling, for all that MacGregor wench cared. One way or another, she was slowly tearing him apart.

The servant hurried over with a fresh flagon. With a low growl, Niall snatched it from him. He downed the remainder of claret in his glass, then refilled it from the new vessel. He'd been drinking for hours. Why couldn't he drown the painful memories? It had always worked before.

But before he hadn't that hot, heavy ache in his loins. The liquor coursing through his veins only stirred it to greater heights, until he felt aflame with desire. Desire for a woman who flagrantly disobeyed him, who mocked his every attempt at friendship . . . at tenderness.

Niall emptied his goblet in one long swallow, heedless of the wine that dribbled out of the sides of his mouth to drip onto his white linen shirt. *She doesn't care.* The thought was like a knife twisting in his gut, but instead of blood, rage poured out.

She didn't care that he'd tried every way he knew to be kind, to ease her way with his clan. She didn't care that she tempted him, set his blood afire. Damn her! He sat here, drinking himself into oblivion, and she felt nothing.

The fury within him burgeoned to explosive proportions, stirring him from his drunken lethargy. Niall staggered to his feet. Why should he be the only one who suffered? Let Anne experience some of the gut-wrenching torment of unfulfilled passion. It wouldn't change anything, but at least it would

ease his pain. And she'd never again be safe in her
self-absorbed little world.

The servants to a man slunk away as Niall made
his unsteady way across the hall. He saw nothing,
all his powers of concentration centered on the corridor at the head of the stairs. A corridor that led to a
bedchamber wherein waited a beauteous, heartless
witch.

Anne raised her eyes from the intricate flowers
she was attempting to embroider on the hem of the
crimson silk gown. Her eyes moved to Agnes, who
was intently working a smaller version of the same
pattern at the gown's neckline. How many hours
had they been busy now since her return from the
Campbell's room? Surely it must be close to time
for the evening meal.

The evening meal. A warm glow suffused her at
the contemplation of seeing Niall this eve. Though
he'd yet to visit her since his return late this afternoon, Agnes had lost no time in informing Anne of
his arrival.

For a fleeting instant Anne wondered why he
hadn't taken even a brief moment to stop by
and greet her, but then she banished the thought
as unreasonable. Niall was tanist and had many
responsibilities that demanded his immediate attention after a week's absence. The evening meal would
be time enough to see him.

With a sigh, Anne shrugged her shoulders to ease
the stiffness brought on by hunching over the
small pattern of flowers, then critically surveyed
the results of her work. The satin stitch of the
leaves and petals was lumpy, the running line of
the stem unevenly spaced, but the flower's colors
were a bright contrast against the crimson fabric. If
one didn't look closely, the embroidery didn't appear
too badly done. Not bad at all, Anne mused wryly,

if one was cross-eyed, half-blind, and besotted with drink.

" 'Twill get easier with practice, lassie," Agnes offered, noting Anne's disgusted frown. "And the Lady Caitlin isna too handy with the needle, either. I doubt she'll see past the fine color and fabric o' the dress herself."

Anne laid aside her portion of the gown and rose stiffly. With a small yawn, she lifted her arms in a stretch. "I hope so, Agnes. I want this gown to be a token o' peace between us. I'm at wit's end in trying to make friends with Caitlin." She shook her head in dismay. "Why, I've never seen a more stubborn, unfriendly child in all my life!"

"Give her time, lassie. Little Caitlin's fast growing into a young woman and has her own cares o' the heart to deal with." Agnes frowned. "The young lord seems sore beset with cares o' late, as well. I havena seen him turn so oft to the bottle. Why, no sooner than he returned this afternoon and he was downing one glass o' wine after another."

At the worried look Anne shot her, the old servant nodded solemnly. "Aye, lass. I passed him in the Great Hall only an hour ago and he was still in his cups, glaring so fiercely none dared approach him." Agnes chuckled. "Well, no matter. He'll pay the price for his foolishness on the morrow."

She cocked an inquiring brow. "If ye'll forgive an old woman's curiosity, how do things go with ye and the young lord? I know I overstep myself in asking, but I care for ye both and—"

"We are barely friends." A bright flush spread across Anne's cheeks. Holy Saints, first Robert Campbell and now Agnes. Why did everyone seem so interested in her and Niall's relationship today? Were her own thoughts so transparent?

She walked over to gaze out the window. "You see better than most how little time he spends with me, the conflict between us. There is naught worth discussing about Niall Campbell and me."

"Aye, yer words are true, but even so I see that old fire, that fire he had for his first wife, flaring to life again." The maidservant came up behind Anne and laid a gentle hand on her shoulder. "And 'tis ye, lassie, ye and no other, who have stirred that fire anew. Does that please ye?"

"Please me?" Anne's gaze caught the first star twinkling in the dark expanse of the night. "What woman wouldn't find the attention o' a man such as Niall Campbell pleasing? For all his blustering male bravado, he can be as kind and gentle as—"

The door separating her bedchamber from Niall's swung open, slamming against the stone wall with a loud thud. At the unexpected sound, Anne and Agnes jumped, then whirled around. There, striding into the room, his face flushed and eyes overbright, was Niall.

He was dressed in snug-fitting trews and his wine-stained linen shirt hung loosely open to expose a glimpse of his strong chest and muscled abdomen. His dark mane was disheveled and, when he moved toward them, his gait was just the slightest bit unsteady.

That he was besotted was evident to both women. When his piercing gaze found Anne, a small tremor shuddered through her. The light that burned in his eyes was hard and cold.

Niall beckoned her forward. "So, there you are, my rebellious little MacGregor. Don't hide so in the shadows. 'Twillna help your plight or lessen your well-deserved punishment. Come here, I say."

Anne glanced at Agnes, searching for some sign of how to deal with this new aspect of Niall Campbell. Eyes wide in apprehension, Agnes stared blankly back.

"Agnes, please," Anne whispered. Try as she might,

she couldn't quite mask the rising fear in her voice. "You know him better than I. Will he beat me? Tell me what to do."

"I—I havena s–seen him q–quite like this, lassie," the older woman stammered. "Truly, I dinna k–know what to tell ye."

"I grow tired o' waiting, lady," his ominous voice cut through the air. "You only add fuel to my anger in your disobedience. Don't make me come to you."

Strange that the wine didn't slur his voice, Anne thought for a brief, disjointed moment. He was still completely in command, his tone unyielding and imperative. To prolong the confrontation would be worse than unwise. It would be foolhardy.

Anne gave Agnes's arm a parting squeeze. "Go now. 'Tisn't fitting you be witness to our personal differences."

Agnes hesitated. "But, lassie . . ."

"Nay, no more o' it." Anne gently pushed her toward the door. "I'll be all right."

With one last, uncertain look, the old woman made her way across the room and out the main door.

Anne watched her go, then turned to face Niall. "We are quite alone now, m'lord." She met his furious glare with a steady one of her own. "Pray, what is my crime to warrant such churlish behavior?"

A fierce oath on his lips, Niall reached her side in two swift strides. He grasped Anne by the waist, pulling her tightly to him. A glittering fire lit his eyes to darkest gold, but Anne's glance barely lingered there.

Her gaze riveted on the red, ragged wound that traversed the left side of his face. Who had dared hurt him so? Her hand moved toward the jagged cut. Niall jerked his head away. He grabbed her arm and wrenched it behind her back.

"You've mocked me one time too many," he snarled, his wine-scented breath engulfing Anne in a warm, heady cloud. "Your punishment is long overdue. But before I lock you in the tower, I plan to first ease this ache between my legs. You're the cause o' it, you know, and 'tis past time I had my rightful taste o' you."

Niall's hand moved to Anne's breasts, grasping the cloth of her bodice in one large fist. Realization of his intent flooded her in one sickening, dizzying surge. With a cry of outrage, she began to struggle in his clasp.

It came far too late. The gown ripped from bosom to waist with one powerful movement of Niall's arm.

Chapter Eight

Anne's hand shot out, meeting the wounded side of Niall's face with a resounding slap. He staggered back, his own hand moving to the reddening imprint of her fingers across his cheek. Surprise, mixed with pain, flickered briefly in his eyes. Then the hard, shuttered expression returned.

With a low growl, Niall pulled her to him, ripping Anne's bodice to expose her chest. He entwined a hand in her hair, pulling her mouth up to his.

The feel of his hair-roughened chest rasping across her sensitive nipples sent an involuntary shudder coursing through her. Then Niall's lips crushed down on hers. Anger at his brutish treatment surged through her.

She caught his lip between her teeth and bit hard. He jerked in pain. In the next instant, he had her head wrenched back.

"Am I too gentle with you?" Niall demanded softly. "Do you mayhap like it rougher? I would have thought not, but the way you bite and claw at me, press your body so tightly to mine . . ."

"There is *naught* I like about you!" Anne cried. "You are a crude, rutting beast to treat me so! Let me go, I say!"

A grim smile touched Niall's lips. He pressed her so snugly to him that her small breasts flattened against the hard planes of his chest.

"I have every right to do whatever I wish with you, lady. Do you deny it? Have you forgotten your vows?"

The reality of her situation slammed home with painful clarity. Anne inhaled a tremulous breath. What had happened between them to turn Niall Campbell into an unfeeling brute, into a—a rapist? Why was he punishing her? What had she done to deserve this?

Hot tears filled her eyes. It didn't matter. He'd never have treated the Lady Anne Stewart in such a manner. The pain of that realization was suddenly more than she could bear—more than the shame of standing before him, her bosom exposed, more than the dread of the rough coupling to come.

With a harsh sob, she nodded her acquiesence. "Aye, m'lord. You have every right indeed." She raised tear-bright eyes to him. "But what have I done to deserve such harsh treatment? Tell me, and I will do all in my power to make amends."

Niall stared down at her, the sweetness of her entreaty piercing the thick fog of his drunkenness. For the first time since he'd entered her room, he saw her as the beautifully stirring woman she was rather than an object of his enraged frustration. His glance moved from her kiss-swollen lips, a streak of his own blood upon them, to the ivory expanse of her bosom.

The pale swell of her soft, pink-tipped breasts, rising with each shuddering breath as she fought back her tears, kindled some deep, primitive response.

She was his and he had treated her like a whore. No matter what she'd done, she didn't deserve such handling.

Shame flooded him. Though he wanted her still, Niall found he could no longer touch her. He stepped back.

"You can never make amends," he rasped, forcing his gaze back to her tear-streaked face. "All you care for is your own wants and needs, and I am tired o' it. Do you hear me? So very, *very* tired."

He strode from the room, leaving the door wide open and Anne staring speechlessly after him. She stood there for a long while, her limbs frozen, her heart twisting within her chest. She had hurt him, but in what manner she still had yet to fathom.

One thing was crystal clear. *She* was the cause of this eve's drunkenness, the source of an anger so great he had almost resorted to violence.

The realization tore through her. Anne floundered in an agonizing maelstrom of emotion. Then reason returned.

No matter what the cause, he had no right to treat her this way. Yet, as reprehensible as his conduct had been, Anne felt compelled to go after Niall. Once and for all, they'd settle the bitter differences between them.

She glanced down at herself and smiled wryly. Her impulse to seek out Niall must first be tempered with a little sanity. Rushing bare-breasted across the Great Hall at supper time would hardly soothe Niall's volatile mood.

Anne crossed her room and closed the door, her glanced already seeking out her clothes chest. It would take but a few moments to don a new gown. Surely, Niall would not have gotten very far by then.

He was not in the Great Hall, though all were engrossed in the evening meal. He'd passed this way, however, for none would have begun eating without him giving leave. Anne paused at the top of the stairs leading down from the sleeping chambers. Once more, her eyes scanned the room for Niall. He was nowhere to be seen.

She hesitated, gathering the courage to cross the Great Hall. The kitchen, storerooms, and stairs to the lower level were on the other side. Though Anne doubted Niall would have gone there, she had to make certain before searching elsewhere.

The conversations at the dining tables lowered dramatically at Anne's approach. She pretended not to notice. Head held high, she crossed before the outright stares and whispered comments, nodding her greeting at the occasional passing servant, who acknowledged her presence. She pushed open the kitchen door. The servants immediately ceased their work.

Anne motioned to Maudie, the head cook. The rotund little woman curtsied nervously before her, the wooden spoon she'd been using to stir a pot of soup still clutched in one hand.

"Aye, m'lady? What is it ye wish?"

"Er, Sir Niall," Anne murmured, lowering her voice for Maudie's ears alone. "I've a need to talk with him. Has he passed this way?"

A distinctly uncomfortable expression settled over the cook's face. "Aye, m'lady," she began slowly. "He was here a few moments ago but soon departed."

"Do you know which way he went?" Anne persisted, vaguely annoyed at the woman's reluctance to volunteer further information.

"Aye, m'lady."

Anne's annoyance grew. "Well, then pray tell me!"

Maudie pointed to the door across the kitchen. It led down the stairs to the servant's quarters. "He went that way, m'lady."

"Thank you, Maudie." Anne gathered her skirts to

head across the kitchen when the cook stayed her.

"M'lady," she began, her pale blue eyes anxiously searching Anne's face. "H–he wasna alone when he left."

"And, pray, who was with him?"

The other woman's eyes couldn't quite seem to meet hers. "He took that girl, Nelly, with him."

The admission sent a frisson of uneasiness through Anne. Though she hardly knew most of the servants, Anne had not failed to notice the striking, flirtatious Nelly. How could one not be aware of her seductive looks and swaying hips, or of the lusty appraisals and ribald comments from the men every time she was in the vicinity?

But what business did Niall have with the serving maid? Before the question fully formed in her mind, Anne knew the answer. In his besotted state, it could be anything—even to his bedding of the woman.

Anne's mouth went dry. Her heart commenced a heavy pounding in her breast. Had Niall taken the woman belowstairs to couple with her? She had to know.

"Thank you, Maudie." Anne backed away. "You may return to your—"

"She's a tart, that one is," the cook interjected quickly, her features softening in concern. "And she's always cozying up to her betters, the Campbell men in particular. Why, I know for a fact she's bedded Hugh Campbell many a time, and 'tis even said Sir Duncan—"

Anne held up a silencing hand. "It doesn't matter, Maudie."

"But if ye'd seen the way she came up to Sir Niall and all but rubbed her body against his and he so befuddled with drink," the woman protested, "ye wouldna be so quick to blame him. He's just a man, with a man's natural appetites, after all."

" 'Tis no excuse, Maudie."

The little cook fell silent. Woman to woman, she met Anne's gaze, then nodded. Maudie curtsied and hurried back to the hearth.

The woman stirred the kettle of soup simmering over the fire, her mouth moving silently. Anne dragged her glance from the hearth to see how much the other kitchen staff had overheard. All eyes were carefully averted, all hands busily engaged.

They know. The realization stirred her to action. With a whirl of skirt and petticoats, Anne was gone, her destination the stairway to the servant's quarters. She'd not allow foolish gossip or speculation to influence her. There could be some reasonable explanation for Niall's departure with Nelly. And, one way or another, she still needed to talk with him.

Yet as her hand traveled along the rough stone wall as she descended the steps, Anne's resolve faltered. The dank mustiness of the ancient corridors wafted up to her on a chill current of air. In the pitifully inadequate light from the flickering torches, the pervasive feeling of dread grew.

She halted and inhaled a fortifying breath. What was she afraid of? Whatever she discovered, it would be the truth. As difficult as it might be to face, it was far better than allowing the doubts to nibble away at her heart.

Anne forced herself onward, her footsteps soundless on the hard dirt floor. The corridor seemed to go on forever. She suddenly realized she'd no idea which room was Nelly's, for she'd never been belowstairs. Perhaps it was better if she turned back now.

A low, husky laugh floated out of the darkness. Anne halted. It came again, followed by the murmur of a feminine voice. Anne forced herself to move in the direction of the sound, down the next corridor that crisscrossed the main one.

A door stood open, a dim red-gold light spilling out to puddle on the hallway floor. The woman's voice came again, this time loud enough to reach Anne's ears.

"Och, m'lord," the woman purred. "I've wanted ye for a such a long, long time and now, at last—"

"Hush, lass," ordered a deep masculine voice, rough with desire. "No talk. Just let me look at you, touch you . . . taste you . . ."

Anne drew up at the door. Her tortured glance took in the scene of a half-naked man and woman standing in the room's opposite corner. It was Niall, his dark mane tumbling down to hide his face as he lowered his head to Nelly's breast.

As his mouth devoured one dusky nipple, the woman threw back her head in triumph. She moaned. Her hands moved up his arms to stroke his broad, bare chest hungrily before sliding down his sides to slip around and grasp Niall's taut buttocks.

As his mouth moved to the other breast, its nipple already pebble-hard, Nelly drew Niall to her and began a rhythmic motion against him. It was Niall's turn to moan now. Clasping her head between his hands, he crushed his mouth to hers.

A light sheen of sweat glistened on his upper torso, glinting off the powerful play of muscles in his shoulders and back. Anne could hear the ragged rasp of his breath as Nelly's undulating hips increased their tempo.

Anne's nails scored her tightly fisted palms. She felt as if she were drowning, the horror of what she was witnessing driving the breath from her body. Yet still she watched.

Nelly's hands moved once again, slipping around to the front of Niall's trews. With impatient jerks of the fabric, she quickly freed his hard, swollen arousal. Then, with a knowing smile, Nelly sank to her knees.

Anne backed away. She whirled first in one direction then the other, attempting to recall which way she'd come.

"Lord . . . Nelly!" Niall exclaimed on a shuddering, blissful breath, and Anne cared no more.

She fled down the shadowed corridors, toward what, she did not know. It didn't matter. The anguish of Niall's betrayal followed swiftly on her heels, mocking her even as she went.

The woman's musky scent, sweetly intoxicating, wafted up to Niall. As she skillfully worked her mouth up and down his engorged, throbbing shaft, he fought hard against the rising need for release. Lord, it had been so long—too long—and now he was as close to losing control as some lad at his first coupling. Ah, but it felt good. So very, *very* good!

Nelly stirred at his feet, pausing to raise her dark, dancing eyes to his. "M'lord?"

Niall's hands moved caressingly in her tumbled mass of hair. "Aye, lass?" His voice was but a thick rasp in the stone-muffled silence.

"Do I please ye, m'lord?"

"Aye." Niall stroked the side of her face. "That you do, Nelly lass."

"Then ye'll take me as yer mistress?"

The maidservant rose, one hand entwining about his neck while the other continued its rhythmic stroking. "I am as lusty as any man and will warm ye through many a cold winter's night. And I am not jealous that ye're bound to another. I'm more than a match for that whey-faced MacGregor wench."

At the mention of Anne, Niall stiffened. The liquor coursing through his veins had worked its mind-drugging magic for a long while now. Long enough to allow Nelly's earthy sensuality to seduce him down here, long enough to relax his strict personal code against sexually involving himself with the servants.

But now its effects had waned, helped along by the memory of Anne MacGregor, striking his conscience like a cold dash of water.

With a low curse, Niall pushed aside Nelly's excitingly stimulating hands and stepped back. He eyed her voluptuous form for one last, lingering moment, then shook his head. "Nay, lass. That can never be." Averting his gaze from her full, pouting breasts, Niall began to dress.

She made a move toward him and laid a hand upon his chest. "But, m'lord. What have I done to offend ye? Just say the word and I will make amends."

Another voice, murmuring almost the same phrases, slipped forward from a distant corner of Niall's mind. Anne. She had been just as confused, just as pleading this eve when he'd stormed into her room and all but ravished her. Yet the look in her eyes had been different, sweetly concerned despite his brutal treatment of her, not at all like the sharp, calculating gleam sparkling in Nelly's dark eyes.

Nausea surged through him. Suddenly, Niall had to get out of a room that seemed to whirl about his head. He backed away.

"There's no need to make amends. I erred in coming down here. I am sorry."

"But, m'lord—"

Niall held up a hand. " 'Tis over, Nelly."

A look of disbelief twisted the woman's face. "I canna believe ye prefer *her* to me. Why, 'tis impossible! She's bewitched ye, she has. That's the answer. That MacGregor slut is indeed a witch!"

Niall strode from the chamber, refusing to listen a moment longer to the edge of hysteria that sharpened Nelly's words to a strident pitch. The voice, however, endlessly calling Anne a witch, followed him down the corridor, grating on his tautly strung nerves until it made his head pound.

Lord, he thought wryly as his steps carried him toward the stairs, he'd have one hell of a hangover in the morning.

Anne thought the dawn would never come. She lay in her bed, tossing fitfully in a futile attempt to escape the memories of the evening past. The recollection of Niall, his powerful form bared as Nelly's mouth settled over his magnificent manhood, came back time and again to haunt her.

She didn't know what hurt worse—the fact he'd not even bothered to bed her before moving to another woman's arms, or that his act was blatant proof he cared nothing for her. Anne was well aware marriages among the nobility were rarely desired by the two partners, that husbands frequently had mistresses. But Niall had not even been interested in trying her, to see what kind of lover she would be.

Yet to say he was totally disinterested in her was not altogether true, either. When he'd come to her chamber last night, he'd admitted she stirred his desires, that he wanted her. True, his lovemaking had left a lot to be wished for in a romantic sense but, for a few moments, he *had* wanted her. Then Niall had stopped, suddenly angry.

He had accused her of thinking only of herself, of being incapable of making amends. Then he'd left, to find solace with that—that woman.

Anne rubbed her throbbing temples. Och, what was she to think? What was she to do?

She laughed derisively. What was she to do, indeed? She was his, vowed for at least the span of a year, and there was nothing she *could* do. Niall Campbell could have all the women he wished, flaunting them in her face if he so desired, and there was nothing, absolutely nothing, she could do. Nothing but bear the humiliation with dignity and pretend it didn't matter.

He'd told her he wasn't ready. It was too soon after his wife's death for him to desire another woman. And he'd told her he never lied.

White-hot anger swelled in Anne. Curse him! He had the soul of a dog! He was a liar and heartless brute! She hated him. How she hated him!

Fury moved her like no amount of pain ever could. Anne leaped out of bed and dressed. She'd not lie abed like some weak, love-crazed girl, helpless to do more than weep her heart out into her pillow.

Her glance moved to the window. The first rays of dawn streaked the sky with a lavender-rose light.

She needed to get away. Go for a ride in the brisk morning air. Sweep clean the clinging tendrils of her romantic dreams and sear harsh reality into her brain. Anne grabbed her cloak and headed toward the door.

Agnes met her halfway down the steps to the Great Hall. The old woman's gaze swept over Anne. Her eyes narrowed in suspicion. "And where do ye think ye're going so early in the morn?"

Anne stiffened, sensing a battle. "I mean to go riding."

She made a move to skirt the other woman, but Agnes stepped in her way. "And who do ye plan to take with ye? 'Tis too dangerous to go riding alone."

Silver eyes glared down at the old servant. "I shall go anywhere I please, and I'll not be accounting to you for my every move. Now, pray, step out o' the way."

Agnes refused to budge. "Does Sir Niall know o' yer plans? If he doesna—"

"You'll run and tell him?" All the old bitterness welled in Anne's throat like some acrid, spoiled wine. "Well, go ahead. I don't care. I know you spy on me for Niall. So run. Go and tell him! But I'm riding this morn, if 'tis the last thing I ever do!"

With that, Anne pushed past Agnes and all but ran down the stairs. The old woman watched her go, a troubled expression on her face. Then she gathered her skirts and made her way upstairs.

The Lady Anne had called her a spy. Well, in a sense she was. But if the lass only knew all the other times she'd not taken information about her activities to the Campbell tanist.

This time, however, she had no choice. It was indeed dangerous for a woman to be out alone. Sir Niall had to be told.

From the shadowed doorway of the keep, a man watched as Anne mounted her horse. His cold gaze followed as she rode away, the stable man shouting after her to wait while he found an escort to ride along. A thin smile touched the man's lips. He chuckled mirthlessly.

"Ride alone, will you, lass? And hasn't Niall warned you o' the dangers outside the castle walls? Mayhap I'll have to teach you a little lesson, a lesson, most unfortunately, that'll be the last thing you ever learn."

He stepped from the doorway, fastening his short-sword to his hip. With long, ground-eating strides, he headed toward the stable.

Loch Awe passed in a blur as Anne pressed her horse onward. Though she didn't consciously plan it, her direction led her toward the small burn where Iain had taken her the day before his departure.

The memory of him plucked at her heart like some bittersweet note from her clarsach. How she missed him! It seemed like years since he'd left. But then, everything seemed like years after the agony of last night.

How could she bear the shame of being hand-fasted to a man who cared so little for her feelings that he wasted no time seeking out the servants? Yet even as she cursed him, Anne knew if Niall had turned his passion toward her in the manner he'd done with Nelly, she'd have welcomed him with open arms. And that, mayhap, was the most painful realization of all.

She desired Niall Campbell. The thought of him stirred her, his tall, powerful body, the dark hair swirling across his hard-muscled chest and rippling abdomen, his iron-thewed thighs. . . .

Anne swallowed hard, an ache throbbing deep in her belly. Och, never to have thought of a man in that way before, and to now have it squandered on one such as he!

With a nudge, she urged her mount to a run, as if the action could outdistance her thoughts. The towering oaks came into view. The noise of rushing water filled her ears. Anne reined in her horse and slid from its back.

The scene was as before. The gnarled limbs of the ancient trees reached across the gurgling burn. Since she'd last been here the flowers had faded, replaced by a lush, emerald carpet of grass. The oaks had leafed out as well and would now provide ample shade from the afternoon sun. Mayhap she'd stay here the whole day, Anne mused, seeking respite from the memories beneath their sheltering arms.

Head lowered in dejection, she walked toward the giant trees. Ah, to hide away from the world for a time, she sighed to herself, to find solace and healing among friends who had seen far greater tribulations than hers. . . .

She sat beneath the trees for a long while, unable to still the restlessness, the sense of unease, that had begun to swirl through her. Finally she stood, following the burn down to the lake. Anne's gaze traveled across Loch Awe, past the narrow outcropping of land where she caught a glimpse of one of

Kilchurn's towers, toward the snowy peaks of Ben Cruachan.

Cruachan, she thought. *The Wolf o' Cruachan*. The name the people had given to Niall, that brave and fearsome warrior.

Though her feelings for Niall Campbell were unrequited, Anne struggled to assure herself that there was still some solace to be found. If he continued to find his pleasure in the servants, she could return home the way she'd arrived—a virgin. And one month had already passed in the year of handfasting. She had only eleven more to endure. Eleven long months to be sure, but not an eternity.

Anne paused at the lake's edge. Her gaze lowered to the gently lapping waves that broke on the grassy bank. She knelt and leaned over to cup a handful of the sparkling liquid, her long hair skimming the water. The movement of a wave caught a lock and carried it on its bobbing surface, to and fro as the current changed directions.

Fascinated, Anne watched her shimmering image reflect in the deep blue water, calling to mind her father's voice many years past. She remembered that day well, a time when she had first entered womanhood.

He had found her swimming naked in a spring-fed pond and, when she was once again dressed, had reprimanded her severely for her unladylike behavior. He had smiled, though, when he'd called her his water kelpie, certain to lure men to their deaths in the water's depths if ever they saw her swimming there. Anne had returned to the pond many times more, but always when her father was away or early in the morn before he arose. She couldn't help it; she loved the water so.

A sudden breeze whipped the lake's surface, sending agitated ripples through her image. Anne watched the wind-churned water as it momentarily obliterated her reflection, then again calmed to a mirrorlike surface. In it, she once more saw herself. But this time she was not alone.

The form of a Campbell warrior loomed behind her but his identity was blurred by the gently undulating water. For a wild, joyous moment she thought it was Niall, come to set things right between them.

Then the man spoke. "Come to the loch to cast your spell over it, have you?" Hugh Campbell snarled. "To poison the water that we drink, mayhap? Well, no matter. I've caught you in time. You shan't escape justice again."

Anne whirled, losing her balance to fall backward into the muddy shallows. She stared up into Hugh's madness-twisted features and the heart-stopping smile of pure malevolence on his lips. Dread ensnared her heart.

She'd been a fool to ride here alone. She should have known there were those in Kilchurn who wished her dead. And now, in her angry confusion over Niall, she had played straight into one of their hands.

"I—I cast no spell over the loch," Anne began in desperation, striving to soothe the madness from Hugh's eyes. "I but watch the water, full o' my own thoughts and dreams. Have you never done the same, Hugh?"

For an instant, the brown-haired man's face softened. A faraway light gleamed in his dark eyes. "Aye, that I have, lassie. Long ago, with a girl named Dora." Then, as fast as it had appeared, the light faded. A cold, furious expression transformed his face. "But Dora wasn't what she seemed, the conniving, heartless bitch," he muttered. "She tried to steal my soul. I was forced to expose her for what she was—a witch."

Hugh moved closer. He towered over Anne, his shadow blocking the sunlight. "She roasted at the stake and I made myself watch. I had to, you see, if I was to purge the memory o' her and her enchantress's body from my heart and soul."

He leaned down and jerked Anne to her feet, his strong fingers gouging the soft flesh of her arm. " 'Tis a blessing for you I haven't the time to turn you over to the authorities. You'll die this day, but at least your suffering won't be that o' my Dora."

With a cruel twist of his hand, Hugh began to drag Anne into the water. She fought him every step of the way. She beat at him with her free hand. She pounded at his face while she kicked at his legs as best she could.

Hugh seemed oblivious to the pain. The crazed, fixed smile on his face never wavered as he dragged her deeper and deeper into the water. Anne screamed. At the cry, Hugh grabbed her about the neck, throttling her.

A sob rose in Anne's throat, a mixture of hopelessness and abject terror. Yet still she fought him as the lake rose now to swirl about her waist. There was so little time left before he turned and pushed her down beneath the water. So little time . . . and nothing more she could do.

As he choked the breath from her, Anne's hands gradually relaxed against the grip on her throat. Hugh shoved her into the cold, dark water. From a place far removed, she screamed at herself to fight on, not to give up.

With one last, superhuman effort, Anne struggled to free herself, twisting and bucking against him. Her head rose to break the surface. She gasped for a precious breath as one of Hugh's hands loosened and moved from her throat. She grabbed at his shirt to pull herself upward. A fist slammed into the side of her face.

Pain exploded in Anne's jaw. Then blackness, horrifying in its finality, engulfed her.

Chapter Nine

"Curse the woman!" Niall groaned as he swung up onto his mount.

He urged the horse out of the stable yard, clearing the castle gate at a dead run. *Of all the morns to have to ride off after Anne*, he thought in groggy disgust. His head pounded, his eyes were gritty and blurred, and his stomach churned unpleasantly. But then when had she ever made things easy for him?

He turned his horse in the direction of the only place, besides Ena's hut, he knew Anne might go—the little burn where he'd found her and Iain that day. Some premonition, nudging uncomfortably at the edge of his consciousness, filled Niall with a rising sense of urgency. Though his swift steed could give no more, Niall couldn't allay his growing apprehension. Somehow, someway, Anne was in grave danger!

The movement of his horse's legs, striking the earth in relentless rhythm, gradually intensified the drumming in Niall's skull. He thought he'd go mad. He lowered his head in an attempt to ease the throbbing agony, the nausea welling inside him. Lord, how, in this sorry condition, would he be any use to Anne if she needed him? He could barely stay astride his horse!

With a supreme effort, Niall straightened. It didn't matter how he felt. He'd borne worse; battle was a pitiless arbitrator when it came to one's injuries. The rules were simple. Ignore the pain and continue fighting—or die. And this time, it might be Anne's life that lay in the balance.

He cleared the top of the hill that overlooked the burn. Niall found her horse, grazing peacefully nearby, but no sign of Anne. His frantic gaze swept the area, finally following the little brook down to Loch Awe itself. There, well out in the lake, was a man, bent over someone. As Niall watched, the man shoved the limp form under the water.

"Cruachan!" Niall roared.

The man in the lake stiffened, then turned. An icy chill spread through Niall. It was Hugh, his hands clenched around Anne's neck. In the next instant he dropped her and began to move toward the shore. Anne slowly sank below the water. Rage exploded inside Niall.

He reached the water's edge just as Hugh gained the shore. With a powerful swipe of his arm, Niall knocked his cousin to the ground, then leaped from his horse and flung himself into the lake. He plowed through the water, his progress an eternity, but at last he reached Anne.

Niall pulled her into his arms. She was waxy pale, limp. "Annie," he rasped, "can you hear me? Lord, open your eyes, lassie." Niall turned, his long strides carrying them swiftly back to shore.

He lay her on the ground, tenderly brushing the wet, tangled hair from her face. A hollow, hopeless feeling swelled inside him, calling forth a memory of another time, another loss.

"Nay, not you, too, lassie," he whispered. With a ferocity he'd never known he possessed, Niall gathered her to him, pressing her tightly to his chest. "Not you, too."

"Move away, cousin."

Niall stiffened. Slowly, he lifted his head. Hugh stood before him, sword drawn, the familiar crazed light gleaming in his eyes.

He clasped Anne protectively to him. "Go to the devil! I won't give her to you!"

The tip of Hugh's sword came to rest against the side of Niall's neck. "She's a witch and I must be sure she's dead. 'Tis for the best, cousin. Unhand her, I say."

A fierce-burning fire in his eyes, Niall lowered Anne to the ground, then rose. He forced a casual motion in her direction. "You're right, o' course. Have at it then."

As he stepped toward Anne, Hugh's eagerness betrayed him. With a swift movement, Niall slammed into his cousin, knocking both of them to the ground. Hugh brought up his sword hilt, striking a blow to the side of Niall's head. Niall's grip loosened. Hugh rolled away.

Shaking the scattering of stars from his eyes, Niall sprang to his feet. His grip on his own sword was none too soon. With a wild cry, Hugh was upon him. Metal met metal as they traded blows. Hugh's madness lent him a power beyond most men. Niall backed off from his cousin's nearly overwhelming strength.

A metallic clang, irritatingly incessant, pierced the smothering fog surrounding Anne. Gradually, consciousness returned and she inhaled a painful, shuddering breath, then coughed. A choking spasm shook her. For a long, terror-filled moment, she thought she'd never breathe again. Then, bit by precious bit, the air began to fill her lungs.

She rolled over onto her stomach and expelled a weak groan. How it hurt to breathe! And her throat . . . At the realization of what had happened, of the danger she still might be in, Anne struggled to rise.

The effort proved fruitless. She had to content herself with raising her head. For a moment, confusion mingled with a nauseating weakness. Her world swirled before her. Then it righted.

The sight of Niall engaged in mortal combat with Hugh filled her with renewed strength. She pulled herself up to rest upon her elbows. He had come! Niall cared and had come to save her!

Hugh was tiring. Niall, however, though the sweat beaded his brow, appeared as fresh and strong as if he'd only begun to fight. His claymore moved with effortless ease, parrying each of Hugh's more awkward thrusts with battle-honed skill.

Relentlessly, Niall drove the other man backward, his face set in grim determination. Hugh, scrambling away from the increasingly damaging blows, finally lost his footing. He fell, the sword still clasped in his hand.

Niall's blade found his throat. "Yield, cousin."

Hugh shook his head. "Nay," he gasped. "I won't yield to one who defends a witch. Kill her first. Then I'll surrender."

"You are mad." Frustration threaded Niall's voice. "Your unreasoning hatred has twisted your mind until you can no longer divine truth from fantasy." He resheathed his sword. "Be gone from me. You are banished from Kilchurn until you can find it in your heart to accept Anne."

Hugh struggled to his feet. "Y–you cannot! You haven't the authority."

Niall arched a dark brow. "Haven't I? Do you

think my father would fail to back me in this?"

"She—she has bewitched you both!" Hugh's dark eyes narrowed. "You will see. The Campbell will soon die, no doubt helped along by her spells. But there's still you, then, isn't there? And you won't be fit to be chieftain, with your devil-whoring witch at your side. Something will still have to be done about you."

"And you're the one to do it, mayhap? Do you conceal your treachery behind a mask of false madness?"

Even as he spoke, Niall regretted his words. Hugh, even as a lad, had never been good at hiding his true intentions. And there was no point in belaboring the discussion at any rate. He'd never wring a willing confession from his cousin.

"Nay." Niall sighed, suddenly weary to the point of exhaustion. "Anne's no witch. 'Tis your madness that makes you see that." He motioned toward Hugh's horse. "Now, no more o' it. Your banishment stands. 'Tis death if I set sight upon you before you come to your senses."

His cousin glared at him. " 'Tisn't the end o' this, Niall. Don't think you've seen the last o' me. I'll be back to finish what I began this day, and no mistake!"

Hugh resheathed his sword and stomped off to his horse. With a despairing eye, Niall followed his cousin's progress until Hugh rode out of sight. One by one, his family was splitting apart. First Iain and now Hugh, both sent away by him—and both because of Anne.

Nay, Niall quickly corrected himself, Iain had been sent away because he suspected him traitor. And Hugh, because he'd tried to kill Anne.

Anne! Niall quickly turned and saw her sitting there, quite alive. For a fleeting moment he was overcome with the impulse to run to her, to gather

her into his arms and tell her how thankful, how happy he was she had survived. But only for a moment.

The look in Anne's eyes was bitter. It rekindled the original emotions that had sent Niall out after her. The wench had the audacity to be angry with him, after all she'd just put him through? Well, two could play this game.

He strode over, refusing to be moved by her sodden, bedraggled appearance or by the purpling bruises on her neck and jaw. He surveyed her indifferently. "Well, madam? What have you to say? You seem determined to get yourself killed."

"And what do you care?" she was barely able to croak. "I'd have thought it would have solved all the problems our handfasting has caused you. Mayhap, for your own good, you were a bit too quick to arrive."

Something exploded in Niall. He pulled her up to him. "Little fool! Why do you say things like that? Why do—" Ensnared in her tear-filled silver eyes, Niall couldn't continue. He gazed down at her and saw nothing but her delicately carved features, her soft, slightly parted lips.

Their glances locked. Something intense flared between them.

Anne's tearful defiance evaporated like the morning mists. Niall's overpoweringly masculine presence, towering above her, banished the memory of last night. Nothing mattered but this moment and the sweet reality of being in his arms. With a small moan, she laid her head upon his chest, her hands entwining about his neck.

Niall stiffened. His hands dropped. Afraid he'd push her away, Anne clung fiercely to him, pressing her body even more closely to his.

After a time weighted slowly on the passing wind, Niall groaned and wrapped his arms about her. "Och,

Annie, Annie," he whispered into her damp tresses, "why do you persist in tormenting me? Do you know the terror I felt this morn when Agnes burst into my chamber and told me you'd gone riding alone? And then when I saw Hugh drowning you, I almost went mad!"

Anne clung to him, not quite sure she was understanding all she was hearing. Niall had been worried, even frantic over her leaving the castle alone? Was it possible? Did she actually mean something to him? If only it were so!

Then what about Nelly? a small voice persisted in asking, squelching the rising joy. *Ask him about Nelly.*

Inhaling a deep breath, Anne released her grip. She leaned back to stare up at Niall. "There's no need to say things you don't mean, m'lord. I'm quite aware your tastes don't run to women such as myself."

A furrow wrinkled Niall's brow. "What are you talking about, lassie? What have I ever done or said to make you believe I don't find you attractive? As crude as my behavior was last night in your chamber, I'd hardly call it the act o' a man who didn't want you."

"Then why did you turn to Nelly?" Anne blurted the question in a painful rush of words, then immediately regretted them. Why, oh why, had she asked? Now he'd only smile smugly and inform her it was none of her business, that he'd do whatever he wanted with whomever.

"Turn to Nelly?"

For a long moment Niall couldn't fathom what Anne was talking about. Then the sickening realization struck him. Anne knew about his tryst with Nelly. But how?

"Who told you? Who—"

"I saw you with her belowstairs!" Now that the truth was out, Anne couldn't seem to curb her words. "You were both half-naked and . . . and soon enough she had you completely exposed and her . . . her mouth was on your—"

Niall gave her a small shake. "Enough, Annie. I believe you were there. But if you were, you must also know that was as far as it went. I couldn't go on."

She lowered her head. "I didn't see anything after that. I didn't stay. I couldn't bear it."

A gentle hand lifted her chin. Warm brown eyes met hers, and Niall's mouth curved up in the beginning of a beautiful smile. "Och, Annie, I didn't bed her. I swear it. She made the mistake of calling your memory back to me, and by then the liquor had begun to wear off. I realized 'twasn't her I wanted. 'Twas you."

He searched her face. Anne's expression was carefully blank, betraying nothing of what she was feeling. Niall sighed. "I know you've no reason to believe me, but I've never done that with a servant before. It doesn't condone my behavior, but I wanted you to know."

Anne cocked a skeptical brow. "Never lain with a servant? Then would you have me believe you came to your first marriage a virgin, m'lord?"

Niall rolled his eyes heavenward. "Lord, Annie, o' course I wasn't a virgin. I was as lusty as any lad. I suppose I meant I've never taken a servant or any other woman for that matter, since I wed. And that includes since my wife died."

"Truly."

Her flat response stirred Niall's growing exasperation. "You're determined not to make this easy for me, aren't you?" A wry grin touched his lips. "Well, I suppose I deserve it. I hurt you and now you're exacting a fair measure o' pain from me in return."

"I am not!" The denial was quick and hot. "I—I haven't a care one way or another what you do!"

"And I say *you* lie, Annie lass."

A spark of deviltry danced in his eyes, melting the last bit of Anne's resistance. She wanted to reach up and kiss him, feel, once again, his body respond to hers. At the thought, a sweet tremor shook her slender form.

Niall noticed the small shudder. "What a dolt I've been to keep you standing out here in this breeze, soaked to the skin as you are. If we don't get you out o' those wet clothes soon, you're sure to catch the ague."

Before Anne could protest it wasn't the cold that had her trembling, Niall swung her up into his arms and strode to his horse. He placed her atop the animal. In the next instant, he was sitting behind her.

Anne felt a momentary rush of disappointment in the failed opportunity for a kiss, then decided all was not lost. As Niall guided his horse to where her own mount waited, Anne comforted herself with the realization that, at long last, she'd managed to exact some admission of affection from the Campbell tanist. And, though a kiss would have been heavenly, riding back to Kilchurn in the strong embrace of his arms wasn't so bad, either.

After a hot bath and bracing toddy, Anne slept well into the afternoon. Then, quite refreshed, she rose and dressed. She decided to catch a breath of air up on the tower walk before seeking out the company of the Campbell, as was their late-afternoon habit.

The wind on the walk was strong. The flag bearing the Campbell arms of a fierce boar's head snapped briskly. Anne was soon forced to seek the shelter of the tower wall.

She had just settled on the rough wooden bench positioned to afford an impressive view of the rolling, tree-covered hills surrounding Loch Awe, when

Caitlin exited the tower stairway. The girl's gaze slammed into hers. Anne stiffened. Caitlin hesitated, then resolutely gathered her skirts and approached.

"Well, are you quite happy with yourself?" the black-haired girl demanded with a sneer. "You knew o' Hugh's hatred for you and yet you insisted on riding out alone, luring him into what he'd no control over. Now he's banished, and all because o' you!"

"Because o' me?" Anne wasn't prepared for an argument over Hugh. "I nearly drowned because o' *him*. I'd hardly say that was much o' a plot to lure Hugh to his destruction. If it hadn't been for Niall's timely—"

"Exactly!" Caitlin swept Anne's protest aside with an imperious wave of her hand. "You knew he'd come to your aid. Why, ever since your arrival my brother acts as if he's a ring in his nose and all you've to do is tug on his rope and—"

"Och, Caitlin!" Anne laughed. "If you think I've such influence over your brother, you've been sadly misled. Niall's his own man and beset with far more important problems than when and how high to jump at my behest." Her eyes narrowed. "And 'twas never my intent to get Niall to banish Hugh. Hugh needs help, not punishment."

Caitlin faltered momentarily, then gathered new ammunition and forged on. "It all comes down to the same thing. You're not wanted here. Even if my brother *is* temporarily entranced with you, he'll soon lose interest. You'll never be half the woman the Lady Anne Stewart was. Niall will realize that in time."

Anne calmly eyed her. "Only time will tell, won't it?"

"Och, aye." Caitlin sniffed. "But in the meanwhile you could well destroy him. Every day the rumors grow that you've bewitched Niall, that you have him

under your spell. By the time he assumes the chieftainship, no one will want to follow him."

"And are you one o' those who believes I'm a
witch?"

The softly couched question gave the girl pause.
"I—I'm not sure I believe in witches." She tossed
her head in defiance. "It doesn't matter what I think
anyway. The rumors are beginning to undermine
my brother's position. If you care even a fig for him,
you'd leave, and be quick about it!"

"And if you cared even a fig for me, you'd have
made more o' an attempt at hospitality toward
Anne," a deep voice dryly interjected.

Both women turned to find Niall standing in the
tower doorway, a grim expression on his face.

"Now, brother, 'tisn't what it seems—" Caitlin
began, hurrying to him.

"'Tis more than evident what's going on here,"
Niall growled. "And I won't have it, do you hear me,
Caitlin? Properly wed or not, Anne's now the lady o'
this castle. She'll be treated as such."

"You're not chieftain yet!" Caitlin snapped back at
him. "Although you seem more than eager to forget
that o' late. I need only obey Father's orders, not
yours."

Niall grabbed his sister's arm. "Then why not pay
him a visit? Let him decide Anne's proper treatment
in this castle."

"N–nay." Caitlin jerked away. "I don't want him
upset, as frail and sickly as he's become these past
few weeks. Besides *she's* won him over, too."

"Och, and has she now? Then more the reason for
you to treat Anne well. 'Tis past time you gave up
this foolish nonsense."

"Nay." Anne moved toward Niall. It was time to
end this battle between brother and sister. "I will
not force my presence where 'tisn't wanted. I know
you mean well, m'lord, but 'twould be too humiliat-

ing, having others coerced into including me when
they'd no wish to."

Soft color bloomed in her cheeks as she held his
strangely piercing gaze. "Let it be, m'lord. You can't
force friendship or respect. It has to be earned."

"Aye, that it does, lassie." Niall's calloused palm
caressed the silken line of Anne's jaw. "And you've
certainly earned mine."

Caitlin glared at Niall, an expression of youthful distaste twisting her pretty mouth. "Och, if you
could only hear yourself! You're so besotted—"

"Enough!" Niall immediately silenced her. "I care
not for your opinion, only for your compliance. I
asked you before and I ask you one time more.
If you cannot find it in you to obey, mayhap you
need time to think upon it. Say, while visiting a few
months with the Lady Mathilda in Edinburgh?"

Caitlin blanched. "But that's so far away, and you
know what a puss Iain's mother is about chaper-
ones. Why, I'd hardly ever be able to see Rory, and
I'd never have any time alone."

" 'Tis your choice."

She stamped her foot. "Och, and you're a hard
one, Niall Campbell!" Then, noting the unrelenting
glint in her brother's eyes, Caitlin's slender shoulders slumped. "Och, what choice have I? 'Twill be
as you ask. Your lady will suffer no further slights
from me."

"Good. Now leave us. I've a wish to speak with
Anne alone."

They watched Caitlin's departure, then turned to
face each other. Anne wet her lips, wondering how
to put her next words. She decided no matter how
she said it, it would probably sound like a rebuke.
"I thank you for your kindness, m'lord," she murmured, "but the difficulty between your sister and
me is too insignificant to concern yourself over.
You've problems o' greater import—"

Niall took her into his arms. His head lowered until his warm breath wafted across her face. "Hush, lass. What I choose to do in regard to you is my decision not yours." His dark eyes slowly surveyed her. "You look well rested. Have you recovered from this morn's swim then?"

She grinned. "Och, aye, except for a tender jaw and sore throat." Anne touched her neck. "I fear I'll wear this circlet o' marks for a few weeks, though."

Niall's gaze dipped to the blue-tinged impressions of Hugh's fingers. He bent and gently kissed Anne's bruised neck.

At the soft brush of his lips, Anne gasped. Her eyelids slid shut in pleasure. "M—M'lord!" she breathed, then gave herself up to the welcoming haven of his arms.

But only for a moment. Then Anne pulled back, firmly removing Niall's hands. Brushing a windswept lock from her eyes, she stared up at him.

At the perplexed look on Niall's face, a small smile touched her lips. There was one matter more between them, until now overshadowed by last eve's scene with Nelly. One matter more, and then she'd give herself up to him without reservation.

"I've a question that weighs heavily upon me, m'lord," she began. " 'Twas the reason I followed you belowstairs last eve."

A glimmer of what was to come darkened Niall's eyes. "Did you mayhap desire the reason for my behavior in your chamber?"

"Aye, m'lord."

He sighed and motioned for her to sit beside him on the bench. " 'Twas many things, lass. Lust . . . anger . . . hurt."

"Hurt?"

At the startling admission, Anne's heart skipped a beat. He'd admitted to his lust, that no longer surprised her. She could understand how she angered him; he spared no words in reminding her of that quite frequently. But to have distressed him in some way!

Her eyes, bright with concern, searched his face. "Pray, how have I hurt you, m'lord?"

Niall turned from her. Leaning his head back against the tower wall, he studied the scene beyond the castle for a long moment. Finally he spoke, his voice low and controlled. "I was a fool to have thought this but I had hoped to forget about last night, and the reason for my confused feelings. But it cannot be. It stands between us as surely as the abyss between heaven and hell."

He turned to her, anguish burning in his eyes. " 'Tis but part o' our ongoing battle over your healing, lass. I came upon you and Davie yestereve in the hall outside my father's chamber. I heard you tell him to meet you later, so you could treat his hand."

At the sadness in his voice, Anne's heart twisted in her chest. Holy Mary, the one and only time she'd tried to heal someone in Kilchurn, and Niall had to witness it! She'd indeed helped little Davie, but all the while had felt so guilty she'd made a vow never to do it again—at least not until she had Niall's permission. And now to have the painful sacrifice been for naught!

"I didn't want to go against you in this. Truly, I didn't," Anne said, placing a hand upon his arm, "but he was such a wee lad and in so much pain. How could I, or anyone, turn from him? Could you, m'lord?"

Niall shook his head. "Nay, I couldn't. I suppose I was unfair to expect you to. But I meant well, lass. Surely you can see that. Already the rumors about you are spreading. Caitlin's words just a few moments ago must convince you o' that. And now that I've banished Hugh, well, tongues are sure to wag. Your healing folk would only add to the talk."

"I know that, m'lord. I try, truly, I do. But it hurts to see folk in need and know I've the skills to aid them, yet not be able to do anything." Anne bit her lip to keep the sob from her voice, but her words trembled nonetheless. "It fair t–to tears my h–heart out!"

"Och, lassie." Niall took her into his arms. "I'm sorry. You know I wouldn't cause you pain." He paused to stroke her cheek tenderly. "You do know that, don't you?"

She managed a tremulous smile. "Aye, m'lord, I think I do."

"Then will you trust me in this for a while longer? Give my people time. Things will die down. Then we'll see about your healing."

"Aye, m'lord. I'll try."

Niall frowned. "One thing more."

Anne's eyes widened. "Aye?"

"Could you find it possible to call me Niall, rather than 'm'lord' all the time? I know 'tis quite proper but it strikes me as rather cold." He crooked her chin with his finger. "And, if 'tis acceptable, I'd rather things not be so 'cold' between us from now on."

Anne's heart sang with delight. "Aye, 'tis quite acceptable to me, m'lor—Niall." She grinned.

Niall stared into her eyes, the look smoldering there igniting an answering flame in hers. His lips, firm and sensually molded, caught Anne's attention as they moved forward. Excitement rippled through her. He was going to kiss her!

The harsh sound of a throat clearing interrupted their heated reverie.

"Er, m'lord," the tartan-clad man began when Niall and Anne turned to meet him. "The Campbell requests your immediate presence in his chambers."

Unconsciously, Niall gripped Anne's hand. "Is there something wrong with my father. Has his condition worsened?"

The man shook his head. "Nay, m'lord. A messenger has arrived from the queen with an important document. Sir Duncan is already with your father. They require only your presence as tanist before breaking the royal seal."

"As you wish." Niall looked at Anne. "This should take but a short time. We'll finish what I began when I return. Will you wait for me here?"

Anne smiled brightly, her whole heart in the action. "Aye, m'lord. I'll wait."

Niall never returned. Instead, he sent Davie to tell her he'd be detained longer than he'd originally anticipated and that he'd meet her at the evening meal. Anne was disappointed, then consoled herself with the thought it was only two hours to supper time. They'd have the rest of the evening together.

The rest of the evening, she thought dreamily, as she dressed. Anne hardly noticed when Agnes slipped the pale blue silk gown with the square, lace-trimmed neckline over her head, or when she fastened the sapphire pendant necklace about her throat. Her thoughts were far away as the maidservant plaited her hair, then tucked it beneath a matching blue silk cap. All Anne could remember was the touch of Niall's lips upon her neck, of the promise that burned in his dark eyes.

Would tonight be the night he'd finally bed her? Instead of the dread she'd first experienced that day of their handfasting, all Anne felt now was eager anticipation at the thought of Niall's hard-muscled body, lying naked and ready, beside hers. How she wanted him, ached to hear him groan her name like he'd done that night with Nelly.

"There, all done," Agnes murmured as she dabbed

a bit of lavender scent at the base of Anne's throat. Her brow wrinkled as she glanced once more at her mistress's bruises. "I only wish ye'd allow me to hide those marks with a bit o' tinted lead powder. 'Tis quite the fashion at court these days."

Anne firmly shook her head. "Nay, Agnes. I won't cover the bruises Hugh gave me. 'Twould seem I've something to be ashamed o'. Besides, if I'd a need to hide anything, 'twould be with one o' my herb concoctions, not that foul lead powder."

Agnes shrugged. "Have it yer way, lass." She gave Anne a small shove. "Now, get on with ye. 'Tis time for the meal to begin and ye dinna want to keep Sir Niall waiting."

No, she certainly didn't want to keep Niall waiting, Anne thought in happy anticipation as she hurried down the corridor. Even the occasional glares and whispered comments as she strode into the Great Hall failed to dampen her rising excitement. Only when Duncan appeared at her side and offered his arm did Anne's happy bubble finally burst.

She eyed his proffered arm. "Thank you, Sir Duncan, but I'd prefer to wait until Niall can escort me to table."

"And 'tis at Niall's express request that I am here, lady." A flatly courteous smile touched Duncan's lips. "He is still in conference with my brother, and said to tell you he didn't know when he'd be done. I'm to lead you to table and commence the meal."

Anne's heart sank. What could possibly be so important that Niall would miss the meal? The hope of a pleasant evening with him vanished before her eyes. It seemed there was always something, some duty or important event, that arose to thwart their budding relationship.

With a deep sigh, Anne accepted Duncan's arm and followed him to the main table, trying mightily to hide the heavy sense of dejection that had suddenly engulfed her. She barely tasted the sumptuously prepared food or noticed the boisterous laughter and talk from the lower tables, so immersed was she in her disappointment. Little by little, as her natural optimism slowly resurfaced, Anne dragged herself out of her misery.

For the first time she paid note to the elegant dress at the main table and the larger than normal amounts of wine being served. With a puzzled frown, Anne turned to Duncan. "Have I imagined it, or are the people more merry than usual this eve?"

A slow grin twisted the corners of Duncan's mouth. "Och, 'tisn't your imagination, lady. There is indeed cause for celebration."

"And, pray, what is the cause?"

Duncan's brows drew up in surprise. "Hasn't Niall informed you o' the queen's charter, delivered just this day?"

Anne fought a surge of annoyance. Why must he persist in making her drag the news out of him? She shook her head. "Nay, I haven't seen him since the arrival o' the messenger. If you'd be so kind as to enlighten me. . . ."

He stroked his beard thoughtfully. " 'Twould be best if you first heard it from my nephew. The news might well upset you. Mayhap he could find some way to soften it."

"Please, Sir Duncan!" An uneasy premonition stirred within her. "He isn't here and I'd prefer not to wait all night. Tell me and see it done."

The older man shrugged, a strange light glittering in his deep blue eyes. "As you will, lady. 'Twas a land grant the queen has finally given us, one we've sought for many years. If you recall, you MacGregors have never had legal title to the lands you've claimed, holding them only on the clan principle. Tradition, however, never carries the same power as a sheep-skin grant."

At the rising horror in Anne's eyes, Duncan gave a harsh laugh. "Aye, 'tis as you suppose. Your lands, m'lady, are now ours."

Chapter Ten

"Why, Father?" Niall demanded, his voice hoarse with frustration. "Why did you do such a thing?"

Robert Campbell straightened in his chair and sighed. "Why obtain legal ownership over Mac-Gregor lands?" He shrugged wearily. "Because I finally tired o' their senseless raids, their burning o' our crofts and theft o' our livestock. 'Twas the work o' fools, this incessant picking at us when they never had any hope o' winning. Duncan convinced me 'twas the only way finally to end the feud. They'd either come to heel or be driven off. I thought 'twas the best course for all, even if the MacGregors were too blind to see it."

"But they've held those lands for centuries, legally or not. 'Tis their heart's blood. They won't give it up, not until the last one o' them is dead. Our feud will now escalate to an all-out war!"

"Even the MacGregors can't prevail against a royal charter. They'd risk banishment, if not proscribement."

Niall shuddered at the word. Proscribement required the clan name be struck from existence, the lands forfeit, and the men hunted like animals with a price on their heads. Yet what other choice would the MacGregors have? Clan honor would never permit them to give up their land, to become little more than tenants to the Campbells.

Robert saw the dark look in his son's eyes. "The feuding had to stop!" he said defensively. "We, too, have our honor, and that honor requires we do all within our power to protect our own. And I meant to be gracious with the MacGregors. Only their chief would've known the full extent o' the grant. 'Twas my bargaining piece." His face brightened. "But now it doesn't matter. Our clans will be joined when you and Anne wed. You can sign the grant over to her as a wedding gift. MacGregor lands will stay MacGregor."

"Somehow," Niall muttered, "I don't think Anne will see it quite so benignly. I wish you hadn't given Duncan leave to tell everyone. I could've used some time to break it to her in a gentler fashion."

His father frowned. "Aye, mayhap that wasn't wise. But Duncan was so happy, so eager to share the news, and now that the feuding's ended . . ."

Niall clamped down on his anger at his uncle's cruel thoughtlessness. In the past, he knew his father would never have been so easily manipulated, but the sickness ravaging his body had also weakened his mind. There was nothing to be done about it. Nothing save to get to Anne as quickly as possible and try to explain.

He gripped his father's shoulder in a parting gesture. " 'Twill be all right in the end. Anne and I will work it out. By your leave, I would see to that now."

Robert waved him away. "Aye, do that, laddie. I've

no wish for the lass to suffer needlessly. Go to her. Tell her the truth o' the matter."

Niall strode from the room. "Tell her the truth o' the matter." He wondered if the truth might not come far too late to assuage the pride of a beautiful, russet-haired MacGregor.

His pace down the corridor quickened to a dead run. The evening meal was sure to have started by now. Anne may have already heard the news about the land grant. He needed to get to her, to explain, to soothe away her fears, or yet another wall would come slamming down between them.

Damn it all! Niall cursed to himself. Why, when they finally seemed to be coming to some sort of understanding, did this have to happen?

He reached the head of the stairs overlooking the Great Hall and paused. He scanned the room for sight of her. Though the meal was over, Anne was still seated at the main table. Even from this breadth of the room, Niall could see her pale, drawn expression, the rigid set of her slender shoulders. *She knows,* he thought with a sinking feeling, *yet is too proud to leave, seeing it as an admission of her pain.*

His clan, however, seemed oblivious to her. There she sat in the midst of the jubilant toasts and joyful revelry, alone and suffering, as beautiful in defeat as in defiance. An overwhelming impulse to go to her rose in Niall.

Anne sensed his presence even before she felt his touch. She tensed, barely controlling the impulse to jerk away. Ever so slowly, she turned to look up at him, making no attempt to hide her contempt and scalding anger.

His dark eyes flashed a gentle but firm warning. "Not here, Annie." He offered her his hand. "Pray, come with me."

She rose, refusing his assistance. "Aye, m'lord. You are right. What I've to say is best heard in private, or this very eve the feud will start anew."

In silence, they made their way to Anne's room. As soon as the door closed behind Niall, she rounded on him. "O' all the greedy, thieving—"

"Are you going to judge and hang me before I've had a chance to defend myself?"

Niall eyed the little spitfire standing before him. Lord, but he'd never seen her so mad or so exquisitely beautiful! All he wanted was to take her in his arms and to kiss away her anger, but he knew the act would never soothe the pain that lay beneath her rage. The only way to do that was first to win back her trust.

Anne glared up at him. "There's naught you can say that speaks more clearly than what you've done, Niall Campbell! You've finally succeeded in destroying us. You must feel so very, very proud!"

"I had naught to do with this, Annie. Today is the first time I knew about the grant."

"And I say you lie!"

He grabbed her arms and pulled her to him. "Damn you, woman! I told you once before—I never lie! Are you so blinded by emotion you can't listen to reason? Am I talking to a fool?"

"The only fool here is you, if you think I or my clan will accept this! We'll fight you to our last breath before giving up our land!" Her voice lowered to a calm flatness. "But then, mayhap that's what you wanted all along. With this royal grant, we now go against not only you, but the Crown as well. What better ruse to annihilate us completely?"

"Damn it, Annie, listen to me!" Niall gave her a small shake. "I'll be chieftain soon. Do you truly believe I'd do something like that? What purpose would it serve? You're the firstborn o' your clan. There are no males with greater claim than you. If we legalize our union at year's end, in a sense we've joined our lands anyway. So you see, there's really no problem."

"No—no problem?" It took all of Anne's control not to slap what she saw as a smug look off Niall's face. "A year is too late! You legally own our lands as o' today. 'Tis no longer ours, don't you see? We'll be the laughingstock o' the Highlands! No wedding a year from now will change that! You've made us look the fool, all but turned us into outcasts. 'Tis done, Niall Campbell, and naught—naught will ever change that!"

She wrenched away, turning her back to him. "I beg leave to return to my people. I have more than served my purpose and cannot bear another day in this castle. If you have even a shred of compassion, you will not humiliate me further."

"Don't even think it!" Niall growled. "You're upset and not reasoning clearly. We had something growing between us, Annie. Will you let the schemes o' others destroy it?"

She whirled to face him, her eyes blazing with silver fire. "And I say you are mistaken, *m'lord*. We have naught. Do you hear me? *Naught!* Don't think to placate me with soft-spoken words. You are no better than the rest o' them! Let me go, I say!"

At the disdainful finality in Anne's voice, the warmth in Niall's eyes faded. In its place grew a hard resolve. If she wasn't clearheaded enough to know her own heart, he'd have to take command. All Anne needed was time. Time to be convinced of his true motives, to find some way out of this quagmire of wounded honor.

Niall shook his head. "I won't free you from your vows. We are handfasted for a year. Willing or no, you'll stay here for that time and not a moment less."

He began to walk toward the door when her tear-choked voice halted him, her bitter words slicing deep to lay open his heart. "I hate you, Niall Campbell," Anne whispered. "Mark well my words. If 'tis the last thing I do, I'll make you rue the day you brought me here."

"W–water . . ."

Niall slipped his arm beneath his father's head. Lifting him, he offered the dying man a sip of water.

The Campbell shot him a grateful smile. With a sigh, his eyes slid shut. Niall lay him down. For a long while he sat there, watching the bedcovers rise and fall with his father's labored breathing.

I'll be chieftain very soon now. The thought gave him little comfort. The position held no joy or attraction for him. It was nothing but a heavy responsibility and burdensome worry. Of late, all it seemed to do was drive one wedge after another between him and Anne.

Anne. When had she begun to fill all his waking moments, become so important to him? Yet now, when he needed her most, she couldn't be further away.

"H–have you talked to the l–lassie?"

Niall shook his head, gazing down at the pain-bright eyes once more staring up at him. "Nay, she refuses to see me. 'Tis well over a week now, and she hasn't budged from her room. My only comfort is that Agnes assures me she's alive and eating."

" 'T–tis my fault. 'Twas my foolish scheme to end the feud that caused this." Robert sighed. "Och, wh–why did I let Duncan talk me into this? Wh–what was I thinking?"

Niall laid a comforting hand on his father's shoulder. "Don't waste your strength worrying over this, Father. I, o' all people, realize how hard the choices are. You made the decision in good faith. You couldn't know what lay ahead. Anne and I will work this out."

"S–she's a sweet lass."

"Aye, Father."

"Y–you care for her, don't you, laddie?"

Tawny-brown eyes met those of bright blue. "Aye."

"B–bring her to me. I m–must say my farewells."

Niall frowned. "She won't come. She holds you as responsible as I for the land grant."

The Campbell's trembling hand grasped his son's shirt to pull him close. "I—I am dying, lad! She'll come."

The effort took all his remaining strength. Robert fell back, a harsh cough wracking his body. He motioned for his handkerchief, but not fast enough to hide the bloody spittle that came to his lips.

Niall winced at the sight. He rose. "I'll do what I can."

Without a word, he strode past his sister and uncle and left the room. Niall's resolve, however, ebbed with each step down the corridor.

Anne wouldn't listen to him. He knew too well her stubbornness, her fierce pride, and knew as well that she now hated him. If it had been anyone but his father he'd never have approached her at this time, for he wasn't fool enough not to recognize a hopeless situation. Yet, somehow, someway, he must convince her. It was his father's last request. He couldn't fail him.

Agnes answered Niall's knock. Her eyes widened when she peeped through the door. "Aye, m'lord?"

"Let me in. I must talk with her."

The maidservant blanched. "Och, nay, m'lord. 'Twill only make things worse. Give her more time, I pray ye."

"There's no time left. Let me in."

His steady gaze held hers until she finally lowered her eyes and stepped aside. Niall strode in, then turned to the old woman. "Leave us."

Agnes shot a hesitant glance across the room, then curtsied and hurried out.

Anne was staring out the window. Her eyes, riveted on some faraway spot, never wavered, though he knew she must be aware of his presence.

"Get out."

Her flat command only reinforced his earlier misgivings. He squared his shoulders and headed toward her, prepared for the battle to come.

Anne stood before the window, her slender form rigid and hostile. The afternoon sun bathed her in a golden hue, setting off sparkling auburn highlights in her long, unbound hair, bathing her delicate features in glowing radiance. Until this moment Niall hadn't realized how much he'd missed her. An intensely painful longing swelled in his chest.

Lord, if only she'd let him hold her, kiss away all the cares that separated them! He knew, if only he could take her into his arms, he could ease the agonizing barriers between them. It had worked before. Dare he try again?

"Don't even think about touching me!" The words escaped Anne's lips in a low snarl. "I swear I'll scratch your eyes out if you do."

Niall inhaled a shuddering breath. Had his feelings been that strong, that palpable, that she sensed them with such ease? His fists clenched at his side.

"I believe you, Annie," he finally replied in a low, pain-rasped voice. "I wouldn't be here at all if 'tweren't for my father." He paused for some reaction. There was none. "He's near death, Annie."

"I know."

Her voice remained flat, her gaze unwavering in its direction out the window. Niall moved a step closer.

"He wants to see you."

"Nay."

It was the answer he'd dreaded. Niall inhaled another ragged breath. "Please, Annie."

The catch in his deep voice sent a frisson through Anne. She wrapped her arms protectively about her. Even now, after all he'd done to her, how could the sound of his voice so easily melt her resolve? *But not this time,* she fiercely reminded herself, *not this time or ever again!*

The effort to deny him, though, brought tears to her eyes. She shook her head. The movement spilled the moisture onto her cheeks. "Nay, I said!"

She turned tear-bright eyes to him, her anger a heavy, heated aura. It was so hard, remembering the pleasant hours spent at the Campbell's bedside, basking in the warmth of his friendship, and all the while he was plotting to steal MacGregor lands.

"I don't care if he's dying!" Anne cried. "I don't care what his last requests are! And I don't care that you've a need to fulfill them. 'Tis your father, your problem. Don't lay it upon me!"

"Don't lay it upon you?" Niall's fists clenched at his sides in a frantic effort to control his impulse to shake her. "Lord, woman! Where else would one lay such cares but at the feet o' a healer? You told me you'd a calling, that you'd never turn from anyone in need. Doesn't your sacred duty extend to the deathbed? If you turn from him now, aren't you gainsaying everything you've devoted your life to?"

She glared at him then, her lips trembling. A wild hope flared in Niall.

"Hate me if you will," he pressed on, sensing she was near her breaking point. "I'm alive and strong. You've many years to exact your revenge upon me. But forgive my father and go to him. A healer's compassion shouldn't recognize clan loyalties."

All the anger, all the fight, fled Anne in one mighty rush, leaving only a hollow, aching void. What was the use? She hadn't the courage to see this through, to sever the emotional bonds that already tied her to the Campbells. Well, to at least one Campbell, at any rate.

And he was dying.

Anne wiped her tears away. "Lead me to him, but remember one thing, Niall Campbell."

"Aye, lass."

"This changes naught between you and me."

Niall eyed her for a moment, then nodded. He walked out of the room.

Anne swept past him when he opened the door to his father's chamber, ignoring Caitlin's horrified gasp and Duncan's muttered oath. Only from a distance did she hear anything, as she leaned over Robert Campbell's bed.

He had worsened so rapidly in the past week. She studied his face, noting the almost translucent skin, the blue tinge to his lips, the sunken, haggard features. Niall had been right. His father was indeed close to death. In spite of Anne's intention to harden her heart to him, the pitiful sight of the Campbell, the memories of his kindness to her, erased her cold determination instantly.

With a small sigh, Anne settled in the chair Niall provided. "Och, m'lord," she murmured, taking his father's thin, cool hand, " 'tis a sad thing to see you like this. Is there any way I can ease your suffering?"

A radiant smile spread across the old man's face. "Och, lassie, y–you've already done it by coming to me." His glance moved to the tall man standing behind Anne. "I told my son you would. D–didn't I, laddie?"

Niall's deep voice, so close behind, sent a curious thrill through Anne. "Aye, Father."

Robert's eyes crinkled with affection, then he slowly licked his lips. "I've a taste for a bit o' broth, laddie.

W—would you send down to the kitchen for a cup o' Maudie's soup?"

"Aye, Father."

The Campbell motioned toward Duncan and Caitlin standing near the window. "T—take them with you. I've a wish for a p—private moment with the lass."

He watched his son lead the others from the room before turning back to Anne.

She eyed him quizzically. "You've certainly regained your strength, and with it your appetite, all o' a sudden."

The Campbell smiled sadly. "I've no hunger. Far from it. I—I but wanted a moment o' privacy with you, lassie. My son wouldn't like me interfering but 'tis a d—dying man's perogative, wouldn't you say?"

"As if you've ever needed anyone's permission for anything, m'lord."

He chuckled weakly, then winced. "Och, lassie, my son has met his match in you. His first wife was a sweet angel, b—but you are as proud and brave as any warrior. Niall will need such a woman in the l—long, dark days ahead." A furrow of concern creased his brow. "Y—you'll stand by him, won't you, lassie?"

Anne couldn't meet his gaze. "There are things between us, m'lord . . . things that cannot be breached."

"H—he needs you, lassie!"

"Nay, m'lord. He has all he needs now, for he has MacGregor lands. He doesn't need me."

"Och, lassie." Robert clasped her hand between his. " 'Twas never Niall's intent to take your lands. If there be fault, it lies with D—Duncan and me. 'Twas our p—plan, and our plan alone, to go to the queen. Niall never knew anything about it.

"In a moment of great a—anger against your father," he continued, "I finally agreed with my brother th—that we should end the feud in any way we could. The land grant seemed the best, the only way."

The Campbell shook his head. "I—I was so tired o' the endless years o' fighting, the destruction on both sides. I only meant to gain control over your clan, not destroy them. I—I might have been wrong," he admitted, raising his eyes to hers, "but I made the best decision I could—for the good o' *my* clan."

Anne exhaled a long breath. "I understand, m'lord."

"Th–then you'll forgive my son?"

"You said he knew naught about the grant. There's naught to forgive."

Robert leaned back and closed his eyes. "Good."

He lay there a long while, his breathing labored, as if the talk had taken what little strength he had. Anne finally made a move to disengage her hand, thinking he'd fallen asleep, but the action only caused his eyes to snap open.

He stared at her a moment longer, then smiled. "Y–you'll stay with him, then? Be a good helpmate and lover? Give him b–bairns?"

"M'lord . . ." Anne paused, as she heard the door open and someone walk in.

"Your word, lass!" Robert gasped. "I've no time left for—"

He choked, the sound hard and gut-wracking. It increased in intensity until he seemed unable to catch his breath. Anne lifted his shoulders to aid his efforts, but it did little good. Robert Campbell's face turned red, then purpled as he struggled for breath.

Anne reached for the cup of water on the nearby table and held it to his lips. The old man took a sip, swallowed, then a strange look crossed his face. A gurgling sound rose in his throat. As Anne watched in rising horror, bright red blood began to spew from his mouth.

Robert clutched at her. A glazed expression dulled his eyes. Anne turned. Her frantic gaze slammed into the serving maid standing there, a covered tray in her hands.

"Niall! Get Niall and quickly!" Anne cried.

Nelly dropped the tray with a clatter and ran. Niall must have heard Anne's cry. He rushed past before the servant even reached the door and was at the bed in a few quick strides.

"Father!"

Anne surrendered the limp form and stepped back. Through a mist of tears, she watched Niall clasp his father to him and murmur something into the old man's ear. Then there were hands pushing her aside, as Duncan and Caitlin hurried forward.

There was little more Anne could do. The lung hemorrhage was fatal. Caitlin's wails signaled the end. Gently, Niall lay his father down and pulled the comforter over his face. Then he took his sobbing sister into his arms, his tortured glance meeting that of Duncan's.

His uncle stood there, glaring back at him, his shoulders stiff, his fists clenched. "You shouldn't have left him alone with her," he spat the words as if they'd a foul taste. "She was but looking for a chance to avenge the loss o' her lands—and you, you fool, gave it to her."

A shuttered look darkened Niall's face. "Have a care, Uncle. 'Tis your grief that makes you speak so."

Duncan grabbed Nelly. "You were here. You saw. Did she give my brother anything? Do anything untoward?"

The dark-haired maid shrunk back from the ferocity of Duncan's anger. "I—I saw the lady give him something to drink, m—m'lord. That is all."

"Was there something in the drink? Did she try to poison him?"

Nelly hesitated, then slowly wet her lips. "She put

some powder in the cup, but what 'twas I dinna know."

With a low curse, Duncan released Nelly and strode toward Anne. He grabbed her by the arm and jerked her to him. "What did you give my brother, witch? Tell me now before I choke the life out o' you!"

For an instant Anne stared up at him, too shocked to reply. Then she began to struggle. "Unhand me! I gave him naught but a sip o' water. I will not stand here and be falsely accused!"

"Do as she says, Uncle," Niall growled in an ominous voice. "I won't dishonor my father's deathbed by this ridiculous scene. Let her go."

Duncan dragged Anne toward Niall. "Ridiculous, you say! Nelly just said—"

"And 'twill be a cold day in hell before I take Nelly's word over Anne's. Now, let her go!"

Niall stood before his uncle, his wide-legged stance emanating an unmistakeable threat. Duncan glared back, his face a mottled red. Finally, he released Anne.

"I've tried mightily to ignore the rumors and malicious gossip spreading through the clan about this woman," he snarled. "But no more, nephew. Witch or no, she has you in her power. Your judgement is tainted, your loyalty suspect, if you refuse even to consider that she murdered your father."

He stepped back from Niall. "I—I'm not sure you're fit to claim the chieftain's feathers!"

"Get out."

In rising dismay, Anne watched as Niall motioned for his uncle to leave. The effort it took for him to control himself, from the furious workings of his jaw to the ragged rasp of his breath, filled her with pain.

Blessed Mother, she thought, wasn't it enough his father had just died in his arms? Must he now be forced to deal with the issue of his right to accede to the chieftainship, not to mention the torment of fighting with his uncle? And why, once again, must she be so intricately entwined in it all?

" 'Tisn't over, nephew!" Duncan spat.

Niall expelled a weary sigh. "Nay, I'd imagine not. But as clan tanist I proclaim a truce between us until my father's buried. Do you agree? For the sake o' our common love for him, can we have peace until then?"

"Aye." Duncan nodded, his reluctance evident. "But only until then."

Niall watched him leave the room, then turned to Nelly and his sister. "Leave us. There is naught more to be done until the preacher has been here. Fetch him for me."

Caitlin opened her mouth to speak, but the words were all but drowned in her tears. She nodded numbly and stumbled from the room, Nelly following closely behind.

"N–Niall?" Anne hesitantly touched his arm. "I—I'm so sorry—"

He stared at her, his eyes burning pools of agony. "Not now, Annie. I—I can't bear much more. Please go to your room and don't leave until I come for you."

She took a step closer. "But I want to stay, be o' help—"

"Please, Annie!"

The anguish roughened his voice to a raw, ragged edge. Anne backed away. She nodded, lowering her eyes to spare herself further sight of his pain, and to hide the hurt that misted her own eyes at his rejection.

" 'Twill be as you ask, m'lord." Anne gathered her skirts and fled the room, but not before the sound of Niall's voice, once more at his father's bed, reached her retreating ears.

"Father," he groaned. "Och, Lord . . . Father!"

*   *   *

From her chamber window, Anne watched the endless procession of mourners arrive the next day. The vibrant hue of various clan tartans, their lairds and warriors come to honor the memory of the powerful Campbell chief, blanketed the road leading to Kilchurn from dawn to dusk. All had journeyed to pay their respect, then prepare for the funeral feast to be held in the Great Hall that evening. All said their good-byes, touching the corpse lying on its bier in the chapel in a gesture to indicate they'd done nothing to contribute to the death, and to gain immunity from future dreams about the deceased.

All, Anne mused sadly, *but I.* She, alone of the castle's inhabitants, had not been invited for the traditional visit. She, who'd come to love the Campbell like a father, who'd held him in her arms as he gasped out his last breaths, was relegated to the prison of her room—an outcast, a pariah. In the past day as the castle bustled with preparations, she'd seen no one but Agnes.

It was from the old maidservant that Anne had gleaned what little information she could about Niall. He was holding up well, Agnes had said, but that look in his eyes.

The old woman had shivered when she'd said that, but Anne couldn't drag another a word of explanation from her. All she could extract was a promise to ask Niall to come to her when he found a free moment. It was Anne's only comfort in the somber hours that dragged by—the anticipation of seeing Niall, of speaking with him.

He arrived just after dusk. For want of anything else to do, Anne was busy putting the finishing touches on Caitlin's gown, a gown she now doubted she'd ever be able to gift the headstrong girl with.

Anne sighed as she painstakingly stitched around

the final neckline flower. Why was every overture she made of friendship twisted into some evil intent? It almost seemed as if someone was purposely thwarting her efforts.

"Who are you making the gown for?" a deep voice inquired.

Anne jumped, stabbing herself with the sewing needle. She rose to her feet, sucking at the throbbing finger, and came face to face with Niall.

Dressed in formal doublet and belted plaid, he stared down at her, his face solemn. The pain in her finger vanished.

"Th–the gown? 'Twas meant for your sister, though I wonder now if she'll ever . . ." Her voice faded.

There were dark smudges of exhaustion under Niall's eyes. His face was drawn and haggard. She wondered if he'd even had time to sleep. Forgotten were the endless hours of worry and pain, as an urge to comfort him filled her. Anne laid down her sewing and took Niall by the arm.

"Come." She pulled him over to a high-backed chair. "You look past weary. Seat yourself and have a cup o' wine."

Niall allowed himself to be led to the chair and seated, but refused the wine. "The vigil begins at midnight and I must keep it at my father's side. Even one cup o' wine, I fear, would put me fast to sleep. And that wouldn't be conduct fitting the new clan chieftain."

"Then they've already accepted you?" Anne's shoulders sagged with relief. "Despite Duncan's threats, there was no problem?"

"There's been no official confirmation or ceremony as yet. That must wait until after the funeral. But did you doubt there'd be any difficulty?"

"All the talk about me, and now the rumors that I'd poisoned your father . . ." Anne hesitated. "Truly, I didn't know what to think."

A determined glint flared in Niall's eyes. "There'll be no problem. I'll see to that." He took her hand and drew her to him. "But I didn't come to speak o' the chieftainship. I came to ask if you wished to accompany me to the chapel? Say your farewells to my father?"

Anne nodded. "Aye. More than anything, I've a wish to pay him my respects." In spite of herself, her voice trembled. "W–would it also be possible to attend his burial on the morrow? 'Tis my right and duty to be there."

Niall frowned. "It might go hard for you. Can you bear it?"

"With you at my side I can bear anything."

"Then, aye, you may come," he replied, his gaze steady, inscrutable. "'Tis past time you left this room. To keep you here any longer would only give credence to the foolish talk."

Anne bowed her head to hide her happiness. Then, mastering it, she met his gaze with a steady one of her own. "I've a confession to make. My words to you, when you last came to my chamber, weren't the complete truth. I was angry, felt betrayed. I said things I didn't—"

A calloused finger touched her lips. "Hush, lass. 'Tis o' no import. You went to him when he needed you. That's all that matters."

She knelt before him and placed her hand on his bare knee. "Then you don't think I did anything to hurt him, do you?"

Though he'd all but implied it, Anne still needed to hear him speak the words. "Truly, I've kept my word and treated no one since Davie. All I gave your father was a sip o' water. I swear it!"

Niall gazed down at her with tired, empty eyes. "I never doubted that for a moment, lass."

Relief washed through her, yet the lack of expression when he'd answered plucked uneasily at Anne's heart. He was so exhausted he was driving himself on sheer will alone. It had to explain the dearth of emotion in his voice, the indifference that deadened his eyes. It had to, or else she'd be forced to believe he'd finally admitted their problems were insurmountable. And that possibility—now, when they were both so vulnerable and needy—was more than she could bear.

She took the big, square hand that lay listlessly on the chair's armrest. Raising it to her lips, Anne kissed it before pressing it to her cheek.

"I wish there were more I could do for you, now, in your time o' sorrow. I never meant to hide away in this room. 'Twas only at your express command that I did so. My place has always been at your side." She kissed his hand once more. "I wanted you to know."

Niall stared down at her, some deep emotion churning in his eyes. Then he sighed, the sound one of ineffable sadness. He took Anne's hand and rose, pulling her up with him.

"Come, lass," he said. " 'Tis time to see my father."

Chapter Eleven

"How *dare* you shame your father's memory? How *dare* you allow *her* in the funeral procession?" a woman shrieked as she leapt in front of Niall and Anne the next morning.

Her eyes were wild, her face tear-streaked and pale. Her hair beneath the plaid that covered her head was tangled and tumbled down onto her face, but Anne still recognized the tormented features. It was Hugh's mother.

"You banish my son, then refuse to allow him to return for his uncle's funeral," Lydia Campbell cried, only half aware she'd begun pounding on Niall's chest. "Yet you permit this witch—"

Gently, Niall captured her arms and held her to him until two serving women hurried over. "Go with them, Aunt Lydia," he said, no trace of emotion in his voice. "Your grief has befuddled your reason. 'Tisn't the time or place to question my decisions. We'll talk later."

He watched the women lead her away, sobbing

as if her heart might break. Then, without another word, he took Anne's arm.

She shot him a hesitant glance as they walked along, but could detect no reaction beneath his stony mask. There were reactions aplenty, however, in the faces of those awaiting them.

Caitlin stood there, a horrified expression on her face. Duncan, a few feet away, had his head bent in heated discussion with the Reformed preacher. Both men, as Anne neared, halted their talk to turn the full brunt of their gaze upon her. From the hostility emanating from them, she knew she'd been the topic of their conversation.

Well aware of Duncan's feelings for her, she ignored him and fixed her glance on the preacher, hoping to determine the extent of his animosity. Malcolm was a short man, with little of the Campbell look about him. His stern visage of dense black brows and beard fairly reeked of fanatical energy and inflexibility. The look in his penetrating brown eyes as he surveyed her was hard and unforgiving.

Anne shivered. One way or another, Duncan had turned another Campbell against her and gained a powerful ally in the bargain.

Concern for Niall filled her. Would his uncle somehow use the preacher and his religious influence over the people to turn the clan against their new chief? It would be easy enough if the rumors of her involvement in the Campbell's death could be twisted into outright lies. Noting the look of malice that curved Duncan's lips as he straightened and began to move toward them, Anne felt certain it was a distinct possibility.

Niall's grip on her elbow tightened as the older man drew up before them. He gave him a brief nod. "Aye, Uncle?"

"I've a wish to speak with you." Duncan's frigid gaze brushed over Anne before returning to his nephew. "Alone."

"You may say what you wish in front o' m'lady," Niall said, a warning smoldering in his eyes. "I've no secrets from her."

The lines about Duncan's mouth tightened. "The matter concerns her. I thought only to spare her feelings."

Anne turned to Niall. "I've no wish to be cause for further discord. I can wait a ways—"

"Nay, lass," Niall growled. "Your place is here, at my side. My uncle can speak his peace now and get it done with, or let it rot."

"Young fool!" Duncan snarled as he took a step closer. "You're set on the course o' your own destruction if you continue on this path! Your loyalty to this woman is sadly misplaced. Will you sacrifice family and clan for the likes o' her?"

"And will you fan the flames o' this destructive feud by refusing to accept her?" Niall shot back, his voice a harsh whisper. "I didn't think you capable o' such petty conduct."

A challenging light flared in Duncan's eyes. "Would you banish me, too, then? You've already driven Hugh and my son away. Strange conduct, indeed, but mayhap all part o' *your* plan to assure none o' your immediate male relatives are deemed acceptable for naming as chieftain over you, not to mention as your tanist. Is that it? Some insignificant laird as second in command would never present a challenge to your chieftainship, would he?"

Niall ran an exasperated hand through his hair. "I haven't time for such foolishness. Let it be, I say, until my father's buried. You gave your word."

"Aye, that I did, and I'll keep it." Duncan sighed, the fight visibly ebbing from him. "Truly, nephew, I meant only to warn you o' what the people would think if you insist on allowing your lady to attend the funeral. Is that not my place, to keep you attuned to the mood o' the people?"

"Aye, Uncle," Niall agreed, his taut-muscled frame relaxing. "But I'll not bend to some whim that is false and unfair, either." He motioned toward the casket. "Now, enough o' this. 'Tis past time we buried my father."

Niall turned to Anne and once more offered her his arm. She hesitated, her glance skittering from one man to the other. Then she placed her hand on Niall's arm.

With each advancing step, Anne's feeling of apprehension grew. Niall may have been fooled by his uncle's apparent submission, but she knew better. The hard, malicious light in the older man's eyes continued to burn even as he'd appeared to acquiesce. Niall's desire to make peace had blinded him to the evil fires smoldering beneath the surface of Duncan's smooth concern.

But Anne, freed of the ties of kinship, had seen the man's true intent. It frightened her. Duncan cared little for his nephew's welfare. And it had begun to appear he wished for yet further conflict to weaken Niall's standing as the new chief.

But why?

Ena's words shot through her mind. "The young lord is in great danger. You must help him."

Fear prickled down Anne's spine. Niall was indeed in grave danger—his position as chief yet unacknowledged, a dangerous enemy made in banishing his unstable cousin, and now his uncle who seemed bent on undermining him.

She glanced up. Niall strode along beside her, tall and proud, his broad shoulders resolutely squared.

Strong shoulders, aye, she mused, but increasingly weighted with new and more serious problems. Problems he'd no one to share with as, one by one, his closest advisers and family slowly slipped away—and all because of her.

For an instant, Anne's eyes burned with unshed tears. Then a fierce determination swelled within her. They were innocent—she and Niall—of any wrongdoing, any fault, in this gathering storm of intrigue and betrayal. The time had come to fight.

And fight she would. She was vowed to the new Campbell chief, the enigmatic and tormented warrior who'd fought the battle for her heart and won. Aye, she'd stand by him to the end. Even if ultimately that end meant death.

The funeral procession wound up the road to the cemetery, the preacher at its head periodically ringing his brass bell, followed by the six clansmen carrying the coffin. Behind them marched the chieftain's personal retinue—his bard and bodyguards who carried his sword and shield, the standard-bearer, piper, then tatter or spokesman, and the two special men designated to carry the chief over running water. Niall came next, Anne at his side. The rest of the family followed. As the procession passed, the other mourners lining the road fell into place behind it.

The sun crept up from behind the hills, the cloud-shrouded sky dampening its light to a hazy glimmer. A misting of rain began to fall. One by one, the gathering pulled their plaids over their heads.

Thunder rolled in the distance. Anne winced at the sound. Wasn't the day miserable enough without the imminent threat of a downpour?

Gradually, a new sound intruded. The rhythmic thud of hoofbeats heading up the hill behind them must have caught Niall's attention as well. He turned. A dark scowl spread across his face. With a growing feeling of unease, Anne turned as well.

A man on a bay horse reined in at the back of the procession then flung himself down and began to make his way through the crowd. Though his dismount was quick, Anne caught a glimpse of his face. It was Iain.

Her unease spiraled as she glanced at Niall. His fists were clenched at his sides. A muscle ticked along his jaw. With the exhaustion that dogged his every movement and etched deep lines into his face, Anne knew the strain of dealing with Iain right now might be too much.

Niall was near his breaking point. He'd been functioning on sheer will alone for too long. But what could she do to ease the tension? How could she help him?

"A truce?" Anne whispered. "Til your father's buried?"

Niall leveled his gaze upon her, his blazing anger fading to one of flat accusation. "You turn my words upon me."

Anne calmly returned his gaze. "What's fair for the father is fair for the son. And, besides," she added, her eyes softening with concern, " 'tisn't the time or place to renew the battle between you. 'Tis no affront to you that Iain attends his uncle's funeral. Let it be for now."

He eyed her for a moment longer, then sighed. "Aye, lass, that I will—for now."

Niall awaited his cousin, his stance still rigid, but Anne knew now there'd be no fight. Her eyes met Iain's. She gave him a welcoming smile.

His mouth quirked in reply, then he riveted his attention on the dark-haired man standing before him. Iain's blond head lowered briefly in greeting. "I came as soon as I heard. I ask leave to attend the burying."

" 'Tis your right."

At Niall's emotionless reply, Iain exhaled a long

breath. There was no forgiveness between them, he realized with a dull ache, only a brief peace for the sake of the dead Campbell chief.

He watched Niall stride on, his glance reuniting with Anne's for a fleeting moment before she turned and followed. Compassion warmed her silver eyes. Iain's gaze never left her as she walked away, a small, delicate contrast to his dark, fierce cousin. Far too kind and good for the likes of him.

Rage surged through Iain. Vainly, he fought back against the destructive emotion, against the frustration that followed quickly on the heels of the admission of his anger. His hands clenched and unclenched with the ferocity of his struggle.

Curse you, cousin, he mentally flung the words at Niall's retreating back. *You don't deserve her, you arrogant, power-crazed fool! You don't deserve her. . . .*

Iain hesitated to knock on Anne's bedchamber door. Sound judgement cautioned against speaking with her, especially now, after all but being banished from Kilchurn. After the funeral, his cousin had lost no time summoning him into the castle's private meeting room.

There, all pretense had been flung aside. Niall had coldly informed him his continued presence was no longer desired. As soon as the meeting to confirm his chieftainship had met on the morrow, Iain was to return to his own lands.

He had considered swallowing his pride and, for the sake of kinship, attempting to make amends. But the hard, unyielding look in Niall's eyes had immediately squelched that. He'd be damned if he'd grovel, beg forgiveness for something that only existed in Niall's jealous imagination.

A large part of Niall's anger toward him had to be exactly that. Jealousy over his innocent friendship with Anne. Not that he didn't want her. He did. Iain was too honest to deny the truth.

But, until this moment, he'd never have considered betraying his cousin, nor attempt to convince his woman to leave with him. He'd risked Niall's wrath in even bringing up the topic of Anne's continued safety at Kilchurn. For his efforts, he'd received threats if he dared even think of seeing her again.

There was something seriously wrong with his cousin of late, but what it was remained a mystery. Surely the death of the Lady Anne Stewart hadn't addled Niall's brains. Iain had seen no sign of it before. But would jealousy turn a man as levelheaded as Niall into such an irrational, suspicious fool? Yet if it wasn't jealousy, what was it?

Well, whatever it was, Iain decided, with this last meeting his cousin's threats and unreasoning attitude had destroyed any lingering feelings of loyalty and affection. Though he wouldn't seek revenge, Iain no longer felt any commitment to support Niall, either.

Anne would be better off with him. *He* would treat her kindly, would give her the love she deserved. And, besides removing her from Niall's cruel presence, he was also rescuing her from the storm of animosity and false rumors rising against her.

In the few hours since his return to Kilchurn, Iain had already heard enough foul tales about Anne to justify a burning at the stake. No, he thought with a small shudder. His plan to take Anne away had come none too soon.

With renewed resolve, Iain knocked at her door. Anne's sweet face greeted him a moment later. He smiled.

"Iain?" Her brow wrinkled in puzzlement. "Why are you here?"

He glanced down the corridor then took a step closer. "I need to talk with you. May I come in?"

She shook her head. "Twouldn't be seemly. Agnes isn't here."

"More the better. What I have to say is best said in private." When she hesitated, Iain grasped her arm. "Please, Anne. You know you can trust me. I wouldn't ask if 'tweren't important."

She eyed him for a moment longer, then sighed. "I know, Iain." Anne stepped back. "Come in."

He waited until she closed the door, then motioned toward it. "Bolt the door. I don't want anyone walking in on us. I can always escape out the window."

Her eyes widened at the fierceness of his request, but Anne complied.

"What is it, Iain? What's wrong?"

" 'Tisn't safe for you here." He walked toward her and pulled her to him. "I want you to come away with me."

" 'Tisn't safe? Come away?" She shook her head. "Truly, Iain, you make no sense."

"Don't I, lass? I haven't been back a day and already I see naught has changed for you. Niall still treats you harshly, the people have yet to befriend you, and the witch talk about you grows to deadly proportions. You're in danger if you stay here another moment!"

"Och, Iain." Anne smiled and patted him on the cheek. "Always my friend and protector. But you needn't worry yourself over me. True, I've made little progress where the Campbell clan's concerned, but 'tis but a matter of time. And once they befriend me, I feel certain the rumors will die. So you see, 'tisn't as bad as you fear."

"And I say you are blind to the truth!" He captured the hand that lay upon his face and turned his lips to it. "You risk much in remaining here, and for what reason? Your vows to Niall?"

Iain lowered her hand to rest upon his chest. "Nay, Anne, you owe him naught. He broke the handfasting long ago when he failed to treat you kindly. Do you forget I was there when he promised to strive for your happiness and welfare?"

He paused when Anne's gaze moved from his. With a firm hand, he grasped her chin and turned her eyes back to his. "You know the truth as well as I, lass. Come with me. I'll love you, care for you as you truly deserve."

Anne sighed. She'd thought time and distance would ease that hunger burning in Iain's eyes. Did he realize how it tore at her heart to have to hurt him? But what choice had she now, even more than before?

"Nay, Iain," she whispered. "I can't go with you. To do so would ruin your life. Niall would come after us. He'd not give up until he killed you. I wouldn't have that upon my conscience."

"And I don't care!" Iain cried. "I love you, Anne! 'Twould kill me if I left you here and something happened to you. Would you have *that* upon your conscience?"

"Nothing will happen." Her voice lowered to soothe his anguish. "Niall will protect me."

"Like hell he will!"

"I know he would, and so do you." Anne gently disengaged herself and stepped back. "There is more, Iain."

At the steady, solemn look she gave him, something inside Iain died. "He has bedded you, hasn't he?"

She gave him a sad little smile. "Nay, but it doesn't matter. I don't love him any less."

A grimace of pain twisted his handsome features. "Nay, Anne! Don't say it!"

"Would my lying change what is?" she asked softly.

"But surely he doesn't love you. I've seen no sign o' it—in his actions or his words."

Anne lowered her head. "I think he feels something for me. 'Tis enough for now."

"Your goodness blinds you to the truth!" Iain pulled her to him. "You'd see that in time. I should take you away, with or without your consent. Far from his presence, you'd soon see your mistake."

"But you won't." She steadily returned his gaze.

He studied her for a long moment, then exhaled a deep breath. "Nay, I won't, for 'twould destroy what there is between us. But if anything happens to you, I swear I'll come back and kill Niall. I'll never forgive him if he doesn't protect you."

"He will. He's a good man."

A dark blond brow arched. "Is he now? I used to think so, but o' late I'm not so certain." Iain smiled down at her, a bittersweet light in his eyes. "I think you're mayhap blinded by your love."

She returned his smile. "Mayhap."

He sighed and released her. "Well, bemoaning what I can't have is pointless. Give me your word that if Niall ever fails you, you'll send word to me. I must know you'll do that at least."

"I know you're my friend."

"Promise me, Anne!"

Her smile widened. "Och, but you're the most persistent, pigheaded—"

"Promise me," Iain persisted softly.

"I promise."

The look in his eyes as his gaze swept over her sent a sad despair rippling through Anne. She'd never meant to hurt him, but what else could she do? She'd sealed her fate when she'd admitted to loving Niall. There was no turning back.

Anne touched his arm. "You should go."

"Aye."

He made no move.

"Now, Iain." She gave him a small push.

Iain forced himself backward, his eyes never leaving hers. When he reached the door, he paused. "Remember your promise, Anne."

"I will."

He slid aside the bolt and opened the door. Not looking back, Iain slipped from the room.

Niall gazed at the flickering tongues of fire lapping their greedy way through the pile of logs. He sat before the hearth, slumped in his chair. In his hand, he clasped an untouched glass of claret.

It was nearly midnight. The castle folk had long ago been sent to bed, but still he sat there, painfully, acutely awake. Niall's eyes burned fiercely. His exhaustion weighted him so heavily even the thought of getting up and walking to his bed required more effort than he was capable of. Yet the blessed reprieve of sleep still eluded him.

Disjointed thoughts whirled through his mind, mocking him with the futility of any possible solution. Duncan . . . Hugh . . . Iain.

Iain. He knew his cousin had been up to see Anne earlier this evening. Nelly, whose primary duties were centered in the kitchen when she was not lustily warming someone's bed, seemed to be all over the castle of late. She had come to him a few hours ago, still hopefully seductive, and informed him she'd passed by just as Anne had let Iain into her bedchamber. Though Niall had thought to deflate her eager confidence with the comment that he knew all about the meeting, he sensed his ruse hadn't worked. Nelly hadn't looked convinced.

His grip about the wineglass clenched. Indeed, what *had* gone on between Anne and Iain in her chamber? He'd wanted to trust her, thought he had, but the news of this latest liaison strained even his newly admitted affection for her. What possible reason could she have for letting Iain visit?

His cousin's motives were more than apparent.

Niall had seen the look in Iain's eyes whenever he gazed at her. Iain wanted Anne.

But Anne—what did she want? With a mighty effort fueled by his anguish, Niall rose and walked to the hearth. Setting his glass on the mantle, he leaned on the wooden overhang and stared, unseeing, into the flames.

Did Anne love Iain? Had they lain together as lovers? He'd kill Iain if they had.

A rage, white-hot and searing, grew within Niall. He was surrounded on all sides by betrayal and the one haven where he'd thought he'd find comfort had never been more than a sweet illusion. The rage subsided at the vision of the beautiful woman that flashed across his mind.

Och, Annie, he thought with a bittersweet pang, *you called to my heart. Yet, when I came, you turned from me, leaving me more alone than I was before. I was a fool to have let myself trust you . . . much less need you.*

Music, soft and lilting, floated to his ears. Niall raised his head, wondering at its source.

It was Anne, playing her clarsach.

He turned from the hearth, his gaze moving to the door that separated their rooms. She was awake. But dare he go to her, as confused and exhausted as he was? He risked betraying too much. It would be wiser to avoid her.

Even as he admitted the fact, Niall's legs were already carrying him toward the door. Though he dare not trust his heart to her, the physical solace of her body was safe enough. She owed him that much at least.

Anne couldn't sleep. Exhausted from the emotionally draining day, she'd gone to bed early but once there, could only toss and turn. A jumble of thoughts and impressions assailed her. The haggard look of grief on Niall's face as they lowered his father into the grave. The strain of the funeral feast from which she'd excused herself as soon as it was considered proper. And then, after everything else, the unexpected surprise of Iain's visit.

That, mayhap most of all, nibbled at Anne, driving all hope of rest from her mind. What was she to do about Iain? The chance of Niall hearing about Iain's visit was too great to ignore. There were too many people in Kilchurn eager for her downfall not to consider the possibility. And if Niall should hear of this latest news from anyone but her, Anne feared it might drive the final wedge between them. More than anything else, Anne didn't want that to happen.

She never wanted to be a problem to Niall again. All Anne desired was to be close, to comfort and support him. To be everything to him, to the extent of his need. He might not love her, at least not like he'd loved the Lady Anne Stewart, but what he was capable of giving she would accept and cherish.

Love was like that, she supposed, especially when it had finally turned your brain to a pile of mush. With a sigh, Anne rose from her bed and donned her warm bed robe. She walked over to stare out the stone-cut window.

What time was it? At least midnight by her calculations. Far too late to speak to Niall tonight about Iain, no matter how desperately she needed to tell him. The admission would have to wait for the morrow.

Her clarsach lay beside the oaken bench beneath the window. Anne picked it up, nestling its sensuously curved frame in the crook of her arm. Her fingers strummed the taut strings, coaxing a hauntingly sweet melody from the vibrating strands. The music soothed her, easing the raw ache in her heart.

How she wanted to go to Niall, to feel the strength

of his arms about her, to bury her face in the comforting warmth of his chest! But that was not to be. Niall's need for rest was of greater import than her petty desires.

She jumped at the sound of the door between their rooms opening, her fingers striking a discordant note on the harp. Anne turned, her startled gaze meeting Niall's. He stood there in the doorway, his stance wide-legged, dressed in only a bed robe knotted loosely at his waist. Through the portion that gaped open from his waist up, a powerful, hair-roughened chest heaved with some barely repressed emotion.

She laid down her clarsach and rose. "What is it, m'lord? Did my playing waken you?"

Niall stared back, a sudden surge of tenderness flooding him. She stood there, her curly mane cascading about her shoulders and down her back, dressed in a simple white nightdress beneath her open bed robe. She looked so beguiling, so sweetly girlish—and so innocent of any wrongdoing.

The anger ebbed, leaving only a curious, quivering ache in the middle of Niall's chest. He was too weary for a battle tonight. Too overwhelmed with the events of the past few days to face the truth. The morrow was soon enough to deal with the unpleasant task of confronting her.

But now, now what he needed was rest. Perhaps Anne's songs, and later her body, would soothe him to it.

He sighed and shook his head. "Nay, lass, I was never asleep. I but heard your music and thought to ask you to play for me. You used to play for my father." His lips curved into a wistful smile. "Will you do so as willingly for me?"

Anne nodded. "Aye."

Niall motioned to her clarsach. "Then bring your harp and come with me."

She followed him into his bedchamber, dark save for the small circle of light cast by the hearth fire. He pulled up a tall-backed chair to face his before the fireplace, then glanced at Anne.

" 'Tis warmest here. Come, seat yourself."

The realization of her vulnerability in Niall's bedchamber struck Anne with the force of a blow. Suddenly, she felt weak-kneed. She had dreamt of this long-desired moment, yet now, when it was finally upon her, she wanted to flee. Too much hung in the balance. She was no longer sure she had the strength to face it.

Anne forced herself to move forward. It was too late to turn back. That choice had been made when she'd revealed her love for Niall to Iain. She owed Niall at least the same honesty she'd shown his cousin. And that honesty began with telling him about Iain's visit this eve. But how to begin? How to tell him without stirring afresh Niall's anger against Iain? Anne settled herself in the chair, but the strings of her clarsach remained silent.

At the worried chewing of her lip, Niall cocked a questioning brow. He motioned toward her harp. "Have you no song for me, lady?"

"Aye, but first I've something to speak o'." Anne imagined he could hear the pounding of her heart from where he stood.

He waved her words aside with a movement of his hand. "In time, lass. But first, a song."

"What would you like to hear, m'lord?" she murmured, both relieved and frustrated to put the matter aside, if only temporarily.

His eyes burned into Anne with a fierce intensity as he seated himself opposite her. "A song o' love," he finally replied, his voice a low growl. "About the enchantment o' a beautiful woman."

Anne swallowed hard. The deeper meaning to his words sent a small shiver of excitement through her. Her fingers, seemingly of their own accord, strummed the opening notes.

"Mayhap you'd like the 'Vision of a Fair Woman' then. 'Tis an ancient Celtic song."

Niall nodded.

His eyes, burning with an inner intensity, so mesmerized Anne that the song flowed from her lips almost without conscious effort. Her voice rose and fell with the melody, breathless at first but growing stronger with each haunting phrase. And all the while, Niall watched her.

"Tell us some o' the charms o' the stars:
Close and well set were her ivory teeth;
White as the canna upon the moor
Was her bosom the tartan bright beneath.
Her well-rounded forehead shone
Soft and fair as the mountain snow;
Her two breasts were heaving full;
To them did the hearts of heroes flow. . . ."

Like some Highland cat he watched her, motionless, tense with waiting, but waiting for what? Anne felt like a doe, alone, poised for flight, sensing danger but not knowing from whence it came. And all the while Niall, the dark, powerful animal, just sat there, watching . . . waiting.

" . . . her countenance looked like the gentle buds
Unfolding their beauty in early spring;
Her yellow locks like the gold-browed hills;
And her eyes like the radiance the sunbeams
    bring. . . ."

The closing stanza ended in a breathless whisper as Anne's throat constricted, smothering with the sense of impending capture. She had never seen eyes quite like his, smoldering golden-brown in the dim firelight. They glowed with some otherworldly fire. They beckoned her toward a heady oblivion she was helpless to resist. Her fingers fell from the strings.

"That night you learned o' the land charter," his deep voice shattered the suddenly heavy silence, "you begged me to free you from our handfasting."

She barely had breath to reply. "A—aye?"

Niall leaned forward. "Do you still wish that?"

The question dissipated the dreamlike trance that had followed Anne into the room. Why was he asking that? Of all times, when she felt herself hanging on the abyss of surrendering everything to him, why was Niall asking such a question?

Did he need some pretense to free himself now that he was about to secure his position as chief? Mayhap he'd finally admitted she was more hindrance than pleasure, that her unpopularity with his clan would never improve.

Or mayhap there was some other reason. Mayhap, just mayhap, Niall was attempting to plumb the depths of her commitment to him. Whatever the reason, it didn't matter. The truth remained the same.

"Nay, I don't wish to be freed from our handfasting." Anne laid her harp at her feet, then squarely met his gaze. "My place is with you, for as long as you'll have me."

"And why do you want to stay, lass?"

Her grip tightened on the chair arm. "Because I love you."

The surprising admission snapped the last of Niall's control. God help him, but he couldn't wait until the morrow! Coupled with her sweet lie just now, her betrayal hurt too much to bear a moment longer.

"And do you?" Niall asked with a mocking smile. "As much as you love Iain?"

"I don't understand." Unease spiraled through Anne. How could he be so calm, so casual, about her heart-wrenching admission? "What have my feelings for Iain to do with you?" She forced the words past her suddenly constricted throat.

Niall shrugged. "I was but attempting to determine the extent o' your loyalty. Whom do you love more, Anne? Iain or me?"

Anne struggled to stand, tears glimmering in her eyes. "You mock me, mock the honest admission o' my feelings for you, to ask such a thing! Why would you want to hurt me like that?"

"Hurt you?" Niall leapt to his feet. "And can anything I say or do compare with what you've wrought by your liaison with Iain this eve? Answer me that!"

She blanched. *Holy Mary, he does know, and because of my hesitation I've lost the chance to tell him myself. He'll never believe I was going to now.*

"I was afraid o' this." Anne sighed, lowering herself back to her chair. Her gaze slid to her hands clasped in her lap. "There are no secrets from you in this castle, however benign they may be."

"Let me be the judge o' that," Niall said, his voice dangerously soft.

Silver eyes rose to meet his. "There's little to tell at any rate. Iain was simply concerned for my welfare."

"And 'twas necessary to seek out the privacy o' your bedchamber to do so?" Niall paused. "Was Agnes with you?"

"Nay."

Even in the firelight, she could see the dark flush that suffused Niall's face. "Naught happened," Anne hastened to explain, panic rising within her. "I swear it!"

"Mayhap not." Niall's voice was taut with barely contained fury. " 'Tis difficult to judge without knowing the real reason for my cousin's visit. What was it, lass?"

She hesitated. The same dilemma confronted her as before. How was she to tell Niall the truth without betraying Iain?

"I await your answer, lady."

The hard edge to his voice prodded her to action. She wet her lips, then hurried on, "I'll tell you, m'lord, and gladly, if only you'll swear Iain will come to no harm because o' it."

"I'll make no oath on that!" Niall snapped savagely. "If you think to protect his deceit—"

"There was no deceit!" Anne cried. "He but wanted to take me away with him, away from all the hatred here against me. He was concerned for my safety, that's all!"

"And I say you lie! You're lovers, aren't you?"

In one quick step Niall was before her, pulling Anne into the unyielding hardness of his body. She gazed up into eyes blazing with anger and, surprisingly, a tortured pain. For a moment, she couldn't find her breath. Then it came, expelled on a shuddering whisper.

"Och, nay. Nay, Niall. I don't love Iain, at least not in the way you mean."

Niall's grip tightened painfully. Anne squirmed in his grasp.

"Niall, please. You're hurting me."

He released her with a jerk, and gave a shaky laugh. "Then we're even. But don't mistake my acceptance o' this as trust. Too many times have your path and Iain's crossed for me to ignore—or forgive!"

"Forgive?" Anne's eyes blazed silver fire. "There's naught to forgive, you suspicious, pigheaded dolt! Och, I don't know why I thought telling you would've made a difference, if I'd ever had the chance! But, nay, so sooner had the deed been done when your people came running to tell you everything. Do you trust me so little you must surround yourself with spies?"

Niall turned toward the hearth, unable to meet her gaze. "I—I can't afford to trust anyone just now. You know how precarious my position as chief is . . ."

"Aye," Anne interjected bitterly, "and I suppose I should accept that I must, o' necessity, be considered a threat to your precious chieftainship."

She paused, as an insight into the source of his continued mistrust suddenly struck her. "But this isn't solely an issue o' jealousy, is it? O' your fears that Iain and I are lovers?" Anne took a deep breath before continuing. "Nay, 'tis o' far greater import, 'tisn't it? Like, mayhap, that Iain is your traitor?"

Chapter Twelve

The color drained from Niall's face. Then a studied mask replaced the fleeting look of surprise.

"What are you talking about? I never said anything about a traitor."

Anne wasn't about to let Niall's momentary lapse of control slip by. " 'Twasn't you. 'Twas my father who spoke o' someone betraying you to us."

"Damn that old man! He swore he'd tell no one!"

"And he kept his word!" Anne hotly defended her father. " 'Twas that day o' your clan's arrival at Castle Gregor. I followed my father to the parapets to hear them request your return. My father was so overwrought at the position he was in, he let slip the fact he'd entrapped you and that there was a traitor. No one heard his words but me. He refused to tell me more, even when I prodded him. And that's the truth o' it, Niall Campbell!"

"The truth as far as you know it," Niall retorted. "But how many others know?"

"My father's a man o' honor. If he gave you his

word, your secret's safe. Besides, to betray you would be to endanger me. He'd never do that."

Niall scowled. "Mayhap not intentionally, but what if he let it slip again?" His fist pounded the mantle in frustration. "Damn, 'twas my only advantage over the traitor, and now I may have lost even that!"

"You don't know that. If I'm the only other one . . ." Anne's voice faded at the piercing look Niall shot her. "Aye." She sighed. "And once again I am asking you to trust me, aren't I? But if Iain's the traitor and I in league with him, you have lost even that advantage."

A sharp pain lanced through her. "It always comes back to that, doesn't it, Niall? You can't find it in your heart to trust me—and never will."

Niall opened his mouth, then clamped it shut. He stared at her, his dark eyes capturing and holding hers until Anne thought she'd scream from the tension. Tears filled her eyes. She saw the dream of a life for them slowly disintegrate in the face of Niall's continued distrust. There was no hope, not anymore.

The tears rolled, unchecked, down her cheeks. "I said I loved you, but 'tisn't enough, is it?" she asked in a strangled whisper. "Well, I can't bear living with your suspicions. 'Tis better for the both o' us if you let me go back to my people."

"Nay."

She swiped the tears away with the back of her hand. "But why? What good am I to you, or to your traitor, be it Iain or any other? You've discovered my complicity and now will guard against me. You can throw me into the dungeons, I suppose, but that would only stir the feud anew. Far better to send me home. I swear the peace between our clans will stand."

"Do you think 'tis that easy?" Niall rasped in a pain-harshened voice.

He flung himself in the chair opposite her, his long legs stretched out before him. "If 'twas, I'd have done it long ago. But I was lost from the first moment I saw you in that little village, your hands bound, proudly defying my men. You *are* a witch, Anne MacGregor," he groaned the admission, "but your spells are o' the heart, not the body. And I can't let you go—not now, not ever!"

"Och, Niall!" Anne sobbed, running to kneel before him.

He straightened in the chair and his arms welcomed her, pulling her to him between his outspread legs. She clung to him fiercely, her renewed surge of tears dampening the thick hair on his chest.

"I've never wished to cause you pain, truly, I haven't" Anne cried. "I know I've been foolish at times, concerned with only my needs and giving little thought to yours, but I swear I'll do better! I'll learn."

"Hush, lass," Niall murmured, gently stroking her hair. "I know, I know."

She raised her tear-streaked face to his, so close now his warm breath caressed her. "Truly?"

"Truly."

Anne sighed and laid her head back on Niall's chest. She knew there'd been no admission of trust in his words, no avowal of love, but tonight it didn't matter. That he accepted the fact she was there and wanted him, that he seemed to want her, too, was enough.

His deep, even breathing soothed her. A languorous warmth spread through her body. She inhaled deeply of Niall's musky, masculine scent. It sent a rippling current of awareness through her.

Her lips moved to his warm skin beneath her cheek and Anne, in a rising tide of excitement, tasted his flesh like one long-starved. Her mouth finally wended its way to his nipple nestled in a swirling sea of hair. She gently laved it before taking it into her mouth.

Niall groaned. "Och, Annie."

Clasping her head between his hands, he turned her face to his. His kiss was gentle, tentative at first, as if he feared the power building inside him. But Anne matched him in growing ardor, her response mirroring his own. She was an apt pupil, Niall realized, her passion for him no less than the passion with which she approached everything in life.

The thought gladdened him like none he'd ever known. Here, at last, was a woman to match his own fiery nature, both in and out of bed. An image of another Anne momentarily floated before his eyes, a vision of a lovely, gentle angel. The vision smiled.

His lips curved in an answering smile as he traced a trail of kisses down Anne's neck. She threw back her head in eager abandon. Her hands moved wildly over him now, spreading Niall's bed robe wider to expose even more of his hot, hair-roughened chest. She pulled back to gaze at his powerfully muscled torso.

Anne inhaled an admiring breath. "Och, you're so magnificent, m'lord!"

"And you're so beautiful, Annie lass,"

His husky admission filled Anne with joy. He did care for her, if only a little. It was enough.

Her hand stroked the side of his face in an attempt to ease the careworn lines that feathered out from his eyes. Tenderness and a fierce protectiveness swelled in her at the pain she saw burning in their depths. Och, how she loved him!

Niall smiled and slipped the bed robe from her shoulders. Before she had a chance to protest, he leaned down and gathered her to him. Lifting her into his arms, Niall crossed the room to his bed.

It was a huge, carven monstrosity, hewn from a giant oak. Though hung with dark green velvet curtains, the bed still reminded Anne of some animal's den. Niall lay her on the soft furs, skillfully sewn into one huge pelt, then stood back to gaze down at her. His breath came raggedly now.

In the flickering firelight, his tawny eyes seemed to glow from his shadowed face. Glowed . . . like those of a wolf. A shudder of terror mixed with a delightful anticipation swept through Anne. Then, in one quick movement, Niall shed his bed robe.

Though darkness hid the details of his body, the outline of his huge form was totally masculine, from his wide shoulders and narrow hips to his firmly muscled arms and legs. *A fine body,* Anne mused dreamily. *A warrior's body.*

Yet though admirable in every way, that outward manifestation of Niall was already known to her. Tonight, she wanted more. She meant to have all of him, in the most intimate way imaginable. Tonight, she'd find her own path to his heart, a path different from his first wife, but one she hoped would someday hold equal importance. It was a sweetly glorious, improbable dream, but tonight Niall Campbell was hers, and hers alone.

At the thought, a delicious ache filled Anne. She raised her arms to him and, with a low groan, he came to her. The touch of his hard body, his long strong legs, pressing so intimately against hers, sent a tremor of delight rocketing through Anne. She surrendered to him in eager abandon. She felt his full, heated arousal brush against her belly.

For a fleeting instant Anne drew away, responding to an instinctive feminine fear. Then reason and her love for Niall urged her back. The hard throbbing shaft was the core of his pleasure. More than life itself Anne wanted to please him, to ease his pain in the age-old healing ritual of mating.

His hands moved over her, hot but strangely soothing, leaving her quivering in their wake. He eased the

nightgown up her body while his tongue seduced its
way into her mouth. Anne welcomed him with a soft
sound of pleasure.

The nightgown moved up past her hips. Niall's
hand lingered there, gliding across her belly with
the lightest, the most tantalizing of touches, until
she trembled uncontrollably in his arms.

"Do you like it, lass?" he growled. "Do you like
what I do to you?"

"Aye!" Anne breathed.

His voice deepened to a fierce whisper. "I want
you wild before I take you. Wild . . . begging me."

Before she could reply, he parted her lips. His
tongue plunged into her mouth to retreat slowly
and plunge again. Anne shuddered, each thrust of
his tongue sending wild jolts through her body. Her
hands moved over him in a crazed abandon, across
his chest, down his arms, over the taut ridges of
his belly.

Niall groaned and jerked against her, his hands
grasping at her gown to pull it up, past her breasts
and shoulders and over her head. The realization
of her total nakedness, lying there so vulnerable
and exposed beneath him, should have evoked a
maiden's modesty. But Anne was beyond caring.
She had yearned for him, dreamt of this moment
for too long to feel anything but a woman's hot need,
and an intense, soul-satisfying sense of power.

Niall's hands stroked the curve of her breasts,
sending delicious waves of heat to feed the ache
growing deep within her. Yet as wonderful as it
all was, nothing could compare to the knowledge
spiraling to full realization.

All her life, since the day Anne had realized the
power men held over women, she had fought against
surrendering even the smallest aspect of herself.
She'd fought against their control, flaunting customs
and strictures of everyday life if they went against her

own desires. She'd paid the price in many ways, yet until this moment she'd staunchly maintained her right to guide her own destiny.

But no longer. Now it was joined with that of the dark man so passionately loving her. Yet there was no loss, no sense of defeat in the realization. Quite the contrary.

Her love for this wonderful, most magnificent of men had opened up the world to her, freeing her— empowering her. Her love only made her stronger. It revealed new mysteries about herself, mysteries both wonderful and life-sustaining. There was no fear anymore, only a wild eagerness to delve further and, in the giving, receive.

The touch of his tongue on her nipple sent fine tremors through Anne. "Niall!" she breathed, arching against him.

He took her more fully then, gently suckling the tender flesh. Anne writhed beneath him, half-mad from the pleasure. Her breath came in sharp little gasps.

Niall sensed she was near her limits, yet wanted to prepare her a little further to ease the discomfort of their eventual coupling. In his heart, despite his accusations to the contrary, he knew Anne was still a maiden. The thought gladdened him in some fierce, primal way.

His hand trailed down her chest, past her flat belly to the soft mound of dark auburn curls. Gently, ever so carefully, he eased his fingers between the velvety lips to find her hot, hidden wetness. She gasped when he reached that secret core and began to massage it.

"Wh–what are you doing?" Anne cried. "Och, I can't bear it!"

"Hush, lass," Niall murmured, moving to silence her with the searing heat of his mouth. "You'll bear that, and more, before I'm done with you."

She went wild then, twisting, turning beneath him, her legs spreading to welcome further exploration. Her uninhibited response ignited a rising excitement in Niall. He knew he couldn't hold back much longer.

His mouth moved to her ear, his tongue caressing the delicate shell even as his hand maintained its frenzied touch upon her. "Do you want me, lass?" he breathed, his voice rough with desire.

"A–aye!" Anne cried, her eyes clenched shut in sweet agony.

"Then tell me." Niall whispered thickly, almost mad with his own need. "Tell me I'm the only man for you, that there'll never be another. I need to hear it. I need to know!"

Her lids snapped open. She gazed up at him, all the love in the world in her silver eyes. "Aye, I want you, Niall. I love you. There will never be another."

He took her hand in his, guiding it down his chest, to his taut-muscled abdomen, to entwine about his thickly engorged shaft. Niall went rigid, a hot, dark look in his eyes.

"Aye, lass," he coaxed, his hand covering hers to pull it up and down his throbbing hardness. "That's the way o' it. T–touch me. I want it. Och, Lord, how I need it!"

Niall gave himself over to the pure pleasure of her tantalizing strokes. He leaned on his arms, his head arched back. The cords of his neck strained with the exquisite sensations shooting through him. His fists clenched at his side. He moaned aloud at the effort it took to slow the fires of his passion.

A seductive, satisfied smile touched Anne's lips. It thrilled her that in her maiden's inexperience she was capable of giving him such pleasure. And it also stirred a need, far from maidenly, to drive him even wilder with desire.

"Please," she pleaded. "I beg you, let us join. I need you so badly."

With a harsh groan, Niall pulled her to him, his mouth parting hers for a deep, violently sensual kiss. Before she could recover from that boldly passionate assault, he shifted his weight on top of her and grasped her hips. In a strong, sure movement he guided Anne to him, fitting her to his need, sliding slowly, unerringly into her.

Anne cried out as he penetrated her maiden's barrier, but the sound was muffled by his insistent tongue that probed and thrust in unison to his hard shaft driving between her legs. The pain subsided quickly, melding with a fierce ache until she could scarce tell one from the other. The sensation of pleasure grew. She thought she'd go mad from the sweet torture. Then Anne could bear it no longer.

A myriad of tiny vibrations, of shimmering delights, coursed through her body until she shook from the ecstasy of it. Anne cried out again, but this time it was a cry of joy.

Niall's pace quickened, his breath ragged and rasping. His own control fled when Anne joined the rhythmic thrusts. Lord, but she felt so soft . . . so wet . . . so good!

He drove himself deeper and deeper in a frenzied race toward satisfaction. And all the while the woman in his arms urged him on, caressing him, whispering words of love and encouragement. No longer could he tell where his body ended and hers began. The fire grew to consuming proportions. At last, with a gutteral cry, Niall plummeted into a swirling abyss of pleasure.

It was early afternoon before Anne awoke to bright sunlight streaming into the bedchamber from the two stone-cut windows. She shifted, stretched lazily, then stiffened at the realization that this wasn't her own room or bed. A warm, hair-roughened body moved against her backside to draw her close.

Last night with its wildly, wonderfully passionate lovemaking came back to Anne in a rush. She smiled, a contented, secret woman's smile, and carefully turned in Niall's arms.

He was still asleep, his recklessly handsome face relaxed, his black mane of hair laying long and tousled on the pillow. For an instant Anne's gaze lingered on his firmly molded lips, lips that had given her such pleasure. Then her eyes, hungry for the sight of him, moved down the full length of his magnificent nakedness.

Niall lay there, completely exposed, the heavy fur thrown aside sometime in the night. Anne feasted her eyes on the broad, flat planes of his hair-whorled chest, admiring the smooth bronzed flesh beneath the dark, wiry crispness. His abdomen was a rippling undulation of muscle covered with a lighter growth of hair that narrowed into a dark river as it plunged down to his tautly sculpted groin.

Anne's glance lingered there, admiring the organ that had driven her to such heights of ecstasy. Even in sleep, Niall was a big man, the heated length of his manhood semi-turgid and full. She ached to touch him, to curl her fingers around that thick evidence of his need, to stroke him once again to full arousal. Anne's hand moved toward him, then fell away.

It would be selfish to wake him. She knew he must be exhausted. Even after their initial lovemaking, Niall hadn't slept for a long while, content to hold and stroke her until his passion flared again.

Their second coupling was gentle. Niall knew, even if she hadn't until he'd carefully sheathed himself within her, that she'd be sore. Her joy at having him quickly muted the discomfort. The eventual release was full of a quiet, yet ardently powerful pleasure.

Afterwards, they'd soon fallen asleep, warm and sated in each other's arms.

Gazing now at the steady rise and fall of Niall's broad, solid chest, Anne contented herself with the knowledge there'd be more of that same loving, time and time again. But, for a while longer, it was enough to let him sleep. Though the Chieftain's Council would meet soon—most likely in another two hour's time if the height of the sun were any indication—in the meanwhile, Anne meant to buy Niall all the rest she could.

She smiled down at him, then moved to slide out beneath the arm clasped so possessively over her hips. At the action, his hand tightened.

Niall's eyes opened to impale her with a questioning stare. "And where do you think you're going?" he growled in a sleep-thickened voice.

Anne's heart quickened as his slumberous glance raked her naked form. "You were asleep. I didn't want to wake you."

"And you see you were mistaken. Your attempt to leave has wakened me instead."

His throaty chuckle vibrated down the length of Anne's body, stirring her desire. The realization brought a flush to her face.

Was she that besotted with his body that all she could think of was coupling with him? She suddenly felt shy. Anne drew the fur up to cover her.

"I—I beg pardon," she stammered, blushing gorgeously. "Truly, I meant only to slip away and let you sleep."

With a dark scowl, Niall grasped the fur and wrenched it away, exposing her silken, long-limbed form. "Don't ever hide yourself from me again. You are mine in every way. There is no shame in our nakedness, or in our desire for each other."

His large hand cupped her chin, lifting her downcast eyes to his. "You want me again, don't you, lass?"

Anne swallowed hard against the tightness in her throat. "Aye."

Niall's mouth curved into a beautiful smile, one of pure, masculine delight. "And I want you, Annie lass."

He pulled her to him, his mouth moving to her face to caress her forehead, eyelids, then down her pert little nose to hover a breath away from her mouth. "I want you," he repeated huskily, "again and again and . . . again."

Anne sighed with happiness and snuggled contentedly against his hard strength. For a long while Niall stroked the sleek line of her waist, hip, and thigh, his look of unguarded pleasure gradually deepening to a thoughtful frown. Her hand moved to stroke his hardening jaw.

"What is it, Niall? What makes you scowl so?"

He raised tormented eyes to her. "You said there'd be no other man but me. Did you truly mean it, or were they but love words, spoken in the heat o' passion?"

Even in his strength Niall was vulnerable, vulnerable because he'd let himself care for her. There was no other explanation for a question such as his. The knowledge sang through Anne with a fierce, exultant joy. She nodded, a soft smile curving her lips.

"Aye, I meant it," she admitted with sweet candor. "You know now I was a maiden when you took me. I told you I loved you. Did my response to you last eve play false my words?"

Niall's eyes smoldered at the memory. "Nay, but still I have one favor to ask, one last proof, let us say, o' your love for me."

Anne exhaled a long, unsteady breath. "And, pray, what is it?"

He unwaveringly returned her gaze. "I want your

promise you won't speak to or be alone with Iain again."

Niall's request left her speechless. How could he ask such a cruel thing? It spoke more eloquently than words of his continued distrust. But was it just of Iain and his possible motives or of her, too? Bitter resentment warred with the knowledge that trust was the rarest of luxuries where a traitor was concerned.

Anne laughed, the sound ragged. "And what will that oath win me? Your undying devotion?"

"Don't mock me!" Niall's fingers dug into the soft flesh of her hip.

"Mock you?"

With a grimace of pain, Anne rolled away from him, scooting off the bed. Stalking to where her bed robe lay, she picked it up and flung it about her. Then she rounded on Niall.

"How can you believe I still mean to betray you after what we shared last eve? Do you think I could give myself to you like I did if, in my heart, I was plotting your death? What kind o' woman do you think I am?"

His brows lifted sardonically and he shrugged. "Women have always used their bodies to get what they wanted."

"Do you seriously think I coupled with you to win your confidence?" Anne cried in outrage. "To lull you into thinking I'm not one o' your traitors? And all the while 'twas Iain's arms I wished to be in?"

Anne's words drove home. Niall flushed in guilty embarrassment. "Nay, Annie, I didn't mean that. I only asked that you not see nor talk with Iain. Lord." He sighed. "I didn't realize I was asking such a sacrifice. I withdraw my request."

"Nay." Anne strode over to stand beside the bed, her silver eyes flashing her displeasure. "Nay, Niall.

You spoke the words, now explain them. Why don't you want me talking with Iain?"

He shot her a hot, angry look. "Because I fear he'll try to use you to get to me and, in the end, destroy us both!"

She returned his gaze and a thoughtful frown puckered her brow. "You don't know your cousin very well, do you?"

"If you mean to defend him—"

"Why are you so certain 'tis Iain?" Anne demanded. "What o' Cousin Hugh and Uncle Duncan?"

"What o' them?" Niall drawled coolly.

Incredulity widened her eyes. "Are you saying you've never considered either o' them? Hugh's mad with ambition, not to mention just plain mad. And Duncan." Anne shivered. "Duncan is cold and heartless. There's something about him . . ."

"Why not add my bastard uncle Malcolm?" Niall offered dryly. "Though a man o' the cloth, mayhap he, too, dreams o' wearing the chief's feathers. Nay, Anne. Because they don't like you is no reason to accuse them o' treachery."

"Yet you accuse one who does like me o' it! I'm not so blind or so emotional that I cannot set aside my personal differences and clearly see the truth o' the matter," she countered, stung by his arrogant assumption to the contrary. "You accuse me o' the same bias you have against Iain."

"That isn't true."

Anne's hands fisted at her hips. " 'Tisn't it? You've resented Iain's attentions to me from the start. Yet what, aside from that, has Iain done to deserve your suspicion?"

"He has much to gain from my death."

"And what o' Hugh and Duncan? Would they not profit as well? They, too, stand in line for the chieftainship. And have you ever considered others in your clan—your lairds, any outlaws you may have banished? Only a fool closes himself to all possibilities."

"Are you calling me a fool?" Fury flashed in Niall's dark eyes. "Next you'll be calling me a liar and you know how I feel about that!"

He climbed off the bed to tower over her. "And, aye, damn you. I *have* and am still considering others."

For an instant, Anne was cowed by his naked masculinity. Then defiance flared. She gazed up at Niall with mutinous eyes. He glared back.

Suddenly, in a long overdue rush of perspective, the total ridiculousness of their argument struck her. A giggle bubbled to her lips.

"What's so amusing?" Niall demanded with narrowed eyes.

"Why, that we're both fools!"

A sound a lot like a soft laugh escaped, in spite of Anne's best intentions not to make Niall any angrier. "Here we are, fighting each other, expending all our efforts in a battle royal, while the traitor stands back and watches. He's no need to do more than that. We'll gladly destroy each other for him."

Amusement tugged at the corners of Niall's lips. The tenseness eased from his body. "We really should join forces."

Anne's expression sobered. "Are you saying you trust me?"

He smiled at her in gentle understanding. "You won't cease until you've forced that admission from me, will you, lass?"

"Nay, m'lord."

"You're a stubborn, defiant little wench."

"Aye, m'lord."

Niall sighed in exasperation. "My name is not 'm'lord'."

She grinned. "Aye, Niall."

His arms opened. "Come here, lass."

With a delighted chuckle, Anne went to him and he carried her down to lie beside him on the bed. She kept the bed robe tightly wrapped about her. Niall's eyes skimmed the offending garment meaningfully.

"I'd like you better without that."

A delicate brow arched in thoughtful consideration. "Do you now? Well, mayhap I'll shed it, and mayhap I won't. I can't quite decide, with my question still unanswered."

"And what question was that?"

A hesitant little smile trembled on her lips. "Do you trust me, Niall?"

His gaze was fiercely tender as he scanned her sweet features. "Aye, lass," he whispered achingly. "I trust you."

Anne slipped the garment from her shoulders and crept into the warm, welcoming haven of his arms. Niall's hands moved down her back, molding her tighter and tighter to the hard length of his body. He leaned over to touch his tongue to her lips, teasing, coaxing them apart. At his insistent probing, she opened. His tongue plunged suggestively into her mouth, and pleasure shuddered through Anne.

Niall's musky scent enveloped her, filling her with the desire to surrender to the needs he stirred within her. Anne's hand slid between them, seeking the hot, swollen organ pressing so eagerly at the junction of her thighs. Och, how they could fight, yet the loving was just as powerful.

The bedchamber door slammed open. In a few swift moves, Niall swung over to grab the dirk that hung by his bed, then shoved Anne behind him.

"Niall!" Caitlin cried as she swept into the room oblivious to the fact her brother wasn't alone. "A murrain! The cattle have a murrain!"

The girl halted, finally noticing Anne huddled behind her naked brother. Caitlin paled, then colored fiercely. Anger quickly replaced the shock.

Her turquoise eyes flashed as she first looked at Anne, then Niall. "So, brother dear," Caitlin ground out the words through clenched teeth, "While our father is barely cold in the grave and our cattle are dying of a pestilence, you lie here abed. And the one woman you choose to couple with is the witch responsible for it all!"

Chapter Thirteen

Niall laid aside his dirk. He handed Anne her bed robe, then donned his. Climbing off the bed, he strode past his sister to close the door.

Then he rounded on her. "You will knock and await permission to enter this bedchamber from now on," Niall growled in a dangerously soft voice. "And you may pack your belongings post haste. You're paying your aunt a long visit in Edinburgh."

The defiance in Caitlin's eyes crumbled. "N-nay! How could you? Haven't I endured enough o' late to have you now all but banish me?"

The girl sank to her knees, weeping as if her heart would break.

Anne ran to Niall's side. If it were within her power, she'd not permit him to send another member of his family away because of her. In time, Anne knew, he'd come to resent her for it. She couldn't live with that between them. She clasped his arm, diverting his frowning attention from his sister.

"Niall," she beseeched him, "don't do this. She's

but a child and overwrought with all that's happened. And she says naught that others don't say. Caitlin has but the courage to speak them to your face while others whisper behind their hands. You can't banish all your people. We must face the problem head on. Any other way would be cowardly."

"Respect for you must start somewhere, lass," he rasped, his eyes dark with pain. "And if I can't command it within my own family . . ."

She gave him a trembling smile. "I know, my love."

Anne squatted beside Caitlin and gently touched her shoulder. The girl jerked away and glared up at her. Anne sighed.

"I know you hate me," she began, "but for love o' your brother, can't you support him in his decision to handfast with me? These past few days have been hard for you, but they've been difficult for Niall as well. You're growing quickly to a woman. 'Tis time you begin to act like one."

Tear-filled turquoise eyes narrowed in anger. "Are you calling me a child?"

"What do you call your actions a few moments ago?" was the gentle rejoinder.

Caitlin wiped away her tears and rose. She squared her slender shoulders. "I don't like nor trust you."

"I know." Anne got to her feet. "But can't you trust your brother and his judgement?"

The black-haired girl shot Niall a pouting glare. "I know enough o' the power o' women over men to think he doesn't know his own mind in this."

"Was Niall so besotted with the Lady Anne Stewart that he didn't know his own mind? Did his love for her weaken his judgement?"

"Nay." Caitlin sniffed reluctantly.

"Then why should he be any less able because he's with me? If you recall, I'm not half the woman she was," Anne said, repeating Caitlin's own words.

"And you don't believe in witchcraft, so what other influence could I possibly have over him?"

Caitlin stepped back, her glance swinging from Anne to her brother. "Och, I don't know. It just seems that everything has turned sour since you arrived. And the talk doesn't help."

"And have you encouraged it?" Niall cut in.

His sister's head lowered. "Well, mayhap a little."

"I need your loyalty in this, Caitlin." Niall grasped her by the arms. "I am sore beset right now. If you, too, turn against me . . ."

Her eyes widened at the slight catch in his voice. "Och, Niall, I won't turn against you. I swear. You're my brother. We're family."

"Then you'll accept Anne?"

Caitlin's glance slid to hers. "Aye, accept her, but that is all. Don't ask me to be her friend."

"Damn you, Caitlin," Niall swore. "Why do you persist—"

" 'Tis enough, Niall." Anne placed a hand on his arm. "Let it be."

His stormy countenance calmed as he gazed down at her. "Ever the peacemaker, aren't you, lass? You've had much to swallow since your arrival here. My clan hasn't met you even halfway. But soon that'll change. I swear it!"

She smiled up at him. "Aye, m'lord. That it will."

"N–Niall?" Caitlin's plaintive voice interrupted their warm glance.

Niall's gaze returned to his sister. "Aye?"

"Must I still go to Edinburgh?"

A dark brow arched. "I don't know. What do you think, Anne?"

Caitlin stiffened, her fierce pride stung at having her fate at Anne's mercy.

Anne gave the girl a gentle smile. "I think Caitlin would be happier here, among family and friends."

"Thank you, m'lady." Caitlin forced the words out

through stiff lips, then bobbed a little curtsey.

Niall frowned, as the remembrance of the original intent of his sister's visit struck him. "You said the cattle have a murrain. How do you know this?"

"I was in the Great Hall when the head herdsman came rushing in. He was very excited as he spoke to Duncan, and his voice carried throughout the hall. I fear the news is all over the castle by now."

"And the cause o' it?"

Caitlin averted her eyes. "They say 'tis witchcraft. Malcolm was there when the news was brought. He immediately raised a hue and cry, all but claiming 'twas Anne's doing. There's trouble afoot, brother."

Niall's face hardened with displeasure. "Aye, that there is."

He waved his sister toward the door. "You may go. I've plans to make."

They watched as Caitlin left the room, then Niall turned to Anne. "This couldn't have come at a more inopportune time. The people will be stirred, fearful and angry." He gave a wry, self-mocking laugh. "And, in but another hour I, in the midst o' all the rising witch panic, must defend my right to the chieftainship."

Anne's glance swept admiringly over Niall's tall, powerful form. She sighed. "I wish I could be there to stand at your side. How many will there be at the Chieftain's Council?"

Niall shrugged into the plaid jacket she held out for him. "With my family and the clan's higher lairds, about twenty men."

"Twenty against one," Anne murmured in dismay.

He laughed and gave her an affectionate kiss before she slipped away to return with his plaid. "I'd prefer to think o' this as a friendly reconfirmation o' my father's wishes than a battle o' wills."

Anne busied herself draping the Campbell plaid

over Niall's left shoulder, then fastened it to hang down his right side with a silver brooch engraved with the clan badge of wild myrtle. When finished with the task, she lifted her eyes to him.

"You'll have enemies there, and no mistake. Be careful."

Niall's gaze was tender. "I'll be careful, lass. Though we Scots are a hardheaded lot, 'twould still take severe misconduct on my part to negate my father's decision in this. And I think I'm man enough to handle a little dissension from my people."

"Aye, that you are." Anne managed a smile. "Man enough and more."

A hot look flared in Niall's eyes. "Have a care, lass. If you persist in talking like that, I'll have to shed all these clothes you've gone to such trouble to dress me in."

"And you know as well as I, 'tis time for you to leave."

Anne's glance swept over him one last time. Dressed in his doublet, trews, and white shirt beneath his plaid and jacket, Niall looked the consummate Highland warrior. The clothing clung to his powerful chest and shoulders, molded tightly to his muscular legs and thighs. Anne's heart swelled with pride.

He had the physical presence to be clan chief as well as the maturity and intelligence. They would be hard pressed to deny him his rightful position. Yet still, she worried.

There was an aura of impending doom hovering over Niall and it frightened her. No, terrified her, for the premonition of death and destruction seemed almost palpable. Anne opened her mouth to beg him not to go, then clamped it shut.

To ask Niall to turn his back upon his people was to ask him to stop his heart from beating or his lungs from inhaling the fresh Highland air. She as heiress to Clan MacGregor understood that better than most. Niall would not be the brave, proud warrior she loved and respected if he didn't face the dangers. But how she wanted to be with him! Wanted it, with all her heart, though knew it could not be.

Niall must face his clansmen alone. Her presence would only stir further resentment and speculation. But Anne's thoughts and all the strength of her love would go with him. Mayhap, in some small way, it would even the odds.

He stepped toward her. "I go off to fight the dragons," he teased huskily. "Mayhap a kiss from a bonnie lassie would send me on my way properly girded for battle."

" 'Tis an honor and more, m'lord," Anne teased back, rendering him a small curtsy.

Then, before he could respond, she moved close to cup his smooth-shaven jaw. Lifting on tiptoe, she planted a gentle kiss on his firm, sensually molded lips.

Niall gathered her to him, forcing her soft curves against the full length of his hard-muscled body. "I had more than a genteel peck on the lips in mind," he growled, and lowered his head toward her.

His tongue flicked over her lips, teasing, then urging them apart. He plunged inside, hungrily exploring her mouth. His kiss deepened, all but consuming her. Anne went limp in his arms, clinging desperately to his jacket for support.

Niall raised his head, an arrogant smile on his lips. "I wanted you to remember me, should I mayhap die in battle. Think you, I've left a lasting memory?"

"A—aye," Anne breathed, barely able to force the words past her constricted throat. "That you have, m'lord."

"Good." He released her and stepped back.

"Niall." Anne stayed him, her hand lifting to lay upon his chest.

"Aye, lass?"

"Your request earlier—that I not speak to nor be alone with Iain."

He went still. "Aye?"

"I give you my promise."

An aching gentleness flared in his compelling eyes. "Thank you, lass." His big hand covered hers. "I don't know anymore if I should have asked it, or if I even deserve your sacrifice in this, but I accept your offer nonetheless. It means a lot to me, especially at a time like this."

" 'Tis all I can do, as little as 'tis."

A wry grin quirked his mouth. "Och, there's a lot you can do for me." His glance strayed to his huge bed. "I'll expect you awaiting me there."

The poignant moment dissipated in the sudden turn of the conversation. Anne considered him briefly. "Well, we'll have to see about that," she began, the hint of a mischievous smile glimmering on her lips. "Mayhap I will, and mayhap I won't. I haven't quite decided."

"Well, take this time then to decide. And I'll see you on my bed when I return."

Niall turned and strode across the room.

"Disgusting, rutting stag," Anne's amused voice followed him to the door.

He paused to give a shout of laughter then, without a backward glance, opened the door and disappeared down the corridor.

Anne returned to her own bedchamber to find Agnes tidying the room. She flushed at the realization the old maid must have guessed what had transpired between her and Niall last eve, then brushed it aside. The blood-stained sheets on Niall's bed would have soon given it away, even if Agnes had not been awaiting her here.

She only hoped the news when it spread though the castle would not stir further hostility against her. Coupling to ascertain if there was sexual compatability was one of the primary purposes of a handfasting. But if Caitlin's reaction were any indication, Anne doubted the castle folk would greet this news with much joy.

Agnes bobbed a curtsy as Anne approached. "Good morrow, m'lady." A knowing, happy light gleamed in her eye. "Did ye sleep well?"

"Aye, Agnes," Anne replied. "I slept well indeed."

She paused, a small frown puckering her brow.

"What is it, m'lady?" the old maidservant asked in concern.

"Och, naught." Anne shook her head and sighed. "I'll just feel better when the Chieftain's Council is over. I am the cause of such animosity here. I wouldn't want that to harm Niall's chances for the chieftainship."

"The young lord can well handle the fools in that room," Agnes staunchly defended him. "He'll win them over, and no mistake."

"Most likely." Anne sighed. "But, still, I wish I could be there to know the charges they bring against me."

"They could be hard to hear, m'lady."

"Aye, but the knowledge might aid my efforts to win them over. I must know what's in their hearts if I've any hope o' changing them."

"There *is* a way," the old woman offered.

Anne's gaze riveted on her. "What are you saying? Is there a chance I could overhear the council meeting?"

Agnes nodded. " 'Tis a secret, one the young lord doesn't even know about. A hidden tunnel runs from the chamber to the storerooms. From there, another tunnel leads to the outside. 'Twas devised for escape in times o' battle."

Anne could barely contain her excitement. "Would you lead me to it? I swear I'd never reveal the secret, save perhaps to Niall, and 'twould help in learning the charges against me. I only ask this in the hope o' aiding Niall."

Hesitation flickered momentarily in the maidservant's eyes. Then, she nodded. "Aye, lass. I'll help ye, but no one must learn o' this. Not for a time, at least."

"Then let us be gone." Anne gathered up her cloak. "There's not a moment to spare."

Few noticed their passage through the castle, for Kilchurn was abuzz with preparations for the evening feast to celebrate Niall's confirmation as chief. Anne knew Niall had ordered things be carried out as if his new rank was a foregone conclusion, fully aware any show of uncertainty would weaken him in the eyes of the council. He had planned for everything, from the feast to the magnificence of his dress, but the true battle had yet to begin in a war of words as Niall defended his right to be chief.

The tunnel leading from the storeroom was musty and dark and strewn with cobwebs. They stumbled along without a torch, for Agnes had said the approaching light might be discovered through the narrow vents on the secret panel separating the council chamber from the hidden corridor. Finally, Agnes gripped Anne's arm, pulling her to a halt.

"The chamber is just up ahead," she whispered. "The tunnel now narrows so only one may pass at a time. Go ahead. I'll await ye here."

Anne gave the old woman a quick hug. "Thank you, Agnes."

" 'Tis naught, lass. I'll do anything for ye and the young lord." She gave her a small push forward.

"Now, get on with ye. The meeting starts even now."

From behind her, Anne could hear the scrape of chairs and rise and fall of deep male voices. She turned and hurried down the tunnel toward the narrow strips of light in the panel wall. As she reached the secret door, the voices faded. Through the slits, Anne saw Niall rise and lean forward on the table, his solemn glance scanning the faces aligned down its oaken length.

She inhaled an admiring breath. The look Niall gave them was bold, penetrating and self-assured. *Even now he begins*, she thought. Pride for the powerful, commanding man filled her. He was clan chief already, if only the others had the wisdom to see it. If only they had the courage to rise above their petty differences and groundless fears.

"As is our tradition," Niall began, his deep-timbered voice reverberating throughout the chamber, "I stand before you, clan tanist and chieftain-elect, to accept your sworn fealty to me as the Campbell. But first, custom allows the occasion to air questions or grievances that might preclude your acceptance o' me. I will tolerate no doubts or lack o' commitment once this council ends."

Niall lowered himself to his chair and leaned back with an air of supreme confidence and lack of concern. "If there are any objections, speak them now or forever bury them in your heart."

There was a heavy silence. Not a few uncomfortably averted their gazes from Niall's piercing stare. For a few heart-stopping seconds, Anne thought Niall had managed to intimidate them with the power of his presence. Then one of the lairds cleared his throat.

"You have something to say, Andrew?" Niall calmly demanded of the man who was one of his most troublesome lairds.

Andrew glared at him. "This council is illegal!"

A dark brow raised. "Och, and how so?"

The laird nervously scanned the others, searching for some sign of support. "There is one o' your family not present. One whose claim to the chieftainship is nearly as strong as your own. Without his presence, how can the decisions made here be considered fair?"

Niall's eyes narrowed. "And are you mayhap speaking o' my cousin, Hugh?"

Andrew swallowed convulsively and nodded. "Aye."

"And what was I to do with him," Niall inquired icily, his glance moving to encompass the entire gathering, "after he attempted to murder the Lady Anne MacGregor? Allow him to remain here and permit him the opportunity to try again?"

"He is mad, nephew," Duncan interjected. "Allowances must be made."

Niall's gaze swiveled to his uncle. "Allowances *have* been made for a long while now. But is Hugh worth endangering an alliance with Clan MacGregor, o' stirring anew a feud we've finally managed to end?"

No one replied.

"I wouldn't deny my cousin his birthright, but the welfare o' the entire clan comes before that o' a single member," Niall softly reminded them. "And Hugh forfeited that privilege when he threatened the peace between our clans."

"And what has Iain done?" Duncan demanded. "He isn't mad, nor has he threatened the lady's life, yet you've all but banished him, too."

Anne sucked in a startled gasp. Blessed Mother, the attacks begin and this one was as deadly as they came. Niall dared not reveal his knowledge of a traitor, yet how could he justify what might

seem an irrational vendetta against Iain otherwise?
And what would Iain say to defend himself?

Niall shot Iain a thunderous look. The younger
man had paled at his father's accusations and, for
an instant, was speechless.

"What's between Iain and myself is personal," Niall
ground out in the sudden silence. " 'Tisn't a fit topic
for this council."

Duncan rounded on his son. "And what have you
to say, lad? Does or does this not bear on Niall's
fitness to be chief?"

Iain's jaw hardened. Watching him, Anne realized
he sensed he was but the pawn in some game being
played out here.

He shook his head, refusing to be dragged in.
"Niall's a hardhearted, stubborn man," he said, "but
that has never been reason to deny a chieftainship.
I won't pretend my affection for him hasn't changed,
but the rest o' it, as he said, is between us."

Surprise mixed with anger flashed in his father's
eyes. "You would support his claim over yours then?"

"His claim was decided two years ago when the
Campbell named him tanist. Why is there suddenly
such doubt afoot?"

Pride swelled in Anne for her friend's honest heart,
even in the face of Niall's continued animosity. Mayhap Niall would now realize Iain wasn't the sort of
man to be a traitor. Mayhap, just mayhap they could
once again be friends.

"Hugh and Iain are not the true issue here!" a
smooth, articulate voice unexpectedly announced.
"There's doubt afoot because Niall's immortal soul
is in danger."

All eyes swung to Malcolm, sitting opposite Niall
at the far end of the table. Anne's gaze followed the
rest. She swallowed a panicked sob. *Och, Niall, here
it comes now.* She glanced back to him and could
have wept with pride.

Niall's face was an expressionless mask. "Matters o' religion are also not a topic for this particular council," he coolly replied. "I govern Campbell hearts and bodies, you govern their souls. I've no intention o' interferring in your domain, unless it endangers one o' the clan."

A sly smile quirked the preacher's mouth. "And what say you to a witch burning? There is now law to back me on that."

Niall smiled back, but the expression never quite reached his eyes. "I obey all laws, but those same laws will be applied in a fair and humane fashion. There'll be no witch panic on Campbell lands, or torture to extract confessions as the only means o' evidence."

"And will you just as fairly consider all accused o' witchcraft," Malcolm persisted, "be they noble as well as peasant?"

"Aye," Niall countered smoothly, though even Anne could see the muscle jump furiously in his jaw. "I haven't changed in my judgements or treatment o' the people, *when* concrete evidence was truthfully given."

"Then," Malcolm said, triumph sharpening his voice, "in all fairness, you are called to judge the Lady Anne MacGregor, named by her own people the Witch o' Glenstrae."

A murmur of excited male voices swirled around the room as Niall sat there, staring stonily back at Malcolm.

"Curse you, Niall!" Anne heard Iain mutter. "I warned you o' this."

Niall, however, seemed unaffected by the turmoil. He paused to pour himself a glass of claret from the flagon at his end of the table. Swirling the burgundy in the glass, he examined its sparkling hues as the others slowly calmed and silence once more fell upon the gathering.

At long last, he raised his eyes to that of his bastard uncle. "And what has that to do with my fitness as chief? That the Lady Anne is called the Witch o' Glenstrae? They are but words, nothing more, as is my title o' Wolf o' Cruachan. Make no further accusations unless you have proof."

"What about the Campbell's death?" the preacher shot at him. " 'Twas said the wench was with him at the last, gave him a cup o' poison."

"She was with him little more than five minutes before the end came. And the word o' a jealous serving maid is hardly a reliable witness. Not to mention," he added, "I later tasted the contents o' the cup and found 'twas only water. Or would you say my word is less than that o' a serving maid, as well, since you seem so determined to condemn Anne?"

"Then what o' the murrain?" Andrew supplied. " 'Tis strange our cattle have been untouched while other clans' died, until the MacGregor woman arrived. 'Tis said she put a curse on our cattle in revenge for the royal grant o' their lands to us. What say you to that, Niall?"

"Superstitious nonsense!" Niall snapped. " 'Tis a pestilence most probably spread from diseased cattle brought here from other clans. The McCorquodales recently had a bout o' murrain and their lands border ours."

"What o' her strange healing skills?" Duncan added quietly. " 'Twas Hugh himself who saw her breathe life back into a stillborn babe. How do you explain that, nephew?"

Niall's head turned to his uncle, the tension rising in his voice. "I'm no physician. I've no explanation for everything, but there is much in nature still unexplained. To attribute the unknown to witchcraft is the work o' ignorant minds!"

"Then the Reformed Kirk, the religion o' our land,"

Malcolm silkily offered, "is a Kirk o' ignorant minds. Is that what you meant to say?"

Niall froze. Though he might himself only pay lip service to this new but hugely popular religion, nowadays it was the heart's blood of most Scotsmen. To ridicule or ignore its power would be folly indeed. For the first time since the council began, Niall was suddenly unsure of its eventual outcome.

Anne saw the look of indecision flare in Niall's eyes. Her heart went out to him. Her greatest fear had been that, like a pack of wolves, they'd drag him down on this very issue. And now it seemed her worst fears were about to come to fruition.

Her nails scored her tightly fisted palms but she made not a sound, expending her efforts in willing all her strength and support to Niall. He finally expelled an exasperated breath and gave a mocking shake of his head, an action Anne knew instinctively was pure bluff.

"I intended naught o' the kind, though all here will admit that ignorance grants little consideration to wealth or status in life. All I meant to say was, as clan chief, I must deal with all issues in a calm, informed manner. How else am I to govern wisely?"

Anne saw the doubts fade from some of the men's eyes and several lean back in their chairs, their minds made in Niall's favor. *Good*, she thought, a tiny ember of hope flaring in her breast. *He is beginning to win them over.*

"Aye, govern wisely, indeed," Malcolm growled, sensing he was losing support on this issue. "And how is that possible, when you seem all but besotted with the MacGregor wench? Besotted so thoroughly," he added, "that some would say bewitched. 'Twould be an easy thing for her to have slipped a love potion into your drink or sprinkled it on your food."

"And 'twould be an even easier thing to care for her because she's a kind-hearted, beautiful woman," Niall countered. "If any o' you had taken the time or effort to get to know her, you might understand that."

"We *have* tried, but there is something about her," Duncan said. "Those eyes . . ."

"They are eyes and naught more!" Niall snapped. "I find your arguments dwindling to the ridiculous. If there are no further issues o' import, mayhap 'tis time to end this council."

"Aye, nephew." Duncan sighed. "Mayhap you are right. There is one issue more to discuss, though, before we swear our fealty."

Niall eyed him. "And what is that?"

"The naming o' your tanist. In times as unstable as these, a successor is vital."

Though he had the leave to name his tanist at his leisure and had planned to wait until the traitor was discovered before doing so, the hearty agreement swelling around the table made Niall reconsider. Gaining the support of these men had been more difficult than he'd anticipated. The tide could still turn if he miscalculated his real influence over them. Niall hated being forced into something he wasn't really prepared for but a compromise in this case might well be the prudent course.

His gaze swept the gathering, considering the merits and weaknesses of each man there. When his eyes met Iain's, Niall stiffened. Though he'd been surprised and more than relieved by Iain's support, Niall wondered what the true motives behind his cousin's actions had been. Iain could have guessed there'd be dissent and chosen the wiser course of appearing to be on Niall's side. A wiser course, indeed, if he'd thought Niall planned on naming him tanist this eve.

If it hadn't been for the issue of the traitor hanging

over his head, Iain would have been Niall's choice as tanist. But not now. He dared not place his cousin in such a position of power. But if not Iain, who?

His glance continued to skim the men, weighing, considering. None of his trusted warriors had returned of yet with any information regarding Hugh's activities or whereabouts, or of any possible traitorous actions on the part of his lairds. And now, more than ever, he desperately needed that knowledge.

Niall's eyes met those of Andrew. Traitor or not, that laird had never been a serious candidate. The man was far too concerned with his own needs. And, without further information, Niall dared not place his trust in any of the other lairds present, either. It would be too difficult to keep a close eye upon their activities, scattered as their holdings were on the huge expanse of Campbell lands. It was wiser to choose a tanist from those close by. It would be easier to watch him. . . .

His gaze passed Duncan. Anne's words about him flitted through Niall's mind. Aye, his uncle was a cold, controlled man, but his advice in the past had always been directed toward the betterment of the clan. Yet, on the other hand, his active involvement in securing the MacGregor land grant. . . .

With a frustrated sigh, Niall rose from his chair. "The choice o' clan tanist is a difficult one, for many issues must be taken into account. Youth and battle prowess must be weighed against the equally valuable attributes o' maturity and wisdom. Sometimes, there is no one perfect individual for the task."

He leaned forward on the table, his next words low and carefully measured. "I possess the youth and battle prowess. Taking that into account, I have decided to draw on maturity in choosing my tanist."

Niall inhaled a deep breath in the anticipatory silence and forged on. "As the first o' my duties as your new chief, I name my uncle Duncan tanist to Clan Campbell."

Chapter Fourteen

As the words fell from Niall's lips, Anne's horrified gaze sought out Duncan. A humble half-smile lifted his mouth but, for a fleeting instant, she caught a triumphant gleam. Was it the triumph of a traitor or an ambitious man?

The men rose from the table to congratulate the new tanist, then left for the chief's installation ceremony. Iain stood there, staring at Niall, who grimly returned the favor. Finally Duncan clapped his son on the back.

"Come, have you no congratulations for your father?" Duncan inquired jovially. "Allow an old man a few years o' power. Then 'twill be your turn."

Iain wrenched his gaze from Niall to stare blankly at his father. "What? Och, aye, you're to be complimented on attaining such a high position. May you bring the wisdom o' years Niall so dearly desires."

He turned and strode from the chamber before

his father could utter a reply. Duncan frowned at his son's retreating back, then turned to Niall.

"The lad's disappointed, that's all," he explained with an apologetic grin.

"I care not for Iain's feelings in this," Niall snapped. "As long as he swears fealty in the ceremony, I'll be content."

"Och, he will, and no mistake. The lad's as loyal as they come."

"So 'twould appear," came the sardonic reply.

Niall motioned for his uncle to precede him. "The ceremony draws nigh. See to the final preparations. I'll meet you in the Great Hall in ten minutes' time with the Lady Anne."

He raised his hand to silence Duncan's attempted protest. "She's my wife in all but marriage vows. And, as such, lady o' this castle and our clan. We will forget what was spoken in this chamber and start afresh. Agreed, Uncle?"

Duncan hesitated, then reluctantly nodded his head. "Agreed, m'lord."

Anne headed down the corridor to her bed-chamber, grateful the feast would not begin for another hour. The tension-fraught atmosphere of the council chamber, combined with the ordeal of the installation ceremony, had drained her energy. The past three days had been exhausting, full of pain as well as joy. Only now, at long last, was she finally able to relax.

Och, for a nice, hot bath, Anne thought with a wistful sigh. *If only there were time. . . .*

Distracted, she rounded the corner and slammed into a hard male body. Sturdy hands grasped her arms to steady her. Anne stared up into dark eyes only a few inches higher than hers.

They were cold eyes. As they gazed down at her, a humorless smile touched the man's lips.

"So where are you going, my wee witch?" Malcolm Campbell inquired. "To procure some potion to put into the Campbell's drink? Or mayhap to chant a few incantations over your witch fire to hasten the death o' our cattle?"

With an angry glare, Anne jerked away. "I do no such thing! Your unreasoning hatred blinds you to the truth!"

A bushy brow lifted in amused tolerance. "Och, angry are you now at being caught in your devilish schemes?"

Once more, Malcolm grabbed her by the arms, jerking her close. "Your time is short, devil's whore. You've bewitched the Campbell with your seductive powers, but my powers are stronger still. Mine are the thumb and leg screws and the fires o' the stake. Think you to prevail against them?"

At the fanatical gleam in Malcolm's eyes, fear shot through Anne. He meant to see her dead. She struggled wildly in his arms. "Let me go, I say!" she cried. "If Niall should hear—"

"He's not fit to rule us," the preacher hissed. "His soul is lost. Even when you're gone the spell can't be undone. He'll have to be tried and burned as the witch's consort that he is."

Niall. She'd never thought of that horrifying consequence. But Niall had defended her and, in that defense, had come perilously close to insulting the Kirk and denigrating its fanatical witch persecutions. Men and women had been burned for far less.

Fear for him drove Anne to the edge of panic. "You mustn't blame him for his loyalty to me," she said in a strangled whisper. "He's a decent, God-fearing man. I beg you. Don't punish him for whatever crimes you think *I* may have committed."

"And what crimes are they, lassie?" Malcolm prodded smoothly, his dark eyes gleaming. "Tell me now. Mayhap there is yet time to save the Campbell."

Dizziness swirled through Anne. The past days had drained her more than she realized. She couldn't seem to find the strength to fight back.

"That's enough, Uncle!"

Iain's deep voice jerked Anne from the hypnotic spell of Malcolm's gaze. In a stunned slow motion, she turned toward him. He looked fiercely angry, but why, Anne didn't know.

"Release her!" Iain demanded. "Now!"

Malcolm freed Anne abruptly. If not for Iain's quick leap to her side, she would have lost her balance and fallen.

"You tread where you should not go," his uncle warned. "Best you leave while your soul's yet untainted by this woman."

"Nay," Iain shook his head. "Best *you* leave before I forget you're family and smite you for your cruel words to this lady."

His uncle's eyes narrowed in disbelief. "You would not dare! I'm a man o' the cloth."

"At this moment, you're not fit to claim such protection. Now, get out o' my sight!"

The preacher backed away, his face mottled in rage. "Young fool! Beware the witch or you'll rue it to your dying day!"

Malcolm stalked away.

Anne inhaled a shuddering breath. "You shouldn't anger him, Iain. He has the power to be a deadly foe."

"The man's a fool," Iain muttered. "Did he hurt you, lass?"

She shook her head. "Nay. But the threats he made against Niall. Och, Iain, what am I to do?"

" 'Tis as I said before," he murmured, tenderly stroking her cheek. "Come away with me, Anne."

At his touch, the memory of her promise to Niall

came to mind. Remorse surged through her but she steeled herself to the difficult task. She'd given her word and would support Niall in any way she could, even if it meant denying herself the harmless pleasure of Iain's company. Even if it meant hurting him.

With a resolute sigh, Anne stepped back. "Nay, Iain. 'Tis as I said before, my place is with Niall." She gave him a gentle shove. "Now, get on with you and don't attempt to speak with me again."

Iain's brow furrowed. "And why not? Has Niall forbidden that, too?"

"I gave him my word." Anne's voice broke. "Please try to understand."

"Och, I understand," Iain ground out. "The man's jealousy has rotted more than his heart. It has now rotted his mind. This is beyond tolerance!"

Anne grabbed his arm as he turned to leave. "You're not going to see Niall, are you?" Anxiety threaded her voice.

"Aye, that I am. I'll have it out with him, once and for all."

"Nay, Iain," she implored. "I beg you—"

"Let him go, Anne."

At the flat command, Anne swung around. Niall stood there in the corridor leading from the Great Hall. In a few quick strides, he was upon them. Gently, he pried Anne's fingers loose and moved her aside. Then, in a quick move, Niall grabbed his cousin by the throat, slamming him against the wall.

"I've told you time and again to stay away from her," he growled savagely. "What more will it take? A dirk between your ribs?"

Anne grasped Niall's arm, tugging frantically. "Stop it! Stop it, I say! Don't do this, Niall!"

He shrugged her aside, his glance never leaving Iain's.

Iain's hand encircled Niall's wrist and clamped down tightly on it. "Release me now," he said in a soft voice, "or there'll be more than one dirk drawn this eve."

Panic rose in Anne. They meant to fight each other, for neither man's pride would allow him to back down. She glanced wildly around, searching for help, and found none. Then, in a flash of inspiration, she relieved Niall of the dirk that hung at his side before hurrying around to take Iain's.

Iain's hand stayed hers. Anne's gaze met his, her silver eyes flashing. "Let it go, Iain."

He eyed her for a long moment then released her hand. Anne withdrew his dirk.

Without warning, she turned and pressed Niall's own dagger against his ribs. He stiffened, going quiet and still, but maintained his grip on Iain.

"Do you mean to kill me, lass?" he drawled, never shifting his gaze from that of his cousin's. "If you do, make your first thrust deep and sure. Otherwise, I swear I'll break his neck before I die."

"And you're a great brute o' a fool," Anne muttered in disgust, "if you think I mean to kill you. I only wanted to get that pigheaded attention o' yours." She pressed the dirk a little deeper, until its tip penetrated his clothes to prick his skin. "And do I finally have it?"

"Aye," Niall gritted. "Now say what you have to say, and be quick about it!"

"You are wrong to treat Iain thusly."

"I told him to stay away from you!"

Anne smiled. "Aye, but I am the one who gave my word, not Iain. Why aren't you throttling me against that wall instead?"

Niall shot her a furious glance. "One thing at a time. I'll see to you later."

"And will you also see to your uncle Malcolm?" she persisted sweetly.

"Malcolm?" Niall frowned. "What has my uncle to do with this?"

"He was threatening me, warning me o' the dire consequences in store for not just me, but you, if I continued with my witchcraft. Iain," she explained, motioning toward the younger man, "rescued me from your churlish uncle. And, just as you arrived, I was informing him that I couldn't speak with him again. Let Iain go." Anne slid Niall's dirk back in its scabbard. "You have falsely accused him."

The request was uttered in a low voice, but the authority beneath it was commanding, nonetheless. Niall hesitated, then released Iain and stepped back. Neither man, however, relaxed his rigid fighting stance, nor extinguished the wary look in his eyes.

"You owe Iain an apology," came the sweet voice beside Niall.

His jaw hardened. "If 'tis truly as Anne says, I beg pardon."

Iain rubbed his bruised throat. "It changes naught and you know it. I don't want your apology, nor will I accept it!"

Anne touched him on the arm. "Iain, please."

He rounded on her. "Leave it be, lass. You've made your choice, and that choice is for him. 'Tis time you start living with the consequences o' his arrogance and mistrust. I only hope he doesn't destroy you in the process o' destroying himself.

"And you," Iain said hotly, his glance swinging back to Niall. "I'm not so sure I made the wisest choice in the council. And that's a decision I may live to regret."

Without another word, Iain strode away. Tears filled Anne's eyes, but they were ones of fury.

"How could you treat him like that?"

Niall studied her impassively. "I apologized. What more do you want?"

Her fists clenched at her sides. "And did you convince Iain o' your sincerity? I think not! You could have tried harder, Niall Campbell!"

A look of utter weariness flooded Niall's eyes. "Aye, mayhap I could've. But this has been a trying day and my patience is worn to its breaking point."

Niall gathered Anne into his arms. "I'll seek Iain out and try again on the morrow. But only for your sake," he hastened to add, seeing the joyous light flare in her eyes. "I still dare not trust him. Not him, nor any man."

She flung her arms around his neck. "Och, my love, you'll not regret it. I swear it!"

He smiled down at her. "Mayhap. Now, where were you going?"

"To my chamber, for a short rest before the feast."

A dark brow arched in feigned consideration. "And have you already forgotten my command before I left for the council?"

Her arms fell from his neck. She began to back away, the full intent of his words rushing back to her. "Well, I could hardly meet you on your bed, when there was a chieftain's ceremony awaiting."

"And now what excuse have you?" A devilish grin spread across Niall's face. "There's nearly an hour until the feast. We have all the time in the world."

Anne grabbed his hand and began tugging him forward. "Then let us hurry, m'lord. I've always had a taste to bed a clan chief. I fear an hour is barely time to satisfy that hunger."

Laughing, Niall followed her down the hall.

Late the next morning, Anne reluctantly rose from Niall's bed. The feast had lasted well into the night, but Anne and Niall had departed for the privacy of his bedchamber as soon as it was considered proper. The door was barely closed before they were feverishly undressing each other. In but a few minutes more, they were entwined on the bed in the throes of passionate lovemaking. Finally, both fell into a sated but exhausted slumber.

After several more hours of langourous love-making when they awoke and a quick breakfast of porridge and cream, Anne bade Niall a fond farewell as he went off to attend to his duties. At her request, Agnes had a bath drawn. Anne was soon lost in contemplation as she enjoyed the soothing water and her maid scrubbing her head.

Her thoughts harked back to last eve's encounter with Malcolm. Though Niall had discounted his uncle's threats, Anne was still worried. The man had the power of religion behind him and that power could not easily be discounted. Not when Niall's very life could well hang in the balance.

She'd do anything to protect him—anything. And that anything included giving up her healing. She'd never thought she could ever compromise on such a vital issue, never imagined she'd be willing to sacrifice the good of many for just one. But Anne had never envisioned loving a man as deeply, as completely, as she loved Niall. And his life held precedent over everything else.

In time, the animosity toward her would cool. She'd be accepted. In the meanwhile, it was too dangerous to sit by and allow things to take their natural course. She had already given Niall her word she'd not heal in Kilchurn but Anne knew now, with a bittersweet pain, there was yet more she must do.

Her visits to Ena must stop if the clacking tongues were to be silenced. Her store of potions and salves would have to be discarded, for they could be used as evidence against her. And her secret herb garden in the forest must be destroyed. Any and all possibilities must be considered. Every threat to Niall's safety must be eradicated. Her physical presence in Kilchurn was problem enough. She'd not knowingly create more.

When her bath was done, she dressed in a simple gown of deep blue wool, then hurried to the chest where she kept her herbal medicines. Not bothering to hide her actions from Agnes, she began to carry the jars to the privy, where she dumped their contents down the long chute. Her task, painful as it was, was carried out with a resolute determination. Only when Anne reached the last of the jars did her resolve waver.

The container of dried foxglove caught her gaze. She had gathered the potent leaves under Ena's watchful eye. Under that same thorough tutelage, Anne had learned of the plant's curative, if sometimes deadly, powers. Holding the jar up now for a final, regretful appraisal, her heart skipped a beat.

She'd put the container away full and had never had the opportunity to use any of the plant, since she'd soon thereafter given her word to Niall not to perform her healing. But the jar was now half empty. There was enough foxglove missing to kill twenty men.

Anne's throat went dry. She rose on unsteady legs. The jar clasped in her hand, she went to seek Agnes.

The old maidservant was next door in Niall's bedchamber, sprinkling sweet woodruff on the freshly laid rushes. Anne crossed the room to shut the door, then returned to Agnes's side. She held up the jar of foxglove.

"Have you taken any o' this plant for some ailment, whether yours or some other's?" Anne demanded, her heart now pounding in her chest. "If so, tell me true, Agnes. There will be no punishment."

Agnes's eyes widened. She vehemently shook her head. "Nay, m'lady. I've never been in that chest. I know naught o' the healing art and would never presume to treat anyone from it."

"This jar is half empty. The last time I looked in my chest, 'twas full."

"Truly, m'lady. I havena knowledge o' such things."

Anne sighed. She trusted the old woman, yet someone had taken the leaves. But who? And why?

"Have you seen any looking in my chest, Agnes?"

"Nay, m'lady."

"Then who has access to this room? Who could come in here and not be found suspicious? I *must* discover who took these leaves."

Agnes pondered that for a moment. "Almost any o' the female household staff. And even, on occasion, some of the male staff, as well. Like just now, when they removed the old rushes and brought in fresh ones. We rarely lock the chambers in Kilchurn."

"Aye, that I know," Anne muttered, remembering Caitlin's unexpected, and most unappreciated, arrival in Niall's bedchamber yesterday morning.

Uneasiness crept through her as she headed to the privy with the jar. Mayhap it was just a well-intentioned servant bent on curing some relative of the dropsy. There were others who knew the healing art besides her and Ena. Mayhap the servant had come upon her chest of herbs one day by accident and had merely helped herself to some of the drugs there. Until she'd reached the foxglove, Anne really hadn't paid much attention to the exact amounts left in the jars. Mayhap that servant had taken samples of most of the chest's contents.

But what if there were nothing missing but the foxglove? And what if the leaves had been stolen for more sinister purposes? There was no known antidote to the plant's heart slowing and eventual heart-stopping effects. Only time and the body's own abilities to rid itself eventually of the drug could save a victim of overdose. And only if that overdose were discovered and halted in time.

A shiver of fear rippled through Anne. *Och, Blessed Mary, don't let my herbs be an instrument o' someone's death!* she prayed. *Not now, not when my position in*

Clan Campbell is yet so precarious. It would be the end o' everything. Everything.

Anne quickly finished disposing of the remaining herbs. Then grabbing up a trowel that she slipped into a fold of her skirt, she made her way back to Niall's room. Agnes glanced up from her sprinkling of the last of the sweet woodruff.

"Where are ye going, m'lady?"

Though she didn't wish to alarm the old woman, Anne knew it would be wise to let someone know where she was headed. "I go to my herb garden in the forest. I won't be there long."

Agnes frowned. "Ye shouldna go alone. Let me accompany ye."

"Nay." Anne firmly shook her head. "I'll be careful. If I'm not back within the hour, you can tell Niall."

"An hour is time enough for harm to befall ye," the maidservant muttered. "At least take Angus, the stable man. He willna talk about what he sees. He and Maudie are too grateful for what ye did for their wee Davie."

Anne sighed and nodded her acquiescence. "As you wish. I'll fetch him on my way out o' the castle."

Agnes's look of relief was enough to make Anne smile. "I'm a trial to you at times, aren't I? I'd imagine the other Anne never gave you a moment's trouble."

The old woman grinned. "Well, she wasna as headstrong nor impulsive. But then she didna have yer fire or fierce spirit, either. Ye're a different woman, to be sure, but as perfect a mate for the Campbell as they come. So, dinna concern yerself with another woman's ghost. The young lord loves ye for yer own self. There's naught more that matters."

Anne sighed. "He hasn't said he loves me, Agnes. His affection for me runs no deeper than that o' the flesh. Not that I'm complaining," she hastened to add. "What he does give me is wonderful. But I don't know if he'll ever love me. I think that emotion may have died with his first wife."

"And I say ye are mistaken, lassie. What the young lord truly feels and what he recognizes can be two different things. I have known him since he was a lad, and I tell ye true. He is happier now, even in the midst o' all these troubles, than he has been since the Lady Anne died. He loves ye, and no mistake. He'll see it soon enough."

At Agnes's words, a fierce joy leaped within Anne. Her eyes glowed with a warm, sweet fire.

"I pray your words come to pass," she murmured. "But, in the meanwhile, I can't stand idly by and allow others to control our lives. I must do all within my power to help Niall. And the one thing more that needs tending to is my herb garden"

Squaring her slender shoulders, Anne headed for the door in a determined flurry of skirt and petticoats. Agnes stood there, staring after her, a fistful of sweet woodruff still clenched in her hand.

Nelly saw Anne leave. A pleased smile twisted the corners of her darkly pretty face. The MacGregor wench was naively unaware that her every movement was being watched. Watched, weighed, and reported back to Nelly's master. He'd paid her well, in and out of bed, to spy on Anne. And it had been money easily earned. As easy as was the theft of the foxglove leaves from the chest in her bedchamber.

Keeping to the shadows as best she could, Nelly followed Anne and the stable man out of the castle and into the forest, until she was certain of the other woman's eventual destination. *The fool*, Nelly thought as she slipped away as unnoticed as she'd come. The wench assumed everyone was unaware of that herb garden of hers.

Well, it had served her master's purpose to let

her think so up until this moment. But when Nelly supplied him with the news Anne was there now, mayhap this time it could finally be used to her downfall. Mayhap she could at last convince her master to kill the MacGregor wench. A crossbow's quarrel straight through her heart would leave no witness or suspect.

Then Nelly could devote all her efforts to comforting the bereaved clan chief. Her smile widened. She could almost feel Niall's large, hard-muscled body shuddering atop hers, hear his cry of passion as he found his release. Nelly's pace quickened. *That* particular errand of mercy would be very, very sweet indeed!

Niall's first order of the day was to find Iain. Though he loathed attempting to apologize a second time, he had promised Anne and would see it through. Summoning up the right amount of enthusiasm would be another matter. Not that he wasn't sincerely grateful to Iain for rescuing Anne from Malcolm's foul clutches. His uncle would be seen to later and receive a stern warning, with dire consequences if it happened again.

But to feel any warmth for Iain or dare lower his guard was out of the question. Though Niall knew it was foolhardy to suspect his cousin to the exclusion of all others, it still served him better to have Iain gone from Kilchurn. If nothing else, he didn't need the added distraction of Iain panting after Anne.

Aye, it was far wiser to send him away, Niall resolved. What went against his grain was having to thank his cousin in one breath then in the next order him back to Balloch Castle. Unintended or not, of late he was beginning to feel the fool in nearly all his interactions with his family.

Frustration roiled within him as he strode across

the Great Hall. A fool indeed . . . And he had the traitor to thank for that.

Iain was in the library, according to a passing servant Niall questioned. He took the steps to the first landing in several quick strides, then stalked down the hall.

The blond man glanced over his shoulder when Niall entered the room. A wary look narrowed his deep blue eyes. He replaced a leather-bound volume on the shelf, then turned to meet him.

Niall inhaled a steadying breath and approached his cousin. "My gratitude to you yestereve was lacking. I truly thank you for helping Anne."

"She's in grave danger here," Iain said flatly, dispensing with the amenities. "You should let her go. Now, before 'tis too late."

Niall's features hardened into a mask of cynical incredulity. "And who are you to tell me what to do with her? If you recall, *I* am the one handfasted to Anne, not you!"

"Yet it seems I am the one most concerned about her welfare," Iain shot back. "If you weren't so stubborn, you might see that. She isn't some prize to be held, no matter the cost. Anne is a living, breathing woman with a life to lose."

"And you doubt my ability to keep her safe?"

Iain saw the anger darken Niall's eyes. He knew he trod on dangerous ground. For Anne's sake, though, Niall must be made to face the reality of her danger.

"You saw how difficult 'twas to win the council over, how many were willing, nay, eager, to attack you. And the strongest argument o' all was the allegation o' Anne's witchcraft. Those aren't accusations you can choose or not choose to deal with in your woman, like infidelity or barrenness. If she's convicted, she's in violation o' the law—and the punishment is a horrible, painful death!"

"I don't need you telling me the obvious," Niall gritted. "I told you. I'll take care o' her!"

"And if you fail, what then, Niall?"

"It won't happen!"

Iain took a step closer and gazed into Niall's eyes. "If it does, I swear I'll kill you."

Niall returned the look of deadly earnestness. "You'll never have that opportunity. I'll be dead before I let anything happen to her."

His cousin gave a mocking laugh. "Indeed, you might be, but then what will become o' Anne, alone, at the mercy o' her enemies?" He gripped Niall's arm. "Send her away before that happens, Niall. Swear to me you'll at least do that!"

Hesitation flickered in Niall's eyes. What if Iain's dire predictions came to pass? If the traitor found some way to kill him, what *would* become of Anne?

Duncan would be chief and Duncan, at the very least, disliked Anne. Would the fanatical ravings of his half brother, Malcolm, influence Duncan against her? And if Hugh was brought back from exile. . . .

Of all his family, Iain was the only one who seemed truly to care for Anne. Niall knew that with a sudden certainty that startled him. Cared for her above and beyond whatever use he might have for her in his role as traitor. If something happened to him, Anne would be safe with Iain.

But even to consider the thought of giving Anne over to him! Niall knew Anne cared for Iain, if only in a sisterly fashion. But that could change, given time and his absence.

Iain was a devastatingly handsome and charming man. The trail of broken hearts, however unintentional, his blond cousin always left in his wake was ample testimony to that. Aye, Anne could well come to love Iain. But to imagine her with another, whispering her love as she lay naked in his arms . . . Lord, it was like a knife gutting his insides!

Yet the time might well come when he'd have to let her go. To save her life, he'd do anything, even if it meant giving her up. But that time had yet to arrive, Niall reminded himself, and he'd not give Iain the pleasure or any premature advantage over him by admitting that possibility.

He was now the Campbell. Now was not the time to show weakness or hesitation. Not to Iain, or anyone!

Niall shook his head, a fierce, shuttered look settling over his features. "I won't swear that or anything to you, cousin. Though your concern for Anne is commendable, if concern is truly what 'tis, it changes naught. She is mine, and mine she will remain."

"And that is all you have to say? All you will do?"

"Aye, for the time being."

"You're a fool, Niall Campbell!"

Niall took a step forward. "Nay, Iain," he said softly, a savage light in his eyes. "You're the fool, for you've finally gone too far. Get you to Balloch Castle this very day or I'll send you to the dungeon."

Iain opened his mouth to challenge Niall, then thought better of it. If he were drawn into a battle with the Campbell, a battle he might well lose even if it were but of words, Anne would ultimately be the one to suffer. And, in the end, this was all about her welfare.

Better to make a strategic retreat, lull Niall into a false sense of victory. It was a bitter pill to swallow, backing down from a man he felt the match of, but Iain knew where his priorities lay. Anne's life was of more import than his pride.

Free, he could still be of use to her. Clapped in chains in Kilchurn's dungeon, he was helpless. Iain forced a grim smile to his face. " 'Twill be as you say, m'lord," he said, bowing low. "This very day I leave for Balloch Castle."

Chapter Fifteen

Niall's long legs quickly carried him through the corridors to Anne's bedchamber, his mood far from pleasant. Iain was right. He *should* send Anne away before it was too late. But how could he do so when he'd just come to know her, and the knowing was so achingly, so shatteringly, sweet? Anne fascinated and challenged him from her gentle goodness to her fiery temper. And the moments they shared in bed. . .

At the recollection of Anne's uninhibited response, Niall's breathing quickened. His loins grew heavy. Lord, but she was so ardent, so hotly satisfying! The thought of letting her go was almost more than he could bear.

He needed her. Only she could drive away the dark loneliness that had so long enshrouded his heart. Only she fulfilled him, like no other woman he'd ever known. He couldn't, wouldn't, let her go.

They would work everything out. Niall had to believe that. Any other contemplation stirred anew the niggling fear that his own needs might be of more import than Anne's safety. The time might come when he'd be forced to face it, but not now. Now, there was still hope.

Her bedchamber was empty save for Agnes, tidying the fresh rushes on the floor. Niall went to her.

"Where's the Lady Anne?"

Agnes whirled around. Should she tell him where her lady had gone? Informing the Campbell of Anne's secret herb garden might stir once again the conflict between them. Well aware their relationship was just beginning to flower, Agnes was loathe to damage it.

"S–she is seeing to some personal business, m'lord," the old maidservant stammered.

Niall's eyes narrowed. "And, pray," he drawled, "what is this personal business you seem so hesitant to reveal? Your loyalty is first to me, Agnes, then to your mistress. I want a full accounting o' where she's gone."

"Aye, m'lord." Agnes curtsied her obeisance. "She has an herb garden in the forest that she slips away to tend whenever she can."

Niall's features tightened with disapproval. Agnes quickly attempted to explain. "I saw no harm in it, for the garden gave her pleasure. She never used any o' the herbs for healing, only dried and stored them in that chest." She gestured to the carved box standing near Anne's bed.

With a low growl, Niall strode to the chest and flung back its lid. " 'Tis empty. Where are these herbs you speak o', woman?"

"Only this morn she tossed them all down the privy. I think she feared them being used against her, o' their existence causing you harm. 'Twas a great sacrifice on her part, I think, m'lord."

"*I have a calling to heal . . . 'Tis sacred to me.*"

Anne's words that night he'd first taken her to see

his father came back to haunt him. She'd given up so much, Niall thought with a surge of remorse. So much, and now even to turn from all thought of healing. . . .

Niall squared his shoulders. There was nothing that mattered more than Anne's safety.

He hurried to his own bedchamber and returned wi"Lead me to her, Agnes. Now!"

Agnes nervously bobbed another curtsy. "Aye, m'lord."

It wasn't supposed to be this hard, Anne thought miserably, the tears, despite Angus's discreet presence nearby in the trees, unashamedly streaming down her face. She dug up yet another feverfew plant, then tore it into tiny pieces before reburying it beneath the earth. Even dumping the jars hadn't tugged at her heart like this.

But these were living things, full of promise, brimming with hope. Hope for the future of her healing—and with their destruction that hope died. But she had to do it. Their death ensured the destruction of all evidence against her. And for Niall, she'd do even that.

A weak breeze stirred through the quiet forest, affording a brief respite from the unusually warm summer day. Anne paused in her vigorous efforts, lifting her damp, heavy mass of hair from the back of her neck. Sadly, she surveyed her garden.

Only half a row remained and all the plants would be gone, torn to shreds and buried beneath the dirt. In but a few weeks' time, the weeds and wild grasses would have taken hold. Soon there'd be no sign a garden had once grown here. Anne wondered if her life at Kilchurn would one day matter as little. No impression, no imprint on anyone.

This time the tears were of self-pity, but Anne quickly wiped them away. Her life at Kilchurn *had* mattered, had made an impression! There was her friendship with Iain, with Ena and Agnes, all friends strong and true. There were glimmers of acceptance from some of the other castle folk as well.

Maudie and Angus had definitely warmed to her after Anne's treatment of little Davie's burnt hand. And several of the serving maids had come to her for advice on feminine ailments, advice that required but a few quick words that any lady of the castle would be able to give. She had been more than happy to assist them, without a qualm that she was going against her promise to Niall.

Aye, Anne consoled herself, Campbell acceptance was indeed slow in coming, but coming it was. All it would take was time. In the meanwhile, she would forge ahead and face what life held bravely with Niall at her side. Her love for him was that deep, that sure.

Mayhap the wind rustling through the trees covered the sound of their approach, or mayhap it was her self-absorbed thoughts, but Anne suddenly found Niall and Agnes standing before her. She climbed to her feet, the trowel still clasped in her hand.

"N–Niall, Agnes," she breathed, her silver eyes swinging from one to the other. "I—"

"Why are you here?" he demanded, anger darkening his eyes. "Have I not told you time and again that 'tis dangerous for you to be alone outside the castle?"

He paused, suddenly aware of his stable man's presence and that he was reprimanding her in front of the servants. "Go, Agnes, Angus," he growled, motioning them away. "Return to the castle."

The old maidservant glanced from her master to mistress, then hurried off with Angus.

Niall waited until the servants were out of earshot. "Well, madam. Why are you here?"

A variety of responses swept through Anne's head, but she decided the flat truth was the best. "I felt the need to visit this garden one final time and destroy the last o' the evidence against me."

"Evidence?" Niall's brow furrowed in puzzlement. "Explain yourself. You speak in riddles."

"Evidence o' my healing," Anne patiently began again. She inhaled a deep breath, then hurried on, "I was there, behind a secret door, when you met with your council. I heard all the accusations brought against me to discredit your claim to the chieftainship. I wouldn't have my conduct used against you again."

"So you disposed o' all your herbal medicines and are now destroying your garden." A look of shattering tenderness flared in his eyes. "Truly, lass, you sacrifice too much for me."

The trowel dropped from Anne's hand. With a cry, she ran to him. They clung to each other for a long, heated moment, the passion building.

Then Anne lifted her eyes, a soft smile curving her lips. "Do you know how much I love you?"

With a wild groan, Niall's mouth came down on hers in rapacious hunger, devouring her joyous offering, demanding more. His tongue plunged into her mouth in fierce possession, then retreated to plunge again and again. Anne arched toward him.

His hands were crazed, moving down her back, massaging her, molding her tighter and tighter to his hard length. The bulging evidence of his arousal pressed, hot and heavy, against her belly. Niall moaned aloud when her fingers traveled down his body to caress him.

"Och, lass!" he cried. "Touch me. Hold me."

"Aye, my love," Anne breathed, her voice a husky whisper. "That I will. Only tell me what you wish, and I will give it to you."

Niall's eyes clenched shut. For a moment, he threw back his head, surrendering to the exquisite pleasure of her touch. Then, with tremendous effort, he straightened. He captured her hand and moved it away.

Anne dragged her passion-heated gaze to his. "What is it, Niall?"

His low, throaty chuckle echoed in the forest stillness. "Naught. I but need a moment o' control to tell you what I wish."

"And what is that?"

"A bairn. An heir." He stroked her cheek. "Yet though I desire that greatly, some part o' me fears it as well. I don't want to lose you in childbirth."

"And won't that childbirth happen one way or another if we continue the frequency and passion o' our couplings?" Anne asked with a smile. "Don't worry yourself. I am strong and healthy. And," she said, her face softening with a gentle, loving look, "I would sooner have a few months in your arms, even if it killed me, than a lifetime without you."

Niall's arms tightened around her. "Don't say that! Don't ever speak o' dying! I fear for your safety enough as 'tis." His mouth lowered to the fragrant tumble of her hair. "Even now, I wonder if my selfishness in keeping you here will be your death. I should send you away before 'tis too late!"

Anne's arms entwined about Niall's neck. She clung to him fiercely, as if to prevent that terrible thought from becoming reality. "Nay. I beg o' you, nay. Let me stay, let me fight by your side. We are not beaten, though our enemies are many. I'm not afraid. If the time comes when I fear for *your* life because o' me, then I will leave and willingly. But not before. I won't desert you!"

"Och, Annie," Niall groaned. "I don't want you to go. I need you. But—"

She pressed a gentle finger to his lips. "No more, my love. The time isn't right to speak further o' this. God willing, 'twill never be right." Her lips curved in a seductive smile. "Besides, I much prefer to speak o' your wish to make a child. This forest seems a most pleasant place to do so."

The rigidness eased from Niall's big body. He laughed. "Och, and does it now, lass?"

Anne's hands moved to the belt that held his plaid in place. "Aye. We can spread out your plaid here beneath the trees and have plenty to lie upon as well as cover us. 'Tis a fine thought. Don't you agree—" She stopped, overcome with a feeling of coldness, of lurking evil. It struck her so forcibly Anne knew it for what it was. Her hands tightened on Niall's belt.

He noted the change, the shudder that wracked her slender frame. He took her by the arms. "What is it, lass? What frightens you so?"

Anne gazed up with fear-widened eyes. "Someone is here . . . watches us," she whispered.

Niall stiffened. "Where? Do you see him?"

She shook her head. "Nay, but I know it all the same. I have felt it before. We're in danger."

"Stay behind me. If we are set upon, flee to the castle."

"But I can't—"

"I have my sword," he rasped in her ear. "I can hold them off until you send help. Now, no more o' it!"

Niall turned slowly, casually. Taking Anne by the hand, he began to lead her across the forest glade toward the castle. All the while, he scanned the area for a sign of an intruder. Despite his vigilance, the warning came too late.

A movement, a flash of something metallic, in the bushes off to his left caught Niall's eye. He lunged to cover Anne. A crossbow quarrel plunged into his chest.

"Niall!"

"Stay back!" he cried, sinking to his knees. "Behind me!"

"Nay!"

Anne gripped his short-sword and wrenched it free. Evading Niall's attempt to stop her, she ran toward the spot where the quarrel had flown, the sword raised high.

Her heart was in her throat, knowing full well another crossbow bolt could come flying toward her at any moment. Her only hope was to take the offensive and pray their attacker was a coward, for to cower beside Niall could well be the death of them both. Many a Scotswoman, and she included, had been schooled in the defensive use of the short-sword. She only prayed their mysterious intruder would not choose to test her on it.

A glimpse of tartan, Campbell colors, was all Anne caught of the disappearing attacker. His plaid was pulled up to cover his head so she saw nothing but a flash of bare, masculine legs and a body, bulked beyond recognition from behind by the belted plaid.

Anne halted and ran back to Niall. He was still kneeling on the ground, both hands about the quarrel's base where it protruded from his chest. His breathing was ragged, his teeth clenched. Before she could reach him, he tore out the crossbow bolt.

With a low groan, he fell, the quarrel clenched in his hand. Anne ran to Niall's side, flinging herself down beside him. She reached beneath her skirt to tear loose a large wad of petticoat. Gently, she turned Niall over and cradled his head in her lap.

Anne opened his shirt to examine the wound. It was high and far out on his left shoulder. She breathed a sigh of relief. It had missed his lung.

From the trajectory of the quarrel and Niall's position, just before he'd lunged to cover her, Anne knew the quarrel had been aimed straight for his heart.

Was it the work of the traitor, some disgruntled clansman or, horror of horrors, one of her own people in Campbell disguise, seeking revenge for the land grant?

She quashed the speculations and shoved her petticoat inside his shirt to cover Niall's wound.

"Well, lass. Will I live?"

At the amusement in Niall's deep voice, Anne jerked her gaze up to his face. He was pale, his brow damp with moisture, but a grin quirked his full, firm lips. She forced a trembling smile.

"Aye, m'lord. 'Twould take more than a puny quarrel to fell a big lout such as you."

He chuckled and the movement brought a grimace of pain. "There you go again, making me laugh when I'm wounded. You're a heartless wench, and no mistake."

"I'll show you how heartless I can be, when I get you back to the castle. Your wound will need cauterizing and I must send for Ena. I have no more salves or medicines, you know."

A large hand clasped her arm. "Nay, lass. I'll allow Ena's ministrations because she is accepted by the clan, but not yours. And even hers I will accept little o', for I must appear to respect the healer sanctioned by the Kirk. And that is Murdoch, our castle physician. I would wish it otherwise, for I trust your ministrations much more than his, but 'tis for your own protection. If something happened, if the wound festered and I died, I wouldn't have you blamed."

"But he'll hurt you," Anne protested. "Mayhap try to purge or bleed you, as if those treatments would aid in the healing o' a wound. How can you expect me to stand by and watch that old fool—"

His grasp tightened, cutting off her protest. "Because I ask it, Annie lass. You said you want to stay with me, to fight our enemies. Well, our battle must be waged in many ways and on many fronts. Some things must be compromised if we're to prevail. This is one such compromise. I am willing to make it."

"But to ask me watch you needlessly suffer!" Tears choked her voice.

" 'Tis the way o' war," he replied softly. "Haven't you the courage for it?"

She studied him for a long moment. "I know not the depth o' my courage, but my love for you is more than sufficient to meet the task. Since you ask it, I'll stand back and watch that simpleton o' a physician treat you. But hear me well, Niall Campbell. If ever the time comes when your life's in danger because o' his ministrations, I will step in to save you. Naught you can ever say or do will keep me from that."

Something flared in the depths of his rich brown eyes. "Then let us pray that day never comes, sweet lass, for I fear it could well mean your life."

Hard, angry eyes watched as Niall, supported by two clansmen, was assisted back into Kilchurn. Anne followed close behind, surrounded by an armed escort of six more men. The eyes, shining with a malevolent light, turned from the sight. Hands clenched knuckle-white at his sides.

Damn the wench to hell! the man cursed beneath his breath. If not for her quick response with the short-sword, he'd have had the time to reload the crossbow and finish off Niall. Taking care of her afterwards would have been easily seen to. But he'd dared not linger to fight off some crazed female with only his dirk and a crossbow for defense. Damn her anyway!

He'd meant to kill her after Nelly had hurried to inform him of Anne's presence in the forest. But when he'd seen Niall there and heard him ask her for a child something had snapped. The memory of another time, another childbirth that had ended to his advantage, came to mind. And now, once again, his claim to the chieftainship was threatened from a similar quarter. Time was running out.

He didn't want peace between Clan Campbell and MacGregor. He didn't want a marriage alliance, an alliance that seemed to be rapidly becoming a reality, if Niall and Anne's passionate response to each other in the forest was any indication. Niall's death was the only solution. The witch would be helpless with him gone and easily seen to.

Things had taken a complicated turn with her arrival at Kilchurn. Plans, so carefully made, were suddenly going awry. It was time to take a more subtle yet even deadlier bent.

A cruel smile twisted the man's lips. Aye, it was indeed time to take a firmer hold on the situation. It was time to use the foxglove. . . .

Anne stayed out of Niall's bedchamber whenever the physician was present, fearing she'd lose control if the man attempted some ignorant treatment that did little but hurt Niall. She was grateful for Ena's presence, for the wiry little physician seemed to respect her advice. Anne only hoped her old friend could successfully temper the man's more outlandish treatments.

Niall said little about what went on during the physician's visits and, though he appeared pale and exhausted afterwards, his wound still managed to mend. But only thanks to Ena's healing salves, Anne thought angrily as she battled to maintain hold of her anger and frustration. Afterwards, she'd spend many hours in Niall's room, reading to him, talking with him, holding his hand while he slept.

At Niall's insistence, Anne was never alone with him, a trusted servant always in attendance. There'd be no cause at a future date, he explained, ever to say she'd slipped him a potion or poison if something untoward should happen. His concern for her worried Anne. Was he in more danger than he'd willingly admit, to now suspect attempts on his life from within his own castle?

Surreptitiously, Anne began to watch the preparation of Niall's food and drink. There seemed nothing out of the ordinary in the kitchen. And Nelly always brought him his meals. Knowing the maidservant's feelings for Niall, Anne doubted the woman would do anything to harm him. She wouldn't be surprised if Nelly attempted to poison *her* food—that would eliminate a rival—but Niall was another matter altogether.

By the third day of his confinement, Niall was climbing the walls from boredom. Against his physician's advice and Anne's concerns, he rose and dressed. Staring down at her from his imposing height, he laughed at her protestations.

"I feel quite well," Niall chuckled maddeningly. "All I want is a short walk in the gardens. 'Twillna require the use o' my arm, and I swear to you, my legs are quite up to the task." He encircled her shoulders with his good arm. "But you may accompany me, to assure my compliance."

Anne stared up into his handsome face. Her heart melted at his boyishly compelling smile. "Och, have it your way." She finally sighed. "You always were a pigheaded dolt!"

"Sweet lass." He grinned down at her. "It warms my heart to hear such words o' endearment fall from your lips. Pray, what else is in that gentle, loving mind o' yours?"

"You're a rogue and a knave, Niall Campbell," she declared in exasperation, "and well you know it!"

"But you'll come with me to the garden?"

"Aye."

A warm, lazy smile teased his lips. "Good."

Kilchurn's gardens were spacious and well-tended. The air was heavily scented with lavender, blooming from the many bushes scattered throughout the walled enclosure. Bright slashes of red and pink roses brightened the area, as did rhododendrons and fuchsias. It was a lovely, peaceful place. As Anne walked along with Niall, she was content.

A girlish giggle from the rose bower, followed by a low male voice, was the first hint they weren't alone in the garden. Niall halted. A dark frown marred his brow.

"Not a word, lass," he whispered. "I've a suspicion my sister is up to no good, and I can well guess who with."

He left her standing there and made his stealthy way to the bower. What Niall saw stirred his blood to a boil. Caitlin and Rory sat on a stone bench, locked in a heated embrace. Rory's hands roved over his sister's slender form, barely pausing at one delectable spot before moving on to another, as if he didn't know where to alight or what to do.

Caitlin, however, seemed well aware what to do. Her hands were tightly entwined about Rory's neck, pulling him against her as they awkwardly but determinedly kissed. Watching the scene of youthful passion, Niall's fists clenched at his sides. Lord, didn't he have enough problems without worrying how much longer his headstrong, highly emotional sister would keep her virginity?

"That's enough, Caitlin," Niall quietly ground out the words.

With a gasp, his sister jumped away from Rory. The lad stared up at Niall, transfixed with terror while Caitlin frantically smoothed her gown and mussed hair. There was nothing she could do, however, about the becoming flush to her face, or her kiss-swollen lips.

"H—how dare you spy upon us?" she demanded, her surprise causing her to take the offense. "You could at least have made some noise to give us a decent interval to compose ourselves!"

Niall cocked a sardonic brow. "Och, and is that the way o' it? And should I have knocked first, too?" His expression hardened with a rare, glacial anger. "Nay, lass," he growled. "You were raised better than this. If I hadn't happened upon you, would he have soon been between your legs, your maidenhood gone? Then who would have you as wife?"

Caitlin sprang to her feet. "How *dare* you speak to me like that? Och, you are a crude, churlish knave to shame me so! And I care not for my maidenhood! 'Tis Rory I love. I'd give it to him gladly!"

Niall's hand shot out to grab his sister's arm and jerk her to him. "Well, since I am now responsible for your conduct and marriageable state, and I don't wish to see you wed to Rory MacArthur, 'tis past time I took firmer measures."

He spared a brief, withering glance for the trembling young man who stood there, rooted to the spot. "Get out o' my sight and my castle. And don't come back!"

Rory fled, almost colliding with Anne who had determined from the tone of the voices emanating from the bower that it was time she get involved. She paused to stare after the lad's rapidly retreating form, then once more gathered her skirts and forged on. The deadly grimness to Niall's voice filled her with rising apprehension.

"He isn't worthy o' you," Niall was saying in a low, furious voice. "Did you hear him come to your defense, or stand up to me for your sake?" He gave her a small shake. "Well, did you?"

Caitlin's mouth opened, then closed, her eyes filling with tears.

"He's but a lad," Anne interjected. "For all his size,

he was no match for you."

Niall wheeled about, a thunderous look in his eyes. "And will you, too, defend the little beggar? I won't have it, Anne!"

She noted Caitlin's startled glance, swinging from her to her brother. In a flash of insight, Anne realized the only way to defuse the situation before Niall in his anger and pent-up frustration took it out on Caitlin was to turn it upon herself. Then, if she could manage to get the girl safely away. . . .

Later, when Niall was back in control, he could see to some fairer punishment for his sister. But not now. Now, all he would succeed in doing was alienating her.

Though she was loathe to anger Niall, Anne knew it was the best of all options. She squared her shoulders and defiantly lifted her chin. "You won't have it, you say?" she deliberately mocked him. "And what would you have me do? Cower in some corner each time I see you about to make a fool o' yourself?"

His features hardened in cold displeasure. "A fool, am I? There's not a man alive I'll let call me that. Do you imagine because you're a woman you can safely do so?"

"Safe or not," Anne shot back at him, "I'll do so, and gladly, if I think I'm right."

She deliberately turned from Niall to Caitlin. "Go to your bedchamber, lass. 'Tisn't fitting you should see your elders argue."

"Aye!" Niall snapped, glancing at his sister as if just remembering she was still standing there. "I'll see to you later."

Caitlin fled without a moment's hesitation, wisely realizing this was not the time to attempt further defense.

They watched her go, then Niall rounded on Anne. "What do you have to say for yourself, madam?"

She had never heard him use quite that silky, dangerous tone before. Anne shuddered. What if she'd made him so angry he never forgave her? What if he turned his back on her forever?

Anne flung the foolish thought aside. Niall was proud, but he was also intelligent. He could be brought to see reason.

"I was wrong to call you a fool, m'lord," she began, honest remorse shining in her silver eyes. "I beg pardon. 'Twas only a ploy to divert your anger from Caitlin."

He subjected her to a cool appraisal, the taut look of rage already ebbing from his features. "And you thought to turn it upon yourself, did you?"

"Aye."

"You risked much. I won't be taunted nor ridiculed before anyone."

Anne's head lowered. "I am sorry, m'lord. Mayhap I chose poorly, but 'twas the best I could think o'."

A long finger crooked beneath her chin to raise it. "Next time," he said sternly, "ask to speak to me in private. If you don't abuse that privilege, I'll know 'tis significant when you use it. Agreed?"

She smiled, relief flooding her. "Agreed."

Niall took her by the elbow. "Come, lady."

He led her into the bower, indicating she sit upon the stone bench. With a bone-weary sigh, he lowered himself beside her.

"I fear my strength wasn't adequate for the emotions o' the past few moments," he said, his face suddenly drawn and haggard. "I have the strangest sense o' fatigue and my muscles feel so weak."

Alarm filled Anne. She slid close, slipping her arm about Niall's waist to steady him.

"Mayhap your wound has broken open. Should I send for help to get you back to your chamber?"

"Nay. Allow me a few minutes more and I will make it under my own power. Though I may have erred in leaving my bed too soon, I'll never admit it to any, save you." He lifted a halting hand to rub his eyes. "Och, but my head aches, and I can't see too clearly."

"How long have you felt this way?"

Niall shrugged. "Off and on for the past two days.

"Then you lied earlier when you said you felt well."

He gave her a mock scowl. "Do you realize that in the span of but a few minutes you've called me both a fool and a liar? What am I to do with you?"

She returned his glare with a resolute one of her own. "Mayhap let yourself heal by staying abed as you should?"

"Aye, mayhap you're right." He smiled tiredly. "I thought my weakness was merely the effects o' my wound. Yet I am healing and these feelings worsen. Don't worry yourself, lass," he said, noting Anne's look of concern. " 'Tis most likely the result o' some spoiled food. It has happened before. I'll get over it."

"Aye, m'lord," Anne murmured. "You're a strong, healthy man. 'Tis certain you will."

Chapter Sixteen

Anne firmly tucked the comforter around Niall. "There," she scolded, "now stay abed! Though your wound looks well, something has weakened you."

He captured her hand before she could move away. "Why not climb in here with me? 'Twould do much to keep me abed."

She shook her head at the suggestive gleam in his eyes. "Och, and aren't you the one who insisted on my never being alone with you? Would you now have Agnes privy to our couplings?"

"You're a hardhearted lass, Anne MacGregor." Niall laughed. "I'll be happy to be well again, so we'll have no further need of a chaperone."

"And I, too, my love." She leaned over to give him a tender kiss. "'Tis most surprising how fiercely I miss our lovemaking. I can never seem to get enough of your magnificent body."

A hot light flared in Niall's eyes. "Or I yours, Annie lass." He dragged in a deep breath. "But, for all my fine words, I wouldn't be up to the task. 'Tis a hard thing when your gut feels sick like mine does. I fear I have no appetite for anything, food or otherwise."

Anne touched his forehead with the back of her hand. She frowned. "Strange, but you have no fever."

" 'Tis spoiled food, as I said before. There isn't always fever with that."

"Mayhap."

Niall smiled at the doubt in Anne's voice. "There's naught to be done but endure. And I'd prefer to endure it in silence rather than tell the physician. Murdoch would only make things worse."

"Aye"—Anne grinned wryly,—"that he would." Her expression grew solemn. "There's something we must talk about, something we never finished in the garden."

"Caitlin?"

Anne nodded. "Would you accept my assistance? This might be better dealt with woman to woman."

"Your help would be greatly appreciated, lass. I swear I can't seem to influence my sister anymore. She used to hang on my every word, scurry to do my every bidding. But no more." He shook his head, confusion in his eyes. "Truly, I don't know what to think or how to approach her."

"She's a young woman now. Though she loves you still, other men will soon claim the special place that before she filled with a sisterly love. And she is proud, as proud as you. You must begin to treat her as the woman she is."

"But she is barely fourteen!"

"Och, Niall," Anne chided gently. "And how many lasses are wed by that age? She is all but grown up."

"Mayhap," he admitted, his gaze lowering in frowning consideration, "but I can't say I like it. She was less a problem as a child."

"Grown women tend to be more o' a challenge— to grown men."

He glanced up, subjecting her to an amused scrutiny. "Och, and well I know that, lass. You've been a handful since the first moment I saw you."

"As well I will be to our dying days, m'lord."

A low chuckle rumbled in Niall's chest. "I wouldn't have it any other way."

Their eyes met and something hot and sweet flowed between them. Anne felt vibrantly alive. Niall's gaze, as it slid down her body, ignited a melting warmth that set her afire. She swallowed hard, knowing she must get away from him before she was overcome with desire.

"By your leave," she murmured, freeing her hand from his firm clasp, "I'd like to visit your sister. She must be worried."

Niall's expression darkened. "She needs to stew a bit. The lass defied me, not to mention risked a scandal because o' her behavior. I meant what I said before. She won't marry Rory MacArthur. I don't like the lad."

"Well, you all but banished him from Kilchurn. There should be little problem where he's concerned for a time. You must speak with her when you are feeling better—as one adult to another. You might be surprised to find she'll then respond to you as an adult."

"Mayhap. But I've still a mind to send her to Edinburgh," he growled. "I threaten her with it constantly o' late, then back down. She's most likely laughing at me for my weakness in that."

"You must do what is fair, no matter the opinions o' others. Your compassion to your sister should not be viewed as a weakness. She's confused and lost right now, bewildered by her budding emotions and physical needs, hurting still from the loss o' her father. You've been more than patient with me, who have defied you far more than Caitlin has ever done. Can't you spare the same patience for your sister?"

Niall sighed. "Go to her, Anne. Talk with her. I'll defer to your judgement in her punishment, but punishment o' some kind she must have. Agreed?"

A slow, tender movement of her delicately sculpted mouth lit Anne's features. "Agreed."

Reluctantly, she rose from the bed and left the room. As Anne walked through the long stone corridor to Caitlin's room, she considered and discarded several ways to approach the girl. A niggling worry ate at the confidence she had shown Niall just minutes before. What if Caitlin refused to talk with her or, worse yet, ridiculed the guidance she'd try to offer? Niall's anger, when he learned of it, would be more terrible than before.

Well, Anne thought as she raised her fist to knock upon Caitlin's door, there was nothing to be done about it. All she could do was try. And try she would, to her very best efforts. In the end, it was all for Niall.

A young serving maid answered the door.

"Jane, 'tisn't it?" Anne asked. "Is your mistress in?"

Jane bobbed a little curtsy. "Aye, ma'am. But she says she isna receiving—"

"Who is it, Jane?" a tear-choked voice interrupted her.

The maid swung back the door to reveal Anne. Caitlin stared at her, a myriad of emotions playing across her expressive face. Then she sighed. "Bid her come in. And you may leave, Jane."

"Aye, mistress." The girl slipped past Anne and closed the door behind her.

Squaring her shoulders, Anne walked to where Caitlin sat on a padded bench by the window. She gestured toward the seat. "May I sit with you?"

The girl's glance moved to gaze out the stone-cut window. "Aye," she murmured dejectedly. "Do what you wish."

Anne settled herself beside Niall's sister. For several minutes neither spoke, Caitlin staring out the window, Anne studying her. Finally, the girl wiped her tears away.

Turquoise eyes proudly met Anne's. "I thank you for your efforts on my behalf in the garden. At first, I was confused as to what was happening between you and my brother. But later, when I'd a time to ponder it all, I realized you deliberately picked a fight with him to divert his anger from me. 'Twas a kind thing to do."

Anne returned her gaze.

"Thinking back," the girl continued, "you've never once been less than kind, turning aside all my rudeness with gentle words and offers o' friendship. I've been a stupid, selfish child."

"There was something gnawing at you from the beginning," Anne said. "Something that affected your acceptance o' me. What was it, Caitlin?"

Niall's sister's eyes widened in surprise. " 'Twas so evident, was it? 'Twas but a foolish dream, but I'll tell you nonetheless. Rory's older sister, Sybil, was greatly desirous o' a marriage to Niall. Rory promised it would assure *our* eventual marriage, if our two clans joined in such a manner. I had hopes Niall might well consider Sybil, once his time o' mourning was done. Then you came to Kilchurn."

" 'Tis only a handfasting, Caitlin. A trial marriage that could well end in a year."

Caitlin smiled. "I saw how my brother looked at you, even from the start. I knew there was no hope for Sybil after that. And even you must now realize he loves you."

Anne flushed. "I know he cares for me, but he's made no offers o' marriage. Truly, I don't know how this handfasting will end."

"Well, I do," Caitlin said. "And I think I will like having you as a sister."

A lump rose in Anne's throat. "Will you now? Then we can be friends?"

The girl took Anne's hand and gave it an affectionate squeeze. "Aye, if you'll still have me." She paused to give a small, self-mocking laugh. "And if my brother doesn't yet banish me to Aunt Mathilda."

Anne smiled. "I think he can be made to see reason. He loves you, Caitlin. He's just sore beset o' late. Be patient with him."

"I–I'll try," the girl said, her eyes filling anew with tears, "but I loved Rory, and now Niall has sent him away, mayhap forever. Och, Anne, what shall I do?"

"Be patient with Niall and with yourself. If 'tis true love between you and Rory, 'twillna die. Even Niall will come to see that. He finds Rory too young to be a fit husband. But time may well alter that impression as well."

"But I will wither on the vine, waiting that long!" Caitlin wailed.

"It seems so, when you're but fourteen, but a woman must learn patience. 'Tis a trait sorely in need when dealing with men, even the man you love. Your time o' waiting won't be squandered if you spend it learning patience. And the eventual reward will be all the sweeter because o' it."

A joyous admiration flared in Caitlin's eyes. "Och, you are so wise. Would that I be, in the few years left until I reach your age."

Anne laughed, warmed by the girl's compliment. "You'll be wiser by far, and no mistake."

"Aye, if you teach me some o' your healing skills, that I will. As lady o' Rory's house, I'll need to know how to aid his people."

Anne's expression grew serious. "Mayhap in time, but not now. 'Twould be too dangerous."

Understanding flared in Caitlin's eyes. "Aye, that I know. But in time . . ."

"Aye." Anne smiled. "In time."

* * *

Niall felt no better upon Anne's return, but listening to her account of her visit with Caitlin filled him with pleasure. He clasped her hand, raising it to his lips to kiss it tenderly.

"You see, lass?" he asked in a husky voice. "We *will* prevail. Even now, you have yet another ally in Kilchurn. One by one we will wear them all down, show them the error of their ways."

"Aye, my love. That we will," she whispered, and watched as he lay back upon his pillow and quickly fell into a deep sleep.

Niall refused the evening meal, stating he had no appetite. Only with Anne's persistent coaxing did he finally take some stew. Then, despite her protestations that it wasn't proper, he insisted she climb into bed with him.

"I don't give a damn how it looks to Agnes," he growled in irritation. "I don't feel well and your presence gives me comfort."

There was nothing she could do or say after that, for Anne would never deny Niall. Her face stained crimson, she lay down next to him atop the comforter. He immediately took her into his arms, snuggled his head upon her breast, and fell asleep.

Late in the night, Niall's agitated movements woke Anne. He mumbled in his sleep, tossing and turning, until Anne was forced to take him into her arms to calm him. As she lay there, concern for Niall's strange illness grew with each passing moment. Gradually, she became aware of his heartbeat, thudding beneath her hand. It seemed slow, unnaturally so.

She lowered her ear to his chest. She'd lain upon him often enough after their lovemaking to know the normal pace of his powerful heart. It was indeed slower than usual.

The first tendril of real fear coiled in her stomach. This was no food poisoning or silent infection. Niall was drugged—and it was most likely the work of her stolen foxglove.

Anne slipped from beneath him, gently lying Niall down and pulling the comforter up to cover him. With her heart pounding, she sat on the edge of the bed and struggled to think clearly, to devise a plan. Niall had become sick in but the past three days, since he was wounded and brought to his bedchamber. He could have only ingested the potent leaves in either food or drink—or in medicine!

Could the castle physician be poisoning Niall? Anne leaped to her feet to pace the room. She knew the little man had made Niall drink a tonic everyday, supposedly to strengthen him and aid in his healing. Could that have been the source of the foxglove? But if so, why? What would have been the man's motives? Surely he was not the traitor.

Nay, he could not be the traitor, Anne told herself, but he might well be working *for* the traitor. But how was she to fight him, forbidden as she was to interfere with the man's treatment of Niall? Well, *she* couldn't . . . but Ena could.

Anne slipped out of Niall's bedchamber and into her own. From there she left. The keep was silent and deserted. None saw her sneak down to the storerooms, where she easily found the hidden tunnel that led to the secret passage out of the castle.

A half-hour later, she was beating on Ena's door. Finally, the old woman peered out. "What is it?" she croaked, her voice thick with sleep. "Is it a birthing, or someone—" She stopped, recognizing Anne. "Lass, what are ye doing here? 'Tis the middle o' the night!"

"Let me in, Ena."

The old healer quickly complied. "Well, lassie," she asked, once the door was shut behind them. "What is it? Is something wrong with the young lord?"

"Aye, Ena. I fear you left too soon. Niall is deathly ill."

"The wound festers?"

"Nay, 'tis more serious than that. Someone has fed him my foxglove."

" 'Tis worse than I feared," Ena muttered. "The young lord . . ."

"Help me, I beg o' you!" Desperation tinged Anne's voice. "His heart has slowed. He's sick, has no appetite, and is terribly weak. He may die!"

Ena took Anne's hand. "Aye, that he well may, if the source o' the drug isna halted. If he takes even one more dose . . ."

"I need you there to stop the physician from feeding him anymore o' his foul concoctions. He may be the one poisoning him!"

"Nay, 'tisn't possible." Ena firmly shook her head. "I've known Murdoch for years. He'd never intentionally harm a body."

"Then who, Ena? Please come back with me. Help me discover the source. Help me stop them!"

The old woman nodded. "Aye, lass. I'll come back. Give me but a moment to gather my herbs. Though nothing but time will ease the effects o' the fairy fingers, I have some potions that might help strengthen the young lord in his battle against it."

"Thank you, Ena." Anne breathed the words in a rush of gratitude. "Thank you with all my heart."

Ena smiled. "We healers must help each other."

The journey back to the castle was slower by necessity, Ena's arthritic limbs stiff in the dampness before dawn. They took the secret tunnel into the castle and were soon back in Niall's room. After a quick but thorough examination of Niall, Ena glanced up at Anne.

" 'Tis indeed the work o' the fairy fingers," she said grimly. "Bring me a cup and some water. I will make him a red clover tea. 'Tis the best o' blood cleansers and an excellent tonic."

She pulled an old pot out of her bag and filled it with the water Anne provided. A short time later, the simmering water was poured over the dried clover leaves to steep.

Finally, Ena motioned toward Niall. "Rouse him as best ye can and lift him. We must try to pour as much o' this down his throat as possible."

Anne slipped behind Niall to prop him up. She gently shook him. "Niall, Niall, my love. 'Tis time to wake. Ena is here. She has a tea for you to drink."

He groaned and mumbled something incoherent, then tried to snuggle into her and go back to sleep. Anne shook him harder, her voice rising. "Wake up, I say. 'Tis past time a lazy knave like you were up and about." She grasped his jaw with one hand and squeezed painfully.

His lids fluttered open then, a confused, startled look in his eyes. "L–lazy knave you s–say?" He glanced around, noting the still-dark windows. "W–why 'tisn't even dawn. You're a heartless lass, Anne MacGregor."

Ena shoved the cup to his lips. "Here, m'lord. Drink this. 'Twill strengthen you."

Niall drank deeply. Then, with an exhausted sigh, he fell back against Anne. The door to his bed-chamber flung open. Ena turned, the cup still in her hand.

In the doorway stood Duncan with Malcolm and several armed clansmen close behind. A scowl of rage twisted the tanist's face. "So," he snarled, "you sneak back here in the dark o' night to wreak your witch's magic on our chief."

Duncan strode into the room, waving the others in behind him. "Seize the old woman. You're all wit-ness to the fact she gave the Campbell some witch's potion."

"Nay," Anne cried, clinging tightly to Niall. " 'Twas only clover tea, a tonic to strengthen Niall. He's so sick, can't you see? Someone has poisoned him!"

"Aye, poisoned him." Malcolm grabbed Anne by the arm. "And mayhap you are as guilty as old Ena."

" 'Tisn't Anne's fault," Ena was quick to intervene. "The Campbell instructed her to obey me in my healing o' him. Ye all know that. She is innocent o' wrongdoing."

Dark eyes, shaded by bushy brows, glared down at her. "She's a witch as much as you. And soon enough you'll both burn!"

"Enough, Malcolm!" Duncan snapped. "The truth will soon come out in Ena's confession." He motioned to the armed clansmen. "Take the old woman to the dungeon. We'll see to her later."

"*Nay!*" Anne screamed.

She slid out from beneath Niall and flung herself at the guards. Duncan pulled her away, capturing her arms to pin them at her sides.

" 'Tisn't wise to align yourself with Ena," he whispered. "She is doomed. Malcolm will soon see to that."

"And why should you suddenly care what happens to me? You've been against me from the start. Why not throw me in the dungeon along with Ena?"

A cold smile touched his lips. "What need have I to condemn you when others will soon do it for me? My hands will be clean no matter what happens. As well I should, I will remain above all the tumult."

She stared up at him, struck speechless by the sheer malevolence of his reasoning. He, above everyone else, would come out as the man of pure motives, forced by law to condemn her and see her burn. And burn she would while Niall lay helpless and near death. Anne knew they'd eventually extract the confession they wanted from Ena. No one could withstand the tortures for long and Ena was a weak, old woman.

Defiance glared in her silver eyes. "We shall see how long you remain above the rabble you so slyly stir. Niall will yet recover, and when he does—"

"Och, I only pray that 'tis so, lady. No one wants for our chief to live more than I." Duncan smiled grimly. "But if he doesn't, I am tanist and must rule as I see fit. And no witch responsible for his death will live.

"Take her away," he ordered the guards holding Ena.

He released Anne only after Ena was led away. "And you, lady, are refused further entrance to this room. I won't have you attempting to finish what Ena has begun."

Anne stepped back from him. Incredulity widened her eyes. "You cannot—"

Duncan arched a graying brow. "Am I not Niall's chosen successor, named before all? My power is second only to his. And, as you see, he is now incapacitated. In all but name, I am the Campbell."

He motioned over Agnes, who had heard the noise from Anne's bedchamber and had entered. "Take your mistress to her room and keep her there. If she dares step again into this chamber, 'tis the dungeon for her."

Agnes hurried to Anne, grasping her by the hand. "Come, m'lady. Come with me."

Tears stung Anne's eyes as her glance moved to Niall, pale and silent in his bed. He was helpless now, at the mercy of others—and someone meant to see him dead. He needed her and she was now denied access to him. But who would protect him, if not her?

"Come, m'lady," Agnes was pleading, a thread of hysteria in her voice. " 'Tisn't the time to defy them.

Please, please, come with me."

She was right, Anne thought. It wasn't the time to defy or fight them. But the time *would* come. She was not yet beaten.

Anne exhaled an acquiescent breath. "Aye, Agnes. 'Twill be as you say. I must obey our tanist."

But only for a time, she silently added as she followed the old maidservant from the room. *The battle 'tisn't over, only begun. At last the enemy, whoever he be, has shown his hand.*

Agnes ushered Caitlin into Anne's bedchamber and shut the door. The girl hurried to the window seat. Anne motioned for her to sit beside her.

"We must keep our voices low," she explained, "for there may be spies. We are far enough from my doors that none should hear, if we talk quietly. And what I speak o' must be known to none or it might cost Niall his life."

"Tell me what you want o' me," Caitlin whispered, a determined light burning in her eyes. "I won't let my brother die."

"Someone poisons Niall," Anne began, "with a drug stolen from my storage chest. There is no antidote. Only time will clear the drug from his body. In the meanwhile, we must make sure he is given no more."

"And how will we do that?"

"You must watch the preparation o' all his meals, bring them up yourself, and feed him. You must not allow the physician to give him any medicines or anything to drink. And you must stay with Niall as much as possible, sleep in his room. Trade off with Agnes when you must, but don't *ever* leave him alone. 'Tis the only way to protect him."

Caitlin's smooth brow wrinkled in a frown. "But who am I to watch? Who is trying to poison my brother?"

Anne sighed. "I'm not certain. Mayhap old Murdoch, mayhap Malcolm or Duncan."

"Nay, not Uncle Duncan!" Caitlin exclaimed with a cry of horror. "Nay, it could never be him. He loves Niall and me like a father."

Anne shot her a wry glance and continued on, "Or mayhap a man outside the castle, manipulating someone within to do his bidding. I don't know, Caitlin. 'Tis the most frightening part o' it all. I don't know whom to trust, whom to suspect." She shook her head in despair. "And I am helpless, save to ask others to do my bidding. Niall needs me, yet I cannot go to him. Help me, Caitlin," Anne cried, her voice breaking. "If you don't, I don't know what I'll do!"

"Fear not, sister. I won't fail you or my brother."

Anne marveled at Caitlin's sudden surge of maturity and strength. Och, but it was so good to have another to bear a bit of the burden, to help where she was not allowed to go. Anne lifted her head.

"You must not reveal our plan to anyone. And that includes Duncan. If the traitor guesses, he will find a way to stop you. We must get Niall strong enough to know his own mind again. Then he will have the power to refuse to eat or drink what 'tisn't safe. Do you understand?"

Caitlin nodded. "Aye, I understand."

Anne gave the girl a gentle push. "Then go and see to your brother. And, Caitlin," she added, as the girl rose to leave.

"Aye?"

"When Niall rouses enough to understand, will you tell him I am near, that I love him?"

Caitlin smiled. "Aye, Anne. I'll say it over and over, for 'twill give my brother the will to live."

"My thanks," Anne whispered.

She turned back to gaze out the window, her hands clenched, knuckle-white, in her lap.

*   *   *

"I couldna see her, m'lady," Agnes admitted regret-fully late the next day. "I am sorry."

Anne sighed. "Do you know if they've yet begun the torture? Och, if only Niall recovers before they begin! Then he can save Ena."

Agnes carefully averted her gaze, finding sudden interest in putting away some fresh linens Anne had been folding. "The guard wouldna say."

"Look at me, Agnes," her mistress commanded, knowing there was more here than her maid cared to reveal. "Tell me true. Have they tortured Ena?"

A look of misery flooded the old woman's eyes. She nodded. "Aye, m'lady."

"H–how does she fare?" Anne asked through a suddenly constricted throat.

"She hasna confessed, but the guard says 'twillna be long now."

"Blessed Mother!" Anne breathed. "What am I to do? Duncan won't allow me down there to see her and refuses to stop that madman preacher. They'll kill her!"

" 'Twould be a blessing. If she died before they could extract a confession . . ."

Anne's eyes widened in horror. "How can you say such a thing? Ena is but a kind old woman. She has never harmed a soul!"

"Aye, m'lady. That I well know. But if she confesses and names ye witch, Malcolm will turn on ye like a blood-crazed hound. Ye'll be tried and burnt before the Campbell has a chance to recover."

"He grows a little better with each passing hour," Anne murmured. "You and Caitlin do your job well."

"But he still falls in and out o' a deep sleep," Agnes stated grimly. "He is confused and weak as a newborn kit. And 'twillna be much longer before Ena breaks."

"Then we must seek help!"

With resolute strides, Anne walked to her small writing desk and pulled out parchment and quill. She scribbled a quick note, then sealed it.

Anne motioned her maidservant over. "Find some man whom you know can be trusted to deliver this. It *must* reach Iain Campbell at Balloch Castle, and quickly. If the man hurries, Iain can be here in two day's time, mayhap less."

Agnes dubiously accepted the missive. "Will he come, m'lady? There's no love lost between him and the Campbell o' late."

"I know that, Agnes. He may not come for Niall, but he'll come for me."

"And isna that a dangerous game ye play? What if the Campbell mistakes yer motives?"

" 'Tis a chance I must take," Anne replied. "I am desperate and must call whatever friends I have to my aid. If Niall turns from me because o' that, there's naught I can do. He said he trusted me. The time has come to put that trust to the test."

She smiled sadly. "Now go, Agnes. Find your man and send him on his way. In the meanwhile, I must go to Duncan and buy time for us all."

Agnes's eyes narrowed suspiciously. "What do ye mean to do?"

"I won't let Ena suffer a moment more for me. I pulled her into this tangled web when I asked her help in healing Niall. 'Tis time I took responsibility for it all."

"But what do ye mean to tell Duncan?"

"That I have been the witch all along, bespelling even Ena to my will. 'Tis the only way to save her."

"Nay, m'lady! Ye'll condemn yerself on the spot. They'll burn ye, and no mistake."

Anne swallowed a panicked sob. "Aye, that I know. More reason to send for Iain forthwith. We have little time to spare."

Chapter Seventeen

Duncan stared up at her from the library desk. He couldn't believe his ears. "What did you say?"

Though her heart was hammering, Anne calmly repeated her words. "Ena is innocent. If there be any fault, 'tis mine. She only helped because I requested it."

"And what did you request?"

She knew what he was hoping she would say. But, though determined to rescue Ena no matter the price, Anne would not easily give him what he wanted.

"Why to save Niall, o' course," she replied, her glorious silver eyes glaring with defiance. "What else would there be? Ena and I use our skills for good, not evil."

"White or black magic, 'tis all the same. 'Tis still witchcraft."

"There was no witchcraft. 'Twas only natural healing."

Duncan leaned forward, his eyes narrowing. "One o' you is a witch. Which one is it, m'lady?"

Anne knew he wanted it to be her. For some reason, he needed her out of the way, had seen her as a threat from the start. But why?

Ena was old, near the end of her life, while Anne was young and had many years ahead of her. She loved Niall, had the hope of a joyous, fruitful relationship with him. By all that was logical, Ena should be the one sacrificed.

But Anne couldn't do it. She couldn't abandon the old healer to such a horrible fate. And there was still hope Iain would arrive in time to save them both. But only if Anne bought that time by diverting Malcolm's witch madness to her.

She graced him with a look of cool disdain. "Ena is innocent. 'Tis I who is called the Witch o' Glenstrae."

An eager light flared in Duncan's deep blue eyes. "Then you admit it? Admit you are a witch?"

"I am the Witch o' Glenstrae," she repeated with exaggerated patience.

"And you'll admit this before witnesses?"

" 'Tis true. 'Tis what I am called. Why should I be ashamed to admit it?"

Duncan rose from his chair and hurried to the door. "Fetch the preacher and a clerk," he ordered the guard standing outside. "Make it quick. We have a confession to hear!"

Anne walked to the window. She gazed out upon the heath and bracken-strewn hills that surrounded Loch Awe. In the sunset, the light glinted off the lake like molten gold. The swans, sailing upon it in graceful elegance, were wreathed in a luminous brilliance. Overhead, a goshawk soared in the deepening twilight, its faint, raucous cry piercing the summer silence.

It was all so beautiful, Anne thought with a bittersweet pang, and she might have just forfeited the right ever to see it again. *Och, Niall,* she silently cried. *What will you think if I die before you recover? Will you hate me for leaving you, or curse me for my weakness? If only I could see you one last time, kiss you, hold you in my arms! I'd whisper in your ear, though you heard me not, that I love you and tried hard to fight. So very, very hard . . . to the bitter end.*

Like the jaws of a trap closing about her, Malcolm, with an ominous-looking black leather case, hurried in. He was followed by a nervous little clerk. After a moment of whispered consultation between the preacher and Duncan, Malcolm's mouth twisted in a triumphant smile. He directed the clerk to take his seat at the desk then motioned to Anne.

"Come here, woman," he ordered imperiously. "Your fate is sealed by your own admission. Cooperate with us and we will spare you the torture."

"How kind," Anne muttered under her breath, as she gathered her skirts and stood before them. She eyed the preacher calmly. "And how may I help you?"

"Don't play games with me, wench," Malcolm snarled. He jerked her to him. "Repeat your confession, word for word as you spoke it to our tanist. That's all I want from you."

"Let her go, Malcolm!" Duncan snapped. "She is still lady o' this house until her confession is duly transcribed and signed. Then you can do with her as you wish."

"All I want is her tried and burned."

"As do I," the tanist soothed. "As do I. But the letter o' the law must be followed or the Campbell will have our heads if, and when, he recovers." Duncan motioned to Anne. "Sit, lady."

She shook her head. "Nay, I prefer to stand and face my tormentors eye to eye."

He shrugged. "Have it your way."

"Transcribe all that is said from now on," Duncan told the clerk. He turned back to Anne. "You've admitted you're the Witch o' Glenstrae. Is that true?"

Her heart gave a jump and hung in her throat. *Holy Mary, here it comes!* She schooled her features into an impassive mask, refusing them the satisfaction of seeing her fear. "Aye, that is what I'm called."

"Did you get that? Did you write that down?" Malcolm glanced over at the clerk who was scribbling furiously.

The man looked up and nodded.

Duncan scowled at Malcolm, then turned again to Anne. "As a witch, what crimes have you committed?"

Anne stared at him, momentarily taken aback. "What? Must I now confess crimes to satisfy you? Wasn't my admission enough?"

"We must know it all!" Malcolm snarled. "Did you poison the Campbell, father and son?"

She shook her head, refusing ever to be party to that accusation. "Nay. Never!"

"She lies!" the preacher cried.

"Write it down," he ordered the clerk. "She'll confess to it sooner or later."

"Nay." Anne moved to stay the clerk's hand. "Write that on the confession and I'll never sign it. I won't hurt Niall with falsehoods such as that!"

An evil grin twisted Malcolm's face. "You'll not speak so bravely after I show you the contents o' my case."

He lifted the black bag onto the desk. "Shall I show it to her?" he asked Duncan.

The tanist eyed Anne. "Nay, not yet. The alleged poisoning isn't important. There are other crimes."

Duncan leaned forward. "Did you put a curse upon our cattle? Give them the murrain?"

"Nay."

His mouth tightened in irritation. "Did you bring a stillborn bairn back to life with your witch's powers?"

Fiona's child, Anne thought achingly. How long ago that day now seemed. It had changed her life, brought her to this moment. But in the same token it had also brought her to Niall.

"I don't know if the babe was truly dead," she forced herself to reply, "but I breathed into its mouth and it moved and cried. I used no witch's powers, only the breath in my body."

"So you *did* bring a bairn back to life," Duncan persisted.

Anne sighed. "Mayhap I did. What does it matter? You've enough to convict me on the admission o' my name."

Duncan turned to the clerk. "Note she brought a stillborn back to life."

He riveted his cold blue gaze upon her. "And will you not admit to bespelling Niall Campbell? To winning his heart and soul as well as body?"

The tanist leaned close, a strange light in his eyes. "Tell us how you did it, how you lured him to your bed."

Nausea welled in Anne. Was even the intimacy of their coupling to be revealed? Dissected on parchment for all to read? It was too much!

" 'Tis private, what goes on between a man and woman." Anne glared at him with all the righteous indignation she possessed. "I will *not* lay it out for all to leer and laugh over. You're his uncle, his family. How can you do this to him?"

A murderous look flared in Duncan's eyes. "I do this to protect him against you, lady. My nephew doesn't know his mind anymore and is hardly fit to rule the clan. When it comes to you, he has turned against his own family. Do you deny it?"

It was so unfair, how he twisted everything, Anne thought miserably. But she'd fight him every step of the way, for Niall's sake, if nothing else.

"And I say, mayhap his family has turned against him, each one for personal reasons, all selfish and unworthy."

Duncan's fist slammed on the desk. "Damn you, woman! My patience with you is at an end!"

He glanced at Malcolm. "Show the witch your bag. Mayhap that will still the sharpness o' her tongue. And if not," he sneered, turning the full force of his contemptuous gaze back to her, "mayhap she'll need a wee taste o' the instruments."

Malcolm shot her a sly smile. With the utmost care and deliberation, he undid the latches and released the belts of the case. Then, one by one, he laid out each piece of cold, black metal upon the desk.

Anne tried not to look, but her eyes froze in horror at the magnitude of man's imagination when it came to torture. Blessed Mother, she thought, how could anyone endure for long under the application of those? Was Ena even still alive?

Anger swelled in her. "You're a madman, the devil himself, to inflict willingly such pain upon another human being! And you call yourself a man o' God! Why, you're lower than the least o' all the creatures you claim to serve! You'll roast in hell for this!"

He slapped her across the face. Something inside Anne exploded. If not for Duncan's quick response, she would have attacked the preacher. Instead, she was pinned within the tanist's iron clasp.

"Calm yourself, madam," he snarled in her ear as she struggled to free herself. "I'd be sorely saddened to have you led out o' here in chains, though Malcolm would no doubt like that."

She dragged in a breath. Duncan was right. They would do what they wanted with her. Any physical defiance on her part would be answered with even harsher retaliation. Her only recourse was to buy time. Only Iain could help her now.

"Aye," she replied, "your words are true. But keep the man from me. If he dare touches me again . . ."

"You've seen enough, I'll warrant," Duncan whispered soothingly. "You'll sign the confession now, won't you?"

Exhaustion flooded Anne in a sudden, mind-wearying wave. Och, what was the use? she thought. There was naught else she could do, not now at any rate. Better to give them what they wanted and bide her time, lulling them into an illusion of victory. But she wouldn't ever admit to betraying Niall.

"Let me see the confession."

Duncan released her and handed her the parchment. Anne scanned the words, noting the only crimes transcribed were her admission to being the Witch of Glenstrae and that she'd brought Fiona's babe back to life. The irony of it sickened her. A name and the saving of a life might be all it took to condemn her to the stake.

Anne signed her name. "There." She handed the parchment back to Duncan with a disdainful flourish. "Is that enough to win Ena's freedom?"

Malcolm chuckled snidely. Anne whirled around. "What, pray tell, is so amusing about that?"

His eyes gleamed with a crazed light. "Foolish woman. Old Ena was never our true quarry."

Anne's gaze swung to the tanist. A triumphant smile glimmered on his lips.

"Aye, Malcolm. That she was."

She should have known, Anne thought, a sickening, trapped feeling coiling in the pit of her stomach. She should have seen it coming.

"But why?" Anne cried. "What have I ever done to you?"

" 'Tis quite simple, really. Your growing influence over my nephew stood in the way of our plans for the takeover of MacGregor lands." Duncan's smile turned pitying. "Innocent victim though you be, I couldn't allow that to happen."

"So you will die, whoring witch," Malcolm interjected gleefully as he moved to Duncan's side. "Die, burned at the stake."

As Anne stared at the two men standing together like some evil, impregnable wall, horror slithered down her spine. How could she ever hope to prevail against men such as they? They were too crafty, too powerful, and far too cruel for any one person to defeat. She'd been lost from the start.

Despair filled her. Her legs wobbled, barely able to support her. Anne clutched at the table, gripping it in frantic desperation.

Ah, curse them, she silently cried, *for they have us all within their power. All—Niall, Ena, myself— and any other who ever dares go against them. By fair means or foul, they will see us all dead.*

The realization triggered something in Anne, stirred that tiny ember of pride, of honor, and justice that her despair had nearly extinguished. Her silver eyes flashed. Her mouth tightened in grim defiance.

"You'll never win!" she cried. "Though you burn my body, you will not break me. My spirit will only come back to fight you anew, joining with all the others who'll rise to the cause until you're defeated at last. For you are wrong—wrong to the marrow o' your bones—and even death won't still the voices against you!"

Anne paced the confines of her small cell, struggling against the panic that clamored beneath a thin veneer of self-control. There was little in the dimly lit room of sweating stone and heavy, moldy air to distract her from the rising fear. Her gaze scanned the cell—the dank, dirty straw that covered the floor, the filthy pallet in the corner, the malodorous, oily torch that sputtered erratically near the thick oaken door.

Her trial had been held the day after the signing of her confession. It had been anticlimatic. Her signature on the parchment had already judged and condemned her. The law, however, required she be given the opportunity to recant. Anne briefly considered it.

In the end, she stood by her confession, for it was the only truth in the whole sordid mess. Though she passionately defended herself, demanding to know why the charges were grounds for witchcraft, her judges refused to listen. Recant was all they said. When Anne refused, irreverently calling them narrow-minded oafs with whey for brains, they sentenced her to death at the stake in the village commons at noon the next day. Anne was tempted to ask why they didn't just drag her out then and there and see the deed done.

But as she stalked the wet, black hole that was her final dwelling place, Anne realized why they'd given her this last night on earth. They knew she'd not sleep. They knew the torments that would assail her, the fear, the sense of helplessness, the utter loneliness. And they wanted it for her. It was all part of her punishment.

Och, if only I could speak to someone, Anne thought in despair. *Agnes . . . Caitlin . . . Iain.* But the two women had been forbidden to see her, and Iain, it now seemed, might not make it to Kilchurn in time. Her only friends and soon they, too, would be gone.

Well, at least Ena had been spared. There was comfort in that. She *had* saved Ena. And Iain, once he arrived, would take matters in hand. Her friends—and Niall, if he survived the foxglove—would at least be safe.

But there was no hope left for her.

Once more the wild fear coiled within her. Anne quickly changed the course of her thoughts. She *must* maintain control. It was all the power she had left over her life. She'd not go to her death groveling and in tears. Niall, whether he lived or died, deserved better than that.

Niall. . . . Anne turned the beloved name over and over in her mind, hearing it in a voice without words. Och, how she loved him! Was he better? Were Agnes and Caitlin protecting him from the traitor, the poisoning? If so, he'd regain his senses soon.

Not soon enough to save her, but soon enough to resume the fight against the traitor and flush him out once and for all. Anne only hoped they'd spare him the news of her death until he was stronger. She didn't want anything to impede his recovery. It wouldn't help her anyway. There seemed nothing on earth that could help her now.

The sound of footsteps, of two people, echoed in the hollow tunnel of stone that was the corridor. Wild hope spiraled within her breast. Were they allowing her a visitor? Was it Iain?

An iron key clanked. The lock turned. The heavy door swung open. Anne took a hesitant step forward, her breath caught in her throat.

It was only Nelly, her head lowered and oddly canted to the left, bearing a tray that held a small, covered pot and a spoon. Without looking up at Anne, the serving maid walked across the room and placed the tray on the floor next to her pallet. It was the only logical spot; there was nowhere else to sit.

Despite Nelly's seething animosity toward her in the past, Anne forced herself to walk toward her. The dark-haired maid was the first person allowed in to see her since she'd been so unceremoniously deposited here today after the trial. Even a word or two about how Niall was doing would be heaven to Anne.

"Nelly." She hesitantly touched the other woman's arm.

The maid kept her back turned. "Aye?" she muttered in a low, sullen voice. "What do ye want o' me?"

Anne swallowed hard. "Please, Nelly. How is Niall? Is he better? I only want to know how he fares."

"He fares well enough." She jerked away. "I must go." Nelly gestured toward the tray. "Ye willna like yer supper. 'Tis nettle soup, flavored only with lard and gristle. The preacher insisted we make it for ye."

"It doesn't matter." Anne sighed. "A royal feast wouldn't tempt my appetite tonight. But thank you for your consideration."

"How can ye be so calm, so kind, when ye're to burn on the morrow?" Nelly cried, whirling to face her.

Anne gasped, hardly hearing the woman's question. A blackened eye and large, purpling bruise marred the left side of the serving maid's face.

"Nelly!" she whispered. "Who did this to you?"

Nelly jerked back, terror widening her eyes. "N–no one," she stammered. " 'T—'twas an accident. I fell . . . fell down some steps and struck my face."

"Nay, lass," Anne corrected her gently, " 'tisn't that kind o' injury. You forget I'm a healer. I know the signs o' a beating when I see it. And I ask you again. Who did this?"

The woman's past mistrust and hostility crumbled in the face of Anne's gentle concern. She buried her head in her hands. "Och, what have I done, what have I done?" she wept. "I have nearly killed the Campbell and will soon have yer soul on my conscience as well. And all to gain the gratitude o' a man who seeks to steal the chieftainship." She gave a bitter laugh. "And this is how he thanks me."

"Who is he?" Anne demanded, keeping her voice low so the guard waiting outside wouldn't hear. "Why did he beat you?"

Nelly raised her tear-streaked face. "Why? Because I failed to slip more foxglove into the Campbell's food, o' course. But Caitlin wouldna let anyone near it. Besides, once I found out Sir Niall was near death because o' me, I lost heart for the task. Though he wouldna take me as mistress, he never failed to treat me kindly."

A dark, angry expression twisted her swollen features. "Not like *him*, who only meant to use me, beating me half to death when I only once failed him. Och, how I hate him!"

Rising excitement rippled down Anne's spine. Her pulse accelerated wildly. The traitor! Nelly was in league with the traitor! Her grip tightened on the serving maid's arm. "Who is he, Nelly? Och, Lord, tell me his name!"

"H–his name?" Nelly repeated, her anger gone as quickly as it had come.

Sudden realization of what she had revealed dawned in her eyes. With a quick movement, the maid wrenched free from Anne's grasp. "Nay," she said, her eyes glazing over in panic. "I canna tell ye that. He'd kill me for certain."

"Nelly, please," Anne implored, her hands lifting in supplication even as the other woman backed away. "Tell me his name. Niall will protect you."

"No one can prevail against him. No one. He is too clever, too powerful."

Nelly stumbled into the cell door.

Anne stood there trembling, a look of entreaty on her face. "Och, please, Nelly."

With one last, wild glance, the serving maid turned and fled. Anne darted across the room after her and slammed into the unyielding bulk of the guard. Cold, implacable eyes stared down at her. He shoved her back into the cell with enough force to make her fall. Anne struck the dirt floor with a painful jolt. She sat there for a long moment, staring up at him.

"Ye willna escape yer just punishment, whoring witch. Not while I'm on duty leastwhiles," the burly man snarled. "And not another word out o' ye this eve or I'll be forced to take the lash to ye."

The thought seemed to please him. His mouth lifted in a suggestive leer. "But mayhap ye want that, whore that ye are. I'd have to strip ye naked to lash ye properly." He took a step toward her. "Would ye like that? 'Tis yer last night on earth. Do ye desire to spend it with a man?"

Anne scooted away, shaking her head. "Nay," she cried, struggling to keep the fear and loathing from her voice. "Lay one finger upon me and I'll call down a curse that'll shrivel your manhood to a useless little worm for the rest o' your days! Just one finger, you brutish knave, and 'twill be all over for you!"

The leer melted from the guard's face as the realization he was dealing with a confessed witch eased to the forefront of his dim-witted mind. Fear widened his eyes. He backed out of the cell, slamming and locking the door behind him. His hurried footsteps pounded down the corridor. A moment later, heavy silence descended upon the dungeon.

A heavy silence, shattered only by the gut-wrenching sobs of the dungeon's solitary prisoner.

They came for Anne an hour before midday, binding her hands behind her. The guards, clansmen she'd met many times in the two months since she'd come to Kilchurn, couldn't quite meet her calm, steady gaze. Gently, almost respectfully, they led her out of the dungeon and through the keep.

Outside was blindingly bright, especially after the damp darkness of her cell. Anne squinted in the sunlight until her eyes readjusted, grateful for the heat that eased the cold ache in her bones. The cart that would take her to the village commons was waiting in the outer bailey. Duncan and Malcolm were already mounted, the tanist in tartan trews, the preacher in blue serge and plain black bonnet.

Anne climbed into the wooden conveyance and glanced back at the keep. High in a stone-cut window, she saw the pale, strained faces of Agnes and Caitlin. She tossed back her head in defiance and smiled up at them. The driver flicked his whip over the pony's back and the cart lurched forward.

It was a glorious, ripe summer's day, birds soaring overhead, a freshened breeze rustling the trees. Anne took it all in, knowing the beloved sights would be her last, drawing on them for sustenance, for courage to face what lay ahead. She thought of home, of Glenstrae and Castle Gregor, of those carefree days of her girlhood. They seemed so very long ago.

She harked back to the eve she'd first met Niall, of her anger at him—and her hatred. That, too, seemed so long ago. Everything, after the last few anguished days, seemed like another lifetime. Even her words to Niall, barely a week past, when she'd stood there in the forest beside her ravaged herb garden. "I would sooner have a few months in your arms, even if it killed me, than a lifetime without you."

She'd spoken those words to ease his fears of childbirth, but they'd been prophetic in another, more horrible way. The truth of them hadn't dimmed, though. She loved him and was glad, oh, so very glad, for the time they'd had. If only he'd remember those words, find the same comfort they gave her.

A crowd had gathered in the commons. They were strangely quiet, shuffling uncomfortably, wearing almost shamefaced expressions.

Anne's gaze swept over them. A soft smile touched her lips. They were good, kindhearted, hard-working folk. They could not help their weaknesses and superstitions. In a sense, they were as much victims of the ignorance and manipulations of their leaders as she was.

Och, Anne uttered a fervent little prayer, would that Niall recovered to lead them again. He, alone, could give them the guidance, the wisdom they so sorely needed.

The cart rolled to a halt. Only then did Anne notice the stake, its base piled high with bundles of fagots. For an instant her courage fled. Then the guards lifted her down. With a proud tilt of her chin, Anne shrugged away their hands when her feet touched the ground. She strode to the stake.

A narrow path had been cleared through the piles of fagots, and a small step placed at the base of the stake. She climbed it, then turned. The guards moved beside her, tying her in place, crisscrossing the ropes across her chest. Anne's breath began to come in ragged little gasps. She fought to steady herself.

The fagots were moved to fill the path before her. A guard, holding a flaming torch, stepped forward. Anne swallowed hard against the lump rising in her throat, stilling the sudden tremors that wracked her body with only the greatest of efforts. She saw Duncan look to Malcolm and nod.

The preacher stepped forward, unrolling a parchment with a slow, practiced hand. He paused to scan the crowd, waiting until he had their full attention. Then he read Anne's confession, carefully enunciating each and every word. Next came the scroll bearing her sentence.

Anne wondered when Malcolm's droning would end. At last the preacher rerolled the second scroll. He lifted his gaze to meet hers and slammed straight into silver eyes filled with a withering scorn. His triumphant gleam faded.

"Vile puppet, inhuman creature!" Anne cried, her voice carrying to the furthest reaches of the crowd. "How dare you call yourself a holy man and still condone such a cruel practice? A practice condemned by the chief himself, who will not allow burnings on Campbell lands?"

"The w–will o' God and the Church is reason enough for your death," Malcolm sputtered. "How *dare* you question such a holy edict? Your defiance o' Church law in itself confirms your heretical origins!"

Anne laughed, her head held high. "And since when is it heretical to save life, to ease the suffering o' others by the healing arts? Answer me that, Preacher."

"That issue has been dealt with!"

"Yet never answered," she firmly countered.

"A–aye," a rough male voice, unsteady in its hesitation, rumbled from the back of the crowd. "Since when has the easing o' pain and misery been grounds for witchcraft? Answer the lass, Preacher."

" 'T–tis her witch's powers that gave her the healing skills," Malcolm hurried to explain. He raised a scroll above his head. "Her signed confession attests to that."

"And how long did ye torture the lass to get that out o' her?" another clansman demanded.

"Aye, how long, Preacher?" yet another shouted.

"Answer them, Malcolm," Anne prodded softly, intruding into the preacher's wide-eyed glance about him. "Tell them about Ena as well."

Malcolm stared at Anne, frozen by the icy gaze she held him in. His mouth moved, but no words issued forth.

Duncan noted the preacher's hesitation, the growing look of fear on his face. The crowd began to mutter uneasily, move about. Though many looked willing to see her burn, there were others. . . .

The moment must be seized. Now, before the people's resolve broke. Duncan signaled the guard holding the torch. "Light the fires. Burn the witch."

The man threw the flaming brand upon the fagots directly in front of Anne. The torch fell into the bundles of dry kindling. With a puff of smoke, the wood burst into flame.

"Nay!" Anne screamed. " 'Tis wrong, what you do! 'Tis evil!"

Even as she spoke, the heat rose to a painful, smothering intensity. The fumes engulfed her. She gagged, then choked.

It was too late. It was over.

Anne bit back a shuddering sob. She closed her eyes as the despair overwhelmed her once and for all.

Och, Niall, my heart's true love, she silently cried. *I tried. Truly I did. Forgive me. . . .*

Chapter Eighteen

His apprehension rising, Iain took the steps of the keep with long, quick strides. It was too quiet in Kilchurn. That more than anything else worried him.

The Great Hall was empty save for the cook, Maudie, descending the stairs from the sleeping chambers. She carried a covered tray. Iain stalked toward her. The woman jumped when he touched her arm.

"M–m'lord!" she gasped, raising tear-reddened eyes. "I—I didna hear yer approach."

"I'd wager not, Maudie." Iain grinned at her. "You were sniffling so loud, you wouldn't have heard a band o' reivers galloping through the hall. Pray, what has upset you so?"

"Dinna ye know, m'lord?" She sighed. "Nay, I suppose not. Ye've been gone from Kilchurn since the Campbell's illness and L–Lady Anne's trial."

Iain gripped Maudie's arm. "Trial? They sent Anne to trial? When?"

"Yesterday, m'lord. And she was condemned a witch."

"Damn them all!" Iain snarled. "Where is she now? In the dungeon?"

The cook's eyes filled anew with tears. "N–nay, m'lord. They took her but a half-hour ago to the village commons to burn her at the stake."

"What?" The incredulous shout reverberated in the silent hall. "And where is Niall to let this happen?"

"U–upstairs in his bedchamber." The woman sobbed. "He's too weak to go to her aid. The lord has been so very, very ill."

"I don't give a damn how ill he is! If he's conscious enough to speak even a few coherent words, he's going with me to the village!"

He wheeled and ran across the hall, taking the steps to the bedchambers two at a time. Panic churned within Iain and he was hard pressed to hold it at bay. Anne was even now at the village commons. Without Niall's presence as clan chief to halt the burning, there was no way to save her.

Niall blinked in the late-morning sun. He felt rested, stronger . . . and hungry. His glance swept the room, finally alighting upon a rounded feminine figure bent over the hearth stirring a pot. He smiled.

"Annie?" he croaked out the name, startled at the hoarseness of his voice. "Is that you, lass?"

The woman at the hearth straightened and turned, ebony hair tumbling down about her shoulders. It was Caitlin. Her eyes widened at the sight of her brother, struggling to raise himself up in bed.

"Niall?" she cried. "Och, thank the Lord! You're better. You've finally left your stupor!"

She ran to the open door separating his and Anne's bedchambers. "Agnes! Agnes, come quickly! 'Tis Niall! He's awake at last."

Agnes hurried into the room. The old maidservant eyed him closely, then turned to Caitlin, drawing her aside. Niall frowned but, try as he might, he couldn't catch a word of what the two women were saying.

"What are we going to do, Agnes?" Caitlin demanded anxiously. "The first word out o' his mouth was Anne's name. How are we to tell him that, even now, she's probably burning at the stake? The news will surely set him back, if not kill him on the spot."

"Och, Lord." Agnes sighed. "If only I knew. I suppose we'll—"

"How much longer will you two women be?" Niall grumbled from his bed. "While you talk, I hear my stomach groaning for want o' food." He glanced hopefully at the hearth. "What's in that pot? Some soup mayhap?"

Agnes inhaled a shaky breath, squared her shoulders, and nodded. "Aye, m'lord. A moment more and I'll dish ye up a bowl o' hearty beef broth."

She turned to Caitlin. "Let him eat first. He'll need the strength to bear what we have to tell him."

The girl nodded.

Gathering her skirts, the old woman bustled to the fireplace. She soon had a spoon and steaming bowl of soup laid out on a small tray. She gestured impatiently at Caitlin, who stood rooted to the spot where Agnes had left her.

"Come along, lass. Pull up a chair at yer brother's bedside and feed him his soup."

"I can feed myself," Niall growled, reaching for the tray that Agnes brought. "You'd think I was helpless as a babe to need such coddling."

Agnes surrendered the tray to Niall and shoved Caitlin down in the chair the girl brought over. "Sit with him, nonetheless. He'll soon tire."

It took only a few spoonfuls. Niall leaned back against the pillows but stayed his sister's hand when she reached for the spoon to feed him. "Nay, lass," he said. "Give me but a few moment's rest. I *will* feed myself this entire bowl if it takes the rest o' the day."

The rest of the day lasted about another five minutes. When he found himself exasperatingly wearied by the attempt to lift another two spoonfuls to his mouth, Niall grabbed the bowl and downed its entire contents. That effort drained him of his remaining strength. He fell back, pale and damp-faced. A triumphant smile, however, twisted his full, firm mouth.

"And, sure, ye'll be one scoundrel o' a patient," Agnes muttered under her breath, "and no mistake."

"I heard that, Agnes," Niall rasped, his eyes still closed. "Except for the voice, you sound just like my Annie."

Caitlin shot her an anguished look.

The door to the bedchamber slammed open, and Iain entered. "Damn you, Niall Campbell! While you loll about at your leisure, Anne soon burns at the stake! Get out o' that bed before I drag you out. You're coming with me to halt her execution or I swear I'll kill you!"

"The hell you say!" Niall roared, jerking up in bed. "What are you talking about?" His narrowed glance swung to encompass Agnes and his sister. "What is Iain talking about?" he demanded in a dangerously low voice. "Where the hell is Anne?"

Caitlin blanched, her mouth moving wordlessly. Agnes, however, took the matter firmly in hand. " 'Tis as he says, m'lord. While ye were ill, your tanist and the Reformed preacher forced yer lady to confess to witchcraft. She was tried yesterday. Even now, she is about to burn."

Niall swung his legs out of bed. "And when were you to tell me? After her funeral?"

A wave of dizziness washed over him. He sucked in a steadying breath. With a superhuman effort,

Niall fought it off, then glanced back at the women. "Get out o' here. Bring some men to help me down to the stables and have my stallion saddled. Iain," Niall summoned him, "help me dress and be quick about it. There's not much time and I've little strength to spare."

The next few minutes were filled with a flurry of activity. Two sturdy clansmen carried Niall down the stairs and out of the keep, then helped him mount his horse. He swayed precariously for a moment, then righted himself. Iain swung up onto his own mount.

"Are you sure you can stay astride?" the younger man asked, a dubious look in his blue eyes. "Mayhap 'twould be better to ride behind one o' the men."

"Nay," Niall muttered, his face white, his lips clenched. "I must appear strong and sure when I arrive there. And I will, if 'tis my last act on this earth."

He signaled his horse. The animal sprang forward, across the cobblestoned bailey and out the main gate. Iain stared after him for a second, then urged his mount on. Niall's black stallion was fast, the finest piece of horseflesh in all of Campbell lands, and Iain was soon left behind.

Niall didn't know when he lost Iain and wouldn't have cared. All that mattered was that he reach Anne before it was too late. If he didn't, Niall didn't know what he'd do. He'd kill Malcolm for sure and most likely Duncan, too.

Malcolm was witch-crazed, obsessed with his single-minded persecution of any he suspected of the black magic. He'd never burn another person on Campbell lands, though. He'd likely not live long enough after today. And Duncan as clan tanist, acting in Niall's stead while he was ill, could have well prevented Anne's burning—if he'd wished to. Why hadn't he?

The answer was too painful to consider, especially now when he needed all his strength to face what lay ahead. Niall urged his horse to its utmost limits as they topped the hill leading to the village. From his vantage point as they galloped down the other side, he could see a large crowd gathered around the stake—and the smoke pouring from the fagots piled around it.

Rage, white-hot and searing, surged through him. Strength, far beyond the capabilities of his weakened flesh, filled him. Blood pumped to his hardened muscles. His lungs heaved for air.

The wild, fierce battle lust to fight to protect what he loved was Niall's only consideration. Raising a fist high over his head, he thundered into the village, the harsh Campbell battle cry on his lips. "Cruachan!"

The people scattered before him. Niall slid to a halt at the base of the stake. A ring of fire and smoke encircled Anne. He could barely see her.

He leaped from his stallion and ran, flinging the flaming wood aside with his bare hands. With a few quick slashes from his dirk, Niall freed Anne.

She fell into his arms. With a strangled sob, Niall gathered her to him and quickly carried her out of the fire.

Iain was at Niall's side in an instant more, his sword drawn. Together, the two men faced the crowd.

"Is she alive?" Iain asked without taking his eyes off the restless, churning mass of people.

"I don't know," Niall replied, his own gaze never wavering as he watched Malcolm and Duncan stride toward them. "I pray to God she is or your father dies this day, along with our bastard uncle."

"And you, too, Niall Campbell," his cousin shot at him through clenched teeth. "I warned you about this very—"

Anne moaned, then coughed, moving restlessly in Niall's arms. Her eyes fluttered open. "N–Niall?"

He glanced down at her. "Aye, lass. 'Tis me. Now hush. Save your strength."

She sighed and again lost consciousness.

The preacher and tanist halted before them.

"You have defied not only the laws o' God, but o' man," Malcolm screamed, ensuring all assembled heard him, "when you freed the witch from her just fate! Put her back, I say! Let the burning be finished!"

Niall took a menacing step forward. "Get out o' my way, you black-hearted fiend! If you utter one more word, I'll cut your foul tongue out, then burn *you* at the stake!"

The man blanched. "And what crimes have I committed?" He gestured toward Anne. "*She*, on the other hand, has confessed, been tried, and sentenced. 'Tis the law that she die."

" 'Tis true, nephew."

Niall turned to face his uncle. "And what were her crimes? Were they so horrible you couldn't have waited until I recovered?"

"She'd bewitched you! Only her burning would free you o' her spell. 'Twas better not to wait."

Tawny-brown eyes, glittering and hard, glared back at Duncan. "Tell me her crimes! Now!"

Duncan's gaze skittered briefly to that of Malcolm's. "She admitted to being the Witch o' Glenstrae and that she'd brought a dead babe back to life."

For the longest moment Niall stared at his uncle, incredulity widening his eyes. "And for *that* you had her condemned? You're a fool, Duncan Campbell! Get out o' my way! I'll deal with you later."

As Niall turned to go, a big, burly villager stepped forward to block his way. Niall's gaze lifted to meet those of the taller man. "Will you prevent me from leaving with my lady, Fergus?" he asked, his calm voice belying the coiled tension of his body. Beside him, Iain lifted his sword.

The peasant vehemently shook his head. "Nay, m'lord. Far from it. But ye look near to collapse yerself and I'd offer my strong back to carry yer lady to yer horse."

Niall and Iain exchanged glances.

"I thank you for your loyalty, Fergus," Niall rasped, "and for the courage it took to stand up for Anne."

" 'Twasn't courage, m'lord. 'Twas good Scot's sense after what yer lady said. To heal others 'tisn't an act o' sorcery. And ye *had* condemned burnings on Campbell lands."

Niall smiled. "Aye, that I had." He stepped forward to lay Anne in the big Highlander's arms. "I'd be honored if you'd aid me with my lady."

Fergus's weathered face broke into a huge grin. "Thank ye, m'lord." With that, he turned on his heel and faced the crowd massed before them. "Get on with ye!" he bellowed. "The day's entertainment is done. The Campbell is recovered and come for his lady. Do any o' ye dispute his right to do so?"

"Nay, Fergus!" a woman cried.

"Not I, either!" Angus, the stable man, stepped forward. "The lass healed my wee Davie's hand. She's no more a witch than any woman here."

"Then out o' my way!" Fergus roared as he plowed forward.

The people parted before him. Niall and Iain followed. Once Niall was remounted, Fergus carefully handed Anne's limp form to him. Iain gained his own horse's back. Without a backward glance, they rode out of the village.

Behind them, Malcolm's enraged cries suddenly shattered the quiet. "You're bewitched, that you are!" the preacher shrieked. "You've defied the law and must be punished! You're not fit, Niall Campbell, to be clan chief!"

*   *   *

Niall was past exhaustion by the time they returned to Kilchurn. It was all he could do to hand Anne down to Iain without dropping her and he did fall himself, when he dismounted. Two clansmen were there to catch him, then carry him up to his bedchamber. Iain followed behind with Anne.

The men lay Niall down on his bed. When Iain made a move to carry Anne to her room, Niall halted him.

"Nay." He motioned his cousin back. "Bring her here. She'll lie by me. I don't want Anne out o' my sight until I know she's recovered from this."

Iain scowled but obeyed. He lay her on the far side of the bed and was quickly pushed aside by Agnes.

"Caitlin, see to your brother's needs," the old woman ordered.

While Caitlin hurried to Niall and began tugging his smoke-stained shirt loose from his trews, Agnes rolled Anne onto her side. She began unfastening her scorched dress then paused, as if suddenly aware of her audience. Agnes raised her eyes to scan Iain and the two clansmen.

"Out with ye, lads. 'Tis woman's work now. We've no need o' your prying eyes."

"I want to stay," Iain protested, "until I know she's truly recovered."

"You heard Agnes," Niall growled from the bed. "As soon as Anne's settled and wakes, I'll send for you."

Iain eyed him with frank suspicion. "I've your oath on that?"

Niall shot him a thunderous glower. "Aye. Now get out."

The three men departed. Agnes returned to her undressing of Anne. Though Anne's face and hands were smoke-blackened, the thorough inspection of her body, once she lay there clad only in her undershift, proved the fire had not yet touched her. Gazing at her sweetly rounded form, Niall fell back with a sigh of weary relief.

If one hair on her head had been harmed, he thought with a blinding flash of anger, he'd have risen from his bed at that very moment and gone after Malcolm. As he watched with hungry, loving eyes, Agnes gently bathed her, then redressed her in a snowy-white nightgown. Just as the old woman finished by tucking the comforter around her, Anne moaned. Niall levered himself to one elbow and took her hand.

"Annie?" he whispered, his voice rough with concern. "Can you hear me? Open your eyes, lass."

Her fragile, blue-veined lids lifted. Silver eyes gazed up at him. For a moment she stared at Niall in confusion, then recognition flared. Color bloomed in her pale face. She smiled, a soft, tender movement of her delicately curved mouth.

"Och, Niall," Anne breathed. "You're alive. I was so afraid for you yet could do naught."

Her glance moved to encompass Caitlin and Agnes. "Thank you, my friends, for doing what I couldn't. You've brought him back to me. I owe you a debt I can never hope to repay."

Niall's glance followed hers. A dark brow arched in irony. "Mayhap they succeeded in saving my life, but they've yet to explain why they almost let you die without telling me."

A small frown marred the smooth expanse of Anne's brow. She turned her gaze back to him. "There was naught they could do, my love. Duncan and Malcolm saw to that. And their first loyalty, as well it should be, was to you. I made them promise to protect you."

"Mayhap," Niall admitted, not sounding at all convinced. "But no matter. We can speak o' it later. For now, I wish to know what happened to you."

"And I need to tend your hands, brother," Caitlin interjected, firmly taking a red, blistered palm in hers.

"Och, Niall," Anne murmured. She sat up and took the hand he'd held hers in, turning it over. "How did this happen? You've burned yourself!"

He glanced from one woman to the other, each holding a burnt palm, and grinned roguishly. " 'Tis naught. I but singed them a bit getting through the fire. But if such action warrants this kind o' attention, I'll be certain to take every opportunity that presents itself in the future."

Anne glanced up at Agnes. "Make a nettle tea and quick. 'Tis too late to prevent the blistering, but compresses soaked in the tea will ease the pain and promote healing."

"Aye, m'lady," the maidservant said, and hurried to the kitchen.

"Caitlin." Anne turned to the girl. "Gather clean bandages and a bowl to soak Niall's hands in."

Caitlin nodded and sprang up, running off to find someone to help her with the task.

"Now, lass," Niall began warningly, "I don't think—"

"Hush, my love." Anne laid a gentle finger to his lips. " 'Tis past time to worry what your people think. I've already been condemned a witch. All our attempts to protect me by hiding my healer's skills have been for naught. I will not hide them again."

"I suppose you're right." he sighed. "But I'll tell you true, Annie. Though I believe my people are finally warming to you, I don't know if we'll ever win over Malcolm. Or Duncan, either, for that matter."

She smiled. "Time enough for that later. First, let me see to your healing. 'Tis all that matters to me."

He pulled her to him, careful to keep his burnt palms off her. "And all that matters to me is how to keep you safe."

His expression darkened and a pained regret smoldered in his eyes. "Do you know how I felt when I heard you were to be burned? I was terrified I wouldn't make it in time, that I'd find you dead, all black and blistered, just like I found Hugh's Dora the day they burnt her. I swear I don't know what I would've done if they'd killed you."

Niall lowered his head to rest upon her shoulder. "Even now, I remember that awful fear, that sickening, helpless feeling in my gut." He dragged in a shuddering breath. His voice broke. "Lord, Annie, I don't know what I would've done without you."

"Och, my love," she crooned, stroking his head. " 'Tis all right. I'm safe. I won't leave you."

He was silent for a long moment. "But mayhap you should, lass." Niall lifted his gaze to her. His eyes glittered with tears. "I should send you away."

A chill, black silence engulfed Anne and, from deep within it, her heart hammered in pain and fear. Pain, that it should finally come to this. Fear, that in the doing, it might eventually sever the bonds between them. She clamped her eyes shut and fiercely shook her head.

"N–nay," she moaned. "Don't ask it o' me, not now, not when I've just gotten you back. Must we speak o' it? Mayhap in time, when our heads and hearts are clearer, our strength returned, but not now."

"You are right," he whispered hoarsely, as loathe to discuss it as she. "Time enough in a day or so when things have had a chance to calm. But not now. I will know, however," he continued, his voice taking on an ominous edge, "what happened to you since I became ill. I must have the facts and I don't want you protecting anyone. Do you understand me, lass?"

Anne nodded. "Aye." She inhaled a steadying breath. "They threw Ena in the dungeon, accusing

her o' witchcraft, when I brought her back to help
rid you o' the foxglove poisoning. To save her and
buy time while I sent for Iain, I confessed to the craft.
You know the rest. Och, Niall," she said, choking on
a sob, "how can there be such evil in the world?"

"The evil that only a narrow-sighted group o' men
in the name o' religion can foster," he snarled. "Did
they torture you, lass?"

"Nay, though they threatened it when I refused to
admit to all the lies spread about me. In the end,
Duncan was satisfied with the meager confession I
signed."

"Aye," Niall laughed bitterly. "That poorest o'
excuses for a confession. What I can't fathom is
the depth o' my uncle's animosity toward you, to
condemn you on such feeble grounds. Malcolm, I
can well understand. In his own way, he's as crazed
as Hugh."

"Do you think all o' this is mayhap tied with the
traitor? 'Twould seem—"

A sudden remembrance struck her. Anne gripped
Niall's arm, excitement threading her voice. "Nelly!"
she cried. "When she brought me my supper last
eve, she spoke o' a traitor, o' working for him. She
was the one who put the foxglove in your food at
the traitor's behest. Och, Niall, find Nelly and get
the truth from her! She knows who the traitor is!"

Caitlin walked in at that moment, a bowl and a
box full of bandages in her hands. Niall struggled
to a sitting position. "Get Iain in here and be quick
about it! Hurry, lass. Now!"

The startled girl hurried back out of the room. A
few seconds later Iain, who must have been waiting
outside the bedchamber, entered. Caitlin was close
behind.

He headed straight for Anne and knelt beside her,
taking her hand in his. "Are you all right, lady?" he
began, his voice taut with emotion. "I came as soon

as I received your message, but still I feared—"

Niall's eyes narrowed, but he shoved the surge of jealousy aside. For the moment at least, there were more pressing matters. "Enough, Iain! Go below and fetch Nelly. I must speak with her immediately!"

"And what is so important about Nelly," Iain demanded, "that I can't have the moment you promised to talk with Anne?"

When Anne made a move to speak, Niall shot her a warning glance. He turned back to Iain. "Why I want Nelly doesn't concern you." He forced his voice to calm. "Suffice it to say, 'tis o' great import to me. Will you fetch her?"

The blond man rose and rendered him a stiff bow. "Aye, m'lord. You are still chief. I must obey."

He glanced at Caitlin. "Come with me, lass. I may need your help."

Iain stalked from the room. Caitlin shot Niall a puzzled glance, then once more hurried out. Anne watched the pair leave, noting the rigid set of Iain's shoulders and proud lift of his head.

She sighed. "Was it necessary to be so harsh with him? Iain has been a loyal friend. If not for his aid, would you have succeeded in your rescue o' me?"

"Nay," Niall admitted, "and I'll see to his reward in due time. But friend though he may be to you, he is no longer friend to me. I still dare not trust him. He threatened to kill me again today, if you died."

"And is that not the heated emotions o' youth?" Anne asked, stroking his face. "He is concerned for me, Niall. That, and naught more."

"Why did you send for him?"

She gave a wry laugh. "Is that not evident? With you as ill as you were, there was no one powerful enough in Kilchurn to stop Duncan and Malcolm. Iain was my only hope."

"O' late he seems more able to care for you than I," Niall muttered. "Mayhap you'd be better off with him."

Anne smiled. "Do you realize how like the jealous lover you sound? Truly, are you jealous, Niall?"

A pair of penetrating eyes leveled on her. " 'Tis hard not to be when your affection for Iain is so apparent."

"And can't a woman have a man as friend?"

"More than friendship burns in Iain's heart for you!"

She returned his hard stare. "I do naught to foster that."

Niall sighed. "I know, Annie. But love isn't the most logical o' emotions. Leastwise, not when it comes to me."

A piercing sweetness flooded Anne. "Are you saying you love me, Niall Campbell?" She propped herself on an elbow.

His brow crinkled in puzzlement. "But, o' course. Surely you knew?"

Anne fell back upon the bed, her eyes rolling in exasperation. "And how, pray tell, was I to know? You've never spoken the words and I'm no seer! Och, you're the most thick-skulled dolt o' a man I've ever had the misfortune to know!"

He grinned roguishly and slid over to her. His long fingers stroked her cheek. "I must be rising in your estimation," he said, his voice low and husky. "I'm no longer pigheaded now, only thick-skulled."

Her eyes filled with tears. "Don't mock me, Niall. 'Tis too important."

His lips lowered to brush tantalizingly, lightly, the sensuous curve of her mouth. "Aye," he whispered. "I well know how important. You are everything to me. I love you, Annie lass, with all my heart."

For a long moment her moisture-bright eyes scanned his face, as if searching for confirmation of his words. Then the tears spilled over. Her lips moved to his.

"Och, Niall," she cried. "My love!"

She kissed him, hard, hungrily, her tongue sliding between his slightly parted lips. Beneath her fingers upon his bare chest, she felt his muscles leap reflexively, then draw taut and hard.

With a groan, Niall drew her to him, his mouth slanting fiercely back and forth over Anne's, his tongue darting out to meet and join with hers. She came to vibrant life in his arms, everything intensified by the terror of the past days, the fear of losing him. A thick, sensual haze engulfed her.

Niall seemed equally out of control. His burned hand moved, seemingly insensitive to the pain, sliding up to her breast, boldly cupping its soft, enticing fullness.

At his touch, Anne came to her senses. Iain and Caitlin would be returning with Nelly any minute now, not to mention the equally imminent arrival of Agnes.

"N–Niall," she gasped, wrenching her kiss-swollen lips from his. "We must stop. Iain will be here—"

As if the words had conjured him, Iain flung open the door and hurried in. His face was pale, his mouth grim. And he was alone.

With an exasperated sigh, Niall rolled away from Anne and sat up against the pillows. "I send you on a simple errand to bring me a serving maid and you come back empty-handed. Why did you bother to return without Nelly?"

Iain halted before Niall. His gaze was fierce yet tinged with a strange horror. "Och, I found her all right," he rasped. "But she was already dead."

"What?" Every muscle in Niall's body went rigid. "What did you say?"

"Nelly is dead, her neck broken," Iain repeated. "I can't be certain when it happened, but from the stiffness o' her body . . ." He paused to shoot Anne a regretful glance. "I'd say 'twas late last night. Do you realize the strength it would take," he continued with a ruthless bluntness, "to break a woman's neck with your bare hands? It requires a very powerful man and, most likely even then, a madness would have to be upon him."

Iain eyed Niall with a cold, unwavering look. "You, m'lord, have a serious problem. It seems there's a madman loose in Kilchurn."

Chapter Nineteen

Anne gave a small cry and buried her face in her hands. "Och, nay." She sobbed. "Poor Nelly. She came to me last night in the dungeon and I saw the bruises on her face. She said he'd beaten her, but I never thought he would kill her!" She lifted tear-filled eyes to Niall. "What are we to do?"

"You speak as if you know who Nelly's murderer is," Iain cut in. "Who is he, Anne? And why did he kill her?"

"Iain—" she began.

"Nay, lass," Niall interrupted, holding her in the iron grip of his dark eyes. "She doesn't know and neither do I," he said, turning to his cousin. "We were about to find that out—from Nelly."

"But you and she both know *why* Nelly was killed, don't you?" Iain persisted. "And, somehow, I sense Anne's welfare is tied in with it."

Niall clamped down on an angry retort. "The welfare o' the entire *clan* is tied in with it. But, for the time being, I don't wish to speak further o' this. Leave us."

The blond man faltered in the silence that engulfed them, a bewildered expression on his face. "The welfare o' the clan? What are you talking about? What is going on?"

Niall's rugged features tightened in anger. "Leave us, Iain!"

Anne laid a hand on Niall's arm, a silent entreaty in her eyes. She glanced up at Iain. "Do as he says, Iain. Please leave us. Now."

His stormy countenance swung from Anne's to Niall's, then back. Iain bowed low to her. "As you wish, m'lady."

He shot Niall one last furious glare and left the room.

Niall rounded on her. "You'd no right to interfere. What's between Iain and me is ours to settle. Don't ever—"

"You're no longer so certain Iain's your traitor, are you?"

He paused, then sighed. "After all that has transpired in the past few days, nay, lass, I'm not. Leastwise, I'm not so certain he's alone in this. Malcolm, or even Duncan, may have a hand in the treachery as well."

"Or even be the ones solely responsible for it." Anne frowned in thoughtful consideration. "And what o' Hugh? He may also be helping from the outside."

"Aye, there's Hugh to consider as well. Damn!" Niall's fist pounded the bed beside him. "The suspicions are eating me alive! Not only has the traitor or his henchmen tried to kill me several times, but he is now murdering others within the confines o' my own castle. And I no longer even have the certainty o' knowing who it is!"

"Iain wasn't even here in time to kill Nelly."

"Aye," Niall agreed, "if he was ever at Balloch to begin with. Though I begin to have second thoughts regarding Iain, I still cannot discount all the possibilities."

He shifted to a more comfortable position. "Think about it, Anne. That day I sent him away, I was shot with the quarrel. Iain could have still been here, fired the crossbow from the forest. And he could have remained here, using Nelly to poison me, then, when she began to have second thoughts, killed her.

"Nay," he said, "Iain's fortuitous arrival to rescue you may have been as well planned as everything else he did. And one thing is a certainty. He never meant to let you die. He wants you for himself. But he needed to make it look like he'd just come from Balloch, to divert suspicion from himself when Nelly's body was found."

"A clever plan, indeed," Anne agreed softly. "Yet if Iain isn't the traitor, how more clever is the real one to divert suspicion so skillfully to others? Don't blind yourself because o' your unreasoning jealousy. Think you on that, Niall Campbell."

Perhaps it was his utter weariness, or the stress of the past few hours, but at her words something snapped in Niall. "And mayhap I wouldn't be so unreasonably jealous," he growled, grasping her arm tightly, "if you weren't so constantly and ardently defending him! Think you on that, lady."

It was too much, after all Iain had done for them. Anger darkened Anne's eyes to stormy gray but, as she opened her mouth to deliver a stinging retort, Agnes bustled in with the nettle tea. Anne glanced at her and forced a smile.

"The Campbell is ready for his hands to be tended. Do you know what needs to be done?"

A small frown wrinkled Agnes's brow as she noted for the first time the sudden tension in the room. "Aye, m'lady."

Anne riveted her flashing eyes upon Niall, then

pried loose his fingers from her arm. "Good. I'll leave you to his care. I've a need for some private time, as I'm certain," she added meaningfully, "does the Campbell himself."

With Niall's wrathful glare burning into her, Anne rose and headed for her room.

Anne slipped out of her bedchamber and quietly, ever so carefully, closed the door. It was well past midnight. Kilchurn was shrouded in silence and sleep. Even the guard stationed outside her door since her return from the stake was snoring soundly.

For the span of an inhaled breath, Anne hesitated. Her courage deserted her. The decision to seek out Iain in his bedchamber had been supremely difficult. The consequences if Niall found her there were terrifying. She risked not only his anger and loss of his love, but Iain's life as well.

But, in the end, it was all for Niall anyway, whether he ever understood or accepted it. Though the common people seemed to be warming to her gradually, little had changed in Kilchurn the past week since her rescue. If anything, thanks to Duncan and Malcolm, the situation was rapidly worsening. It was time to take matters into her own hands.

With that resolve to bolster her, Anne gathered her skirts and quietly made her way down the hall.

Someone, and Anne was convinced it was either Malcolm or Duncan, had notified the queen of Niall's flagrant disregard for the law. Even now, a royal representative was on his way from Edinburgh to judge the facts and report back to Queen Mary. Niall risked losing his chieftainship, if not his life, should the findings go against him.

In the meantime he was besieged with local officials and various Campbell lairds. All protested the course of recent events, already magnified beyond reason by rumor and speculation. Though Niall had managed to turn aside most accusations and dispell many of the false tales, sending the majority of his lairds back home satisfied with the true facts, the grumblings and unhappiness continued. Anne could see it in the faces of some of the castle servants, many of the clansmen, and, most especially, in Duncan's eyes.

His animosity had evolved into outright hatred, a hatred he made little attempt to hide. Even Caitlin, who spent many hours with Anne each day filling her in on the current state of affairs, was distressed by her uncle's unbridled rancor. The girl would pour her heart out to Anne, hurt, unable to understand what was happening.

Before her very eyes, Anne saw the Campbells being split into factions, one turned against the other. And all, it seemed, because of her. Though she was innocent of cause, it mattered not. It was tearing Niall apart.

He'd avoided her ever since they'd argued that day. He was still angry over her defense of Iain, and she refused to ignore his continued unfairness toward the younger man. It broke her heart to be yet another source of pain and problem to Niall, but what was she to do? Accept a wrong being perpetrated upon an innocent man? Watch Niall make a monumental error in judgement and not stand up to him over it?

She couldn't do it. To ignore a wrong went against everything Anne was and believed in. And she'd never betray her principles, not even for love.

Yet love, in the end, was what was leading her down the darkened corridors toward the room of a man whom she'd promised Niall she'd not speak to, much less visit alone. But what choice was there? Anne well knew Niall's stubborn pride. He'd fight until he was overcome and destroyed. And that destruction now seemed imminent if something wasn't done soon.

She would leave Niall, go back to her people. For some reason unknown to her, Anne had become the focal point of all the dissension. In her absence, she hoped the conflict would die. Niall's jealousy would end and he'd be able to separate Iain's desire for her from the possibility his motivations were that of a traitor.

Without that additional issue to distract him, Niall could at last turn all his efforts to discovering the real traitor, to strengthening his precarious position as Campbell chief. And perhaps the witch fever that Malcolm continued to stir would also calm. Indeed, what would anyone care about a witch who was no longer among them?

Iain's room was easy to find, for Caitlin had inadvertently revealed its location one day. It was a lucky thing she had. Anne dared not ask anyone about it or Niall would have known soon thereafter. Iain was the only one she could trust not to go to Niall. Iain, though his ultimate motives might be different, would help.

She reached his room. Before she could lose any more of her courage, Anne tried the latch. Though she hated sneaking in to wake Iain, it was better than risking possible notice by tarrying in the hall and knocking at the door. Blessedly, the latch opened, and Anne slipped inside.

For a moment she stood there, searching out the bed in the dimly lit chamber. A sudden thought assailed her. What if Iain were not alone, had taken some serving maid to his bed? Anne hesitated, then decided to move closer before she woke him. If he had a companion, she'd leave as quietly as she'd come.

Only one body lay in the bed. Anne touched Iain's bare shoulder. He flipped over and grabbed her arm. Before she could cry out, she was wrenched up against him, a dirk's blade pressed to her throat.

"Who sent you," Iain rasped in her ear, "and what do you want?"

Anne froze, the knife too dangerously close to dare struggle. " 'Tis me, Iain," she whispered. "Anne."

"Anne?" The blade lowered from her throat and he turned her face to his. "Lord, Anne," he groaned, "what are you doing here? If Niall finds us . . ."

"I—I know, Iain." She shoved herself to a sitting position. "I wouldn't have come, if I didn't need your help. I don't know what else to do."

He levered himself up in bed and resheathed his dirk. The comforter fell away, the flickering candle-light revealing a muscled expanse of broad, lightly haired chest and taut abdomen. She flushed, rea-lizing he was naked beneath the bedclothes, and averted her eyes.

Iain saw her embarrassed movement and smiled. "Would you like me to dress?"

Anne jerked her gaze back to him. "Nay. There's no time. What I have to say, I must say quickly and leave. 'Tis too dangerous for me to linger."

He stared at her. "What do you want from me, lass?"

A lump rose in her throat, but she forced her words past it. "I want to leave Niall and go back to my people. Will you help me do that, Iain?"

"Why, Anne? Why do you want to leave Niall?"

"Because I am a danger to him, even to the poss-ible loss o' his life. He won't willingly let me go, so I must do it for him."

"I could take you to Balloch Castle," he offered softly. "I would protect you from him."

Anne vehemently shook her head. "Nay, Iain. 'Twould only make matters worse. I'll hurt Niall enough in the leaving. I won't hurt him in that way, too. I ask only that you make arrangements for an escort for me back to Castle Gregor."

"I can do that." He frowned. " 'Twill be difficult getting you out o' Kilchurn unnoticed, though. Niall has you watched at all times now for fear o' further harm befalling you. How did you manage to slip from his bed without him waking?"

She lowered her head. "We sleep apart, have so since he rescued me. We argued . . ."

"Over me, no doubt."

"It changes naught, Iain. I can't stand by and watch Niall go to his destruction. Will you help me or not?"

Iain nodded. "Aye, you know that I will, lass. I'll send you a message when the arrangements are made. Be ready. It could well come at a moment's notice." He paused. "The difficult part is still how to get you out o' Kilchurn."

" 'Tisn't a problem. I know a way. Just tell me where you'll meet me and I'll be there. And, Iain," she said, touching his arm, "you're not to go with me. Niall must not suspect you're involved in this."

"Damn him! I care not what he thinks! Besides, he already knows my feelings on the matter."

"But he won't be sure you were involved if you're here and I'm gone. I'll leave him a letter, making it appear I managed it all myself. That I sent word to my father and 'twas MacGregors who were waiting to take me away. You've only to find men who can keep our secret. Can you do that?"

Iain nodded. "Aye. I know a few, enough to get you safely home."

Anne rose from the bed. "Good. I must go now, Iain."

He stayed her with a light touch on her arm. "Anne?"

She glanced down at him lying there, a golden-haired, handsome young warrior. "Aye?"

"In time, may I come to visit you?"

"You're my friend, Iain. You'll always be my friend."

His blue eyes darkened. "And Niall will always be your love? Is that it?"

She gave a sad little nod. "Aye."

Niall strode into his bedchamber and flung himself into one of the hearth chairs. Lord, but he was weary! The day had begun badly as it was and the arrival of the queen's envoy had only made it worse. After the initial flurry of preparing accommodations and seeing to his needs, it had been necessary to spend long hours with the man, addressing all the charges brought against him. Not surprisingly, his bastard uncle, Malcolm, had been his accuser.

Niall thought the inquiry had gone well, that the royal envoy had been satisfied with his answers. The final decision, however, rested in the hands of the queen. It was all that prevented him from banishing Malcolm from Campbell lands. Niall smiled grimly. For a time more he must be patient, but once he'd received official absolution of the crimes brought against him by his bastard uncle. . . .

If everything went as he hoped, in but a matter of days Niall would be free of at least one of the thorns in his side. Just one of many, he reminded himself, but it was still progress of a sorts.

The arrival of the last of his warriors sent out on the secret mission had only added to the day's stress. None had returned with any useful information. There seemed no true disloyalty among his lairds. Normally, that would have been the best of news, but not now. Now, he desperately wanted to find the traitor outside Kilchurn.

Hugh remained somewhere in the mountains near Ben Cruachan. His cousin ran with a large group of outlaws who appeared content with periodic cattle raids upon nearby crofts. In time, Niall would have to see to their capture. But not now. Now, it was enough that Hugh stayed away from Kilchurn and made no overt attempts against him.

If only he could catch the traitor in a false move. Even Duncan was now kept at arm's length after a heated argument over his uncle's ruthless persecution of Anne. Though the tanist claimed he was borne along on the tide of law and religion in condemning Anne—and regretted it deeply—Niall found the act hard to forgive. For all practical purposes, Niall was now alienated from all the closest male members of his family.

His glance moved to the door that separated his room from Anne's. Aye, he mused glumly, and alienated from Anne as well. The continuing dilemma of her loyalty to Iain over what he saw as her expected commitment to him ate at Niall. Now, more than ever, he wanted her, needed the solace of her body, her love. But her stubborn devotion to his cousin was more than Niall could bear.

He knew he was being an irrational, jealous fool, knew his feelings were clouding his judgement, but why couldn't she understand, be there for him when he needed her most? Aye, needed her most of all while he fought through this quagmire of doubts and suspicions. If only. . . .

Niall rose from his chair. His long, lithe strides carried him across the bedchamber in a matter of seconds. There were ways, aside from strong words, he reminded himself meaningfully, to bring a woman to heel. He knew Anne's body as well as his own—the slim, ripened form, the tantalizing curves and graceful hollows.

The pleasure he'd gain in exacting her apology stirred him wildly. All Niall wanted, all he could think of, was Anne.

She was not in her bedchamber. Niall frowned.

Where could she be? It was nearly time for the supper meal. Mayhap she was already below, awaiting him in the Great Hall. He turned to reenter his room when a bit of parchment on the table near the door caught his eye.

His name in Anne's feathery scrawl was written upon a small scroll sealed with red wax. Uneasiness coiled within Niall as he picked up the letter and broke it open. How strange that Anne would choose such a manner to communicate with him.

His eyes narrowed to glittering slits as he read her words. "Niall, twice before I begged you to let me return to my people. I ask you no longer. Even now I am on my way home, my clansmen having come for me. 'Tis over between us. I beseech you, don't follow. 'Tis better I am gone from your life."

The letter was signed simply "Anne."

Niall groaned, throwing back his head, his eyes clenched in pain. The parchment crumpled in his fist. How could she do this to him? How could she be so cruel, so hardhearted? It wasn't like her. . . .

His eyes snapped open. Nay, it wasn't like Anne at all. Someone had surely said something to frighten or to convince her she was saving him by sacrificing their love. A fury smoldered inside him. Niall pondered all possibilities—and alighted on the most obvious culprit.

Iain. It *had* to be Iain. Who else would she listen to? And who else but Iain desperately wanted her to leave?

With a harsh cry, Niall stormed from the room. He paused only long enough to send the guard to gather more men, ordering him to bring them to Iain's bedchamber. Then Niall strode off.

For a brief moment he considered going back for his sword, then decided his dirk would be more than adequate. He'd not give his cousin opportunity to attack. He'd strike first to win the advantage.

He paused outside Iain's bedchamber to withdraw his dirk, then walked in without knocking. Iain was sitting by the fire, a book in his hands. He seemed not at all surprised at Niall's arrival. Iain calmly closed the volume and laid it aside. His gaze when he looked up at Niall was cool, unperturbed.

Niall's temper exploded as he advanced on Iain. Grabbing the front of his shirt, he pulled his cousin to his feet and pressed the dirk to his throat. Iain tensed but said nothing.

Niall pushed the knife a little deeper. Blood welled at the blade's tip, trickling down Iain's neck and chest to stain his shirt. He didn't move.

"How long?" Niall demanded hoarsely. "How long ago did she leave?"

He pulled the dirk back a little.

"Two hours," came the terse reply.

"Damn you!" Niall cursed. "Why did you do it? Why couldn't you leave Anne and me be? You've finally gone too far, cousin. Now you haven't even Annie's influence to protect you!"

"Do you think I care?" Iain snarled in return. "Anne is safe now. From Malcolm, my father, and most o' all, from you. She was in more danger from you than them, for you professed to care for her, to protect her, and didn't. Your selfish needs blinded you to her danger, and always will. I am glad I helped her escape and naught, *naught* you can do to me will change that!"

Something inside Niall shattered, severing his emotions from all rational control. *Kill him!* a voice screamed inside his head. KILL HIM. *End his life once and for all!. End at least one of your problems with one clean thrust of your blade. Then Anne can come back and all will be well. . . .*

The sound of the guards rushing into the room wrenched Niall from his violent thoughts. His rage-clouded vision cleared. Once again he saw before him his cousin, a man who refused to lift a hand to defend himself. To ram the dirk home now would be murder. No matter what Iain might ultimately be—a traitor, a murderer—Niall was neither.

He removed the blade from Iain's throat and shoved him back into his chair. "You won't escape your well-deserved punishment. 'Tis only delayed until I return with Anne."

Niall motioned to the guards, secretly pleased by the spark of anger that flared in Iain's eyes at his mention of bringing back Anne. "Take my cousin down to the dungeon and clamp him in chains," he ordered his men. "I'll deal with him later."

Iain leaped to his feet. If not for the drawn swords instantly pointed at him, he would have attacked Niall. As it was, his powerfully muscled form trembled with barely suppressed rage as he permitted himself to be bound.

He'd not allow the guards to lead him away, however, without firing some parting words. "You've also gone too far, *cousin*," Iain cried. "This won't set well with the clan. Beware your followers, for you may soon have none to lead!"

All the doubts about Iain flooded Niall with renewed force. He gave a harsh laugh. "Spoken like a true traitor," he sneered, then signaled the guards. "His presence sickens me. Get him out o' my sight!"

Their band had gotten a late start. Before departing Campbell lands, Anne had paid Ena one last visit. The old healer was well, recovered from her terrifying stay in Kilchurn's dungeons. Their farewell had been tearful, for neither knew if they'd ever see each other again.

Now, the day was edging toward twilight. Anne's gaze moved to the setting sun. They'd been on the road two hours and had at least another two more before reaching Castle Gregor. It would be well into the night before she arrived home.

Anne glanced at the men riding with her. There were four of them, all "broken men" from other clans who'd pledged their loyalty to Iain in return for the protection of the Campbell name. As an underchieftain of Niall's, Iain had considerable power and resources of his own. Yet Anne couldn't help but worry about him. Niall could have a fearsome temper when pushed far enough and Iain would never back down.

With a small shudder, she shoved the anxiety aside. There was nothing more she could do to ease the rivalry between them, save leave them both. That in itself might be all that was needed. She hoped, she prayed that it would be so.

Once again, Anne glanced toward the mountains. Amid a wild landscape, Ben Cruachan towered over the land. Its lower slopes were heavily wooded, thinning as the elevation rose to bare and lumpy crags, the summit split into two cones. The mountain exerted a vital, powerful influence over Campbell lands—bold, proud, compelling. So much, she realized with a bittersweet pang, like the dark man she was leaving behind.

She loved Niall, would always love him. But Anne wasn't certain there could ever be a life for them together. Mayhap in time things might settle down, tempers and unreasoning fears might fade. But that might be a long while from now.

Niall was a virile, lusty man in his prime. He could well tire of waiting and take another wife. Their handfasting only bound them for a year, less than ten months more. And Anne knew how dearly Niall wished for an heir.

Tears, maddeningly frequent of late, filled her eyes. There was nothing else she could do. If she must give him up to save him, so be it. Her love could do no less. It was enough that he lived. It had to be.

Up ahead, the call of a sparrow hawk rent the silent evening. From behind them came an answering cry. Her companions exchanged narrowed glances, reining in their mounts. Unease spiraled through Anne. There was something not quite right.

The thunder of horses pounding over the hills that bordered the road filled the air, mingling with harsh shouts and battle cries. Iain's men closed in around her, drawing their swords. In a clash of horseflesh and metal, the attackers, twenty strong, were upon them.

Screams of pain as blades cut into living flesh, the squeals of terrified horses, rose to surround Anne in a horrifying cacophony. Her companions fought bravely to protect her, taking down several of the enemy before finally falling to the overwhelming odds. Almost before it had begun, the battle was over.

Anne sat there on her horse, alone amid the carnage, her traveling gown splattered with blood. She swung her gaze around the band of men encircling her. From the plaids they wore, they were Campbells, but not ones she recognized. What did they want from her? Indeed, who *were* they?

The sound of another rider drawing up behind her sent a premonitory prickle through Anne. There was a malevolence emanating from him so tangible it was as if he'd run his finger down her spine. She stiffened, dreading the confrontation to come. Slowly, she turned in her saddle.

"So, we meet again, whoring witch." Hugh Campbell chuckled evilly. "And once more you are totally at my mercy."

He motioned to Anne. "Bind her. We must be off. 'Tis too dangerous to linger so near Kilchurn."

She unsheathed her bodice knife. "Kill me now, Hugh, for I will not go with you. Let me die with these brave lads and have done with it."

"And spare you the torment I've planned for you this night?" He grinned, his glance skimming her slender form. "I think not. I've a taste to know your witch's charms before I kill you. You're a special lass to have enchanted a man such as Niall Campbell. I'll know the reason why."

"Take her." He backed his mount away.

Four burly warriors surrounded Anne. She slashed out as the nearest one grabbed for her, leaving a deep gash in his arm. He cursed and drew back, clutching the wound.

Another arm snaked about her waist, nearly unseating her. Anne wheeled, her dagger arcing toward her newest attacker. She'd meant only a glancing cut, but the man leaned forward at the last moment. The blade went deep, into the outlaw's gut.

With a strangled cry, he loosened her and toppled from his mount, her dagger still embedded in his belly. Anne's gaze followed him, horrified at what she'd done. The momentary distraction was all the advantage the other men needed.

One grabbed her by the hair, pulling her to the ground. Another two leaped down to pin her roughly there, wrenching her arms behind her to bind them tightly. In the next instant, she was pulled back to her feet.

Hugh rode up. "You'll pay for that, wench! I don't sell the lives o' my men lightly. When I'm done with you, each and every one will have you in turn. Then I'll slowly, but ever so thoroughly, choke your life away."

"Never!" she cried. "Never, do you hear me! I'll kill myself before I let that happen!"

A cruel smile touched his lips. "And when will you have that opportunity, devil's whore? We'll guard that precious life o' yours with our own. Until we're done with you.

"Come, let us be gone!" Hugh commanded.

Turning his horse, he galloped off over the hills, headed toward Ben Cruachan. Anne was lifted up into the arms of a nearby man, her mount left standing where it was. In a flurry of hoofbeats and choking dust, the outlaw band headed out after its leader.

She glanced over her shoulder as they rode away. Behind her, ten bodies, all dressed in Campbell plaids, were sprawled bloody and lifeless on the ground. And nearby, heedless of the slaughter, her horse moved to graze upon a succulent patch of grass.

Niall, accompanied by one of his warriors, galloped down the road. He'd kept up the frantic pace for well over an hour now and, from the spacing of the hoofprints in the dirt ahead, knew he should soon overtake Anne's much slower party. Though there were four men with her to their two, he felt confident they could physically overpower them if the need arose. He only hoped it wouldn't come to that. He dreaded endangering Anne in a fight.

An unnatural stillness lay upon the scene that greeted him as he crested the next hill. Bodies were scattered on the ground not far below. In the deepening twilight, the distance made it difficult to make out form or sex. With his heart in his throat, Niall urged his stallion on, checking his speed only when he reached the bodies. His horse skidded to a halt. Niall was off its back in an instant.

He ran from one form to the next and quickly ascertained Anne was not among them. Relief surged through him. He began to examine the bodies more closely. Four he recognized as Iain's men. The other six he knew as men he'd banished as outlaws. In the belly of one, Niall found Anne's dagger.

"You little wildcat," he whispered in admiration.

He withdrew the knife and wiped its blood-stained blade clean on the grass. "Keep fighting them, Annie," he rasped. "I'm coming."

Niall slipped her dagger into his belt and swung onto his horse, readjusting the claymore that hung at his back. His clansman quirked a questioning brow.

"Their track leads toward Ben Cruachan," Niall explained. "Return to Kilchurn and bring a party o' forty men back on this trail. I'm riding on."

"But they are a large group, m'lord," his warrior protested. "At least ten, if not fifteen, men. Even ye canna take on that many alone."

"If luck is with me," Niall muttered grimly, "I won't have to. But I don't know who has the Lady Anne, so I can't fathom the danger she is in. I must go on. Now off with you," he commanded, "and don't waste an extra moment in returning. I'll need your help soon enough, one way or another."

"Aye, m'lord."

The man reined his horse about and galloped back in the direction of Kilchurn. Niall watched as he disappeared over the hill, then urged his own mount onward. Two hours time would be lost before his men arrived again at this spot. And, from the looks of things here, the outlaws had at least a half-hour lead. Time was against him. Time and the unknown enemy who now had Anne.

Anne paced the confines of the small tower room, anxiously casting about for any means of escape. The narrow slit of window precluded its use. The room's single door was bolted from the outside. At the base of the winding stairs was a guard, with the rest of Hugh's men camped outside.

She ground her teeth in frustration. So many obstacles to overcome, each one nearly impassible in its own right. And so little time left before Hugh came for her.

They had ridden up into the mountains for well over two hours before arriving at the ancient stone tower. The repairs inside, however, were of a more recent nature. Anne wondered if this were the boyhood haunt of Niall, Iain, and Hugh. It would explain Hugh's use of it now to carry out his depraved revenge against her.

Anne halted at the door, a sudden thought assailing her. How had Hugh learned of her journey back to Castle Gregor? She knew Iain would never have betrayed her and the preparations had all been made in secret. Had someone seen them leave and sent a message to Hugh? Or had some spy in Kilchurn overheard Iain as he made the arrangements? In the end, it didn't matter. She was now the prisoner of a madman.

A madman. Iain had said there was a madman in Kilchurn, that day he'd discovered Nelly's body. Was Hugh that madman? He hated Niall. Had he mayhap been manipulating Nelly from the outside to do his will? And, indeed, mayhap he even stalked Kilchurn at times. Though Agnes seemed to think differently, mayhap Hugh also knew of the secret tunnel into the castle. And mayhap would use it again, once he was through with her.

Fear roiled through Anne. If Hugh were the traitor, Niall was in terrible danger, and there was nothing she could do to warn him. Nothing indeed, Anne realized, with a sudden surge of impotent anger, nothing . . . but die at the hands of a witch-crazed traitor.

She sagged against the door. Blessed Mary, what had she ever done to deserve this? How had she sinned, to escape one horrible death only to fall prey to an even more gruesome one?

The burning at least would have been quick, if

excrutiatingly painful. But to be raped by Hugh, then all of his men before being murdered was an even more fearsome fate. At the stake, Anne still had her dignity, but even that would be stripped from her before this eve was done. Och, but she hated being so helpless, so. . . .

Footsteps, climbing the stone staircase, echoed hollowly in the tower. Anne lunged back from the door. Panic rose like bitter gorge in her throat. Once more she scanned the room for a sign of a weapon, for hope of escape. There was none. The chamber was empty save for a threadbare bed.

The door unlocked with a metallic clank, swinging open to reveal Hugh standing there. Anne held her ground, refusing to cower before him. Defiance flashed in her eyes. With her head thrown back, her shoulders squared, she looked so much the warrior that Hugh momentarily faltered.

Then the old madness crept into his eyes. "Your spells will serve you poorly this eve, witch!" he spat. He held up a small bag tied around his neck. "I have an amulet to protect me."

Hugh waggled the sack before her eyes and giggled. "Does it frighten you? No? Then mayhap this will strike some fear in your heart!"

His hand moved to his groin, where the hard swell of his manhood bulged. He grinned at the horrified flicker of Anne's eyes toward him, then turned to shut and lock the door. Hugh dangled the key from his finger as he faced her.

"Do you want this, lassie?" he taunted, moving toward her. "Well, come and take it." He slid the key down the front of his trews to rest beside his hardened organ, his grin widening suggestively. "I'll let you have it, you know, if you come and get it."

Anne backed away as Hugh inexorably advanced, until she stood against the bed. She inhaled a steadying breath. She must confront him, must get the key.

And if that required touching him, sliding her hand into his trews to do so, then she would. She would do whatever it took to get that key. He'd quickly discover she was no shy, fearful maid.

Her hand moved toward him, toward the belt that bound his trews. A strange, excited light gleamed in his dark eyes. Anne undid the belt and let it drop to the floor. Her hand was captured in an iron grip, however, when it moved again toward him. Hugh twisted her arm behind her, then grabbed her other arm to pull it back to join it.

"Did you think you'd get the key so easily, my beauteous little witch?"

His head lowered to hers. His hot breath wafted across her face. Anne fought back a surge of nausea. Hugh's body moved closer, intimately pressing into hers. She squirmed against him.

"Aye, that's it," he said, his voice rough with desire. "Rub your body against mine. Make me stiffen even more."

Anne froze. Everything that was in her screamed to get away from him, but she forced herself to maintain contact. If she fought too hard, she'd never have a chance at the key. And the key was everything—her one hope of freedom.

Hugh chuckled, a cold edge of irony in his voice. "You're just like all the other sluts. You'll sell your soul to the devil to get what you want. Only this time, the devil is in league with me. 'Tis all part o' our plan. Your death will begin the feud anew. Niall will finally fall."

His mouth descended, grinding roughly, painfully, over hers. At the same time, he levered himself against her, forcing Anne off balance. An icy, awful fear shot through her. She fought to maintain her footing but the effort was to no avail. With a choking cry, Anne fell onto the bed, Hugh atop her.

Chapter Twenty

Niall watched the tower for a long while, studying the movements of the men outside, gauging
where the guards were and where Anne was probably being held. The room at the top of the winding
stone staircase was the most likely spot. And the
only means of escape was back down those stairs.
Even if he managed to reach her, they could well
be trapped in the tower room if the men outside
were alerted. Whoever had brought Anne here had
planned well against any rescue.

The realization filled Niall with rage. As far as he
knew, only two other kinsmen besides himself knew
of this old tower. Hugh, Iain, and he had spent many
a summer's day here, repairing the crumbling struc-
ture. It had been a labor of love for three idealistic
lads, steeped in tales of the glorious deeds of brave
Campbell ancestors.

But idealistic no more, Niall thought with a bitter
pang. Time and cruel experience had soured those

high aspirations. Soured them all, for each in his own way.

Hugh had gone mad with his unrequited ambitions and the searing betrayal and loss of his beloved Dora. Iain, at the very least, coveted Anne. And he, he had become so weighted with cares and responsibilities and eaten by suspicions that he dared trust no one.

Niall's mouth twisted with grim humor. Two men dreamed of power and would stoop to anything to get it. And the other who possessed that power was slowly being destroyed in the battle to protect it.

Tonight, one of them would seal his fate. Niall would soon have his proof. Whoever's followers these were, one of the men could be persuaded to reveal the traitor, either with money or torture. All Niall had to do was wait. His own men would soon arrive. Then the renegades would be easily overcome.

Niall crept forward to gain a better view. At the back of the building, covered by thickly overgrown ivy, was another door. Niall prayed its entrance, hidden from sight in a darkly shadowed corner under the stairs, had yet to be discovered.

It could serve him well when the time came. If orders had been given to kill Anne in the event of an attack, Niall could quickly gain access and fight off any guards stationed inside. Her abductor had not thought of everything, he wagered.

He settled behind the bracken and low shrubs that grew close to the far side of the tower. By his calculations, his men were still an hour's ride away. Niall shifted to allow his huge claymore to rest more comfortably against his back and eased himself down to rest upon his elbows.

He gazed up at the blackened sky, scattered with twinkling bits of light. How close the stars seemed here in the mountains. One could almost reach out and touch them.

Once more the remorse surged through him. He and his two cousins had lain outside just like this so many summer nights ago, watching the star-studded sky, speaking of their dreams, of honor and kinship. They'd been so close then, vowing to stand beside each other in battle and life, swearing to eternal loyalty. What had happened?

A cry from high in the tower drifted to Niall's ears. He heard the men outside chuckle, then settle back around the fire to talk in low, amused voices. Niall rose to a crouched position behind the shrubs.

It was Anne's voice and the sound had been one of fear. He dared not wait a moment longer. Even if he'd have to take on the outlaws without his men, he had to go to her. Anne was in danger.

With swift, stealthy strides, Niall made his way to the ivy-covered doorway. He slashed away the obstructing leaves with his dirk, then grasped the door handle. At first it would not turn, age and rust binding it stiffly, but Niall's determined strength finally worked the corroded metal free. He shoved open the door.

The metal hinges creaked in the stone-muffled interior. Niall froze. Footsteps moved toward him. He slipped in, his dirk clenched in his fist.

The man's hand swung to his sword when he saw the open door, but Niall was upon him before he had a chance to shout an alarm. Two quick thrusts of his dirk and Niall had disposed of the guard. He dragged the body into the shadowed corner and cautiously crept into the main room.

The guard seemed to be the only one on watch in the tower. Niall slipped up the winding staircase, bloodied dirk in hand. From overhead came the sounds of a struggle, another muted feminine cry. His blood stirred hotly. Someone was harming his woman. That person would die.

He reached the door and pulled down upon the handle. It was locked from the inside. Niall tried the door with his shoulder, slamming into it with increasingly harder blows. The thick oak stood firm. Frustrated rage exploded within him.

Niall pounded on the unyielding wood. "Anne, open the door!" he cried in a low voice. " 'Tis Niall, lass. Open the door and let me in!"

He heard the sound of a slap and another strangled cry. Niall went mad. He threw himself against the door again and again, heedless of the men pouring into the tower below.

Hugh's hands roamed over her body, tugging at Anne's clothes, while the weight of his body pressed down, pinning her to the bed. She struggled against him in rising panic, flinging her head from side to side to evade his hard, wet mouth. A large hand captured her breast, squeezing it viciously.

Anne cried out, then stilled. Hugh's fingers found her nipple, teasing it to a hardened nub.

He grinned down at her. "You like that, don't you, little slut? I thought as much." He grasped her hand and guided it to his groin, fitting her fingers to his swollen arousal. "You'll like *that* even more, once 'tis inside you."

"P–please," Anne forced her voice into a husky plea, "let me feel your flesh beneath my hand. Och, I want it so!"

"Then have it," Hugh rasped, his breath ragged with desire. "Have it all!"

He took her hand and slid it inside his trews. Anne's fingers glanced off the key, laying warm and metallic beside his aroused organ. She controlled the impulse to grab it. *Too soon*, she told herself. *'Tis too soon.*

Hugh covered her mouth with his as he began to rub himself against her. Anne fought down the surge of renewed nausea, willing her mind to remain clear. *Bide your time, Annie girl,* she inwardly cried against her rising fear and disgust. *Your chance will come.*

From somewhere, Anne heard a strange thudding sound. She wrenched her attention from Hugh's groaning sighs and found the source of the new noise. It was coming from the door. Someone was pounding on it!

She heard a voice, calling her name. Niall's voice! Anne grabbed for the key, tugging it free. Hugh yelped angrily and reared back from her. With one hand he grabbed Anne's wrist, capturing the hand that held the key. With his other, he slapped her hard across the face.

Anne gave a strangled cry. From somewhere deep within her, an instinctual feminine reflex responded. Her knee jerked up and jammed hard into Hugh's momentarily vulnerable groin. He screamed in agony and fell off her.

She leaped from the bed and ran across the room, the key clenched in her fist. Fingers jerky with desperation, Anne unlocked the door and began to pull it open. A hand tangled in her hair, then wrenched her backward. She lost her balance, stumbled, and fell.

Niall burst into the room. He paused to take in Anne and Hugh, then slammed the door shut and locked it. The key was deposited beneath his belt.

Hugh released Anne and backed away. Niall advanced, pulling Anne to her feet. He noted her tousled hair and the reddened imprint of Hugh's hand on her cheek.

"Has he harmed you in any other way?" Niall demanded softly, stroking the swollen side of her face.

"Nay," she whispered.

Niall turned to Hugh. Behind them, a shout of voices and pounding on the door began. Niall smiled grimly. "You'll die before they get to you," he snarled to his cousin. "I won't spare your life a second time."

"Or I, yours!" Hugh cried.

With panther quickness he sprang, grabbing for the dirk Niall held in his hand. The two men grappled wildly. Hugh's foot went out to entwine about Niall's lower leg. The movement was so swift, so unexpected, that it toppled Niall.

Both men fell heavily to the floor. Niall's head struck hard. For an instant he saw stars. It was enough opportunity for Hugh. He twisted the dirk in Niall's grasp until it was pointing toward Niall's chest. Then, with all his considerable strength, Hugh threw himself down upon Niall.

Anne screamed a warning, but it was too late. With all the power in his hard-muscled body, Niall twisted the dirk upward. Hugh fell, impaled on the blade.

For a stunned moment Niall lay there, then gently shoved his cousin off him. He sat up, cradling Hugh in his arms. Anne came to kneel beside him.

The dirk protruded from the middle of Hugh's chest. Even as they watched, the injured man turned ashen. Blood bubbled from his lips. Niall held him close, forgetting all past animosity, remembering only the boyhood friend. In the background, the pounding on the door worsened, as if it were now being battered by some kind of log.

"Why, Hugh?" Niall groaned. "Why did you do this?"

"W–why?" Hugh whispered, his eyes already beginning to glaze. "Because *I* should have been ch–chief, not you. 'Twas my birthright. But no m–matter. You've won naught. The devil himself . . . is yet to be d–dealt wi—" With a gurgle, Hugh's voice faded. His eyes rolled back in his head.

A large log shattered the door, splintering its way halfway through the wood. Anne glanced from it to Niall. He seemed oblivious to the danger.

"Niall!" She shook him by the shoulder. "Hugh's dead. Let him go. His men are almost upon us!"

He lifted tormented eyes. "Wh–what?" His gaze moved to the rapidly disintegrating door.

With a savage curse, Niall bolted to his feet, reaching for his claymore. He grabbed Anne, shoving her toward the nearest corner.

"I'll try to fight them out o' the room and down the stairs!" he shouted above the rising din. "Stay close behind me. If there's a chance for you to get out o' the tower then, run and don't look back. My men are on their way."

"I won't leave you!"

"You *will*!" he snapped back, moving into his warrior's stance, his two hands gripped about his sword. "I command it!"

Anne's lips tightened in a mutinous line, but she knew it wasn't the time to argue. What Niall needed from her now was help, not hindrance. With a sickening crash, the door gave way.

The outlaws spilled into the room. They formed a half circle before Niall, three men deep. Slowly, they moved forward. Niall was forced to back into the corner to keep any from slipping around behind him.

"Surrender while you can," he growled. "Even now, my men draw near."

"Surrender?" a large burly man at the forefront demanded. "To what? We've naught to lose but our lives. Ye took all else away when ye named us outlaws. And I, for one, want a taste o' yer blood before I die!"

He sprang at Niall with a fierce cry, the others surging forward behind him. Niall met them with the solid length of his claymore, cutting down the burly leader in a few quick strokes. The rest fell back to a more respectful distance from the longer span of Niall's sword.

Niall took advantage of their hesitation. He advanced. Slowly, doggedly, he battled his way across the room, forcing the pack of men out the door and down the stairs. Anne followed.

For a considerable time Niall fought with effortless strength. But the weight of his giant sword, as well as the cramped confines of the staircase which hampered its full effectiveness, eventually wore him down.

His movements slowed. His reactions became sluggish. More and more frequently, the outlaws were able to leave their mark upon him.

Niall began to bleed from several minor wounds. His mighty chest heaved with the strain of his exertions. The sweat rolled down his face and soaked the shirt to his broad, muscular back.

Hiding behind him, Anne sought desperately for some way to help. He could not go on much longer before someone caught him in a false move and delivered a disabling if not fatal blow. She needed a weapon.

Gingerly, Anne climbed over the next man Niall cut down, then bent to pry his fingers from around his sword. It was a short-sword, similar to the ones with which she'd been trained. Feeling more useful now, Anne followed Niall down the stairs.

Time lost its meaning as Niall hacked his way to the first floor. His arms felt like lead weights. Every blow he parried now vibrated excrutiatingly up his arms. He knew he couldn't fight much longer. Though eight men lay dead or dying behind him, seven more fought or waited to fight him still.

The tower's doorway loomed like some gateway to heaven, though he knew he dared not leave the confines of the tower. To do so would allow his attackers opportunity to come at him from all sides. If he could just hold them at the doorway. . . .

A movement at the door caught his eye. In an instant slowed in time, Niall saw a crossbow lifted to a shoulder—and aimed directly at his heart. With a hoarse cry, Niall lunged aside, shoving Anne along with him. The quarrel flew by, missing him by a hairsbreadth.

The outlaw nearest Niall took advantage of his opponent's lowered guard. He sprang forward, his blade slashing into Niall's sword arm. Niall tried to recover, to raise his claymore to parry the second thrust, but his badly wounded arm was unequal to the task. His attacker's sword drove home, this time into Niall's thigh.

Niall sank to his knees, his weapon clattering to the floor. The man stepped forward. His sword lifted to deliver the killing blow.

"Cruachan!" Anne cried, and leaped in front of Niall. With all her strength, she thrust her sword toward the outlaw's midsection.

He halted, his arm frozen in its arcing descent. The man looked down stupidly at his belly. Then, with a choking cry, he fell.

From down the hill, an answering Campbell battle cry was heard. The remaining men hesitated, then turned, and fled. The pounding of hoofbeats grew louder. Shouts, mingled with screams, filled the air.

Anne ran to the doorway. A familiar face rode by. She sagged in relief. It was over.

Turning, she went back to where Niall lay, bleeding on the floor.

It took several hours before Niall was strong enough to travel after the cauterization of his deep arm and thigh wounds. He still insisted, however, on riding back to Kilchurn on his own horse, Anne clasped securely before him.

"Why did you leave?" he whispered into the fragrant tumble of her hair after a time of silent riding down the road. "Do you know what it did to me, to have you desert me in my greatest hour o' need?"

Anne glanced back at him, her cheek grazing his lips. "I left to save you from further danger, danger that was mounting against you because o' me. I couldn't stand by and watch you fall, knowing I was the cause."

She choked back a little sob. "And, even after the events of this night, how has anything changed? Now Hugh's death will be added to your wrongs, for once again I was the cause."

"Nay," Niall replied gruffly. "Hugh was but a pawn manipulated, I'd wager, by the traitor. You heard him say I still had the devil himself to deal with. The traitor must have been using Hugh to further his foul means, just as he did Nelly. But no more. We took several o' the outlaws prisoner. I'll get the truth out o' them now."

He chuckled grimly. "And I have Iain just where I want him as well. I threw him in the dungeon when I discovered he was involved in helping you leave."

"But 'twasn't Iain's fault," Anne protested. "I went to him, begged him to help me. He never had any intent o' abducting—"

"Who else but Iain knew o' your leaving Kilchurn? And who else wanted you for himself?"

"Nay, you are wrong," she countered stubbornly. "Think about it, Niall. If 'twas truly Iain's plot to steal me away for himself, he'd have never involved Hugh. Iain well knew Hugh's hatred for me. Yet he stayed behind at Kilchurn. Nay, Iain wouldn't have taken me this way."

"Your words have merit," Niall admitted. "But if so, who *was* behind the scenes, playing Hugh in such a black-hearted way? The traitor—"

"You are wrong, Niall Campbell, if you still think it to be Iain!"

A wry grin twisted Niall's firm lips. "Ever the loyal friend, eh, Annie? Well, we'll find out soon enough now. Until then, I must consider all possibilities. Even Iain."

"And I say I am no fool! I can look into a man's heart and see what's truly there. How else would I have put up with a pigheaded dolt like you for so long?"

Niall's big chest rumbled with a chuckle. "A pigheaded dolt, am I? So, we are back to that again? Fine gratitude, indeed, for saving your life."

Anne smiled and slipped her arm about Niall's waist. "Aye, m'lord. 'Tis why I love you, I suppose."

"And I, you, lass." His expression grew solemn. "When this is over and settled, I want to take you as wife. Will you have me as husband?"

Silver eyes, luminous in the moonlight, stared up at him. "You wish to wed me?"

"Aye."

She laid her head back upon his chest, snuggling against him. "I would like that, very much indeed." Anne gave a small, pensive sigh. "If only the traitor would let that be . . ."

The darkness hid the tense, anxious look that passed across Niall's rugged features. "Aye, my love. That fight, I fear, is yet to be won."

"So, he persists in flaunting the MacGregor wench before us," Duncan growled. "The Campbell has sealed his fate with this last o' his foolish efforts."

"Aye, that he has," Malcolm snarled beside him. "And this time he won't win."

Iain glanced at the two men, then back down from the castle parapets to the party of riders drawing up before the closed gates. It was dawn, the first faint rays of light just filtering over the distant horizon.

He'd been free of the dungeon, thanks to his father, from the moment a force of Niall's men had ridden out to reinforce their leader in his rescue of Anne. And, in those hours since, the Campbell tanist and his half brother had worked to convince him that Niall Campbell was no longer fit to rule the clan.

It had been a relatively simple task. Iain's anger and disgust at Niall's judgements of late, most particularly when they dealt with Anne, had finally come to a head when his cousin had confronted him in his bedchamber. He didn't understand the man anymore, much less respect him. And Iain could never follow someone he didn't respect.

"He isn't fit to lead our clan," his father had said. "Surely you can see it now. His power has gone to his head. He's crazed with it. Why else would he turn first against Hugh, then you, accusing you both o' treason? 'Tis a surprise he even named me tanist, as close in the family as I am to him. I can only surmise he chose me because I am old and no threat to him as your and Hugh's youth are."

"Hugh is mad, Father," Iain had replied. "I can well understand why Niall banished him. He tried to kill Anne."

"Aye, but not why he turned against you. Niall's mad, I tell you. As mad as Hugh, in his own way. For the clan's sake, if naught else, we must unseat him before he drags us all down to destruction!"

Though misgiving roiled inside Iain, he'd grimly nodded his assent. There was too much awry of late, but whether it stemmed from Niall's strange behavior or from another source, Iain had yet to fathom. One way or another, some decisive action had to be taken.

" 'Twould seem so," he'd sighed his acquiescence. "For the clan's sake—and Anne's."

Now a niggling question again eased to the forefront of Iain's mind as he watched Niall's party halt before Kilchurn's gate. How had the outlaws known about Anne's departure and eventual destination, to be waiting for them on the road? He had told no one, save. . . .

"Ho, guard!" Niall shouted, reining in his stallion just shy of the drawbridge. "Open the gates!"

Duncan leaned forward between the crenelated wall. "Nay, nephew, 'twill not be! Not until you renounce your right to the chieftainship. You are no longer fit to be the Campbell!"

Niall's grip tightened around Anne. "Damn him," he muttered. "What is Duncan's game?"

Anne's glance swung up to where the three men waited. "I don't know, but Malcolm and Iain stand with him. Surely Iain isn't party to this."

"You think not?" Niall rasped. "Mayhap there has been more than one traitor all along—and they are my two uncles and cousin."

"Och, Niall! What will you do?"

"I have no choice. I must demand they send out a champion to fight me."

She gripped Niall's arm. "Nay, you can't! You are injured. You've ridden all night without sleep. The man would kill you!"

He shot her a roguish grin. "Have you so little faith in my warrior's abilities? Did I not, with only a wee bit o' aid from you, hold off fifteen men until help arrived? The stakes are different now, but just as high. I can do it again. I have to."

Niall turned back to the parapets. "I claim right to do battle for the chieftainship!" he shouted in clear, ringing tones. "Send out your champion!"

Iain exchanged a glance with his father. "You misjudged Niall if you thought he'd give up easily."

Duncan shrugged. "Did I? He is tired, wounded. Killing him won't be such a difficult task for a man such as you. Go down, Iain. You are his match, and more in the condition he is in. I'll name you my tanist once Niall is dead. And you can have his woman in the bargain."

His son's gaze narrowed. "I thought you hated Anne, believed her a witch. Why would you now offer her to me?"

"Aye, brother," Malcolm heatedly interjected. "That wasn't part o' the—"

"She's no more a witch than you or I," Duncan replied, raising a hand to silence the preacher, "but I dared not disobey the law. However, since the royal envoy already confided to me there was no case against the lady, I have little problem now with giving her to Iain."

He turned to his son. "You do want her, don't you, Iain?"

Iain stared down from the parapets, his eyes seeking out Anne, possessively clasped in Niall's arms. "Aye, I want her," he admitted softly. "But she loves Niall and would never have me the way I want her to. Nay," Iain finished, his deep voice raw with emotion. "I'll fight Niall for her safety and because he's no longer fit to be chief. But not to have Anne. If I kill him, she'll never be friend to me again."

" 'Tis for the best, at any rate." Duncan gripped his son's arm. "Have a care how you fight Niall. Work to tire him and wait for your opening. Give no quarter for he'll give none, not for a cause such as this. One mistake and, wounded as he is, he could well kill you."

Iain jerked away. "You needn't lecture me on battle techniques. I'm well aware o' Niall's prowess with the claymore. I know the fight could go either way."

"Go then," Duncan growled. "And don't fail me."

As Iain strode away, he heard his father bellow down to Niall that his champion would soon meet him. His long strides carried him to his bedchamber where he quickly girded himself with his own claymore, while keeping a firm rein on his emotions.

There was no time left for doubts. No time to ponder the turn of events that had led to this moment—a battle to the death with his cousin and boyhood friend. Yet as strong a hold as Iain kept on his feelings, he couldn't help but wonder if something outside them all hadn't driven them to this sad course of events.

It was an uneasy, sickening feeling, but it crept back to haunt him again and again as he strode back through the castle to the outer gate. He, Hugh, Niall, and Anne. All driven, all manipulated, but why? And by whom?

Kilchurn's gates swung open. Iain walked through, claymore in hand. At the sight of him, Niall cursed softly. Anne gave a small cry.

She grabbed his arm. "Nay, Niall. Not Iain. I beg you. Don't fight Iain!"

He swung to face her, his eyes blazing pits of light. "Damn you, woman! I didn't choose to fight him. He did! Accept it, once and for all. He's the traitor. And accept the fact that you must finally choose between us!"

Niall advanced toward Iain. "You've dreamt o' this day, this very moment, for a long while now." He raised his sword before him. "Come, cousin. Let us do battle and I will show you the fate o' traitors!"

Iain glared back at him. "I'm not a traitor! Your own arrogance has brought you to this day!"

"Then let my arrogance win it for me!" Niall declared, swinging his sword.

His opponent moved quickly to parry the blow. The metallic clang of swords meeting, the grunts of two men straining with all their might to overcome the other, filled the air. Back and forth they thrust and hacked as the minutes ticked by with lumbering slowness, neither giving quarter.

Sweat beaded Niall's brow. His recent wounds tore open to brightly stain his bandages. He began to tire. Iain worked him around the battle area, quickly settling into a defensive posture in an effort to conserve his own strength while draining Niall of his.

Niall's hard-driving offense required more power and effort, but Anne knew it was the only tactic he dared use. He must overcome Iain before his strength drained, ebbing away as inexorably as the blood now streaming from his wounds. It was a dangerous ploy, yet the only one he had left.

The gamble paid off. Iain, once more inching back from a particularly vicious onslaught, stumbled over a rock jutting from the ground at an odd angle. He lost his balance. Niall took quick advantage and slammed into him.

Iain fell, his weapon still clenched in his hand. As he hit the ground, Niall's claymore was at his throat. Iain gazed up into eyes glittering with a murderous light—and saw his death.

Niall lifted his sword to deliver the fatal blow. "Die, you craven coward! Die the traitor's death you have earned!"

"Nay!" Anne screamed, and flung herself onto Niall's sword arm. "Don't do this. I beg you!"

Disbelief twisted his features. "You would beg for his life, knowing he meant to kill me? Get out o' my way, Anne! I won't have you shame me by begging for him in front o' all."

"And would you rather live with the shame o' knowing you killed an innocent man?"

"What would you have me do?" he tersely demanded. "Allow him to fight me again? Who would you rather sacrifice, Iain or me?"

"He isn't a traitor!"

Something hardened in Niall. "And if you're wrong, I could well die. Do you wish to take that chance? Choose, and choose now, Anne."

"I don't want either o' you to die!" she cried. "I love you, Niall. You are everything to me. But I can't condemn an innocent man to death because o' that love. I can't, I *won't* choose."

He stared at her, his eyes suddenly bleak. "Then I'll choose for you." Niall sighed, the sound weary and defeated. "And I only hope you can live with that decision."

He stepped back, motioning for Iain to rise. "Come, cousin." He lowered his sword to his side. "Anne claims you're no traitor. Prove the truth o' it to her— and me."

The younger man climbed to his feet, his blue eyes narrowed in suspicion. He lifted his sword to Niall's chest. Niall didn't move.

Iain pressed the tip deeper, until blood welled at its point. Still, Niall did nothing. Confusion furrowed Iain's brow. He glanced at Anne.

Fear, stark and vivid, glittered in her eyes. "Iain, please. Don't do it. I trusted you. I've always been your friend. *Don't do it*."

His eyes turned back to Niall, his sword lowering to the ground. "I can no more hurt her by killing you," he whispered thickly, "than you can by killing me."

The claymore was resheathed in the scabbard hanging at his back. "And Anne's right. I'm no traitor!"

"Then who?" Niall rasped. "Who *is* the traitor?"

"Kill him!" Duncan roared from his perch high on the walls. " 'Tis past time for the misfortunes o' our family to be righted, for the chieftainship to pass into our hands. Kill him, Iain, and the chieftainship will finally be ours!"

Three pairs of eyes turned to gaze up at the Campbell tanist, the truth of Duncan's treachery filling each with a private horror. And all the while the man raved down at them, the realization he could no longer twist them to his evil intent driving him over the brink of madness.

"Kill him!" he screamed. "None will follow him anymore, not with that MacGregor witch at his side! I've seen to that. We've got MacGregor lands. We've weakened them with the feud I've stirred all these years. We can soon have it all. Don't fail me like Hugh and Nelly did. You're my son, Iain. You'll be chief someday. Kill the arrogant bastard. Be done with it!"

Iain shook his head. "Nay, Father!" he shouted back. "*You* are the one who has failed us all. You have shamed our family with your treachery. I'll have no part o' it!"

"Then die, as will the witch and Niall Campbell!" Duncan screeched.

A crossbow appeared in his hands.

"Get down, Iain!" Niall cried, pulling Anne behind him.

The crossbow glinted in the early-morning sun, aimed straight at the Campbell chief. Something flashed. With a cry, Iain flung himself in front of Niall. A quarrel sunk deep into his chest.

He fell. Anne screamed and fought to go to Iain. Niall held her firmly behind him.

High on the parapets swords gleamed as clansmen rushed to halt the tanist, slashing up and down until the blood streamed from their razor-sharp blades. Duncan's voice rose, assumed an agonized intensity, then faded in a strangled cry. "Kill him! Kill him! Kill hi—"

Chapter Twenty-One

Anne saw to the arrangements for care of Iain's injury, then watched them carry him off to his bed-chamber. She turned to Niall.

"I should look at your wounds now. After your battle, they're sure to need tending."

"Shouldn't you see to Iain first?" Niall asked. "He's hurt worse than I and the physician may need help removing the quarrel."

She arched a quizzical brow. "I didn't think you'd want me near him."

He studied her for a moment in thoughtful silence. "I was wrong about him."

"Tell Iain that, not me," Anne shot back, a ripple of anger in her voice.

Niall sighed. "I will, have no fear. But I wanted you to know, too. I've been wrong about so much these past few months. I trusted no one, not even you at times."

"I know."

Anne forced the tension to ease. It wasn't Niall she was angry with, not really. They were all on edge after the violence of the past night and today's confrontation in front of the castle. But what if he were also saying he'd erred in his feelings for her? It was foolish to ask, but she needed to know.

Her eyes lowered. "And were you also wrong in loving me?"

Niall lifted her chin. "Nay, never that, lass," he rasped, a fierce tenderness smoldering in his eyes. "Never that . . ." He hesitated. "Would you like to go to Iain? See to his proper tending?"

A radiant smile lit Anne's face. "Aye, for a wee bit o' time, if you will. The quarrel missed any vital organs, but I'd like to see Iain's wound properly cleansed and dressed so it will not fester."

Niall motioned her forward. "Then go, lass. I'll be here when you return."

Love flared in her eyes. Then, gathering her skirts, Anne hurried off.

Murdoch had just finished removing the quarrel from Iain's chest. Anne found her friend in his bed, pale and pain-wracked, his eyes clamped shut. She knelt and took his clenched fist in her hand. Gently, she pried open his long, strong fingers to entwine them in hers. With her other hand, she moistened a cloth and wiped his sweat-damp brow.

Iain's lids fluttered open. Eyes, as blue as Loch Awe on a summer's day, gazed up at her. "You shouldn't see me like this," he whispered.

"And what do I see," she countered softly, "but a very brave man? 'Twas wonderful what you did for Niall, putting yourself between him and the crossbow."

He smiled wanly. "I couldn't betray your trust. You never failed to champion me, even in the darkest moments." Iain's mouth twisted in self-disgust. "Even when I unwittingly failed *you* and sent you into a greater danger than Niall ever did."

She put a gentle finger to his lips. "Hush, Iain. Save your strength. 'Tis o' no import, whatever you may have done. Let us tend your wound."

"Nay, a moment more, lass." Iain caught her hand. "Let me confess what I did. Only then will it be truly over."

"Then tell me."

He dragged in a steadying breath. "I told my father o' my plans to help you escape Kilchurn. I needed his assistance in procuring men who could be trusted. Knowing his animosity toward you, I felt certain he'd be more than happy to help send you back to your people. Little did I realize he'd betray you instead to Hugh." Iain shook his head in disbelief. "Lord, what a fool I was! Never once did I suspect the depth o' his treachery."

"Don't blame yourself, my friend. He fooled us all. He'd had years to plot and plan, from the beginning o' the feud until now. And he was such a clever man. He knew how to turn the weaknesses o' others to his own gain." Anne stroked Iain's cheek. "But he had no power over strength. Our friendship saw us through."

"Aye," Iain agreed gruffly. "Our friendship, and the love between you and Niall. I only hope to find such a love someday." He grinned wryly. "One that's equally returned, o' course."

Anne laughed. "And are you trying to tell me, Iain Campbell, that no lass has ever fallen in love with you? Why, you're one o' the handsomest Highlanders I've ever set eyes on!"

His grin faded to a sad wistfulness. "There's never been a lass like you, Anne MacGregor."

"But there will, Iain," Anne whispered fervently, moved by the ineffable tenderness of his gaze. "One who's my match, and more. One who's truly worthy o' a man as brave and good as you.

"Now, not another word," she said, rising to her feet. " 'Tis time to see to your injury. I can't tarry here all day. Niall's wounds need tending, too."

A dark blond brow quirked in surprise. "He let you come to me first?"

"He *sent* me to you."

"I hope we can someday be friends again." Iain sighed. "We were once, you know. The best o' friends."

"And you will again. But I think the course o' your friendship will depend more upon you than Niall."

"Och, and how so?"

"Niall's a proud man. He'll feel awkward around you for a time, imagine he's not worthy o' your acceptance or forgiveness."

Iain's expression darkened. "As well he should. He was unreasonable and arrogant."

"Aye." Anne nodded. "But he knew from the day my clan captured him that a traitor was involved. Right or wrong, he suspected 'twas you. So, he couldn't very well confide in you and your attentions to me were so easily misinterpreted in light o' those suspicions. Niall thought you were using me in some way to further your plotting."

Iain frowned in thought. "It explains many things." Blue eyes rose to hers. "I'll talk with him. In time, we'll work out the problems between us."

"Good." A teasing light flickered briefly in her eyes. " 'Tis past time. I grow weary o' being the peacemaker between you two."

Anne motioned to Murdoch. "Let us see to Iain's wound."

The old physician nodded and shuffled over.

It was a glorious late July day. Sparrow hawks and golden eagles soared overhead, their hoarse screams rending the deep, summer silence. The purple-pink heather was just beginning to bloom on the hills.

Fragrant lavender, growing along the side of the road, perfumed the air with its delicate scent.

Anne's gaze swept the familiar landscape as their party rode along. The scene stirred a memory of that day, now nearly three months past, when she'd been riding the opposite way, toward Campbell lands. Then she'd been handfasted to a man she despised, her life in a shambles.

Now she was going home, to MacGregor land, if home could ever again be anywhere Niall wasn't. She glanced at him. His attention was momentarily diverted, speaking with Iain who rode beside him. Anne's eyes softened with love.

He'd been so busy in the past month since Hugh and Duncan's deaths. The queen had accepted the royal envoy's findings. All charges against Niall had been dropped.

Once Hugh and Duncan's funerals were over and the two men properly buried, Niall had lost no time in banishing Malcolm from Campbell lands. He couldn't find it in his heart to forgive a man who countenanced, if not actively supported, Duncan's treachery. Malcolm had been escorted away, unrepentant to the end, raving about witchcraft and Anne's guilt.

In the long days Niall and Iain both spent recuperating from their wounds, Anne had begun Caitlin's lessons in the healing art. The ebony-haired girl was an apt pupil, showing a real talent for the craft. Slowly, as she gained confidence and enthusiasm for her new skill, her lovestruck preoccupation with Rory MacArthur eased.

The time not spent with Anne in learning to mix the various concoctions and potions, Caitlin used to talk with her brother. Anne couldn't help but laugh at Niall's surprise at the depth of his sister's maturity. She had chided him, telling him he'd have known Caitlin better if he'd cared to take the time.

He'd laughed and pulled her into his arms, admitting that, once again, she was right.

There was much, indeed, to be thankful for in the past days, including Niall's surprising offer to take her to Castle Gregor for a short visit. Anne knew it had been a great sacrifice on his part to spare the time for what was essentially a frivolous journey. She was grateful and loved him even more because of it. But there remained one small doubt to nibble away at what would have been her complete happiness.

Since the night he'd rescued her from Hugh's evil clutches and asked her to be his wife, Niall had never again mentioned marrying her. Anne wondered about that. After much thought, she could only find one reason for his reticence on the subject. Niall regretted the offer.

Not that he treated her any differently. Far from it. As soon as his wounds were sufficiently healed to permit more vigorous activity, he'd ardently taken her back to his bed.

Nay, Anne mused, with a woman's secret satisfaction, there was naught lacking in their coupling.

She knew she should be patient, trust that Niall would broach the subject when the time was right. She was not one to nag and would never force him to wed because of a prior offer mayhap made in haste. Niall would come to her willingly or not at all.

But therein lay the problem. Niall wanted a child. Anne now carried that child. She'd had to laugh at her own naivete, her a healer, in missing the signs for so long. It must have been the strain of the past several weeks, the preoccupation with the danger they'd all been in, but it had taken Agnes sitting her down and pointing it out for Anne finally to admit the truth.

The realization filled her with a fierce joy, but that same joy was muted by the knowledge that

Niall would wed her now, if only for the child. And Anne wanted him to want her for her own sake. So she swore Agnes to secrecy, knowing well the old servant would respect a woman's right to reveal the news in her own time.

She was foolish, Anne knew, to doubt Niall's devotion to her. He gave himself to her in every way with the heartfelt abandon of a man in love. In every way, Anne sighed, as she redirected her attention to the road ahead. In every way—save one. And that was the final commitment of marriage vows.

As they neared the village of Glenstrae, a large crowd of peasants began to line the road. Anne turned a questioning gaze to Niall.

He grinned back. "Your people, m'lady. Turned out to welcome you home."

A suspicious half-smile curled the corner of her mouth. "Another o' your surprises, m'lord? I wonder what else that devious mind has in store for me this day?"

"You'll have to wait and see, won't you?" he drawled in reply.

Niall glanced at Iain. "What say you, tanist? Will she like what I have in store for her?"

Iain chuckled. "I don't know. She was none too pleased the last time we were here. You may find, cousin, you've more trouble on your hands than you bargained for."

"Whatever are you two men talking about?" Anne demanded in exasperation. "I don't like being left out o' this conversation, much less your plans."

Niall smiled. "Have patience, my love. In due time, all will be revealed."

She opened her mouth to tell him exactly what she thought of his suggestion when a woman with a child in her arms ran forward from the crowd. It was Fiona.

"Her name is Annie," the young peasant said, lifting a fat, healthy infant up to Anne.

Tears filled Anne's eyes as she took the baby in her arms and cuddled it to her. "Isn't she beautiful?" she murmured to Niall.

A tenderly possessive light flared in his eyes. "Aye, lass, that she is. And someday we'll have bairns o' our own, just like her."

Anne flushed and quickly handed the baby back to its mother. Had he guessed her secret, or had Agnes broken down and told him? She forced herself to smile at Fiona.

"Come to the castle soon and we'll spend more time with the bairn. I've a wish to know my namesake better."

"Aye, m'lady," Fiona agreed happily. "Why, this very eve I'll be there for you. The whole village is coming."

"Come along, Anne," Niall urged her on, taking hold of her horse's reins. "Time enough to visit later. Your father awaits."

Anne glanced from Fiona to Niall in momentary confusion, then nudged her mount to catch up with Niall's. "What was she talking about? What is the whole village coming for?"

He shrugged. "Mayhap your father has something special planned. We'll find out soon enough."

"Aye, I suppose we will," Anne muttered, still bewildered.

Their arrival in Castle Gregor was a joyous affair. After the usual greetings, Anne found herself bustled upstairs to her old bedchamber by Agnes and Anne's two married sisters. While all happily gossiped, her clothes were unpacked and belongings put away. Then Megan, Anne's youngest sister, brought out a gown of shimmering ivory silk. Its neckline was a simple, rounded scoop edged with the finest lace, the sleeves long and snug, the dress fitted in bosom and waist before flaring gently to the floor.

" 'Twas Mother's," Megan offered, her voice tear-choked with memories. "We'd like you to wear it today, in honor o' the joining o' our clans and an end to the feud."

" 'Tis too beautiful for a simple feast," Anne protested.

"But ye'll wear it, nonetheless." Agnes stepped forward and began unfastening Anne's traveling gown. "Ye willna begin yer visit here by hurting feelings. Yer sisters wish for ye to wear it, and wear it ye shall."

Anne protested no more. She allowed herself to be undressed and bathed before donning the beautiful gown. The MacGregor tartan was then draped over her shoulder and fastened with the clan brooch. Her hair was brushed until it gleamed and fastened away from her face in a simple, feminine fashion, allowing the thick mass of russet curls to tumble about her shoulders and down her back.

Finally, as the sun slid behind the mountains, Agnes stepped back to admire their handiwork. "Ye're so beautiful, m'lady," she whispered.

Anne smiled at her loyal maidservant. "Only because you have made me look so."

A firm knock sounded at the door. Anne's sisters were suddenly in a flutter. She cocked a quizzical brow and hurried to open the door.

Niall stood there, grinning back at her. He was dressed in his belted plaid, a snowy-white shirt beneath, a blue bonnet bearing the three eagle feathers denoting his rank as clan chief perched rakishly atop his ebony hair. He looked the picture of a Highland warrior, full of barely restrained power and masculine vitality. *A fine, brave Highland warrior*, Anne thought with a surge of pride. *And mine.*

Niall offered his arm. "Come, m'lady."

A questioning light glimmered in her eyes. "What are you about? 'Tis a half-hour before the feasting begins."

"We go to see your father. We have a few things unfinished to discuss."

She placed her hand on his arm. "As you wish, m'lord."

Alastair MacGregor, dressed as well in full Highland regalia, was awaiting them in his chambers. His eyes softened when he saw Anne. He walked to her and placed his hands on her shoulders.

"You look so like your sainted mother in that dress," he said with a husky catch in his voice. "I'm proud o' you, lassie." His glance momentarily strayed to Niall. "Have you found happiness with the Campbell?" Alastair's piercing gaze returned to her. "Did I do well in giving you to him?"

Anne's eyes moved to Niall's. A soft, loving smile curved her lips. In spite of it all, in spite of the lingering doubts she had about the depth of Niall's commitment, she was content. She loved him with all her heart, would stay with him as long as he would have her. And mayhap, someday, even that last, little misgiving would finally be eased.

She turned back to her father. "Aye, I am happy with him. You did well, Father."

"Good. Then I grant him his request."

He faced Niall. "You may take my Annie as wife."

"W–wife?" Anne's grip tightened on Niall's arm. "You want me as wife?"

"And why not?" he demanded. "Didn't I already ask you before? Why would I have changed my mind?"

She flushed, not quite able to meet his fierce-burning gaze. "I . . . You never spoke o' it since. I wasn't sure."

"There were preparations to be made and I wanted to surprise you." Niall took her chin and lifted her eyes to meet his. "I thought you'd like being wed here, where it all began with our hand-fasting."

"Here? When?"

"Today, my love. In but a few moments more."

"Och, Niall!" Anne breathed, the aching tenderness in her voice mirrored in her eyes.

"But first, I have a small wedding gift for you."

He motioned for her to follow him to her father's huge desk. Niall unrolled a large parchment scroll, then picked up a quill pen and offered it to her.

Anne frowned in puzzlement. "What is this?"

"The grant deeding MacGregor lands to clan Campbell. I wish to give them back as my wedding gift."

Hot tears flooded Anne's eyes and spilled down onto her cheeks. "Thank you," she whispered.

She shot her father a quick, joyous glance then, taking the quill, signed the scroll.

Niall rerolled it, handing it to the MacGregor for safekeeping. He once more offered her his arm.

" 'Tis time for a wedding, m'lady."

Anne smiled up at him, all the love in her heart shining in that single glance. "Aye, m'lord."

With Alastair following, he led her out of her father's chambers and down the long, stone corridors to her clan's Great Hall. They paused at the head of the stairs to a room lavishly decorated with pine and heather, ribbons of crimson, green, and white interwoven among the branches. In the deepening twilight, hundreds of candles illuminated the huge chamber, casting a soft glow upon all the faces gazing up at them.

Iain was there, good friend and true, smiling his encouragement. Caitlin, Agnes, and Anne's sisters stood around him, tears of joy in their eyes. And, in the mass of people, Anne saw Fiona and Donald, little Annie proudly cradled in her father's arms. At that moment the babe gurgled loudly.

Niall chuckled. "That's a bonny babe you helped birth, lassie. May ours someday be as lively and healthy."

A small, mischievous giggle escaped Anne. Tawny-brown eyes shifted back to her.

"And, pray, what is so amusing?"

She tossed her head. "Och, naught, m'lord, save you may soon rue those brave words. Babes can be very noisy and demanding, as well you'll discover in but another eight months' time."

For a moment Niall stared, as realization of her meaning slowly dawned. Then, his mouth lifted into a beautiful smile. "Truly? We—we're to have a babe?"

She nodded. "Aye, m'lord."

"A babe," he repeated, as if not quite able to comprehend the revelation. He grinned at her in startled pleasure. "You've had a few surprises o' your own, I see."

"Aye, m'lord."

"Well," Niall remarked with feigned casualness, "I always said a spirited filly, if gentled well, was o' greater value than some plodding nag."

Anne's silver eyes flashed. "And there you go again, Niall Campbell, comparing me to a horse!"

He threw back his head and gave a shout of laughter. Then, to the accompaniment of the wailing bagpipes, he led her down to their wedding.

Dear Reader,

I hope you enjoyed CHILD OF THE MIST. I have a similar type of book coming out in 1994, a fantasy romance entitled DEMON PRINCE. Set in a land of knights and ladies, magic and superstition, it is the tale of Aidan, firstborn son of the queen of Anacreon, and Brianne, a beautiful peasant girl. Conceived in an unholy union between his mother and, unbeknownst to Aidan, the necromancer, Morloch, the young prince has grown up shunned by all due to his birthing curse of the "evil eye." Renouncing his right to the throne, Aidan roams distant lands as a mercenary until the eve of his thirtieth birthday when the law requires he return home. His kindness in rescuing Brianne from a pack of outlaws sets them on an inevitable course that not only binds their lives but their hearts as well in a desperate battle to save Anacreon from the evil Morloch. But in the end will love be enough to free the tormented Aidan from the curse of the DEMON PRINCE?

For those of you who also enjoy futuristic romances or are interested in giving this exciting new type of book a try, FIRESTAR, my fourth futuristic, will begin yet another trilogy. This time, the threat to the Imperium is much more external. In the absence of the Knowing Crystal, the Volans, an alien race of mind slavers from a neighboring galaxy, renew their efforts to seize control of the Imperium. Gage Bardwin, the famed Imperial tracker, is sent to a distant planet to spy on purported Volan activities.

There, he is captured and offered to Meriel Corba, a royal princess, as a stud for the sole purpose of impregnation. The ensuing passion and eventual betrayal sets the stage for their tempestuous relationship as both are inexorably drawn into the battle against the Volans to save the Imperium. FIRESTAR will be a Summer 1993 release.

I love hearing from my readers. For a list of all my currently available books and a personal reply, please write me at P.O. Box 62365, Colorado Springs, Colorado 80962. A self-addressed, stamped envelope is appreciated. In the meanwhile—happy reading!

Kathleen Morgan

Kathleen Morgan

Valentine Sampler

The sweetest gift of all...

Leisure Books is proud to present this collection of Valentine love stories by three of today's bestselling contemporary romance writers!

Written in the Stars by Parris Afton Bonds. Disillusioned by the singles scene, Sarah discovers her soul mate in a different kind of singles game: tennis. And once she starts playing to win, the score changes from 40-love to Advantage Sarah.

The Magic Time Machine by Rita Clay Estrada. Theresa has always wished she could go back in time to find the man who got away. And when she steps into J.D.'s fantasy-oriented nightclub, she isn't about to waste her only chance to make her wish come true.

Branson's Daughter by Lynda Trent. Born on the wrong side of the tracks, Hannah is looking forward to the Valentine Day's reunion of her high school classmates. She'll show them all what a success she's made of her life—especially the boy she wasn't good enough to love.

__3378-X $4.50 US/$5.50 CAN